W9-AMN-970

## "Why do you try to hide what you are?"

Jessie stiffened, and her eyes turned suspicious. "And what's that?"

"A woman." He struggled to find the words to express what he meant. His eyes went unconsciously to her throat, exposed by the open collar of her mannish shirt. "You know, dressing like that. Acting tough."

"I *am* tough." Jessie crossed her arms over her chest and stared back at him with blazing eyes. "I'm not trying to hide anything."

Stephen looked at her, unable to do anything else. He suspected that when her hair lay loose across her shoulders, it was a glory to behold. He wondered if any man had ever seen it loose. If any man had ever turned her soft. "But you're very pretty. You could look . . . enchanting."

*Enchanting!* The word stunned Jessie into silence. No man had ever suggested such a thing. Finally she said, "Your fever's worse than I thought. You must be delirious."

Dear Readers,

As you may already have noticed, we have something a little bit different for you this month. The handsome gentleman on the cover of Kristin James's aptly-titled *The Gentleman* is one of two brothers whose stories we'll be bringing to you this month and next. Follow Stephen Ferguson from the East, where he's been brought up with wealth and gentility, to the rugged West, where he spent the first few years of his life. The family reunion that follows strikes sparks, but they're nothing compared to the flames that are ignited between Stephen and tomboyish Jessie Randall, who soon starts dreaming of being the kind of lady who could attract her very own gentleman.

And the excitement doesn't stop there, because next month, Dorothy Glenn's *The Hell Raiser* tells the story of Sam Ferguson, the brother who was left behind to make his way in the hard and dangerous Montana mountains. Sam is rough and tough—but even the toughest man can melt when he meets the right woman. Read *The Hell Raiser* and find out who she is!

In months to come we'll take you from East to West, Europe to America—even to China. Join us and watch the past come alive. It happens every month in Harlequin Historicals.

Leslie Wainger
Senior Editor and Editorial Coordinator

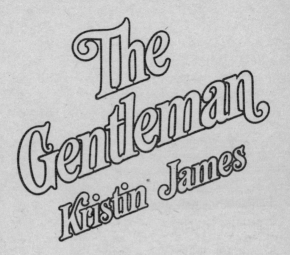

# The Gentleman

## Kristin James

# Harlequin Books

TORONTO • NEW YORK • LONDON
AMSTERDAM • PARIS • SYDNEY • HAMBURG
STOCKHOLM • ATHENS • TOKYO • MILAN

Harlequin Historical first edition April 1990

ISBN 0-373-28643-0

**Books by Kristin James**

Harlequin Historicals

*Satan's Angel* #1
*The Gentleman* #43

---

## KRISTIN JAMES,

a former attorney, is married to a family counselor, and they have a young daughter. Her family and her writing keep her busy, but when she does have free time she loves to read. In addition to her historical romances, she has written several contemporaries.

# *Prologue*

*1866*

The young boy watched his mother hurry around the cabin, stuffing clothes into a big cloth bag with handles. There was something odd about her manner—a nervousness and haste—that made Stephen excited and fearful, all at the same time.

He gripped his wooden whistle more tightly in his fist. It was his favorite toy; his big brother, Samuel, had carved it for him with his pocket knife. Samuel was the person Stephen loved most in the world, next to Mama. He seemed to Stephen a grand and glorious person who could do all the things for which Stephen was too young. He was kind, too, letting Stephen help him, and often playing with him. And on cold winter nights, when Stephen snuggled up against Sam's back, he felt safe and protected not only from the cold, but from all the other dangers of the world, as well. Stephen was convinced that there was no one else in the world as wonderful as his big brother, no one as intelligent or brave or skillful.

This morning, Papa had taken Samuel into the woods with him to work. Stephen had wanted to go, but, as usual, he was not allowed. He was too young. He hadn't fretted about it. It was too common an occurrence to get upset about. Besides, he enjoyed the lessons he always had with Mama in the morning. He knew the alphabet and his numbers now, and he was starting on reading and doing sums.

But today there had been no lessons. Mama had hurried through the dishes, then had begun scurrying around their small cabin, packing.

Now she shut the bag and took a long, slow look around the one-room house. There was something in her eyes that made Stephen want to cry. He went to her and leaned against her leg, one hand clenching her skirts. She glanced down and summoned up a small, brittle smile to reassure Stephen. She put the bag on the floor beside the door, then sat down at the table and began to write on a piece of paper.

Stephen followed her and watched her, still leaning against her a little, his elbows planted on the table. "Whatcha doin', Mama?"

"Writing a letter to your papa."

"Why?"

"Because we won't be here when he and Samuel get back, so I'm telling him where we're going."

"Oh. Are we going to town?" His voice rose in anticipation. The closest little community was far away, and they went to it rarely.

"Yes. But farther than that, really."

Stephen's eyes, big and brown and heavily lashed, widened expressively. "Farther than town?" He couldn't imagine such a thing.

"Yes. All the way to St. Louis. Do you remember St. Louis?"

He shook his head.

"Of course not. You were just a little thing when we left. We used to live in St. Louis. We had a sweet house there, with a flower garden in the summer. And there was a big river. You loved the river. Sometimes we'd go down to visit your grandpapa at his company, and he'd take you and

Samuel on one of the ships." She smiled reminiscently, her eyes misting. "We're going to see Grandpapa and Grandmama again."

"Is Sammy coming, too? And Pa?"

The brief animation that had touched Eleanor Ferguson's face died abruptly, and she shook her head. "No. They'll be staying here."

Stephen frowned, not liking the idea, but his mother forestalled any more questions or comments from him by jumping up and taking down her bonnet. She tied it under her chin, then popped Stephen's hat onto his head. "Come now, we must be going, or we won't reach the stage station at Curryville by nightfall."

She took Stephen's hand and went outside. They walked across the yard to the shed, where she led the horses out and began to hitch them to the wagon. Stephen watched her, the funny empty feeling in his stomach growing. Though he had given up the habit long ago, now his thumb popped into his mouth. His mother finished harnessing the team and came around to lift Stephen onto the seat.

Then she returned to the house and came out a moment later, carrying the bag. As she stepped out the door, Stephen heard the sound of cheerful whistling. He twisted on the wagon seat to look.

A boy came around the side of the house, smiling and whistling. When he saw them, he came to an abrupt standstill and stared, astonished. "Ma?"

Stephen waved at his brother, pleased that he had come. His mother just stood as though rooted to the ground, staring at Sammy. Then, abruptly, she turned and almost ran to the wagon. She threw the bag over the end gate. She bent and kissed Sammy, then climbed onto the wagon seat beside Stephen.

"Come on!" Stephen called to his brother, gesturing with his hand. "We're going to see Grandpa. I'm taking my whistle."

"Ma! Where are you going? Can't I go, too?" Sammy ran to the side of the wagon.

Stephen looked at his mother. Her face was as white as paper, and there was such sadness in her eyes that it made him cold inside. "Mama?"

Tears gleamed like crystal in his mother's eyes and spilled over onto her cheeks. "Goodbye, sweetheart. I love you. Mama loves you." Her voice broke, and she turned her head toward the front. She clicked to the horses. "Giddap!"

"Ma!" Samuel's cry pierced the air.

"No!" Stephen grabbed his mother's arm, tugging at her to stop. "Sammy come! Sammy come, too!"

"He can't," his mother said brokenly, slapping the reins.

Behind them Samuel began to run, calling out to them. Stephen struggled to his knees on the seat and turned to look. "No!" Stephen cried. "No! Sammy! I want Sammy!"

"Mama, don't go!" Sammy held something aloft in his fingers, dangling it enticingly. "Don't go, Stevie! I'll take you fishing—"

Stephen cried and screamed, choking on his sobs. He stretched out his hands toward his brother, his fingers clutching uselessly in the air. "Sam—my! Sam—my!"

Eleanor shut her eyes, tears pouring down her face, and slapped the reins across the horses' backs. The animals picked up their pace, and the wagon lumbered away, leaving Samuel behind them.

# Chapter One

*September, 1888*

Stephen Ferguson stood beside the polished walnut casket, his hat in his hand. He was a tall, slender young man with thick brown hair and chocolate-colored eyes. His features were even and handsome, and his eyes were so thickly and darkly lashed that only a very firm, even stubborn, jaw and a wide mouth saved his face from prettiness. He was dressed in a black suit, cut to perfection, with a black mourning band tied around his arm. Even in sorrow, he looked every inch the elegant gentleman.

He gazed at the coffin, covered with a magnificent spray of roses, creamy white, which his mother had loved. Tears pricked at his eyes. He had known that one day he would, in all likelihood, be standing in this place. But he had never expected it to be so soon, so sudden. His mother had been only fifty-two, too young to die. Five days ago he had been going about his normal life in New York City, managing the McClellan and Caldwell Shipping Office, learning his grandfather's business from the ground up, as he had been doing every day of his life for the past five years. Then there had come the telegram that his mother had had a brain seizure and was seriously ill. He had jumped on the first train west, arriving in St. Louis in time to see her alive. He had taken her hand and talked to her, had gazed at her familiar, beloved face, but she had not opened those fine brown eyes, so lovely and calm, and looked at him; she had not spoken. Eleanor Ferguson had died without regaining consciousness. Now he was standing, watching, as her coffin was lowered into the grave. They were all dead now—his father, his brother, his mother, even Linton Caldwell, who had been like a father to him. All of them gone from him forever.

He glanced at his grandfather beside him. The old man was holding up well. He was in his late seventies; his hair was thinning and pure white, and the hands that gripped the hat in front of him were splotched with age. But there was no fragility in that old body. His back was ramrod-straight, and his fingers didn't tremble. Stephen knew a warm, amused pride; it was foolish to think that Hiram McClellan would give way before anything, even grief.

On the other side of Hiram, his wife leaned heavily upon his arm. Though ten years younger than her husband, she was not as strong. Tears leaked from her eyes beneath the black veil, and her heavily lined face was as pale and crumpled as old parchment.

Though the iron in Hiram McClellan would not let him show it, Stephen knew that he suffered, too. Two years ago his long-time partner, Linton Caldwell, had died. And now Eleanor, his only child. Stephen knew that his grandparents would need him more now than ever. He felt the familiar bonds tightening around him, squeezing him. That thought was quickly replaced by guilt. It was wrong of him to feel that way, he knew. His grandparents had taken him and his mother in, had raised him lovingly and with the best of everything. He owed them; more than that, he loved them. Such things were more important than any restlessness he might feel now and then. If at times he daydreamed of seeing other places, doing other things, he quickly rid himself of those dreams. He was a man who understood and accepted responsibility, who had been brought up to do his duty as a gentleman should.

A soft, gloved hand slipped into the crook of his arm, interrupting his thoughts, and he turned his head to smile down fondly at his fiancée. Elizabeth Caldwell was an attractive young woman, taller than average, with cool green eyes and thick black hair. She was intelligent and refined, everything a man could ask for in a woman. Stephen didn't think that he had ever seen her with a hair out of place or heard her utter a word that wasn't proper. She was a lady through and through, the perfect wife for a man in his position. Moreover, they had been friends since they were children. Her father and Stephen's grandfather had been partners in the shipping business since before the war, and the two families had been as close as if they were related. Elizabeth and Stephen had grown up together. It seemed only natural and right—and was the wish of both their families—that they should marry.

Elizabeth gave him a sad, comforting smile. They turned and walked from the grave site, his grandparents behind them. They stepped into the black-draped funeral carriage, and the slow procession began to wind its way out of the cemetery.

Throughout the afternoon at his grandparents' house, there was a constant stream of visitors offering their condolences. It was the custom, and Stephen knew that he had to politely greet them and accept their sympathy, but he found it difficult to maintain a polite social mask. He was aching with grief inside, and he would have liked to retreat to his room, where he could be alone with his sorrow. Of course, he did not.

But he was grateful when Elizabeth laid her hand on his arm and said, "I'm feeling a trifle faint, I'm afraid. Could we walk for a few moments in the garden?"

"Of course." He had never known Elizabeth to come close to fainting in her life. She was employing a polite subterfuge to allow him to get away.

He excused himself from the small group of people to whom he had been talking and led her out to the formal gardens at the rear of the house. He let out a long sigh, relieved to be in the tranquillity of the garden, away from the people and the social obligations. "Thank you, Elizabeth. I badly needed an excuse to slip out. How did you know?"

She smiled faintly. "I've known you long enough to spot the signs. You looked tired and . . . trapped."

"You were right, as always." He took a deep breath of air, and they strolled along the pathway to a bench beside a small pool. Darting bright goldfish glimmered in the water. They sat for a while, gazing at the fish. Elizabeth took his hand and squeezed it.

Stephen pulled his mind from the sad subject around which it had revolved for so many hours and tried to focus on Elizabeth. "How are *you*?" he asked. "I'm sorry. I've been so absorbed in my own problems that I haven't even inquired after you."

Elizabeth shook her head. "No need to apologize. Your problems have been much larger and more important." Tears shone in her green eyes. "Eleanor was such a dear, good person. I shall miss her terribly. I remember how I felt when my father died. It seemed like the end of the world to me."

"He was a good man."

Elizabeth nodded. "If only he were alive now . . ."

Stephen glanced at her, his eyes narrowing. "What's wrong, Elizabeth? Is your stepmother bothering you?"

Elizabeth's mouth thinned into a bitter line. "I can manage her. But she is . . . bothersome. She thinks she has the right to order my life. She—no, I shan't trouble you with petty nonsense at a time like this."

"No, go ahead. It isn't petty nonsense if it's troubling you. What is she doing?"

"She wants me to marry."

"What? You mean, she wants us to marry soon?"

"No. She wants me to marry someone else."

Stephen stared. "Someone else? But—" He stopped, struck by a thought. "Elizabeth, do you wish to marry another man?"

She glanced up, startled. "No! Oh, no. I have no desire to marry him at all."

"Then how can she think that you will? We are engaged."

"She realizes that. But she is pressing me to break my promise to you and marry—" She gave a sigh and looked away from him. "Judge Thorpe."

"Judge Thorpe!" Stephen shot to his feet. "Is she mad? The man must be twice your age!"

"Almost. But he seems to have formed some sort of liking for me. He has asked her permission to court me, and Netta gave it. He's a very powerful man, wealthy and influential. Netta craves power."

"I had no idea. How long has this been going on?"

"For some months now. I have tried to tell her that I am engaged to you, but she refuses to listen. She keeps inviting him to teas and parties, and she drags me along on any occasion when he might be at a function."

"I'm sorry. You should have written me about this. I shall speak to her."

Elizabeth shrugged. "Unfortunately, talking to Netta doesn't do much good. She believes exactly what she wants to."

"You shouldn't have to stay with her. We should be married. I'm sorry. I've been remiss. Your year of mourning was over long ago. I've been so busy in New York that I hadn't realized how much time had passed."

Two years ago, when Linton, Elizabeth's father, lay dying, he had been filled with anxiety about what would happen to Elizabeth after he died. Linton had begged Stephen to marry Elizabeth, to take care of and provide for her, and Stephen had promised readily. He couldn't have refused Linton anything on his deathbed, and besides, he had more or less expected to marry Elizabeth all his life.

Stephen had immediately asked Elizabeth to marry him, and she had accepted. Of course, it would have been improper to have a wedding before the year of mourning was over, so they had waited. Her mourning had ended some time ago, but Stephen and Elizabeth had been content to drift along, not choosing any definite date for their wedding or making plans. Now it seemed as though Netta Caldwell would force their hand.

"We shall set a date," Stephen went on, "for as soon as possible. That should spike Mrs. Caldwell's guns."

"Oh, but I don't want you to marry me because of Netta's disagreeableness."

"I'm not marrying you just because of Netta. We are already promised to marry. We should have done so earlier." Stephen looked down at Elizabeth. He wondered what she felt for him. Did she love him? He wasn't sure. They were good friends. But was there a bright, compassionate love burning inside her for him? He couldn't quite imagine it. Elizabeth was far too sensible and proper.

He knew that he loved Elizabeth, but it was a quiet, fond sort of love. There was none of the passion that he had felt from time to time for a mistress. Nor did he sit around pining for her presence and boring everyone around him with descriptions of her eyes or hair or beautiful white shoulders, as many of his acquaintances were wont to do over whatever lady had most recently seized their fancy. Sometimes he had wondered what it would be like to experience that kind of passionate, consuming love. The affection he held for Elizabeth seemed a rather tame thing compared to that.

However, Stephen was quick to remind himself, he probably wasn't the type of chap to throw himself so wholeheartedly into love. Besides, those passionate affairs usually wound up with the friend trying to drown his sorrows in a bottle or discovering bitterly that his goddess was a mere mortal, after all. The mutual respect and friendship he and Elizabeth had for each other were a much firmer foundation on which to build a marriage.

"Then let us think about when to do it," Stephen went on. "Surely, once we set a date, your stepmother will have to accept the fact that you are going to marry me."

"I'm not sure anything is that easy where my stepmother is concerned. But I *will* think about a date." She paused and smiled at him. "Thank you. It's kind of you to trouble yourself with my problems at a time when you are facing such grief of your own."

"Nonsense. I will always be here to help you. Whatever is wrong."

They sat for a few minutes in companionable silence before they rose and returned to the house to continue their duties. It was some time before the flow of visitors slowed to a trickle and then stopped. By then, Elizabeth had returned home with her stepmother. Stephen asked one of the servants to have his supper brought to him on a tray, and he retired to his room.

His valet, Charles, was there, as usual, waiting for him. Stephen wished he was not. He would have liked to be alone, and he started to snap at the man to get out, but he refrained. It wasn't Charles's fault, after all, that he was British and retained a British servant's rigid view of what was right and proper. Charles would have been horrified at the idea that Stephen might dress himself and even more astounded that Stephen did not think of himself as alone when only his valet was with him.

When Charles had helped him into his dressing gown and fussed over his clothes to his satisfaction, he finally left the room, and Stephen flopped onto his bed with a sigh. He lay staring at the dark green tester and thinking of his mother. Eleanor had been his only family—Eleanor and his grandparents, and he knew it would not be too long before they were gone, too. He could hardly remember his father and brother. He had been only five when Eleanor had taken him from his father's home. He had never seen Papa or Sammy again. Only a few months after they arrived in St. Louis, Eleanor had told him that both of them had died in a timber accident. At first he had thought of them often, but over the years the memories had faded, until he couldn't even clearly remember what they had looked like.

He had asked his mother questions about them, but the sadness that had come into her face at such times soon stopped him from mentioning them or the life he had known before. His grandparents had disliked his father; he had gathered that much from remarks his grandfather had made. Once Grandpapa had told him that Eleanor had left his father because Joe Ferguson was a crass, uncivilized brute. After that, Stephen had felt that Grandpapa was always watching him, afraid to see some part of that uncivilized brute come out in him. Due to the rigid social training he had received, it never had, except perhaps in the sport of boxing, which he had taken up while at college, at Princeton. Though it was a gentleman's sport, his grandfather had frowned over it. Stephen thought he would have preferred him to take up fencing or sculling.

But his mother, unlike the old gentleman, had never blamed Joseph Ferguson for anything. She had said only that she could not stand the loneliness and the vast emptiness of the land, or the freezing climate. Later, when Stephen was grown, he thought he understood why she had left. It must have been a rough, lonely life in the wilds of Montana for a woman who had grown up in this wealthy, civilized household. She had known only refinement and culture, and there had been servants to do everything for her. It must have been a hellish struggle for her out there.

Out there. He didn't exactly know where it was. No one had ever spoken of it except as "that uncivilized place," and he couldn't remember enough about it to identify it. All he could remember was looking up at immense trees all around him—and the security and warmth of lying in his bed at night, snuggled up against his brother.

Stephen sighed and sat up. Why the devil was he thinking about such things now? Was it because his mother, his last link to that shadowy life, was gone? Now there was no one who could really tell him why she had left her husband and, even more puzzling, her older child. Now there was no one who knew what his brother had looked like, or who could describe their cabin or tell him its location. He had always thought that one day he would ask his mother where they had lived, and he would travel there to see it again and to stand beside his father's and brother's graves. Now he would never do it.

This fact swelled the discontent within him. Over the course of the past few months, he had been feeling more and more wound up . . . burdened . . . trapped. Something inside him longed to break free, though he wasn't sure exactly what he wanted to break free from. There was something about having the mantle of responsibility for the business slide more and more onto his shoulders, about setting a date for the wedding, about losing his childhood with his mother's death, that made him feel as if he was being smothered.

There was a discreet tap at the door, and Harrison, the butler, stepped into the room. Stephen was surprised. Harrison was the most important in the social scale of the servants, and he rarely came upstairs on any errand.

"Sir." The butler made a faint bow with his head. "I hope this is not an inconvenient time."

"No. That's quite all right." Stephen looked curiously at the small wooden box the butler carried in his gloved hands. "What is it, Harrison?"

"I have known your mother since she was a girl," he began in his slow, careful voice. Stephen wondered where this was leading. Harrison had already offered him condolences on his mother's death. "In some ways she looked upon me as a friend, I think, despite the differences in our stations. After she was taken ill, she called me to her room and gave me this." He extended the box. "She told me that if she died, I was to give this box to you, sir. She trusted me, you see, not to pry into the contents."

"Of course. There's no one *I* would trust more." Stephen reached out and took the box from him. "Thank you."

He smoothed his hand across the mahogany top, tracing the outline of the mother-of-pearl rose inlaid there. He hardly noticed when Harrison quietly left the room. Stephen opened the lid, and the faint scent of his mother's lavender sachet wafted out. Tears stung his eyes. He closed them, remembering when he and his mother had first moved to his grandparents' house, and he had often awakened in the night, crying. His mother had always come to him, shooing away the nanny his grandparents provided, and taken him in her arms. He remembered the soft, warm comfort of her embrace and the scent of lavender that clung to her bed robe.

Swallowing, Stephen dashed the tears from his eyes and sat down to look through the box. On top lay a pale gray envelope, which he recognized as his mother's stationery. On the front, in his mother's elegant copperplate handwriting, was his name. He took out the envelope and tore open the flap, then pulled out the sheet of paper inside and opened it. It, too, was written in his mother's hand, although the writing was shakier than he had ever seen it and filled with blotches. He began to read.

Dearest Stephen,

I am very ill, I fear. The doctor looks grave and tells me it is possible that I could have another seizure. Therefore I am writing you to tell you something that I have never had the courage to say. I have committed a great sin against you, though you must believe that I did it with a good heart, my sole concern being your happiness.

I imagine you remember that when you were very young, I took you away from your father and brother and returned to live with my family. Never think that I did not love your father, for I did. Joseph Ferguson was a good man, and I loved him dearly. But I was weak, ill and frightened, so I ran home. I took you with me because you were young enough that you needed your mother and because I could not live without at least one of my sons. But I could not bear to take everything away from Joe, his wife and both his sons. Samuel was older than you and very close to his father, and it was obvious that he already loved the same way of life that Joe did, so I left him with his father. Please believe me when I say that I did not leave him for any lack of love for him. It broke my heart to do so.

You were young enough that I expected you would quickly forget Joe and Sammy, but I had not reckoned with your devotion. Night after night you had bad dreams and woke from them crying. Daily you asked me where Sammy and Papa were and when we would go back to them. It tore my heart to see you so unhappy. Finally, I could think of nothing else to do, so I told you that they had died, hoping that this, at last, would free you from your thoughts of seeing them again and enable you to forget them and be happy once more. After a time, it seemed to work. You gradually accepted that they were gone, and you began to forget. You became happier here.

But I had lied to you. In fact, they did not die. To the best of my knowledge they still live in Montana, in the town named Nora Springs.

As the years passed, I realized what a wrong I had done to you. When you grew older, I knew that you could have met your father and brother and gotten to know them. First because of my weakness and then because of my foolish lie, I had deprived you of your rightful family.

Yet I compounded my sin by not telling you the truth then. I feared that you would hate me for the lie I had told you, for the years that I had deceived you and kept you from Joseph and Samuel. I let the time pass, putting off telling you the truth, and with each year, my deception grew worse, so that I was more and more terrified of revealing what I had done.

But I cannot die with this sin on my soul. I have to tell you now and hope that you will not hate me. No matter how foolishly or selfishly I may have acted, I love you more than I can tell you. I hope you will forgive me.

I am entrusting these letters I have written to Samuel to you. I know you will see that they reach him.

I leave you with all my love.

                                                            Mama

Stephen read the letter through, then his eyes went back to that single earth-shattering paragraph. His father and brother were alive. He sat back, the letter fluttering down to his lap. *Samuel. Papa.*

*They were alive!*

He returned his attention to the box in his lap. On one side of it sat a small stack of letters in envelopes, tied together with a pale blue ribbon. On the top envelope was written his brother's name. He ran a finger over the black ink, as though it were some sort of link with his brother and the life buried deep in his memory.

Next to the letters lay a small wooden whistle, crudely carved. He picked it up. It was his toy; he could remember that. He had worn it on a string around his neck, except when the nanny or his grandmother discovered it and ordered him to take the cheap thing off, for it ruined the look of his expensive little suits. Gently he rubbed it between his thumb and forefinger, recalling the times he had sat fingering it just that way when he was a child, and the momentary comfort it had given him. Sammy had made it for him. There was a moment's flash of memory of a small, rough cabin and of towering, thin trees. Evergreens of some kind, so tall they dwarfed even a grown man.

Beneath the whistle lay a set of two small, ornate silver picture frames fastened together by delicate hinges so that they closed, holding the pictures inside. Stephen opened the frames. Inside the two ovals were miniature portraits done in oil by an expert hand. In one frame was a portrait of a young boy with the same coloring as his own. The face, too, was similar to his when he was a child, though a little blunter, perhaps. The boy was smiling broadly, and the portraitist had captured the blend of boyish mischief and innocence in his young face. Stephen's heart began to pound in his chest. It was Samuel.

On the other side was a portrait of an older man; he looked to be about Stephen's age now. He stared out of the picture without a smile, but there was a certain lightness around the eyes that made one think humor lurked inside him. His face was rougher and heavier than Stephen's, but the eyes and the shape of his mouth were like his. There was no denying the family resemblance. It was his father.

Seeing their faces, memories came tumbling into his mind: the smell of his father's pipe and the feel of flannel beneath his cheek as he sat on his father's lap; sitting beside Sammy in front of the fire and watching him whittle;

laughing as the man in the picture swung him up above his head and set him on his shoulders. He could remember, too, that last morning and the terrible ache in his chest, the gut-wrenching fear, as Mama rode with him out of the yard, leaving Sammy behind them.

Stephen snapped the portrait set closed and leaned his forehead against his palm, the picture frame cool and hard against his skin. They were alive. All these years he had gone his way, living his life alone, they had been there, alive. He was flooded with a thousand questions, but, more than that, he was filled with emotions that pulled and tore at him. They were his flesh and blood, his family. He had to see them.

He would leave immediately, he thought. Pack his bags and go, staying only long enough to tell Elizabeth and his grandparents where he was going. Grandpapa would no doubt be furious, but Elizabeth would be her usual calm, collected self, pointing out that with their wedding at least a year away, his being gone for a few months would hardly matter.

Stephen jumped up, shutting the box, and went to the wall to yank on the bellpull. When his valet answered a few minutes later, he set him to packing his clothes, ignoring Charles's startled, curious stare. Then he trotted down the stairs to his grandfather's study. On one wall hung a large map of the United States, including its western territories. Stephen found Montana—how far north it was!—and dragged his finger up and down across the territory until at last he found the name he was seeking. It was a little dot in the northwestern part of the state, practically all the way to Canada, in the mountains along the Flathead River: Nora Springs. That was where he was going. That was where he would find his brother and father, so long lost to him. Excitement shivered through him.

Nora Springs, Montana!

* * *

The pace of the horses began to quicken. Stephen pulled aside one corner of the window curtain and peered out, wondering why the tired horses had speeded up. He saw a small wood hut and barn ahead, with a corral beside them, and he realized that they were approaching another way station. He sighed. He had been hoping that they were at last about to reach his destination, but obviously this wasn't Nora Springs.

Stephen let the curtain fall and leaned his head back. It had been a long, tiresome journey. He had told his grandparents what he intended to do, and, as he had expected, his grandfather had been set against it. Elizabeth, of course, had been understanding. She was an independent female who didn't need her fiancé around all the time, and since the wedding was set for a year away, there wouldn't be any problem with his returning in time. She understood his amazement at learning that his father and brother were alive, and she fully agreed that he should reestablish relations with them.

He had started on the trip almost immediately, accompanied by his valet. Stephen had tried to talk Charles out of going, knowing it would be a difficult trip into a part of the country that was still rough and wild, but Charles had pleaded to come. He was mad about the West. Stephen had more than once found him reading a pulp magazine about the exploits of some Western hero or outlaw. So, in all conscience, Stephen had felt that he could hardly leave Charles behind, and he had finally agreed to let the Englishman go with him.

He had set out eagerly, excitement welling in him. He was curious and eager, not only at the thought of seeing his family again after so long, but also at the idea of traveling west, seeing new territory, stepping into a land that was unknown and still untamed. As the train had rolled north and west, he had been glued to the window, watching the famil-

iar land change into the vast sweep of prairie and finally into
the near-desolation of the flatlands of Montana. It was so
empty, sparsely dotted with sagebrush, and so immense.
And the sky! It seemed bluer than he had ever seen before,
and somehow higher, wider, arching over the great land all
the way to the horizon like a huge, inverted blue bowl.

The railroad ended in Missoula, and from there he and his
valet had had to take the stage northwest to Nora Springs.
They'd had to wait three days before the next stagecoach left
for Nora Springs, and then, to his amazement, the stage ride
had taken more time than the much longer trip by train from
his hometown. They were climbing up into the mountains,
and the straining horses went slowly. They had to stop frequently to change teams at the small way stations. At first
Stephen had been so entranced by the magnificent scenery
of the rugged mountain country that he had scarcely noticed the discomfort of the journey. But finally even the
towering mountains, soaring pines and swiftly running
creeks couldn't distract him from the jolting of the poorly
sprung coach or the choking dust that came in through the
windows. Their progress was agonizingly slow, and they had
to stop at night in the small, airless way stations, where they
slept on hard cots, dined on tasteless food and breathed in
the perpetual smell of dust and horses.

In vain Charles brushed Stephen's suit in the morning and
pulled forth a freshly starched white shirt. Within minutes
he was coated with road dust again. The passengers, all
male, slept and dressed in a single large dormitory-style
room. Stephen noticed that the other passengers cast sideways looks of amazement at Charles as he scurried around
freshening Stephen's clothes, shaving him and helping him
dress. Stephen, who had spent almost his entire life being
waited upon by servants and living among people similarly
used to being waited upon, felt suddenly embarrassed about
it. This was a hard country, and the men who lived here were
hard, too. There were calluses on their hands, and their skin

was dark and rough from the sun. Their daily lives were a
struggle to tame nature, and he could see in their eyes a kind
of stunned amusement at watching a man who had to have
help to get dressed.

Stephen wasn't sure which he felt the most: embarrassment at appearing a ridiculous figure to the people around
him, or astonishment at being the object of anyone's
amusement. Never before in his life had anyone regarded
Stephen as weak or soft. He was a man of strength in the
world in which he lived, a gentleman of honor as well as a
businessman of some wealth and power.

Because of this unaccustomed uneasiness around his fellow passengers, he kept to himself, conversing little with the
other men. It made the journey even more tedious. On the
train he had talked with several men who were glad to tell
him about their part of the country and themselves. On the
stagecoach, his only respite from boredom was looking at
the scenery.

When they pulled into the way station, Stephen stepped
out of the stagecoach with the other four passengers and
walked around, working out the kinks in his muscles. He
wondered how much longer it would take to reach Nora
Springs. It was only midmorning. Surely they would make
it there today. It would be a great relief to spend the night in
a real bed in a hotel instead of on one of those miserably
hard cots.

He leaned against the corral fence, watching the station
worker and driver switch the horses. A slender lad in a large
floppy hat joined the others and began to help them. Both
men greeted him with a smile and a clap on the shoulder. He
worked quickly and efficiently, his fingers nimble, though
he obviously lacked the others' strength, and all the while he
kept up a running conversation with the men, laughing as
he talked.

When the stage was ready to pull out, the lad climbed up
on top with the driver and his shotgun rider. Stephen

guessed that he had begged a ride off them, paying for it with his help and lively conversation. Stephen found himself thinking about the boy as the coach started forward again. There was something about him that nagged at Stephen, but he couldn't decide what. His expressive face had been intriguing. It was a trifle small, almost effeminate, and because of that and his size Stephen guessed him to be barely in his teens. Yet his movements as he worked with the horses had been smooth and practiced, with none of the gawky awkwardness of youth. Stephen frowned, wondering why it was that the boy stayed in his mind. There was something about him . . . but he couldn't put his finger on it.

Finally Stephen gave up with a mental shrug and leaned against the side of the coach, trying to nap. But with the ruts and bumps in this crude road, it was difficult; every few minutes, the movement of the coach would jolt him awake, rapping his head sharply against the wall. Even with his eyes closed, Stephen could tell that they were climbing again. He hoped they would not have to stop and get out and walk to the top, as they'd had to do before at a few particularly steep inclines. Then he felt the coach begin to shift downward and pick up speed. The ground seemed to level out, yet still the horses moved at a good clip. Stephen glanced at his watch. They'd been traveling for over an hour. Could they possibly be coming to yet another way station? The horses were fresh, but still, it had been a hard haul for them uphill.

He pulled aside the window curtain and looked out. To his amazement he saw buildings ahead of them. He opened the curtain wider and glanced around. They were in a valley, with the mountains all around them, and the coach was moving along a road beside a wide strip of water. This was no mountain creek but a river. And the town . . . His pulse quickened. Could it be Nora Springs at last?

They reached the edge of the town. There was the marker: Nora Springs. Stephen's stomach tightened into a knot. He was close to meeting them. What would it be like? Would they be instantly family? Or remain strangers forever?

The coach pulled up to the side of a small building and stopped. A couple of men were standing on the porch. One was young and rather nondescript. The other was older, with a great deal of gray in his hair and thick beard, and he chewed incessantly. The older one spat a stream of brown juice into the street, then called, "Hey, Jess!"

"Hi, Burley. Carter." The lad climbed nimbly from the coach, jumping the last couple of feet to the ground. "What are you two lazing around for?" He glanced toward the driver. "Thanks, Harry."

"Anytime, Jess. You know that."

"Yeah," the younger man on the porch joked. "Your ma cooks too good a meal for anyone to refuse you a ride."

"That's the truth, sure enough," the driver agreed genially as he, too, climbed down.

Stephen and the other passengers emerged from the stage and stood waiting in the yard. The driver went around to the rear and unfastened their luggage. Stephen took the bags from his hands, but Charles hurried forward.

"Mr. Stephen, sir! I'll take them." The valet sounded thoroughly shocked at the idea of Stephen handling his own luggage. He seized both leather bags and inspected them, shaking his head over their condition. "There. Two scratches. Those clumsy oafs. I knew they weren't paying attention to what they were doing."

Stephen smiled faintly. "Hard to travel without doing any damage to the bags. And I expect you'll have to let me carry them. There's still the trunk, and you will need help to carry that." He glanced around. No sign of a porter. Before this trip that would have surprised him, but not now. His glance fell on the boy, now standing in front of the porch, thumbs hooked in his pockets, talking to the other men. "Here, boy!" Stephen called to him. Since the lad had needed to cadge a ride off the stage driver, he would undoubtedly be willing to earn some money. Stephen dug in his pocket for a coin. "Where's the best hotel in this town?"

The boy and the two men on the porch turned to look at him, their faces blank. Stephen flipped the coin toward the lad, and he caught it in an automatic gesture, but he still stared at Stephen uncomprehendingly.

"Help my man with the trunk and take us to the best hotel," he explained. Was the boy slow-witted? "You. Boy." What had the driver called him? "Jess."

Every line in the lad's body stiffened. He planted his hands on his hips and his feet apart, anger radiating from him. "Are you talking to me?"

"Yes, you." Whatever was the matter with him? One would think Stephen had just insulted him instead of offering him a job. "Well, do you want the money or not?"

The men on the porch guffawed, and the driver and shotgun rider joined in. One of the men pointed at the boy, hooting with laughter, saying, "Yeah, *boy*, why don't you carry the gentleman's bags?"

Jess shot a fierce look at the man who had spoken, then turned to Stephen. He reached up and swept his hat from his head. A pair of long, bright red braids fell down his back.

Stephen stared. Good God! The boy they called Jess was a girl!

## Chapter Two

Jessamine Randall had never understood why it was necessary, in order to be a woman, to wear encumbering petticoats and skirts. Being a girl of independent mind, she refused to wear them and instead wore trousers and flannel shirts that she got in boys' sizes at Swenson's Mercantile, just as she did her heavy work boots. She knew her wearing them worried and horrified her mother, but after all, it was her mother who had introduced her to the practice.

Jessamine's father, a chopper in Ferguson's lumber camp, had died when Jessamine was a young girl, crushed by a tree that had fallen the wrong way. His death had left Jessamine's mother, Amanda, destitute and heartbroken. There had been men who had wanted to marry her, but she had been unable to bring herself to do that so soon after her beloved husband's death. Fortunately, Mr. Ferguson had been kind enough to give Amanda a job by which she could support herself and her child. She had cooked for the men in the lumber camp, and, raising Jessamine in that rough place, with the bitter winters of northern Montana, it had made sense to dress her daughter in boys' clothes. She was to regret it later. Jessamine, always a tomboy and the pet of most of the tough men in the logging camp, resisted any later attempt on her mother's part to dress her as a girl.

After all, it made no sense. It was much easier to do her work in the simple boys' clothes, and they were warmer, too. Besides, she had no interest in looking like a lady. In fact, she saw very little advantage to being a woman. The men held all the interesting jobs, while women like her mother did nothing but cook and clean up after them. It was the men who had the adventure and the fun, whether it was felling trees or sawing them into lumber or tallying figures in Joe Ferguson's mill. It was men who held the power and made the money. A woman was doomed to have none of those things and could make her way only in some menial occupation or by marrying. Jessamine had no intention of doing either one.

She didn't plan on marrying and having babies like Marian Sloane, who slaved her life away for a husband and eight children and looked like she was fifty years old when she was barely thirty. Nor did she intend to cook and clean and scrape by like her mother. She wouldn't wear dresses; she wouldn't learn how to flirt with a man, or try to please him. There was no way that she would allow something like love to lead her into a life of servitude and pain like her mother's—like that of all the women she knew.

No. That wasn't the way for her. She called herself "Jessie," not "Jessamine," that long, flowery name her mother had given her. She eschewed feminine dress and actions. And she set out to learn everything she could about the business she had grown up in until finally, when she was seventeen, she had been able to prove to Joe Ferguson that she knew his operation inside and out. He had given her a real job in his mill. It wasn't femininity that had gotten her there, she knew; it was brains and determination. And the only way to get those things noticed was to make the fact that she was a woman as *un*noticeable as possible.

The result of all this effort was that the men around the mill and camp pretty much accepted her as one of them, but they did so with an indulgent, teasing air that infuriated

Jessamine. They were constantly playing practical jokes on her to try to get her to react with a feminine shriek of terror or rage, or making jests about whether she was a girl or a boy. Therefore, any reference to her sex, especially mistaking her for a boy, which was one of the men's favorite games, was guaranteed to arouse her ire. So when this stranger called her a boy and demandingly tossed her a coin to carry his bags, anger surged through her.

Jessie swung around, glaring at him, ready to take him down a few pegs. But instead, when she looked at him, her jaw dropped, and she could only stare. She had never seen a man like this before. He was dressed in a suit, something few men around here wore, except for the banker and the undertaker. But his suit bore little resemblance to those of the banker or the undertaker. His was not black, as theirs were, but a pearly gray and made of a soft, obviously expensive cloth. The style was different, too, and it had been tailored to fit him exactly. He wore thin gloves that were gray, just like his suit, and on his feet were not work boots, nor even sensible, ordinary shoes, but elegant black leather shoes that followed perfectly the line of his feet and were polished to a high gloss—or had been before they met the dust of the road. Around his neck he wore a silk cravat, fastened with a discreet pearl stickpin.

She had never seen a man dressed as elegantly, as softly, as *beautifully*, as this. She'd always heard that gamblers were fancy dressers, but none of the ones who'd come through Nora Springs could hold a candle to this man. What was he that he dressed this way? He was a city slicker, that was for sure. He didn't look like he'd last a day out here; she was amazed that he'd managed to make it this far.

He was staring at her with an equal amount of amazement, obviously dumbfounded at seeing a supposed boy turn into a girl right before his eyes. It was a look Jessie had seen before. Well, let him stare. She told herself she didn't care.

"I—I'm terribly sorry," he said finally in a well-modulated, refined voice. "I didn't realize—that is—well, I beg that you will forgive my rudeness."

Jessie had never heard anyone talk quite like he did, either. Even Elias Moore, the banker, who used big words and whose grammar was the best around, didn't speak so smoothly, with that upper-crust accent.

"That's all right. It's happened before." Jessie strove for a nonchalant tone. She wasn't about to let a man, especially a . . . a *popinjay* like this think that he'd hurt her feelings. She shot the coin back to him, using her thumb to give it graceful, careless spin in the air. Then she turned and spat. It was a talent one of the young loggers had taught her when she was six, and her mother had whipped her hide more than once when she'd caught her doing it as a little girl. She didn't do it anymore, but this man's high-toned speech and obvious horror at seeing a woman dressed and acting as she was had gotten her back up. She'd show him. "There ain't no hotel here," she added, purposely making her voice rougher than it naturally was. "Leastways, not one fine enough for a fella like you. They sleep four to a room, and you have to walk a block to get a bath."

Stephen's eyes had flown wide open when he saw her spit, and the news of the primitive living conditions left him almost speechless. He had never imagined anything like this. "I see."

"Best you can do is a boardinghouse. My mother runs the nicest one in town, and she's got an extra room, if you want it."

Stephen hesitated for a moment. The gray-bearded man spoke up. "She's right. Ain't no place better'n Miz Randall's."

"Well, yes, all right, then. That is, if there's somewhere for Charles." He glanced at the man standing a little behind him and to one side.

Jessamine glanced at the other man. She'd scarcely noticed him hovering there, she'd been so occupied in looking at his companion. He wasn't half as nicely dressed as the one who did all the talking. "She's only got one room. 'Course, you and your friend could share."

"Heavens!" Charles exclaimed, looking so appalled that Stephen could hardly keep from smiling. "Surely there must be servants' rooms."

Jessie looked at Charles, understanding dawning on her. "Servant?" Her gaze swung to Stephen, more astonished than ever. "You travel with a servant?"

Charles drew himself up stiffly, oozing British disdain from every pore. "A gentleman always takes his valet wherever he goes."

Jessie gazed at Charles as if he were some rare form of flora or fauna. "Does he, now?"

Stephen shot Charles a look that made him subside, then turned to Jessamine. "Now, Miss...uh, Randall, I believe it is? If you could give us directions to this establishment..."

"Better than that. I'll take you myself. It's on my way."

"That's very considerate of you. I would appreciate it."

"Sure." Jessie started toward the trunk, saying over her shoulder, "Charles, if you'll grab hold of that end, I'll take this one. It's not too far to Mama's house."

Stephen moved quickly, interposing himself between her and the trunk. "Miss Randall!" His voice was shocked. "You cannot carry my trunk!"

Jessamine shot him an amused glance. "Oh, yeah? I'm strong enough."

"I couldn't possibly allow a lady to lift something like that."

"A lady?" Jessamine repeated, blinking. She couldn't remember ever being called that before.

"I will help Charles carry it," Stephen went on.

"Master Stephen!" Charles protested. Stephen knew that he would consider it an outrage for his employer to pick up something, but Stephen quelled him with a look.

"I have managed to carry a few things in my life, Charles."

"Yes, sir." Charles's thinned mouth and stiff posture conveyed his utter disapproval, despite his acquiescence.

Jessie glanced from one man to the other. They were a strange pair. She wondered if this was the way men from the city always acted. She shrugged and reached for the two bags on the floor. "Doesn't matter to me. It's your trunk. I'll take these, then."

Stephen stared. Never in his life had he seen a woman pick up her own luggage, let alone someone else's. The women he knew would stand around for hours waiting rather than do something so unfeminine. But then, this woman obviously didn't care about appearing feminine—look at the way she dressed!

His eyes followed the pull of her denim trousers across her backside as she bent to pick up the carpetbags. Damn! Obviously he hadn't been paying attention earlier when he'd assumed she was a boy. She might be slender, but curves like that couldn't belong to a boy.

"Miss Randall, please, no. I'll send Charles back for them."

The men on the porch had been watching the whole scene with interest. Stephen's courtesy immediately struck them as weakness and tickled their rough sense of humor.

"That's right, *Miss Randall*." The younger man mimicked the way Stephen addressed her, using a falsetto voice. "Them bags're too heavy for a *girl*. Oh, no, I'm wrong—for a *lady*. Ain't that right, Jess?"

Stephen glanced at the man, frowning. These were low, crude sorts of men, the kind he wouldn't ordinarily have paid any attention to. However, they had no right to address any woman—even one dressed in pants—in that sneering way. He was just about to let them know that fact in no uncertain terms, but the girl took the wind out of his sails by swinging around and addressing them first.

"Yeah!" she retorted, dropping the bags and planting her fists on her hips pugnaciously. "I reckon that's who I am, to a lead-bottom, belly-crawlin', beer-swillin' know-nothin' like you!" She turned to the older man. "I don't know what you're doing, Burley, hanging around trash like this."

The older man grinned. "Well, now, Jessie, I was just wondering the same thing."

Jessie picked up the bags and stalked off down the street.

Stephen's eyebrows rose at Jessie's retort. Looking at the man's reddened face, he decided that there was really nothing he could add to what she had said. He glanced at his valet, whose normally expressionless face was now torn between laughter and disapproval. "Come on, Charles. I think we'd better follow the lady."

"Yes, sir."

Jessamine led them away from the stage depot along the main street of Nora Springs. The town, Stephen thought, was as crude as the men they'd just encountered. Wooden buildings stood on either side of a wide dirt street, hard-packed now, but marred by deep wagon ruts and holes that gave mute evidence to what it must be like in the spring, when it rained and the street turned to mud. Very few of the wooden buildings were painted, except for the identifying lettering—often misspelled—across the doorway. There was one major street crossing this one, on which sat a few more businesses. The only buildings of any note were a rock-walled bank with bars on the windows and a large, rambling wooden structure that Stephen could not identify. Once across this street, they seemed to have passed out of the downtown area, and now they walked past houses of all sizes and quality.

As they walked, Stephen came up alongside Jessie, carefully walking between her and the occasional traffic along the street. When she crossed to the other side of the street, he moved so that he would be on the other side of her, again next to whatever vehicles might pass. Jessie wondered why. Stephen, used to being courteous, didn't even notice what he had done. Walking between a woman and the street was as natural to him as eating or sleeping—or any of the other conventional courtesies that were drummed into all well-brought-up boys' heads.

Jessie glanced at him from time to time. There was something familiar about him, though she couldn't quite put her finger on what it was. It was almost as if she recognized him, as if she had seen him before, or seen a picture of him. But she was sure she hadn't; she would have remembered anyone like him. Still, the feeling nagged at her. She wished she could figure out what it was.

She came to a stop in front of a large, pleasant house with a wide, welcoming porch. It was painted a pale blue, with clean white shutters. There was even a low picket fence around its wide yard, along with a few bushes planted along the foundation.

"This is my mother's house," Jessamine stated with pride.

"It's lovely," Stephen answered honestly. After most of what he'd just seen, this well-cared-for place looked like a palace, even though it was modest compared to his family's mansion in St. Louis.

"Yes. Mama's very proud of it." It was obvious from Jessie's face that it was the nicest place she had ever seen. Stephen wondered if she had been outside the territory, or even outside Nora Springs. "Let's go in, and I'll introduce you to Mama. Then I have to get to work."

Work. Stephen was unused to women working, too. He knew they did, of course. After all, there were the maids and the housekeeper who worked in his home. And there were the women, mostly immigrants, who worked in the factories. Obviously this woman had little money, so that, like those women, she had to work. But why didn't she work in her mother's boardinghouse? And whose house could she clean around here? Besides, she didn't look like the poor, pinched-face, pale women who worked in the factories, or the subservient maids, with their downcast eyes.

He followed her up the dirt walkway to the house and onto the porch. Jessamine swung the door open and went inside, calling her mother. Stephen and Charles followed her into the hallway and set down the trunk with relief. An older woman bustled into the room, wiping her hands dry on a spotless apron. Everything about her was spotless. Her hair, which had once been the color of her daughter's but was more faded now and showing streaks of gray, was pulled back softly and curled into a roll at the back of her head. Her skin, redhead fair, showed wrinkles around the eyes and mouth, but they were lines of laughter, smiles and kindness, and they gave her a soft, loving look. Her eyes were a paler blue than her daughter's, as if they, too, had faded over the years. She was short and a little plump, and there was a sweet, motherly look to her, but there was also something in her eyes that said she had seen many things and few of them were kind. Stephen liked her immediately.

"Hello, I'm Amanda Randall," she said a little breathlessly, her eyes sweeping down Stephen's elegant clothes and taking in Charles hovering behind him.

Stephen bent over her hand as if she were a wealthy, highborn lady. "Mrs. Randall. It's a pleasure to meet you. You have a lovely home."

"Thank you." Color rose in Amanda's cheeks, and she almost bobbed a curtsy. Jessamine might never have seen a man like this, but her mother had grown up in Baltimore, and she knew a high-class gentleman when she saw one. "Goodness, Jessie, why didn't you ask the gentleman to be seated in the parlor?"

Jessamine shrugged and rolled her eyes. The way her mother was acting you'd think a prince had walked into her house. "He just came to see about a room."

"I was told that Mrs. Randall's rooming house was the nicest to be found," Stephen explained.

Amanda beamed. Her daughter frowned. Whatever was the matter with her mother? Just because this sissified stranger bowed over her hand like he was going to kiss it and talked sweet, she acted like he was something special. Jessamine couldn't see what was so great about him. Why, he couldn't even go anywhere without dragging a servant along to take care of him, like a little boy with his mother.

"Thank you," Amanda answered him. "I can guarantee that it's the cleanest. I'm afraid we have only one room available, but if you'd like to look at it, Mr ... uh ... ?"

"Forgive me. I haven't introduced myself." Stephen had been so startled by Jess's transformation into a girl that he hadn't even thought to tell her his name. "You must think I'm terribly rude. My name is Stephen Ferguson."

"Ferguson!" Both women exclaimed, staring at him.

"That's who you look like!" Jessamine went on. "I kept thinking and thinking you looked like somebody I knew. It's Sam. You look like Sam Ferguson—kind of."

Of course, he wasn't as muscular as Sam, and his shoulders weren't as wide, nor his arms as powerful. And he was paler. Sam's heavier, rugged features were handsomer, she thought. Samuel Ferguson had protected Jessie many times throughout her life, and he was nothing short of a hero to her. As far as she was concerned, no man could compare favorably to him. But she could see the similarity between the two men. They were almost the same height, they had the same thick black hair, and the lines of their lean-hipped bodies were much alike.

"Of course," Amanda chimed in. "Are you related to Joe and Sam?"

Stephen's throat tightened. It felt strange to say it. "I'm Joseph Ferguson's son."

Amanda's jaw dropped. "You—you're—"

"Who?" Jessamine asked impatiently. "What are you saying, Mama? Sam doesn't have a brother!"

"Yes," Amanda corrected quietly. "Yes, he does. Joe had—has another son."

Jessamine stared, first at her mother, then at Stephen, then at her mother again. "But how—who—how come I didn't know?"

"Some things are private, Jessie. Joe Ferguson doesn't go around spouting off about his life to everybody."

Jessie felt hurt. Why had Sam and Joe never told her? Joe often ate at her mother's house. She and Sam were friends. It seemed unfair that her mother knew about it and she didn't. Why, even her own mother hadn't told her.

"Well!" Amanda was saying. "This is quite a surprise. Oh, Joe is going to be so happy to see you." She turned to her daughter. "Jessie, you must take Mr. Ferguson to the mill to meet Joe. I mean, that is, to see him." She sighed and beamed at him. "This is wonderful."

"I was going there anyway," Jessie said, her voice a trifle surly. She felt as though this man was to blame for her feeling of exclusion from her surrogate family, and though she knew that was silly, she couldn't keep from being annoyed with him. "If you want to come along, it's all right."

"Jessie! A little more courtesy to our guest, please."

Jessie grimaced.

"Thank you," Stephen told her. "I would appreciate it very much if you would take me to my father." He glanced at Amanda, and she saw an instant of vulnerability in his dark brown eyes. "If you're sure that he'd want to see me. I—I'm not quite sure of my reception."

"Don't worry about that. He'll be thrilled to see you. He's never forgotten you."

"Nor have I forgotten him."

Jessie clomped over to the front door in her heavy boots and turned. "I'm ready to go, if you're coming."

"Give the poor man a bit of time to freshen up from his journey," Amanda told her daughter, fixing her with a stern look. "Let me show you to your room first, Mr. Ferguson."

"No, that's not necessary. I'd rather go right now to see my father."

Jessamine opened the door. "Come on, then. Let's go."

They walked into the center of town and up the major cross street on which Stephen had seen the odd-looking building. Stephen realized as they continued to walk that it must be this building, with its great pile of dirt and the odd conical side building, toward which they were heading.

Neither of them said anything as they walked. Stephen realized that Jessie was miffed about something, though he couldn't imagine what. She appeared to be a rather touchy young woman. But now he asked curiously, "What is that building?"

She gave him an odd look. "The mill? Why, that's Ferguson Sawmill. Don't you know?"

"No. I'm afraid I know very little about my father. So they cut up these pines I saw on the way here?" His voice rose a little at the end in question.

"Yeah. They have a logging camp, too, where they fell the trees. Sam's up there. He runs the camp. Mr. Ferguson, Joe, takes care of the mill. That's where I work, too."

He glanced at her, surprised. "You work at a sawmill? But what could you do there?"

Jessamine's features tightened. "Just 'cause I'm a woman it doesn't mean I'm stupid or helpless."

He was taken aback yet again by her harsh words. Why was this young woman so angry about everything? "I didn't mean that you were. It's just, well, a lumber mill hardly seems like a place for a girl to work."

"I'm not a girl. I'm full grown. And there's hardly anything about the lumber business that I don't know. I could run that mill myself if I had to. I do the books for Joe, and the correspondence. I help wherever he needs me." Her chin lifted a little defiantly. "I've been with Joe Ferguson for years."

"Ah, I see. Years when I haven't been. Is that right?"

Jessie glanced at him, surprised at his perceptiveness. "Well, yeah. That's right."

"Then I'm glad he's had such a loyal helper as you."

Jessie didn't quite know how to answer that. She stuck her hands in her pockets and walked faster, pulling ahead of him. Stephen found his eyes drifting to her denim-clad legs. He'd never seen a woman's legs so revealed before, except in a house of ill repute. They were not bare, but the denim, worn to softness, outlined her shapely curves, and seeing the shape of her legs and derriere in broad daylight on a public street sparked a flicker of excitement. It was bold; it was brazen; it was titillating. Yet there was nothing about Jessie Randall that suggested a woman of easy virtue. Stephen had the feeling that if he was to make an overture toward her, she would probably hit him with a hard right hook.

He realized how he was ogling her legs and tore his eyes away. Whatever was the matter with him? He had other, more important things to think about than some graceless hoyden's legs.

When they reached the sawmill, Jessamine ran lightly up the stairs to the upper floor ahead of Stephen and reached for the door handle. He had to almost run to grab it first and open it for her. She looked at him oddly. He was beginning to think that she had never met anyone with manners.

Inside the mill, he was assaulted by a piercing, high-pitched whine that made him want to plaster his hands over his ears. The girl didn't seem to notice it. She waved toward the left, where he could see that most of the factory lay. She said something, too, but he couldn't understand it over the loud, irritating noise. She turned toward the right, leading him down a hall, where it was minimally quieter. She walked into a large room, obviously an office, and closed the door behind her, cutting out some of the noise. On the other side of the room lay a door, and Jessamine went straight to it. She knocked on it twice, loudly, and Stephen heard a gruff rumble of a voice on the other side.

Jessie opened the door. "Uncle Joe, there's somebody here to see you."

"Tarnation," Stephen heard, followed by more unintelligible words.

Jessie shook her head. "You'll have to come see him."

Moments later, a middle-aged man stuck his head out the doorway. His thick black hair was liberally sprinkled with gray, and his hard frame was beginning to blur with excess weight. He wore a plaid flannel shirt tucked into denim trousers and heavy work boots on his feet. He frowned at Stephen. His face went slack. "What the hell...?"

Joe Ferguson took a step or two, and Stephen moved the same distance closer to him. Joe stared, unable to speak. Stephen's heart was pounding, but at least he'd been prepared for this. His father hadn't. Stephen took another step forward. "I—I'm Stephen Ferguson. I—"

"Stephen! Stevie?" Ferguson glanced around, as though he would somehow find in the room an answer to his confusion. "You can't—"

"I'm your son. My mother was Eleanor McClellan Ferguson."

Joe shook his head. "I can't believe it." Tears filled his eyes even as a wide grin spread across his mouth. "Stevie!"

He came closer, wonderingly, looking into his son's face, so familiar and yet so unexpected. When he reached him, he threw out his arms and pulled Stephen to him in a fierce hug. "It *is* you! I never thought I'd see you again." He squeezed him, then stepped back to look him over once more. He shook his head. "It seems impossible. My God, you were just a little boy."

"Five. It's been twenty-two years."

"Twenty-two years." Joe shook his head. "I can't believe it. Come in, come in." He pulled Stephen into the inner office and closed the door after them.

Jessie stood, looking at the closed door. Who was this man? Why had she never heard of his existence? Joe hadn't even introduced him to her.

She made her way over to her desk and plopped down in the chair behind it. She shuffled some papers around, but she scarcely noticed them. Her mind was on Joe and the man who had appeared out of nowhere claiming to be Joe's son. Did Sam know about him? she wondered. What would Sam say? Would he be thrilled to see the stranger, too, or was he as much in the dark as she had been?

But he must know. How could Joe have a son who was clearly an Easterner? A son who was younger than Sam? It didn't make sense. Curiosity overwhelmed her feelings of exclusion and resentment, and she sat doodling on a pad of paper, her eyes staring vacantly, trying to figure out the puzzle of Stephen Ferguson.

He was different. He bothered her. He had from the first moment she saw him—even before she knew he was Sam Ferguson's brother. Somehow he disturbed her equilibrium. When he had looked at her earlier, she had been aware for the first time in years of the masculinity of her clothes. For some reason it had hurt when he had mistaken her for a boy. She didn't know why. He was a useless sort of a fellow; one look at him, and anybody knew he couldn't take care of himself out here. She doubted that he'd ever slept in the open; he wouldn't have the strength to wield an ax in the forest, or the skill to be a sawyer in the mill. Hell, he probably couldn't even ride or use a gun. He wasn't anyone; she shouldn't care for a second what he thought of her.

Yet for some reason—maybe it was his elegant clothes or those heavily lashed eyes that gave him the handsomeness of Lucifer before the Fall—when his amazed eyes had run down her body to her clunky boots, she had become acutely aware of what she looked like. Suddenly her hands and feet had seemed too big. She remembered the stains and dirt on her pants. She thought about the awful carroty color of her hair and the fact that it was straggling out from her braids, as it always did. She felt clumsy and embarrassed, which she strove to hide under her usual air of uncaring defiance.

Thinking about her reaction, Jessie frowned. It was stupid to let the man upset her. It wasn't as if he was someone about whose good opinion she cared. What did it matter if he stared at her as if she were some strange form of wildlife he'd never seen before? So what if he considered her unfeminine? She'd never had any desire to be feminine.

She tossed her pencil onto the pad with a loud sigh, disgusted at the way her thoughts kept circling around Stephen Ferguson. She shoved back her chair and strode out of the room and down the hall into the mill. She was used to the high-pitched whine of the buzz saw and the heavy thrum of the steam engine that powered it, as well as the thumping and clanking of machinery and chains, and she didn't notice the incessant din any more than she did the fine sawdust that drifted through the air and caught on her hair and clothes. She stood for a moment watching as the head sawyer and his dogger maneuvered one of the long pine logs into position for the spinning saw. The saw bit cleanly into the wood, and chips and sawdust flew thickly. The very air seemed to vibrate with the power of the machine. Jessie watched, enthralled, as she always did.

A hand curled around her arm, and she jumped. In the midst of all the noise, she hadn't heard the man's approach. She turned and looked up at a large man with a mane of thick, long, dark blond hair and a reddish-blond beard, stained brown around his mouth from tobacco juice.

He was the only man she knew who was bigger than Sam Ferguson; his neck and shoulders were bunched with muscles so thick it seemed almost as if he had no neck at all and his head sat directly upon his shoulders. Sawdust covered his hair, beard and clothes, and even clung to his skin. His name was Frank Grissom, and he had worked in the mill practically his whole life. Once he had been the best dogger Ferguson Mill had ever had, though he had never had the supremely accurate eye to be a good head sawyer. Now he was the mill's foreman. Jessie disliked the man, but she had to admit that he was good at his job; there wasn't a man in the mill who dared disobey one of his commands, and he knew the running of the mill from the ground up.

He smiled at her, displaying a set of stained teeth from which three were missing, lost in one or another of the fights he'd had over the years to establish and maintain his dominance. He smelled like tobacco and days-old sweat, and Jessie tried to breathe through her mouth so that she wouldn't smell him. He pulled her away from her vantage point and with him into the relatively quiet hall.

"Hello, Jessie," he said, still grinning. "You looking for me?"

Jessie gave him a flat, blank stare. For some reason Grissom had taken a shine to her; it amazed her almost as much as it appalled her. She had never considered herself pretty, dismissing her fiery hair as orange, her white skin as a nuisance and her blue eyes as pale. As a result, she couldn't imagine what any man would see in her. But then, Frank Grissom didn't have much taste or gumption, as she well knew. He seemed dead set on her.

It was a decided nuisance. As long as Joe or Sam was with her, Grissom would never dare approach her, but if he caught her alone, he always managed to put his hand on her arm or shoulder and grin at her, leering, as he was doing now, and he would talk to her in what Jessie supposed he must think was a sexually stimulating way. The only thing his heavy, often vulgar comments aroused in her was disgust, and the feel of his hand anywhere on her made her skin crawl. Just as bad was seeing his mean little eyes sliding over her body as if he was trying to see right through her clothes. She had never liked Frank Grissom, thinking him a small-brained bully of a man, but in the past year, since he had started to pursue her, she had grown to despise him.

Joe and Sam would never have allowed him to bother her if they had known about it. A few months ago Sam had heard him make a suggestive remark to her, and he had given him a choice, in a low, deadly voice, between talking to Jessie like that and keeping his job. Grissom, of course, had apologized to her sullenly. Jessie knew that if she complained to Sam, he would get rid of Grissom. But that was just the problem. Grissom was a good foreman, and if he was fired, it would mean that Sam would have to come back from the lumber camp, or Joe would have to assume the extra workload. With all the other problems they were having, the last thing Jessie wanted was to add to the Fergusons' troubles.

Besides, it would gall her to hide behind Sam or Joe. She was proud of being able to take care of herself just like a man took care of himself. Sam, by whom she measured all other men, would never go running to his father or any other authority to get rid of someone who was bothering him. He would take care of it himself. And that was what Jessie was determined to do. She could handle Frank Grissom without dragging the Fergusons into it. Eventually, no matter how annoyingly persistent Grissom was or how thickheaded, he was bound to get the message that she wasn't interested in him.

She had spent the past few months avoiding being caught alone with him, and when she had been unable to avoid it, she had made it clear that she discouraged his pursuit of her. But avoiding him greatly limited her freedom of movement, particularly around the mill, and he was so thickheaded that she was beginning to wonder if he would ever realize that she didn't want to be around him.

"I been thinkin' about you all day," Grissom went on. "Thinkin' maybe we could take a little walk tonight."

"I don't think so."

"Then how about tomorrow?" He smiled and reached out to lay his hand on her shoulder.

Jessie quickly stepped back. "No."

His grin grew. "Not scared of me, are you, Jessie?"

That was a taunt sure to arouse a reaction in her. She squared her shoulders and faced him, her chin going up. "I'm not scared of you or any other man."

"Then how come you keep hidin' from me? Huh, little Jessie?"

Her eyes flamed. "Don't call me that."

"Why? You are, you know. So little my hands could go clean around your waist and then some." He started toward her, his hands reaching out to demonstrate the narrowness of her waist.

Jessie stepped to the side, knocking his hands away, and moved around him. "It looks like a person has to hit you in the head to make you understand! I am not interested in you, and I have no intention of taking a walk or doing anything else with you. Ever. Now, is that clear enough?"

His upper lip curled into a sneer. "Yeah, that's clear. Think you're too good fer a man like me, don'tcha? Who you waiting for? You think young Ferguson's goin' to go after you?" He snorted. "You're wasting your time if that's what you're hopin' fer."

Jessie flushed. "I'm not hoping for anything. I just don't plan to waste my time with you!"

She swung around and marched toward her office. Behind her, she heard Grissom's obnoxious laugh. "When you get tired of waitin', just let me know! I can make you forgit ol' Sam!"

Jessie shuddered. As if any woman who wanted Sam Ferguson would even look at a man like Frank Grissom!

She slammed into the office and plopped down at her desk. Frowning, she snapped open a ledger book and got to work.

# Chapter Three

Stephen followed his father into his office. Joe sat on the edge of his desk and motioned Stephen toward a chair in front of it. For a long moment they simply looked at each other.

For years Stephen had had only a vague memory of his father, remembering mostly his size and his voice. The miniature in the mahogany chest had brought back his face, but Stephen had studied it so often on his journey that he was no longer certain how much he remembered his father and how much of his memory was taken from the portrait. Now, looking at Joe, he knew he remembered those eyes—bright, alive, a chocolate brown so deep they looked black. The eyes hadn't changed. His hair might now be salt and pepper instead of black, and his face might have thickened and grown lined, but the eyes were still his father's, and he knew them. He knew *him*.

"It's been so long." Joe shook his head wonderingly. "I'd given up hope of seeing you again. Are you still living in St. Louis? Married? Children?" He laughed a little nervously. "It's odd. I know you, yet I don't know you at all."

Stephen smiled. "I feel the same way." This man was his father, and he felt the pull of the basic connection, yet Joe was also virtually a stranger. "I'm not married, no children. But I am engaged. I've lived in New York City the past few years, but it looks as though now I'll go back to St. Louis to live."

"Your grandparents? Are they still alive? And—Nora? How is Eleanor?"

Joe knew the answer instantly from the pain that filled Stephen's eyes before he even said a word. "She's—she died quite recently. It was very sudden."

"Dead?" His father seemed to shrink, as though something had drained out of him. "No. So young?"

Stephen nodded. "We were shocked. The doctors said it was a stroke, a seizure in her brain."

Joe shook his head slowly, staring at the floor, as though seeing something that lay only in his mind. "Such a beautiful woman, Nora was. I lost her long ago, but still . . . it saddens me."

"In a way, that's why I came."

"To bring the news to Sam and me?"

"Yes, I suppose, but more than that. You see, until after her death, I didn't know where you were, or even that you were still alive."

"What?" Stephen's statement startled Joe out of his reverie. "What do you mean?"

"I thought you were dead, both of you."

"Well! I guess that explains why you never came before. I reckoned you'd just forgotten about us, or maybe didn't want to see us."

"No. No, you mustn't think that. As soon as I learned that you were alive, I came here."

Joe smiled. "I'm glad. But tell me, why would you think we were dead?"

"It's what Mother told me. Apparently, when we first returned to St. Louis, I was so unhappy, always wanting to come back, that she decided to tell me you were dead. So I would accept it and get over it. Later, she was afraid to tell me the truth, to admit that she had lied to me. So she let it go on."

Joseph Ferguson sighed. "Ah, poor Nora. She never could bear to see anyone fret, especially you. It doesn't surprise me that she'd say that. She was inclined to get rid of a problem the quickest, easiest way possible. She didn't always stop to think about what it would mean in the future. I can't say I regret her impulsiveness. She married me the same way."

"Then you don't regret marrying her?" Stephen studied him, wondering if he still felt bitter toward the woman who had deserted him so many years ago.

"No. How could I regret it? Those were the happiest years of my life, and they brought me two sons. A lot of sweet memories." He shrugged. "I don't believe in letting bitterness or hurt corrode what was beautiful before the pain. You can't ever lose memories, unless you destroy them yourself." He smiled faintly and levered himself away from the desk, moving across the floor to look out the window. "I'm not saying I'm a saint. There were times after she left when I cursed that woman. I laid the cause of all my grief at her feet. But I knew, deep down, that she wasn't to blame any more than I was. She missed her family and the life she'd had in the city. She hated the cold and the loneliness. The life here was too hard for her. She couldn't bear to live here any more than I could bear to live anywhere else. For months I could tell how unhappy she was. I knew she loved me, and I knew I still loved her. We just weren't meant to be together all our lives."

He turned to his son. "I wanted her to be happy. She didn't take everything from me. She left me Sammy. I knew it tore her heart out to do that. She did it only out of love for me, so that I wouldn't be left with no one."

"You're very understanding."

"Just realistic. You can't expect a rose to thrive in the snow. I always knew a man like me was lucky to have her for however little time I did." His face lightened. "And now I have both sons again."

Stephen swallowed. He could feel tears pricking his eyelids, and he didn't know what to say. His father returned to his perch on the desk and leaned over to pat his leg.

"Ah, I can't wait for you to see Sam again. He'll be so happy. Do you remember how close you were as boys?"

Stephen nodded and reached into his coat pocket. "I remember him very well." He held out his hand toward Joe, palm up, the little wooden whistle resting in it. "He made this for me. I can remember carrying it around everywhere I went. As I recall, there was a terrible scene once because we left it behind when we went on a visit."

"Yes." Joe picked it up and turned it over in his fingers, examining it. "I remember him making it. It was one of the first things he whittled. He still does, you know, whenever he's just sitting. Makes all kinds of things."

"Where is he? Does he work here, too? When can I see him?"

"Not for a while, I'm afraid. I run the mill, and Sam's in charge of the lumber camp, out in the woods where we cut the timber. It's a good day's ride there and back. But he'll be in town in a week. Our main saw blade broke, and we had to order a new one. Right now we're using one of the old ones, not as big or as good. The new one's coming in on the train next week, and Sam's going to Missoula to pick it up, so he'll be through here. You can meet him then."

"Oh." Stephen's face fell a little. "I had hoped to meet him right away. But, of course, if I can't..." He paused, then asked, "But couldn't I ride out to the camp tomorrow and see him? I mean, surely I could rent a horse somewhere in town, and you could tell me how to get there."

His father frowned. "I don't know. Of course you could get a horse—you could have mine. But trying to find the camp by yourself wouldn't be a good idea. You aren't used to the area. You could easily get lost."

"Not if you gave me directions or drew me a map. I'm usually rather good at finding my way."

Joe looked troubled. "That's in a city. It's different here. There's no road to the camp. You have to follow landmarks, which you aren't familiar with, and then there are the trees and the mountains that cut off your view and make directions confusing. Even the distances seem different because of going up and down hills. I don't think it's a wise idea. I understand that you'd like to see Sam sooner, and I wish you could, but—" He stopped, and his scowl eased. "'Course, I could send somebody with you. Jessie, for instance. I could spare her tomorrow."

"Oh, no, please, that's not necessary."

But Joe was already crossing the room to the door. "Sure it is. It'll keep me from worrying."

Stephen knew that Miss Randall didn't think highly of him. He'd seen the faint contempt in her eyes as they swept over his clothes, and the way she'd looked when she found out he had brought his manservant along with him. It was clear that she thought he was an overdressed, incompetent dandy. She would not be happy about having to lead him out to Sam's lumber camp.

Nor did he want her along. She was an odd creature, and he wasn't sure how to act with her. Besides, it galled him that she thought him negligible, even an irritation. From the time he had grown into manhood, he had been considered a very eligible bachelor, and he was accustomed to women trying to arouse his interest, not to a woman who was, at best, laughing at him. He was used to being pursued in a delicate, feminine way, to being flirted with and admired, to having a woman look at him with big, limpid eyes as he talked, as if hanging on to his every word. He had often found that irritating, but with Jessie Randall, he'd discovered that the reverse was even worse.

"Jessie!" Joe called to the girl sitting a few feet away, absorbed in a ledger book. "Come here, girl. I guess you know my son, Stephen, seeing as how you brought him to me."

Jessie rose and came to the door at his request, but she only looked coolly at Joe as he spoke, offering no response to his words.

"Of course, now that he's found us after all this time, he wants to see Sam right away. He wants to go up to the camp. Why don't you show him the way up there tomorrow?"

Jessie's eyebrows shot up, and she stared, momentarily speechless. The condition didn't last long, however. "But, Uncle Joe, I've got work to do. There's the payroll to figure, and it's the end of the month besides. I have to—"

"And who do you think did those things before you came along, I'd like to know? I think I can manage to do the payroll. What I'm not too good at anymore is sitting in the saddle for any length of time. You know, since I rebroke that leg four years ago, it's been real hard for me to ride."

"I know, but—" The last thing Jessie wanted to do was to play nursemaid to this fancy Easterner. And it hurt that Joe found her so easily expendable that he would take her away from her work to lead Stephen Ferguson around the woods. He couldn't have said more plainly that what she did could be done by anyone, that it wasn't important. She had spent the last few years trying to prove how well she could handle this work, how much she belonged at the sawmill even though she was a woman, and here Joe was, as much as saying that she wouldn't be missed.

However, she could hardly refuse to do it, no matter how much she hated the idea. Joe had helped her more times than she could count, and now he was asking her for *her* help. She couldn't turn him down, especially not when he reminded her of the pain it would cause him to ride. She turned her gaze toward Stephen, her anger and frustration focusing on him. "Sam'll be in town in a week! Why can't he wait till then?"

"Wait?" Joseph Ferguson repeated. "You're asking the man to wait after he's already waited over twenty years?"

"Well, if he's been content that long," Jessie asked bluntly, "why in tarnation can't he hang on a few more days?"

Ferguson grimaced. "Sam's his brother. It's only natural."

Jessie's mouth tightened. She couldn't very well tell Joe that she thought his son was a selfish, spoiled rich boy who was used to having people do everything for him. It was obvious that if he wanted anything, he expected everyone else to drop whatever they were doing and get it for him. But if Joe couldn't see that for himself, she wouldn't hurt Joe's feelings by telling him.

"Please, no," Stephen spoke up, rising from his chair. It couldn't be any plainer how much she disliked him. If Joe forced her to take him to the camp, her dislike would only get worse. "I shan't need Miss Randall's help. Honestly, Father." The name slipped out, surprising him. "I can find my way perfectly well by myself. All I'll need is a map."

"A tenderfoot always thinks that," Jessie retorted. She didn't want to take him, but his almost haughty assurance irritated her. He was the kind who thought he knew everything. No doubt he thought that they were just country bumpkins. "But there aren't any street signs here."

"I am well aware of that, Miss Randall." Stephen's voice turned icy, his annoyance unconsciously heightening his upper-crust manner of speech. "However, I have managed to find my way around quite a few places in the world that were no more familiar to me than this one. Whatever you may think, I'm not entirely helpless."

"Now, Stephen, we didn't mean that," Joe began placatingly.

But Jessie interrupted him. Crossing her arms, she fixed Stephen with a flat stare. "It's different out here. Sometimes a map doesn't help. It can be dangerous."

"Dangerous?" Stephen's voice was filled with disbelief.

"Wild animals—wolves, bears, that kind of thing. Not to mention the fact that sometimes there are human animals who would as soon kill you as look at you."

"You sound like one of those preposterous magazines Charles is always reading."

"No, she's right about that," Joe agreed. "It's not a safe or easy country. A smart man carries a gun when he rides into the timber—and he makes sure he knows how to use it."

Stephen stiffened. "And that's why you want her to lead me there? To keep me safe? You want me to take a girl along for protection?"

"Now, don't get in a taking about this. I don't mean anything bad, son."

"Nothing bad! You mean, other than thinking I'm too stupid to find the lumber camp and such a weakling and a coward that I need to hide behind a woman's petticoats? No, forgive me, this woman doesn't wear such things, does she?" He shot a glare at Jessie. "No doubt skirts would impede your wrestling a bear or firing a gun."

"No more than lack of brains keeps some people from talking," she retorted.

"All right, now, you two. I don't want a full-scale war here in my office."

Jessie set her jaw mutinously, but with an effort Stephen reined in his temper and gave his father a nod and a thin smile. "Of course. I apologize. My words were quite uncalled for." He sketched a bow in Jessie's direction. "Miss Randall, I hope you will accept my apology. I was rude. Father, I appreciate your concern. However, I fear that you and Miss Randall have underestimated me. I've taken care of myself for some years now. I am able to ride, and I have a good sense of direction and have never gotten lost, even in the old section of Paris. If, in fact, the woods are that dangerous, then I shall ask you to lend me a firearm with which to protect myself. But I intend to ride out to see Samuel tomorrow, and I shall do so alone."

For a moment there was silence, during which the two men looked at each other expressionlessly. Then a grin cracked Joe's face. "No denying you're Sam's brother," he said. "I thought you looked like a reasonable man, but it's apparent that you're just as bullheaded as he is. All right." He shrugged. "I can see I can't stop you. I'll draw you a map tonight. You can borrow my horse and gun."

"Thank you." Stephen returned his smile. "Now, if you will excuse me, I should return to Mrs. Randall's and get settled."

"Sure. I understand." Joe paused. "You're welcome, you know, to stay with me. I'd like to have your company. The only thing is, I recently rented out our house and moved into a room here at the office. It didn't make much sense having all that space with Sam living at the camp and me spending most of my time here."

"All right." It seemed odd to him that his father would be renting out his house and living in a single room at the mill office. He wondered if it was an indication that Ferguson Mill was having financial difficulties. There wasn't any tactful way to ask. He would have to watch for signs of it in the next few days, and if it did look as if the mill was struggling, he would be able to help his father and brother out of the problem.

"Then I'll see you at supper," Joe went on calmly. "I take most of my meals at Amanda's. Best food in town. Ain't it, Jessie?"

"Of course." Jessie watched Joe, puzzled. She'd never known him to capitulate so easily on anything.

Stephen left the office, brushing past Jessie with a nod. Jessie watched him go, then turned to Joe as soon as the door shut behind Stephen. "Joe, you aren't serious, are you? You aren't going to let him ride out tomorrow!"

"What else can I do? He may be my son, but he's a grown man. I can hardly keep him from it."

Jessie shifted nervously. She felt guilty for being reluctant to take Stephen to the camp. That had probably gotten his back up. Then she'd had to go and point out how dangerous it was, something that would insure any man's being determined to do it just to prove he wasn't afraid. She had practically pushed Stephen into going alone tomorrow. If he got lost or was jumped by a mountain lion or encountered one of the hundred other deadly things the mountains had to offer, it would be her fault. Joe would never forgive her.

"But, Joe, think of what might happen to him. Remember that fellow from Massachusetts who came out here two summers ago? He fell off the side of the mountain, and they had to send him home with both legs broken."

"I remember. But I have no authority over Stephen. He hardly even knows me."

"You can't just give up and let him do what he wants. I don't want to waste a day leading him around, but I don't want you to lose a son, either!"

Joe smiled. "Then perhaps you'll do me a favor."

"What?" Jessie eyed him warily. He obviously had a scheme in mind, and he had just as obviously maneuvered her into a position where she had to agree to do it.

"Follow him. Don't let him know it. Just stay close enough to get him out of trouble if he needs it. If nothing happens and he manages to find his way to the camp, then he'll never have to know. But if he loses his way or gets on the wrong side of a bear, you can rescue him."

It wasn't a task Jessie relished. She didn't like the idea of sneaking along behind anybody, spying. And it still would be a waste of the entire day. But she knew that if she didn't do it, Joe would, and his damaged leg would ache terribly. Besides, her guilt wouldn't let her refuse, nor would the knowledge of all the good and kind things the Fergusons had done for her and her mother over the years. "You know I will, if that's what you want."

"It's the best solution I can see." Ferguson smiled and patted her cheek. "I knew you'd be a sweet girl about it."

Jessie grinned. "I'm always wax in your hands, Uncle Joe."

He rolled his eyes. "Well, if only you'd told me that years ago, I might have been able to keep you on the straight and narrow."

"I doubt it."

"You're right."

Jessie turned and started toward her desk. She paused and looked at Ferguson, her expression serious again. "I noticed you didn't tell your son why you've taken to sleeping in the room under the office."

He shrugged. "No use dumping my load of troubles on the boy the minute he appears. He's got a whole different life to lead in St. Louis. I doubt he'll be here long. I don't want to take up what little time I've got with him talking about whatever bastard damaged our saw blade. Besides, what good would it do to tell him?"

"I guess you're right," she admitted. Stephen Ferguson didn't look like he'd be any help in finding and stopping whoever had broken into the mill a few weeks ago and broken the main saw blade. "But I wish you'd tell somebody. I don't like the idea of your staying here alone. What if he tries something else? You could get hurt."

Joe assumed a wounded expression. "It's nice to know that you think I couldn't handle the sneakin' coward by myself."

Jessie sighed. They'd been through this argument before, from the moment she and Joe looked at the blade and realized that it hadn't just broken but had been deliberately ruined. Joe had been staying at the mill ever since, hoping to catch the man in the act of committing another crime. But he refused to hire anyone to help him. He refused to even tell Sam about it, saying he didn't want his son leaving the camp to come help him in town.

"All right," Jessie said, raising her hands in surrender. "I know it's useless to argue with you."

She walked to her desk and sat, pulling the ledgers to her. But her mind wandered from the numbers to the more intriguing topic of the identity of the person who had damaged the blade. Who could it be? There weren't any rival timber businesses around that might want to grab Joe's share of the profit. And she could see no reason anyone else would want to hurt the mill; it could only damage the economy of the whole town, dependent as it was on the timber business. Joe suspected it was someone with a grudge against him or Sam. Jessie was inclined to agree, since it made little sense otherwise. Still, she couldn't imagine anyone holding that heavy a grudge against the Fergusons.

Shrugging, she pushed the thought out of her mind and tackled the ledgers once again. If she was going to waste the whole day tomorrow, she'd better put in some extra work now.

Jessie pushed the swinging door open with her back and turned into the dining room, balancing a heavy bowl in each hand. The men who ate at her mother's table were all large and hard-working; they had hearty appetites, so supper each evening was a large meal, consisting of several platters and dishes of food, which Jessie usually helped Amanda to carry in.

Most of the men were already seated at the long table when she entered the room that evening. One man, however, stood to the side, hands clasped behind his back, as if he was waiting for something. It was Stephen Ferguson.

It was all Jessie could do to keep from gasping when she saw him. He had changed out of the clothes he had worn this afternoon. That fact alone was amazing—how many times a day did this man change clothes?—but what nearly caused her to lose her composure was the way that he looked in them. Jessie had never before met a man whose physical appearance could be so... well, dazzling, almost. Stephen had obviously washed away the dust of the road. His hair was its true deep black, glossy and thick, and his features seemed sharper and more distinct. The suit he wore was black, and though Jessie had thought there could be nothing more elegant than the gray suit he had worn earlier, this one was. Instead of a jacket and waistcoat, he wore a short frock coat, fitted close to his body. A snow-white shirtfront gleamed between the lapels of his jacket, and around his neck was a white cravat, fastened with a costly gold stickpin. Matching gold cuff links glittered at his wrists.

There was nothing ostentatious about him. The cravat pin and cuff links were his only jewelry. Jessie had seen other men, usually gamblers, who wore more than one gold ring, as well as huge jeweled tiepins, jeweled cuff links, and gold watches and chains with ornate little fobs dangling from them. No, Stephen Ferguson's manner of dress was quiet, even reserved, but only a fool would not have seen that years of gentility and wealth lay in what he wore.

It was a style that suited him. He was heartbreakingly handsome, and the expensive simplicity of his clothes provided a perfect frame for his good looks. Jessie thought wryly that Stephen Ferguson probably had no lack of ladies competing for his favors in his slick, rich world. She thought of her denim trousers and flannel shirt. They were much washed and faded, the pants almost white at the knees and the shirt with a pocket that had torn away at the corner. Jessie could imagine what a plain country bumpkin she must look to Stephen, and she could feel the heat of embarrassment rising in her face, even as she told herself that she didn't care what a man like that thought.

"Miss Randall," he said to her, nodding slightly.

"Mr. Ferguson." She kept her voice cool and hoped that her face looked uncaring. She walked past him to set down the bowl and reached toward her chair to pull it back.

Much to her surprise, Stephen pulled the chair out for her. She stared at him for a moment, then glanced at the chair. Somewhat cautiously, she sat down and started to pull it up to the table, but she found that he was pushing the chair in, too. She had lifted her bottom partway off the seat to pull the chair, and when he pushed it in, the chair hit the back of her legs and she plopped down ungracefully. Color flooded her face, and she kept her eyes turned down.

He walked away, and she followed him out of the corner of her eye. Her mother had entered the dining room and set her dish down, and now Stephen was jumping to pull out her chair, too. Jessie was chagrined to notice that her mother accomplished being seated with grace and ease, smiling a thank-you at the young man. Jessie began to eat quickly and silently, glowering at her plate. She felt embarrassed, which irritated her, and she disliked Stephen Ferguson for being the cause of both feelings.

Most of the men fell to their food with concentration, just as Jessie did, but her mother, Joe and Stephen kept up a lively conversation as they ate. Jessie noticed that several of the men kept shooting curious glances at Stephen, though none of them showed open amusement or contempt, as she had half-expected they would. J.D. Bowden, the little bank clerk, practically fawned over him. That was to be expected. Though he couldn't aspire to Stephen's modish attire, he was the sort who would be impressed by it. He, too, never worked with his hands, spending his days counting up Elias Moore's money, and no matter what the weather, he dressed always in the same outfit of conservative black suit and white shirt with celluloid cuffs and a collar so stiff and tight he looked as if he was about to choke. Jessie suspected that he had already assessed Stephen's wardrobe and added up its total expense; the cost in itself would be enough to make Bowden admire him.

It was the fact that the three other men treated Stephen with deference that surprised—even annoyed—Jessie. They were laboring men, and Jessie couldn't understand why they didn't think Stephen Ferguson was a useless decoration of a man. There were just some people, she supposed, who must be awed by the trappings of wealth.

Amanda and the Ferguson men made a few attempts to draw Jessie into their conversation, but her brief replies soon made it clear that she had no interest in being included, and after that their conversation flowed onward with never a glance or remark in her direction. Even though she realized that she was being silly, the fact that they left her out made her even more disgruntled.

After supper Jessie helped her mother clear the table and clean the dishes. "Well," Amanda said without preamble once all the men were out of earshot, "you certainly weren't friendly to our new guest."

"I didn't see any reason to butter him up," Jessie replied coolly.

Amanda stopped, one hand on her hip, and gave her daughter a long look. "You think that's what I was doing?"

Jessie shrugged, unwilling to meet her mother's eyes. She knew Amanda had not been buttering him up. Her mother didn't believe in it. That was what made it even worse; Amanda must actually like the man. "Well, I don't know anything else to call it."

"He's a charming young man."

"You like all those airs and graces he puts on? I think it's silly. Like putting you and me in our chairs—as if I wasn't capable of sitting down by myself!"

"He was being polite."

"Polite! Polite's a man tipping his hat to you or saying please and thank you and excuse me."

"Or a man opening a door for you, or letting you walk through first—or pulling out your chair for you."

"Well, I never said I liked those things, either."

"That's because very few men do them for you. The men out here are rough. Most of them don't have much polish or sophistication. But they'd treat you with more courtesy if you didn't always act as if you were a boy. Why, you've worked at it so hard, everyone practically thinks you *are* one!"

"Well, I don't need all those polite folderols. What good do they do?"

"They make you feel special. Feminine. Surely you wouldn't mind it if men treated you like a woman?"

"I don't want to be treated like a woman. I want to be treated like an equal."

"Wearing trousers and clumping around in boots doesn't make you an equal." Amanda, who had started picking up the utensils from the table as they talked, paused to point a fork at Jessie for emphasis. "It makes them not respect you."

"That's not true!" Jessie retorted, stung.

"You know what you look like when you dress that way? A *boy*, not a man. And not a grown woman, either. Just a child. You know what I think? I think you wear those clothes because you're scared."

"Scared!" Jessie let out a short, indignant laugh.

"Yes, scared."

"I ain't scared of nobody."

"You're scared of yourself. Or men, or something. You're scared to act like a woman, to admit that you are one."

Jessie stared. She and Amanda had argued most of her life about the clothes Jessie wore, but she had never before heard her mother speak so harshly or bluntly about it. "Mama!"

Amanda sighed. "I'm sorry, honey. It's just that when I see a nice young gentleman like that Stephen Ferguson come into town, so handsome and charming, I always wish that you would—"

"Stephen Ferguson! Mama, you can't be serious! You think that I would have any interest in a man like that? A dandy? A greenhorn? Why, he's so ignorant he doesn't even know that he doesn't know anything. He looks like somebody just took him out of a bandbox, all clean and starched and pressed."

"Jessamine Randall! I'm ashamed of you. Judging a man by the clothes he wears or where he comes from. It's what's inside a man that counts, not how he dresses."

"I'm not! I mean, well, this is different. It's not just the clothes he wears—it's everything about him. Why, he even carts a servant around with him everywhere he goes. Can't he dress himself? I bet Stephen Ferguson can't do a single thing that's useful, and even if he could, he wouldn't, because it might dirty his jacket, or maybe even his hands." She made an expression of mock horror.

"You certainly think you know a lot about the man for a girl who's hardly spoken to him."

"I saw him. I heard him. I've seen how he acts."

"I know." Amanda pulled a long face. "So polite, so charming—terrible of him, isn't it?"

Jessie rolled her eyes. "Mama, you might as well give up. I'm not interested in any man, and most especially not in Stephen Ferguson. How could I feel anything for a man I can't even respect?"

"I don't know, Jessie," Amanda said, shaking her head. "I just wish you could find a man you could respect. But I don't know how that's going to happen if you don't stop comparing every man you meet to Sam."

Jessie smiled fondly. "But Sam's the best. There's no one like Sam."

Amanda sighed. "I know. I know. But he's not the man to pin your hopes on."

"I know Sam would never marry me!" Jessie would never admit that she had entertained that daydream more than once. She had always declared that she never intended to marry, but she knew deep in her heart that if Sam were to ask her, she wouldn't hesitate for a second. She had practically worshipped him ever since she could remember. As far as she was concerned, Sam Ferguson could do no wrong, and it made her want to burst with pride and joy whenever he smiled at her or said that she'd done a job well. "I'm not stupid. I'm not the kind of woman he'd marry. Besides, he thinks I'm still a baby."

Jessie knew Sam would never feel love or desire for her. He treated her like a younger sister—or, really, more like a younger brother! Even to think of marrying Sam was like crying for the moon. She'd never get it, and she wouldn't waste her time thinking about it.

"It's not that you aren't good enough for him," her mother went on reassuringly. "Any man would be lucky to marry you. But Sam is a lot older than you, and he's known you since you were knee high to a grasshopper. He cares for you, but . . ."

Jessie shrugged, unwilling to let her mother see that she cared how Sam felt about her. "I know, Mama. And I know it's not the way a man cares for a woman he's going to marry. It doesn't matter. I don't want to get married. I'm happy as I am."

Amanda's look was a little skeptical, but she didn't say anything. Arguing with Jessie only turned her stubborn as a government mule. They finished cleaning the table in silence.

Jessie went upstairs to her room, where she undressed and washed up quickly, then pulled on her modest white cotton gown. She turned down her bed; she was used to going to sleep early and rising early. But tonight she felt unaccountably restless, and she didn't lie down immediately. Instead she wandered to the window and stood looking out. Beyond the town stood the dark bulk of the mountains; a full yellowish moon hung suspended at the top of one peak, as though it had been speared by the dark thrusting point. She leaned against the window frame and gazed at it, dreamily lost in contemplation.

A scraping noise brought her out of her moonstruck trance, and she glanced into the yard below. A man stood in the side yard, clearly illuminated by the full moon. He was smoking a cigar; now and then it glowed red as he drew on it. He was turned away from her, so that she could not see his face, but she knew who he was. It was Stephen Ferguson, stepping outside for a last cigar. Polite, of course—he wouldn't dream of stinking up her mother's house with a cigar.

Jessie watched him. He, too, was gazing at the moon hanging over the mountains. She wondered what he thought as he looked at the sight. She couldn't imagine anyone from the city really understanding that wild, stark beauty, feeling it to the depths of his soul, as she did. Yet he stared, as intent and motionless as she had been.

He'd do better to come upstairs and go to his bed, she thought with a touch of acerbity. If he didn't get up early tomorrow morning, he'd be hard pressed to make it to the camp and back in one day. She grimaced. Stephen Ferguson probably wouldn't even roll out of bed until eight or nine o'clock. He was a gentleman of leisure, after all.

Jessie sighed. She didn't want to wait that long on him. Heck, she didn't want to have to follow him at all. But she'd promised Joe, and she would never go back on her word. She'd trail him until he got lost, then take him by the hand and lead him to the camp. It promised to be a long, boring day.

Below her Stephen turned, dropping his cigar and stubbing it out. Jessie jumped to the side of the window so that he wouldn't see her if he happened to glance up. She watched him as he walked into the house. In the moonlight his face was pale and handsome. She supposed that most women would find him attractive; they probably swooned all over him. But not her. Not her.

# Chapter Four

Much to Jessie's surprise, Stephen Ferguson came down to breakfast the next morning at six o'clock, when Amanda first started serving. Jessie was sitting at the table, sipping a cup of coffee and wondering how she was going to pass the time until he got up, when he walked through the door.

Her eyebrows rose in surprise, not only because of the early hour, but because of his dress. She had expected him to wear another one of those fancy suits. He was as immaculate as ever, not a hair out of place or a wrinkle in his clothes, but he wore simple denim trousers and a dark blue flannel shirt, with a sleeveless leather vest over it, just like any man around here might wear. He even had on riding boots, though they were of a smooth, glossy brown leather so polished that one could see one's face in them.

He smiled at her expression. "I thought casual clothing might be in order today. I went to Millburn's General Store yesterday afternoon and purchased these. What do you think? Do I look like less of a tenderfoot now?"

His tone was gently mocking. Jessie shrugged sourly. "Don't matter how you look. It's what's inside that counts."

He chuckled. "Can't get the better of you, can I, Miss Randall?"

"Don't feel bad," she told him cockily, lifting her chin. "I don't know any man who can."

His eyes were bright with amusement. "I imagine that's true."

"So, are you getting an early start?"

He nodded, dishing up eggs, bacon and biscuits from the sideboard. "Yes. I thought that was wisest. My father indicated that the way was rather rough and slow-going."

"Do you ever talk like a regular man?"

"Pardon?" He glanced at her in surprise.

"I said, don't you ever talk just like people?"

He paused, as though turning her statement over in his mind, then said, "Yes. Just like *some* people. But apparently I don't speak as the people around here do. Is that right?"

She made a brief grunt of amusement. "That's right."

"Is that why you don't like me?" he asked calmly. "Because I'm different?"

"I didn't say I didn't like you."

"Perhaps not. But somehow I've received that impression."

"I can't help what you think."

"Then you do like me?"

"I didn't say that, either."

"Then what are you saying?"

"I'm saying I don't know you, and I don't think about you one way or the other."

"I see. Well, that certainly puts me in my place."

Jessie set down her cup and pushed her chair from the table. Talking to Stephen Ferguson made her feel slightly uneasy. Besides, she had planned to saddle up before he left and wait for him outside town, but to do that now she would have to hurry.

"Well, it's been real nice chatting with you, Mr. Ferguson."

"The feeling's mutual."

"I'll see you around."

"Off to work so early? I hope I haven't chased you away."

Jessie stiffened. "Nobody chases me away. I have things I have to do, is all."

He nodded. "Of course. Goodbye, Miss Randall."

"Yeah." She turned and walked through the kitchen door, very aware of his eyes following her.


Thirty minutes later, Jessie was seated cross-legged on a boulder, hidden from the road by a thick stand of trees and elderberry shrubs, waiting for Stephen to ride by. Her horse was nearby, tied to one of the low branches of the elderberry.

At last her patience was rewarded by the sound of a horse's hooves thudding against the packed dirt of the road. Jessie scrambled off the rock and over to her horse. She laid a hand over the mare's muzzle to keep her quiet and watched the road through the branches of the bushes. In a moment Stephen passed by on the horse Joe had lent him. He was moving at a canter, glancing all around him curiously. Jessie stifled a sigh. With the way he was gazing at the scenery, he was bound to miss the cutoff he was supposed to take, as well as the identifying landmarks. His mind obviously wasn't on what he was supposed to be doing.

She untied the horse as she let Stephen get well ahead of her. Then she led the mare to road and mounted her from a fallen log. She started down the road after Stephen Ferguson. She didn't worry about losing him; she had the imprint of his horse's hooves in the damp soil to follow, and she knew of two or three places along the way where she would have a high, panoramic view of the area through which he was traveling.

To her surprise, Stephen did not miss the road that cut off to the lumber camp. Road—they all called it that, but in reality it was little more than a track, just wide enough to allow the supply wagons up to the camp. Here, the ground was covered with a soft cushion of pine needles, and it was difficult to follow the trail. So when she came to the edge of a clearing, Jessie stopped and shinnied up a tree to look for him. She managed to catch sight of Stephen disappearing into the trees at the opposite end of the long, narrow clearing. He was still on the right path.

Jessie climbed down, gave him a few moments to get into the trees, then crossed the clearing herself. So far, he was exceeding her expectations. It was another forty-five minutes before he lost his way.

It was the stream that did him in. Stephen had followed the map for some time, feeling a little smug at finding the proper path. But when he had come upon a tumbling, narrow creek he had been so delighted that he had dismounted and cupped a handful of the icy water. As his horse drank, Stephen squatted and examined the pebbled bed of the stream. It was covered with rocks ranging from small to tiny, so smooth and flat they looked almost as if they had been laid, like a road. The rocks were colored in shades of rose, blue, green and yellowish tan, as well as flat black and charcoal gray. He found when he picked up a few and held them in his hand that they dried to a dustier, duller shade, but under the water they glistened brightly, giving the clear stream almost jewel-like tones.

Unconsciously, he moved slightly downstream, leading his horse, as he gazed at the rocks, bending now and then to pick one up. So when he finally crossed the stream, he came out further southeast than he had intended, and as he turned north to correct his mistake, he passed several yards away from the yellowish rock that was the next landmark on the map. It didn't take him long to realize that he must have missed the rock, and he retraced his steps, to no avail. He began to roam, searching for it, and soon found himself in a stand of lodgepole pine, thoroughly confused.

Stephen took a deep breath and struck out through the woods. He had to find his way out and get on the path. He couldn't get lost, not after the way he'd shrugged off Joe's warnings. That strange girl who worked for his father would have a good laugh at his expense. His lips tightened at the thought of her laughing in his face, and he pushed on through the trees. Eventually he came out of the stand of tall, narrow pines and into a small alpine meadow. He sighed with relief.

He had been climbing ever since he had left town this morning, and now he was quite high up. All around him was a soaring, magnificent view of the mountains and valleys, so grand it took his breath away. Stephen thought that he had never seen a land so wild and untamed in its beauty.

But it wasn't long before unease encroached upon his wonder. He still didn't know where he was. Had he come out of the trees above, below or to the side of where he had gone in? Now able to see the sun again, he could move northward, but if he was starting off from the wrong place, his northward movement could take him far to one side of the camp. He understood now why his father had been so concerned about him going alone, how difficult it would be to find something as small as a camp of men in an area as vast as this and how easy it was to miss or mistake a landmark. It had been foolhardy of him to try to ride to the camp without a guide.

Damn! Why had he been so stubborn? Why hadn't he listened to the wiser counsel of his father, who knew this part of the country? Why had he had to get his back up at the amusement on Jessie Randall's face, so that he'd insisted on doing this alone? Idiotic male pride, that was all it had been. He had hated to think he had to be led by a mere slip of a girl. He had hated for Jessie to think so, too.

With a curse, Stephen swung down from his horse and began to walk across the clearing, thinking. It did no good to bewail his stupidity. What he needed to do was get out of this situation.

As he paced, deep in thought, he heard a sound and turned. At the far edge of the clearing sat a person on horseback. Stephen straightened, a smile beginning on his face. Thank God, someone had happened along. Now he could get directions to the lumber camp. He mounted quickly and trotted across the meadow. Across from him the stranger also started forward.

As they drew nearer, Stephen could make out the person's features, and he realized it wasn't a stranger. He reined up short. It was Jessie Randall.

Blood rushed into Stephen's face. Of all the people to come across him! Why did it have to be her? Everything she had thought about him would be confirmed.

Then he realized that she couldn't have just happened by; that was far too coincidental. She must have come after him. His father had sent her to make sure he didn't get lost. His humiliation was complete.

He waited for her stiffly, his face a blank mask to hide the embarrassment and frustration burning within him. It had taken years of rigid social and business training to acquire that polite, expressionless veneer, which allowed others no glimpse of his weaknesses.

However, to Jessie, riding across the meadow toward him, the frozen expression on his face merely looked like arrogance. It irritated her. Imagine that! Here he was lost, exposed to danger from wild animals, starvation, thirst and the chill of the nights. And here she was, coming to save him. But all he could do was sit on his horse, looking haughty, as if she were a servant who had showed up late for her job. Jessie gritted her teeth and pulled to a stop a few feet away from him.

"Mr. Ferguson," she said, with a brief nod.

Stephen read the clear contempt in her eyes, and he had seen the little smile on her lips as she rode toward him. His feeling of humiliation deepened. It was obvious that she thought of him as something less than a man. He didn't stop to analyze why her opinion of him should matter. He just reacted to his inner writhing by setting his spine straighter and his eyes harder. "Miss Randall."

Jessie glanced around the meadow and raised a mocking eyebrow. "Stopping for a rest?"

Stephen clamped his teeth together so hard that a muscle along his jaw jumped. His embarrassment sizzled into anger. She hadn't a drop of womanly gentleness, prodding at his sorest spot like that. "Hardly," he ground out, his eyes cold and hard as marbles. "As I'm sure you are well aware, I have lost my way."

"Oh, really? I couldn't tell it from your face."

"I'm sorry." His tone indicated that he was anything but sorry. "Didn't I grovel enough for you? Was I lacking in the proper amount of humble gratitude?"

Jessie's cheeks flamed at his sarcastic tone. "I didn't say that!"

"But it's what you meant, isn't it? I was aware that you had no interest in being a woman, looking and acting the way you do, but I didn't realize until now that you don't want a man to act like a man, either. What suits you? You play the man while he whimpers and crouches at your feet?"

"Act like a man!" She whipped off her hat, and the sun glinted off the red-gold of her hair, plaited into a single braid as thick as her wrist.

Strangely, a tendril of lust curled through Stephen's abdomen. She looked wild and fierce and untamable, a challenge to his maleness, and he knew a sudden, aching need to conquer her in the most basic way. It was so swift and piercing a desire that it almost took his breath away. He knew that he wanted to curl his hand around that thick red braid and pull her to him. He wanted to kiss her as hard and as deep as he could, until she softened and trembled. The idea left him so stunned and thrumming with lust that he could not speak, could only sit and stare at her as she railed at him.

"What do you know about acting like a man?" Jessie continued hotly. "I never met anybody who acted less like one! You're more a tailor's dummy than a man. It's obvious that you don't know how to do anything, that you have to take a servant along with you to do the hard work, that you're a—a—"

"A what?" he snapped, as irritated with himself and his bizarre, lustful reaction to her as he was irritated at Jessie herself. "A greenhorn? A tenderfoot? I believe that's what you called me before. I'm not a Westerner, so I'm not a man? Isn't that what you're saying? This may surprise you, Miss Randall, but there's a lot more to this world than this one little spot in the Montana Territory. In most places, being able to cut down a tree or blaze a trail through the wilderness or spit tobacco and hit a bug at ten feet is not the measure of a man. In a great deal of the world, culture, courtesy, a good mind, a strong character, a sense of honor and duty—these are what make up a man. Not thick muscles or a sure aim with a gun."

"Fancy words!" Jessie scoffed, unable to come up with any adequate retort.

"No doubt that makes them valueless to you," he responded dryly.

"You're twisting what I said. I never said that a bull neck or a bullhead was what made a man."

"No? Then what is your beau ideal?"

"My what?"

"Your perfect man?"

"He's—he's someone you can respect, someone you can look up to. He's strong and quick, but his mind's sharp, too. He knows how to take care of himself. And he can take care of other people. He comes when you need him, and he does what has to be done. He's truthful, loyal and brave. He doesn't go back on his word."

Jessie's face had softened as she talked, until she looked almost dreamy, staring off into the distance, her eyes glowing.

"Somehow I feel this is a real man you're describing." Stephen's tone was sharp; he found her moony expression decidedly irritating.

She looked at him with wide, honest eyes. "I am. It's Sam. Samuel Ferguson."

"My brother."

"Yes."

"I'm glad to hear that my brother is such a paragon." Stephen wondered if Samuel knew that this strange young woman was so enamored of him. Perhaps he did. Perhaps he encouraged it. Her behavior might be strange, but there was no denying that she was a pretty woman, with that thick, flaming hair and big, brilliant blue eyes. Any man might want her for his mistress—if he was able to put up with her sharp tongue and outrageous ways. She would never do in St. Louis or New York, of course, but out here...

His mind turned away from the idea, reluctant to accept her as Samuel's mistress. After all, she was a young girl still, and despite her peculiarities, he suspected that she was rather innocent. Her mother seemed every inch a lady. He didn't like to think that his brother would take advantage of Jessie's obvious admiration for him.

Jessie glanced at Stephen. She felt a little foolish for having revealed her admiration for Sam. She hoped he wouldn't make a joke about it to Sam. She couldn't imagine why she'd said such things to him. Or, frankly, why she'd said any of the other things she had. Joe, even Sam, would probably have been appalled at her verbal attack on Stephen. However arrogant or sissified he might be, he was, after all, their flesh and blood. And her mother! Jessie hated to even think what *her* reaction would be.

She wasn't sure why she had gotten so angry. She had expected him to get lost before she even set out. In fact, he had done better and gotten farther than she had expected. And what did it matter to her if he was an indolent, useless ornament of a man? It was nothing to do with her.

It was just that she had had a little trouble finding him, and she had even begun to worry that she might not be able to. It had been scary coming through the stand of lodgepole pines, unable to follow his tracks on the carpet of needles, and she had been swept with relief when she had emerged into the mountain meadow and seen him. She'd ridden toward him, smiling with relief. Then she had run into the blank wall of his face.

Stephen hadn't been pleased to see her. You would think that someone who was hopelessly lost would be happy to see a rescuer. But not the high-and-mighty Mr. Stephen Ferguson. Oh, no. He'd just looked annoyed, as though she should have arrived earlier. Then, in that superior tone of his, he had accused her of wanting him to grovel and lavish her with thanks, and he had made a few sarcastic jabs about her lack of femininity. As if she weren't a woman just because she liked to wear comfortable clothes! Or maybe it was because she was more competent than he was that he thought she wasn't womanly enough.

His smug, biting comments had been like a torch to tinder, and she had immediately flared up. Jessie didn't understand how a nice man like Joe Ferguson could have such an exasperating son. She couldn't think of any other man who got on her nerves as easily as Stephen did. She thought he liked to do it.

Jessie squared her shoulders. Well, she wasn't going to give him the satisfaction of setting her anger ablaze again. Let him be as annoying as he liked. She would simply ignore him.

The rest of the ride to the lumber camp was a silent one.

The camp lay in a man-made clearing in the forest at the end of the narrow track Jessie had followed. There was a large, rough log building with a steeply pitched roof in the center of the clearing, and a smaller one to the side.

"That's the bunkhouse," Jessie explained, pointing to the bigger building. "And that's the cook shack. Over there are the stables, and that little house there is the headquarters. That's where Sam stays."

A man emerged from the cook shack and dumped a bucket of dirty water onto the ground.

"Hello, Cookee," Jessie called.

The short, slight man looked up and grinned. His hair was white and thinning, and half his teeth were missing. "Well, hi there, Jess. Wasn't expectin' ta see you 'roun' here."

"I made a surprise trip. Is Sam around?"

The man gestured toward a ramshackle building. "He's in there, doin' some scribblin' and figurin'. I reckon he'll be glad for the interruption."

Jessie grinned. "I reckon." She turned toward Stephen, and her smile died abruptly. "Come on."

She led the way to the building Cookee had indicated and jumped lightly down, tying her horse's reins to a nearby bush. Stephen followed suit. His heart was beginning to pound, and his throat swelled with excitement. Finally, after all these years, he was going to see Sammy again. He didn't know whether to grin or run.

He followed Jessie into the low building. A large, dark-haired man sat at a table near the window, his head bent over his work. He glanced up curiously at the sound of Jessie's entrance.

"Howdy, Sam," Jessie greeted him.

"What the hell are you doing up here?" Sam responded, jumping up. "Is Pa all right?"

Hastily Jessie reassured him that Joe was fine. There was a narrow bed against one wall, and a man lay on it. He was awakened by their voices and sat up. Stephen recognized him as the older man from the stage depot the day before. What was it Jessie had called him? Burley, he believed.

The old man stared at Stephen, and his mouth dropped. "Hellfire 'n' brimstone!" he exclaimed. "If it ain't the dude!"

Sam's eyes slid across to Stephen, really taking him in for the first time. He went utterly still as he gazed at him.

Stephen looked back. His heart was pounding in his chest. It was so strange to look at this man and see the resemblance to himself, to remember the boy he had been and see traces of that child in his face. Sam was about Stephen's height, with the same wide-shouldered build, though he was far more heavily muscled. His hair was dark, but still a shade lighter than Stephen's, and a black mustache spread across Sam's upper lip. His features were heavier and rougher than Stephen's, and his skin was weathered by the elements. Still, there was no denying the resemblance.

"Hello, Sammy."

"Stephen?" Sam's voice slid upward questioningly. "My God."

Sam started toward him, and Stephen thought he meant to hug him. But before he reached him, the dawning wonder on Samuel's face faded, and he hesitated, then held out his hand to shake Stephen's. The gesture was formal, even remote, and Stephen could see the wariness in his eyes. His brother wasn't too sure whether he liked having him return.

Stephen's heart fell a little. After his father's happy greeting, he guessed that he had expected too much from Samuel. Sam had been only a boy when he left; he had grown up without Stephen. No doubt Stephen was little more than a distant memory to him; being the older, he wouldn't have remembered him through the years with the warmth that Stephen had felt. Stephen wouldn't mean that much to him anymore.

Stephen managed a smile. There was really no reason Samuel should welcome him back with open arms. It had been the dream of a boy to think that he would.

"It's been a long time," Sam said slowly.

"Yes, it has. Twenty-two years."

They continued to talk awkwardly, their conversation filled with long pauses. Sam moved restlessly around the room, seemingly unable to stay still.

Stephen grew more and more uncomfortable. The two of them had little to say to each other. With Joe, the conversation had flowed fast and free, very naturally.

Stephen told Sam about their mother's death, but Sam expressed no sympathy. "Don't expect me to mourn her," he told Stephen. "She means no more to me dead than she did alive."

An angry retort in defense of his mother rose in Stephen's throat. He pushed it down and glanced away. He loved his mother, but, after all, he had experienced her gentle kindness and love all his life. Samuel hadn't really known her. No doubt the main thing he remembered of Eleanor was her leaving him. Stephen supposed that nothing could ever make up for that. He felt saddened and suddenly tired.

There was nothing else to say between them, Stephen realized. He took out the packet of envelopes Eleanor had left for Samuel and gave them to his brother. Sam took the ribbon-tied bundle and tossed it down onto the rough table without even looking at it.

Again there was a long silence. Behind Samuel, Jessie shifted uneasily. She shot a glance at Sam. She knew how he felt about his mother. That subject was a closed book, one he never opened. She understood; she couldn't imagine a mother who could so callously take off and leave her son behind. Worse yet, she'd taken one son, the favored one, and left the other behind. Unwanted. Unchosen. Sam had carried that pain within him most of his life, though, being the kind of man he was, he never talked about it.

She was sorry that Stephen had come along and reminded him of it. Still, she couldn't help but feel a little sorry for Stephen, much as she disliked the man. She knew well enough that it wasn't any fun to face that cold-fish stare of Sam's; it shriveled her right down to her toes. And, after all, Stephen wasn't responsible for what his mother had done. It wasn't his fault that Nora Ferguson had wanted him and not Sam.

Jessie had suspected that Sam wouldn't be as happy to have his long-lost brother turn up as Joe had thought he would be. But there was no point in letting the meeting degenerate into a fight, which was the direction Sam seemed to be heading in right now. Joe wouldn't like it for anything if she brought back his baby boy all bruised up at Sam's hands.

So she stepped forward, planting herself between the two brothers. "We'd better be going. I told Uncle Joe we'd be back before dark."

Stephen hesitated, then agreed. There was no point in prolonging this painful experience. Perhaps if Sam was given a little time he would come around. Stephen paused at the door and looked at his brother. "Goodbye, Sam. I'll see you again before I leave."

"No doubt you will. I'll be down in a few days. I make sure I see Pa every week or so," Sam said pointedly.

Stephen stepped off the porch behind Jessie and followed her to their horses. "Is he always that friendly?" he asked as they swung up into their saddles.

"Sam has his reasons." Jessie flared up in Sam's defense. "I don't reckon it would feel very nice to know that your mother didn't want you."

"It wasn't like that," Stephen began, then gave up. There was no reason to try to explain his mother to this girl. Instead he changed the subject. "I'm sorry. I had hoped to see something of the operation here. I know very little about the lumber industry."

Jessie rolled her eyes. "That's obvious. There's nothing to see here now. Chopping only goes on in the winter. Sam and the cook are just getting the camp set up for the men. They won't arrive until the first of next month."

"They work in the dead of winter?" Stephen looked at her curiously. "I would have thought it was just the opposite. How can they move the logs with all the snow?"

"They use the cold." Even though she didn't like this man, Jessie was never reluctant to talk about the business she loved. "The road monkeys water down the skid so it's icy, and the sleds carrying the logs just slide right down."

Stephen frowned. "I don't see how they would keep from wrecking, then."

Jessie was surprised that he understood enough to recognize what the problems would be. "That's why the hay men, the drivers' assistants, run along throwing hay on the road in front of the sleds when they need to be slowed down."

"I see. You certainly seem to know the business."

Jessie shrugged. "I grew up in it. My pa was a chopper, and after that Ma worked for the Fergusons. Now I do."

She continued to tell him about the timber business, explaining how the choppers felled the trees, using a double-cut saw and working in teams of two, and going on through the entire process until the logs were driven down the river after the spring thaw by the most agile and daring of the crew.

Stephen listened with interest and asked curious questions that surprised Jessie with their perspicacity. After she ran down on the subject of felling the tall trees, Stephen began to ask her about the vegetation around them. She identified the trees and bushes, pointing out the lodgepole pines, the elderberry bushes, the mountain willow trees that clustered along the banks of the streams and a dozen other things. Though his interest in the country amazed her, she was equally surprised by the fact that, even though he must be disappointed by Sam's unfriendliness, he did his best not to inflict his bad feelings on her, instead keeping up a lively discussion.

Here was a man, she thought, who kept his temper under control. It wasn't a characteristic she was used to seeing in men. She wasn't sure what she thought about it. It seemed false, yet it was also rather pleasant and warming to think that he would change his behavior so that it would not bother her. After their argument this morning, she had been certain that she hated Stephen. Now she wasn't quite as sure.

The sun was low, about to sink behind the mountains, and shadows broadened around them. They crossed a swiftly running creek, safely shallow at this time of year, and emerged from a grove of trees into a small clearing. Jessie turned to say something to Stephen, so she missed the glint of sunlight on metal that flashed on the hillside.

But she heard the crack that echoed through the valley, and she saw Stephen jerk, his face showing more surprise than pain. One hand flew up to his chest, where red suddenly blossomed on his new shirt. He'd been shot!

# Chapter Five

Stephen's horse shied at the noise of the rifle blast, and as it did, another shot rang out.

"Get down!" Jessie screamed, leaping off her horse and pulling the rifle from the saddle scabbard.

Stephen's horse danced and reared, and Stephen fell heavily to the ground. The horses took off as a third shot slammed into the ground behind Stephen's body. Jessie darted to Stephen, firing her rifle as she ran. She threw herself across him, shooting blindly in the direction from which the shots had come, but she couldn't pinpoint the exact location, so she had no chance of hitting anyone. Her only hope was that her return fire might frighten their attackers away before they could finish off the job.

Beneath her, Stephen groaned and tried to rise. Unceremoniously, Jessie shoved him down. "You want to get killed? Lie still!"

"Get off of me! Damn it!" He managed to wiggle out from beneath her. "I'm not hiding behind a woman while she—"

Jessie ran out of bullets.

The air was suddenly, heart-stoppingly quiet. The scent of cordite burned in their nostrils. Jessie lay motionless, her body tense, waiting. Beside her, Stephen was equally still. Jessie knew she was out of luck if the shooting started again, for she had grabbed only the rifle from the horse, not even thinking of the extra ammunition in the saddlebags.

"Come on." She grabbed Stephen's arm and jumped to her feet, trying to pull him up with her. "Run for it!"

Stephen staggered to his feet, and they ran, stumbling, across the clearing and into the trees. There were no shots. They melted deeper into the trees and stopped, staring at the hillside where their attacker had been. Seconds passed as they waited tensely.

Jessie drew a steadying breath. "He must have run off."

"Or decided to come down the mountainside and finish it close up."

Jessie shot Stephen a disgusted look. "You're a real cheerful—" She stopped short.

Stephen was leaning heavily against a pine, his face drained of color, his eyes narrow slits. Red stained the front of his shirt. When he was first shot, Jessie had been afraid he'd been killed, but when he'd started talking and moving and had even managed to run, she had assumed that the wound was minor. Now she realized how wrong she had been.

"Good God." She leaned the rifle against a tree and went to Stephen, swiftly unbuttoning his shirt and pulling the sides apart. He had taken the bullet in his left shoulder. His chest was bathed in blood.

She pulled his shirt the rest of the way off and tore it into strips. She wadded one up and pressed it against the wound. Stephen's breath hissed in, and his face turned paler, but he said nothing. With a shaking hand, Jessie took his arm and turned him so that she could see his back. There was no hole, which meant that the bullet was still inside him. Jessie held the bandage against his shoulder, waiting for the flow of blood to slow or end—and also for the shaking in her limbs to stop.

She couldn't let him die. She had to get him to town, where the doctor could care for him. Jessie glanced around, wondering if even now the assassin was circling through the trees, stalking them. She had to fetch the ammunition from her horse. She had to bandage Stephen's wound before he bled to death. What should she do first?

Jessie closed her eyes, concentrating on regaining her calm. She must have a plan of action. First things first. She couldn't go searching for her horse and leave Stephen here bleeding, or she'd be taking a corpse to town. Therefore, step one was to bandage him.

It restored her confidence somewhat to make the decision, and her fingers worked quickly and with only a slight trembling as she tossed away the blood-soaked pad and folded up a new one to replace it. "Here. Sit down while I bandage you."

She put his hand on the pad where hers had been and had him hold it. Then she tied the remaining clean strips of his shirt together and wrapped the resulting long strip tightly around his chest and over his shoulder several times. When she was finished, she sat back on her heels and checked her handiwork. It was a sloppy bandage, nowhere near her mother's quality. She had watched her mother work on wounded men over the years and had picked up what to do, but she had never been very good at it. However, the thing was tight enough to stop the blood flowing, and that was all that was necessary. Besides, it was all she had time for.

She glanced at Stephen's face. His eyes were closed, and his skin had a gray tinge to it. Jessie bit her lip. *Oh, please, God, don't let him die.* "I'm going after the horses," she told Stephen.

He gave a little nod to signify that he had heard.

"I'll be right back," she added, guilt swelling in her at the thought of leaving him alone and defenseless. But she had to find the horses, and she obviously couldn't drag him along with her while she did it! She couldn't even leave him a weapon; the gun was useless without the bullets. "Here."

She laid the rifle beside him. "There aren't any bullets in it, but maybe you could scare him off."

"Sure." Stephen opened his eyes and mustered up a faint smile. "He'd probably quake in his boots to see me holding a gun."

Jessie smiled, a little reassured. Surely he wasn't near death if he was able to joke. "Just rest. Maybe some of your strength will come back."

She knew she was lying—weakness from loss of blood didn't abate that quickly. But maybe he didn't know it, and her words would make him feel better.

Jessie rose lithely to her feet and peered around her. She could see no sign of their horses. The gloom was rapidly deepening beneath the trees. Before long she wouldn't be able to see her hand in front of her face.

She started off rapidly in the direction the horses had gone. Her eyes moved constantly, looking for any sign of the horses—or the killer. He could be sneaking through the trees right at this moment, looking for them. She had to make sure she saw him first.

Finally Jessie spotted a glimmer of white ahead of her. Her horse was a brown and white paint. She took the chance of whistling softly. There came a whinny and a movement. She could see the mare now. Jessie crept cautiously forward. She couldn't afford to spook her. She murmured the mare's name in a low voice, extending her hand as though there were a treat in it. The mare shook her head, setting the bridle jingling, and walked toward Jessie. The animal's fear had left her, and she was content to rejoin Jessie, snuffling against her hand for the nonexistent apple or carrot. She blew out and rolled her eye at Jessie accusingly.

"Sorry, girl. But you get us back to town safe and you can have anything you want. That's a promise."

She couldn't see a sign of Stephen's horse anywhere. Well, it didn't really matter. At least she had ammunition, as well as the pistol in the saddlebag, and they could get to town on one mount.

Jessie led the horse to where Stephen was. He sat in the same spot, leaning against a tree, his eyes closed. "Stephen." She bent down and said his name again, gently pulling his hands and taking the rifle from him. Stephen's eyes fluttered open, and he looked at her in confusion.

"It's me. Jess," she told him. "I got my horse. I couldn't find the other one, but we can both ride mine to Nora Springs. It's not far." As she spoke, she was reloading the rifle.

Stephen's eyes cleared, and he nodded. Good. At least he was awake and aware of what was going on. He got clumsily to his feet, wincing as his movements intensified the pain in his chest. Jessie put her hands under one of his arms and pulled to help him up. It occurred to her that Stephen had gone through it all—the shooting, her bandaging and now getting up—with hardly a murmur, even though his wound must be throbbing with pain. It surprised her. She never would have figured this man would show any signs of stoicism.

"Now you'll have to mount the horse," she told him, leading him over to the mare.

Stephen looked at her, his eyebrows rising. "I'm not sure I can." He grasped the saddle horn with his right hand, but then did nothing more than lean against the horse.

"Damn! Excuse me."

Jessie realized that Stephen was apologizing for cursing in front of her, and she had to clap a hand over her mouth to stifle a giggle at the absurdity of his unwavering courtesy even in this deadly situation.

"I feel so weak." He sounded faintly surprised.

"You've lost a lot of blood," she explained.

He nodded. "It seemed rather much. But then, you see, I've never been shot before."

Was this man real? Hysterical laughter bubbled in her throat. "Well, that makes two of us," she said crisply to quell the hysteria. "I've never seen anyone shot, either."

"Really?" He glanced at her. "My man Charles tells me it happens all the time out here."

"Not that I've ever noticed."

"Perhaps they usually refrain around ladies."

Jessie grimaced. "Do you plan to stand around here cracking wise all evening, or are you going to get on this horse?"

"Actually, I was hoping to avoid it." Stephen's face was as white as paper, and sweat dotted his upper lip. "I don't think I have the strength." He stepped back. "Tell you what: you ride into town and get help. I'll wait here."

"Don't be foolish. He might come back."

Stephen didn't ask who. His head wasn't clear enough to figure out why, but it was obvious that someone had tried to kill him. "I know. But what good will it do for you to be here, too, still struggling to get me on this horse? He'd simply kill both of us."

"I'm not leaving you." Jessie tried to smile to lighten the moment. "Your daddy would kill me for sure if I left you behind to die. At least this way I have a chance."

Stephen shook his head but didn't argue anymore. Jessie glanced around and found the stump of a fallen tree a few feet away.

"Over here." She led him and the horse to the tree trunk. "You can use this stump for a mounting block. It'll work. I've often gotten up that way. You can put your hand on my shoulder to help you climb up on the stump. Don't worry, I'm strong."

He nodded, braced himself with a hand on her shoulder and stepped onto the stump. It was difficult, and it made his head swirl for a moment. Jessie reined the horse in close, and, still balancing with his hand on her slim shoulder, Stephen climbed awkwardly into the saddle. His feet dangled ludicrously below the stirrups, and he was slumped in the saddle, both hands around the horn, but at least he was on.

Jessie hopped lightly onto the broken trunk. "Scoot back as far as you can, so I can get on in front of you. Then you can hold on to me to keep from falling off."

Again he nodded, then moved back, his hands leaving the saddle horn. Jessie swung carefully into the saddle, her movements almost as awkward as his had been, for she had to bring her leg over in front to keep from kicking Stephen. She settled gingerly into the saddle. It wasn't big enough for two people, even people as slender as they were. The saddle horn pushed into her abdomen and the tender mound of her womanhood, and her bottom was cupped by Stephen's legs and pelvis. She found the position acutely embarrassing. She had never felt any part of a man's body flush against hers before, especially *that* part!

She gripped the reins tightly, reminding herself that this was no time to be thinking of trivial things like that. If she didn't get Stephen to the doctor in time, he could die. She tapped the mare's sides, urging her forward. Jessie didn't dare ride fast, much as she longed to, for she knew that Stephen would never be able to stay in the saddle. As it was, he was curved over her back, his head against hers, his arms wrapped around her waist, using all his strength just to stay on.

The slow, rocking gait of the horse rubbed Stephen's body against her. She could feel his thighs, his chest, his arms, sliding up and down her with every step. And in front the saddle horn pressed into her intimately, rubbing in a way that was somewhere between pleasure and pain. Jessie's breasts tingled, and she could feel the nipples puckering, as they did in the cold. Good Lord, what was the matter with her? Had she lost her mind? She couldn't remember ever feeling this bizarre licentious glow deep within her. It seemed insane, horrifying, that she should feel it now, with a wounded man hanging over her back and a killer maybe on their trail. It must be the shock; the whole incident had rattled her so badly that her mind was flying off in strange directions.

But she couldn't ignore the fact that in reality it was flying off in only *one* direction.

She was enormously grateful when at last she glimpsed the dark bulk of the buildings of Nora Springs ahead of them. It was night now, but the moon gave enough light to follow the path and pick out the shapes of the town. Jessie continued the nerve-rackingly slow pace into town. She could tell from the laxness of his body that Stephen had lost consciousness. He was hardly even holding on to her now, and she knew he'd pitch off into the road if she moved any faster. As it was, he was beginning to list to one side, and she had to stretch one arm awkwardly backward to keep him in the saddle.

She rode straight to her mother's house, and as she drew near, she began to shout for Amanda. By the time she pulled to a stop in the street, her mother was on the porch, holding up a lighted kerosene lamp and peering into the dark. "Jessie? Is that you? What's the matter?"

"Yeah, it's me. Ma, get the doc. And send the men out here to get Stephen off the horse."

Amanda didn't waste time with questions but stuck her head in the door and shouted urgently to the men who roomed there, then hurried into the street, holding up her lamp to illuminate Jessie and her burden on the horse. Amanda drew in her breath when she saw Stephen Ferguson leaning so limply against Jessie's back. "Oh, no! Lord in heaven, what happened? Did he fall off his horse?"

"He's been shot."

"Shot!" Amanda gasped, but she didn't have time for any more questions. Several men were running out the door and across the yard in answer to her summons, and she whirled to them to issue commands. Within seconds, one of the men was racing down the street to Doc Holzworth's house, and several others were carefully pulling Stephen from the saddle.

Jessie felt his weight leave her back, and she relaxed gratefully. It was over. She had done all she could, and now the responsibility was lifted from her shoulders. She slid from the saddle and gave the reins wordlessly to one of the men. Every muscle in her body hurt, and she was embarrassingly close to tears.

She followed her mother into the house and up the stairs. She could have stayed downstairs, could have gone into her room and fallen into the utter softness of the big feather bed. She could have closed her eyes and let the fear and tiredness drain out of her, could have slept and left the care of the wounded man in Amanda's capable hands. Instead she found herself trailing after the little procession into Stephen Ferguson's room. Somehow she could not let go of her responsibility for his life.

The men laid him on the bed and stepped back to give Mrs. Randall access. Carefully she cut through the primitive bandage Jessie had stuck on his chest and peeled it away. The pad stuck to his wound, dried stiff with blood, and she had to soak it before she was able to pull it off.

Stephen's eyes flew open, and a groan escaped his lips. He looked at Amanda without recognition. "Jessie?" He glanced around. "Jessie?"

"I'm right here." She stepped forward into his line of vision. "We got back home all right. The doctor'll be here in a few minutes."

A smile wavered on his lips. "Good. You're—safe then? Nothing happened?"

"Nothing."

He nodded. His eyes slid toward Amanda. "And you're—uh, Mrs. Randall. Am I right?"

"Yes. But don't worry your head about it. You lie still and let me tend to this wound."

Stephen's servant shouldered through the crowd of men in the hall and stopped just inside the door. He drew in a shocked gasp and stared, frozen. "Master Stephen!" he exclaimed finally and moved forward. "What happened to him? What's wrong?"

Jessie glanced at him. He looked as though he might start wringing his hands and crying at any moment. Her mother answered him, her voice calm, "He was shot. But he'll be all right."

Charles gripped the back of a chair, his eyes fixed on his employer. "You'd be better off going back to your room and letting Ma tend to him," Jessie told him.

"No. No, I couldn't leave him."

Jessie shrugged and turned to watch her mother, ignoring the man. Amanda soaked a cloth and began to clean the blood from Stephen's chest until the small, dark red hole made by the bullet was clearly visible. Jessie watched her mother's deft hands work. How light her mother's touch was; she never gave unnecessary pain. Jessie hadn't bothered to learn such things, hadn't thought them useful. "Serving skills," she had dubbed them with scorn, much as she had her mother's cooking and cleaning. But now she could see how, at times like these, they could be worth far more than any strength or intelligence.

"Is he going to be all right, Ma?" she asked, her hands twisting together.

"I don't know. First that bullet needs to come out." Amanda glanced at the men still crowded in the doorway. "Tom, has anyone notified Joe Ferguson?"

"Yeah. Burton ran down to the mill right after Jessie and him rode in. We sent for the marshal, too."

"Good." Her gaze swept over the men, and she spoke with a quiet, almost maternal authority. "Why don't you men go back to what you were doing? You aren't helping this man any, standing here gawking."

"Anything I can get you?" Tom asked, as the others began to move away.

"Jessie'll get it for me." Amanda turned toward Charles. "Why don't you go, too? There's nothing you can do for him."

"I couldn't, ma'am."

Amanda shrugged and turned to her daughter. "Help me get these boots off him. We might as well make him as comfortable as possible."

Jessie went to Stephen's feet and began to pull off one of his boots. They were tight-fitting and difficult to remove, although the fine, supple leather helped somewhat. Jessie had never removed a man's boots before, and it felt strange to do so, almost intimate. She remembered the way his body had felt behind her, the heavy weight, the warmth, and color rose in her face. She hoped her mother would mistake it for the flush of exertion, not embarrassment.

"Here, Miss, Madam, allow me." Charles came up beside them. A touch of humor gave his drained face some life. "I think this is one thing which *I* can do better."

Amanda and her mother turned the task over to him and walked away from the bed. "What happened, Jessie?" Amanda asked in a low voice.

"Somebody shot him. I don't know who. They were hidden on the hillside in the trees. All of a sudden I heard a shot, and there was Stephen with blood on his chest."

"Someone hunting, do you think? An accident?"

Jessie shook her head emphatically. "No. It couldn't have been. Ma, he shot three times. Three times! He hit Stephen with the first shot, then he fired again. But Stephen's horse was jumping around, and Stephen fell off. Then the fellow shot again. Nobody fires at you three times by mistake."

"No." Amanda's forehead creased. "But who? Why?"

Jessie shook her head. "I don't know. Nobody even knows Stephen."

Joe Ferguson burst into the room. His face paled when he saw his newfound son lying still on the bed. "Oh, my God. I thought—I couldn't believe it when they told me. How— what—Jess, girl, what happened?"

Jessie started to repeat her story for him, but just then Rob McSweeney pounded up the stairs to the door of Stephen's room. He was frowning. "Miz Randall, the doc ain't there. His wife said today's his day to go to Ransom. He sees people there every other week. She said he always spends the night there, and he won't come back till tomorrow." He paused and looked at her. "What do you want me to do? Ride to Ransom for him?"

"No," Joe Ferguson snapped. "Stephen could die by the time you got there and back." He turned toward Jessie's mother. "Amanda, you'll have to do it yourself."

Amanda looked horrified. "Oh, no, no. I couldn't take out a bullet."

"Remember the doctoring you did at the camp in the old days? There wasn't a doctor then. You got to where you could do most everything. Hell, I bet you're better than a lot of doctors."

"But it's been so long. I've forgotten how...."

"You don't forget skills like that. They come back to you, whenever you need them. Shoot fire, woman, remember the time Swede Gustafson got liquored up and shot Blackie Roscoe?"

"Yeah." Amanda snorted. "Over Delia Culbertson."

"And how about the time you cut that piece of wood out of Dave Wilson's leg and sewed him up again, good as new?"

"Yes, but ... but what if I make a mistake and I kill your son?"

"Amanda, if you don't help my son, you'll kill him sure."

She looked at him for a moment. "You're right. I'll do it."

"No!" Stephen's valet shrieked. "No, you can't! You mustn't. You're not a doctor. You'll hurt him. Send for the doctor. Let him do it. Mr. Ferguson is a wealthy man. He can pay for any inconvenience, any—"

Amanda fixed him with a stern look. "No amount of money can bring that doctor here in time to save him. His father wants me to help him, and I'm going to. If you're going to argue and fuss, then Joe can put you outside. If you want to help Mr. Ferguson, then you shut your mouth and do what I say. Do you understand?"

"Let her do it." They all turned, startled, to look at the bed, from which the weak voice had come. Stephen's eyes were open, bright with pain but obviously alert. "I trust her, Charles. Mrs. Randall has my permission to take out the bullet."

Charles nodded and stepped back. Amanda turned to Jessie. "All right. Jessie, I'm going to need your help."

Amanda rattled off a list of the things she would need, and Jessie shot downstairs to get them. She worked quickly, trying not to think about what lay ahead. Her mother had had to practice a lot of rudimentary medicine when she cooked at the camp, and Jessie had helped her. But that had been several years ago; Amanda had given it up when Dr. Holzworth moved to Nora Springs. The thought of helping her mother get a bullet out of Stephen made Jessie queasy.

But she couldn't think about that. She had a task to do.

When she returned, she found Joe, the valet and her mother clustered at the head of Stephen's bed. The bedside stand had been pushed up tight against the mattress, and two kerosene lamps at full blaze sat upon it. Another lamp sat on the dresser. The room was a bright contrast to the dark hall outside. On the bedside table also sat a washbowl, several folded towels, a pair of tweezers and a threaded needle. Jessie's stomach pitched and turned, and she had to swallow hard.

She handed her mother the kettle of hot water and the two sharpened kitchen knives, then took the bottle of bourbon out of the crook of her arm. She poured a healthy shot into a glass. Her fingers trembled.

Jessie walked to Stephen's bed. He opened his eyes and looked at her. "You going to help her cut me open?" His voice was so faint she could hardly hear him. "Bet you'll enjoy that."

Jessie swallowed again. "Sure." She hoped he was too weak to notice the tremor in her voice. "You need to drink this. It'll make you feel better."

She slid her hand under his head and helped him lift it, and he drank from the glass. After a swallow, he coughed and shot her a disgusted look. "What the devil is that? Take it away. Cheap whiskey."

Jessie grimaced. "Sorry, I'm sure you're used to the finest brandy. But we can't always get it out here. Now drink again."

"Don't want to." He shook his head.

"You need to." She hesitated and glanced at Joe, then at Stephen. "For the pain."

"Oh, my God!" the valet gasped.

Stephen's eyes opened, and he focused on her. "What? Aren't you going to use chloroform?"

Jessie shook her head. "We don't have any."

"The doctor..."

"He took it with him. I asked McSweeney. This is—this is all we've got."

Jessie didn't know what she expected—crying or pleading or a sudden recanting of his decision to let Amanda take out the bullet—but she certainly hadn't expected what he did. Stephen gazed at her unblinkingly for a moment, then said, "Pour me another shot."

When she deemed him inebriated enough to take the edge off his pain, Amanda came forward, a small kitchen knife and the tweezers clutched in her white-knuckled hands. She looked at Joe. "You ready to hold him?"

He nodded. Amanda glanced at Stephen. His eyes were open, though foggy from the liquor, pain and loss of blood. He wet his lips, and Jessie could see him struggling to make his words come out sensibly. "Have a' it." His voice was slurred; his eyes wandered.

Amanda swallowed and bent over his wound. "All right. Hold him."

Charles, kneeling on the bed beside Stephen, bore down on his good arm to keep him from thrashing around, while Joe gripped his shoulder and arm tightly on the other side. Jessie stood behind her mother, watching, waiting to hand her whatever she asked for.

Amanda began to probe the wound, and a low groan escaped Stephen's lips. Jessie's stomach tightened.

"I'm going to have to make a cut," Amanda said, bringing the knife down to Stephen's skin. The valet made an odd noise, and his eyes rolled back. He fainted, collapsing on the bed beside Stephen.

"For Christ's sake." Joe swore and released Stephen to reach over and shove the servant aside. "Jessie, get up here and hold him."

Jessie crawled onto the bed and gripped Stephen's arm and shoulder tightly. She turned her head so as not to see the knife bite into his flesh, but she knew from Stephen's muffled oath and hissing breath when it did. Stephen's arm was taut and hard as stone beneath her. He was far stronger than she'd guessed. Each time her mother hurt him, the muscles beneath Jessie's hands bulged, and once, weak as he was, he raised her several inches off the bed.

It seemed as if it was taking her mother forever. Jessie glanced over and saw Amanda probing the wound with the tweezers. She turned away quickly. Another groan came from Stephen. Jessie found herself praying frantically inside her head. Abruptly Stephen's muscles relaxed beneath her. She glanced at his face and saw that he had finally sunk into blessed unconsciousness. Thank heavens!

A moment later her mother exclaimed, "Eureka!" Slowly, carefully, she removed the tweezers and held them up. A mangled, blood-smeared piece of metal lay between the prongs. Amanda laid the bullet on the table and wiped her hands on a towel, then picked up her needle, pressed the flesh together and began to sew with tiny, delicate stitches. Jessie continued to keep her face averted, wondering when her mother would finally be through.

"That's it." Amanda stepped back from the bed.

Jessie looked down at Stephen. The skin around the wound was bloody, but the wound was closed, held by small blue stitches. She began to tremble. Amanda went to wash the blood from her hands before she bandaged Stephen. Joe stopped her and enfolded her in his arms. Jessie crawled off the bed, hesitated for a moment, then hurried out the door. She ran down the back staircase and into the yard.

The evening air was chilly against her face, and she was glad to feel it. Amanda had done it. And Jessie had managed to stand her ground and do her job, too. But now her stomach turned and heaved, and she ran behind a bush to be thoroughly and violently sick.

It was some time before Jessie was composed enough to creep into the house and up the stairs. She went to her room and washed her face, then glanced in the mirror. Her skin looked sallow in the dim light, and her eyes seemed huge. She sat on her bed, took off her boots and lay against the cool coverlet. She still felt jittery inside, the result, she guessed, of the danger and fear she had faced earlier. She didn't think she could sleep.

She thought of Stephen and was embarrassed to remember how she had rushed out of his room. She hadn't even stayed to help her mother clean up. She wasn't usually that weak. Wondering how he was, she stood and went quietly down the hall to his room. The door to his room stood open a fraction, and she peeked inside. A kerosene lamp, turned low, lit the room dimly. Her mother stood beside the bed, smoothing out the covers. The lamp cast her shadow huge and dark against the opposite wall. Stephen lay on the bed, so still it made Jessie's heart beat a little faster in fear. Was he still alive? He looked so pale, so motionless.

She eased the door open and tiptoed inside. Amanda turned and gave her a little smile.

"How is he?"

"It's hard to tell. Right now he's resting comfortably. But when he wakes up, I'm afraid the pain will be fierce. And there's always the danger of a fever. However, he's a strong young man. I think he'll pull through all right."

Jessie came nearer. The sheet lay over Stephen's chest, but did not cover his shoulders and arms. A white strip of gauze came up over one shoulder, adding a touch of vulnerability to the masculine set of his shoulders. His eyes were closed in deep sleep; his eyelashes lay thick and dark against his cheek, absurdly beautiful. Something twisted in Jessie's chest. "I should have been watching better."

"Oh, honey, there was nothing you could do." Her mother slipped a reassuring arm around her shoulders. "You couldn't know someone would be hiding, planning to shoot him."

"Maybe not, but Joe asked me to look after him, and I promised I would. Then I didn't. I just showed him the way. I didn't keep an eye out for danger. And I should have. I was careless."

"I'm sure Joe doesn't blame you. How could you have guessed that someone would ambush you? Even if you'd been more alert, there's nothing to say you would have seen the killer before he shot young Mr. Ferguson. It probably would have happened exactly the same way."

"At least then I would have known that I'd done my best. But now I have to live with the fact that I didn't."

"Maybe you weren't perfect. I don't think anyone expects you to be—except maybe you. But think about this: that young man was lucky to have you along. If you hadn't been there, he'd be dead right now. What if he'd gone alone, or Joe had sent someone with him who wasn't as quick or as sharp as you? You protected him. You chased away the killer. You brought him home alive. You saved him, Jessie. I think that's how Joe feels about it."

"I guess so." She gazed at the immobile face. How handsome Stephen looked in repose, as though no flaw could spoil his elegant features. He was very different from Sam—up close, at least. She liked the way Sam looked better, of course; harsh experience had given his face character. Still, there was no denying that this man was wickedly handsome.

He was also tougher than she would have guessed. He had made that ride into town without a murmur of complaint, even though each step must have jarred his wound. Then he had grimly endured Amanda's probing for the bullet in his shoulder, with only a bottle of whiskey to ease the torment. Nor had he lost his head and panicked during the shooting. He had gotten up and run with her to the trees when she had told him to, and he had sat there gamely with the empty rifle in his hands while she had searched for the runaway horses. Stephen Ferguson had earned her grudging respect tonight. Maybe there was some of Joe's and Sam's iron in him, after all.

"I'll watch him tonight," Jessie told her mother. "You go to bed."

Her mother glanced at her, surprised. Usually Jessie hated sickbeds and avoided nursing duties at all costs. "If you'd like."

Jessie nodded.

Amanda hugged her daughter, laying her head against the girl's bright red one. "He'll be all right. I know it. He can't die now, just when Joe's finally gotten him back."

Amanda slipped out of the room, closing the door softly behind her. Jessie pulled a straight-backed chair up beside the bed and sat in it. The lamplight flickered, casting shadows across Stephen's face. Jessie reached out tentatively and laid her hand across one of his. In his sleep, his hand turned over, and his fingers curled around her hand. Jessie settled herself to wait out the night with him.

## Chapter Six

Stephen woke up and immediately wished he hadn't. His head was pounding, his mouth was dry, and his left shoulder felt as if it was on fire. He groaned and rolled his head to the side, closed his eyes and hoped that this was another one of the harsh, violent dreams that had been plaguing him all night long. But he knew it wasn't. The pain was too sharp, too real. He opened his eyes again. He was in a strange bedroom furnished simply and inexpensively.

His valet bent over the bed, his long, plain face concerned. "Sir? How are you feeling? Are you in pain?"

With some effort Stephen bit back an oath. "Of course I'm in pain. What do you think I'd be, with some woman cutting on me?"

He remembered now where he was and most of what had happened. He'd been shot while he and Jessie were riding to town. Then Jessie had dragged him home—what a courageous, quick-thinking girl! After he'd been shot, he had gone in and out of consciousness, and he had only jumbled memories of the ride home and being carried into the Randall house. Unfortunately he had come to quickly enough when Amanda Randall had started poking around in his shoulder, searching for the bullet. He remembered Jessie standing there, propping up his head, urging him to drink a bottle of rotgut whiskey. He had gotten drunk, though he couldn't recall that it had helped the pain; at least it had finally knocked him out.

It was no wonder his head was pounding and his mouth tasted so foul. He had a hangover as well as a bullet wound in his shoulder.

"I'm most sorry, sir." Charles looked deeply troubled. "I tried to stop them, but they insisted that it was the only way. They told me there was no doctor in the town. I never heard of such a thing."

Stephen remembered Joe Ferguson holding him down with all his force, Jessie helping him, while Mrs. Randall went to work. His father's face had been grim and his eyes almost tortured as he kept Stephen still. Stephen thought that nothing could have shown his love for his son more clearly than that expression.

"They are tough people here," Stephen murmured. He tried to imagine his lovely, delicate mother out here, and he failed. It was no wonder she had run to St. Louis. He couldn't picture her handing a man a bottle of whiskey and going in with a kitchen knife and a pair of tweezers to take a bullet out of him.

"Mrs. Randall left strict instructions to let her know when you awoke."

Stephen nodded. "Of course. Go tell her."

His servant left the room, and a few minutes later, Amanda Randall swept into the room, followed by Charles, who was carrying a tray. Stephen had expected to see Jessie with her mother, and he knew a curious sense of disappointment when she did not walk into the room.

"Well, now," Mrs. Randall said, smiling and coming over to the bed to pick up his hand. "I won't ask how you're feeling this morning, for I'm sure it must be awful. But I will say I'm terribly glad to see you awake and not feverish. It's a good sign." She was a soft, maternal woman, and her presence was soothing.

"Thank you." Stephen tried to squeeze her hand in his, though he found he was too weak to exert much pressure. "You were an angel to do what you did."

She chuckled. "That's not exactly what you were calling me last night, as I recall."

"I'm sorry. I was half out of my head. I don't know what I said. If I offended you—"

"Oh, no, no, I was only teasing," she hastened to reassure him, her kind face showing worry. "You were in pain, and I paid no attention to it. Believe me, I've heard much worse in my life—and not always from a man I was cutting a bullet out of."

Stephen smiled faintly. He felt unutterably weary. His shoulder throbbed. His eyes closed and fluttered open again. "Where is Jessie?"

"Jessie? Down at the sawmill. I tried to get her to sleep in this morning—she sat up half the night, watching you. But I couldn't reason with her. She said Joe would need her more now than ever. Maybe she's right. He was worried something fierce about you." Amanda smiled. "But I told him not to fret. I knew you came from strong stock. I figured you'd pull through, just like Sam would."

Stephen's eyes drifted closed again, and he opened them with an effort. "Sorry," he mumbled, fighting the exhaustion that threatened to overwhelm him. "I'm just so tired...."

"Of course you are. Sleep is exactly what you need. But first, I want you to eat a little broth. You lost a lot of blood last night, and you need to build it back up. I made you some good, strong meat broth. Charles, help hold his head up, please."

Stephen felt ridiculously weak. He couldn't even lift his head by himself. His valet had to put his hands under Stephen's head and prop him up while Mrs. Randall fed him a few spoonfuls of beef broth. At the first sip, his stomach almost revolted, but gradually it settled, and he was able to

eat a little. Then Amanda let Charles lay him back down.
Stephen was asleep before she got out the door.

"Do you know anyone who might wish to harm this Mr.
Ferguson?" the marshall asked Joe. He stood with his hat
pushed back on his head and his thumbs hooked in his belt,
his face expressionless, as it had been all through Jessie's
retelling of what had happened to her and Stephen on their
ride home last night. Having told it to her mother and then
to Joe, she was getting rather tired of relating the events, but
Marshall Wayman, who had been given the facts by Joe last
night, had insisted on coming by the sawmill this morning
and hearing Jessie's story himself.

"No. It plain don't make sense." Joe shook his head, a
perplexed look on his face. "I mean, he's only been in town
a couple of days."

"Yeah," Jessie agreed. "God knows he's an irritating
creature, but surely in so short a time he couldn't have gotten on anybody's nerves enough for them to want to kill
him."

"Maybe it *was* an accident," Joe offered.

"Three times?" Marshall Wayman looked skeptical.
"Didn't you say they shot at him three times?"

"Yes. They couldn't possibly not have realized they were
firing at him."

"Maybe it's somebody that ain't from around here," the
marshall suggested. "Maybe it's a fella that followed him
from St. Louis to kill him. Something to do with something that happened back East."

"Why not do it there, then, instead of going to the trouble of following him out here?" Joe snapped.

The marshall shrugged. "You sure he couldn't've been
aimin' at you, Jess?"

Jessie shot him a disgusted look. "Well, he sure was a hell
of a bad shot, if he was. He fired three times, and all of

them were close to Ste—Mr. Ferguson. Not me. Besides, who'd want to kill me, either?''

"Well, I know a few people you've riled a mite now and then." Marshal Wayman gave a sly little grin. "But I wouldn't think it'd be enough to shoot you. More likely it was robbers. They saw that fancy city dude and figured he was easy pickin's, so they shot him and were going to ride down and take his money."

"There's only one problem with that. He didn't look like a rich tinhorn. He went out and bought regular clothes for the ride, and he looked just like you or me or—" She stopped abruptly, and her eyes widened. "Joe...you know who he looked like?"

Joe understood immediately. "Sam? You're saying somebody thought he was Sam?"

"Wait a minute," Marshal Wayman stuck in. "This Eastern relative of yours looks enough like Sam that somebody'd confuse 'em?"

"He's not just a relative, Marshal—he's my son. Sam's brother. They don't look exactly alike. Standing this close to him you'd never mistake Stephen for Sam. But they do favor. He's tall and has black hair and the same sort of frame."

"From a distance, it wouldn't be hard to mistake him for Sam," Jessie added. "Especially since it was getting on toward twilight. And he was riding with me. Everybody knows Sam and I are friends. Anybody could have seen me riding out in the direction of the camp that morning."

"Yeah, and I told several of the men at work that you'd gone to the camp," Joe added. "They asked about you 'cause they hadn't seen you around."

"So knowing I'd been to the camp and seeing this man who looked like Sam with me, naturally they'd assume it *was* Sam."

"They could have figured you had the payroll for the camp on you." The Marshal began to weave a story. "They followed you, and—no, that don't make sense. They'd've shot you when you were riding to the camp. They wouldn't figure Sam had the payroll when he was riding toward town."

"Maybe they weren't wanting to rob Sam."

"Ah, Jessie, now don't start that up," Joe groaned.

"Why not?"

"Start what up? Jessie, Joe, what's goin' on?"

"Somebody broke the main saw blade—on purpose," Jessie explained. "They're trying to hurt Joe."

"I thought that was an accident." Marshal Wayman looked confused.

"That's what you determined," Jessie said, unable to keep a trace of resentment and scorn out of her voice. "You said you reckoned it must have been an accident. There wasn't anything to show it had been tampered with."

"Yeah. So why do you say it had been?"

"'Cause it didn't just break. I know it didn't. It was fine the night before when the mill closed down. The next morning, first thing, it broke. And it broke so clean. No pieces of metal flying all over the place, just that big split right across the middle, so it fell into two pieces. Why would it break like that, unless someone weakened it along a line? Joe thinks so, too. He's been spending the nights in the mill since then."

The marshal swung his astonished gaze toward Joe. "Why didn't you tell me?"

Joe shrugged. "I got no proof, and neither does Jessie, no matter how convinced she is that she's right. It's all speculation."

"Well, it wasn't speculation that somebody took shots at a man who looked like your son. Now, who do you think might have broken that blade of yours? Who'd want to hurt your mill? Or you?"

Joe sighed. "That's just it. I can't think of anyone who would. Somebody with a big grudge against me or Sam, I reckon. Maybe he broke the blade, thinking that'd hurt our business so bad we'd be in real trouble. But when it didn't, when Sam just ordered a new one and we went on with the smaller one, then he might've figured he'd better hurt Sam directly.''

The marshal shook his head. "This is hard to believe."

"I know. I been racking my brain, trying to remember if I've ever done anything to anyone that would make them this angry, make them want to take revenge on me. Especially something this serious—I mean, the saw blade was one thing, but trying to murder my son . . . !''

Wayman sighed. "I guess I'll have to ride out there tomorrow and look around, see if I can find anything on the hill to show who might've been there." He reached for his hat and started toward the door. He paused and looked back at Joe and Jessie. "If you think of anything, let me know." His face turned stern. "Especially you let me know if anything else strange happens. You understand?''

"Sure." Joe nodded. "I reckon the coward's already hightailed it out of here, thinking he'd killed Sam."

"Maybe." He didn't look convinced.

After the marshal left, Jessie and Joe sat silently for a moment. Then Jessie sighed.

"Maybe we ought to tell Sam now. I mean, there's no way to hide that his brother got shot. And if they're going after Sam, he ought to be on guard. Ready to fight back.''

"Sam's always ready to fight back," Joe replied, his mouth curling up into a grin.

"You know what I mean. On the lookout for danger."

"Yeah. I thought of that. I don't want someone sneaking in on him at the camp and hurting him. But sure as fire, if I tell him, he'll be camping out at the sawmill. He probably won't even go get the blade because he won't want to leave me and the mill alone. He'll say Burley can go by himself.''

"Well, we'll just have to convince him to go. After all, that fellow might try to stop Burley from bringing in the new blade. Sam ought to be there to make sure nothing happens to it."

"Right." Joe's expression lightened. "We'll use that argument on him." Then he frowned. "You know, that might just be the truth. Damn! There's no way to keep him safe. I'd rather it *was* an enemy chasing Stephen out here from St. Louis. At least Sam wouldn't be in danger—and Stephen wouldn't be lying there half-dead just because he came to visit us."

Jessie reached out and laid her hand on his arm. "It's not your fault that some lunatic is out to get you. Stephen was just unlucky enough to get in the way."

"And you."

"I didn't get hurt."

"Maybe not this time. But what about the next time? Suppose you get in the way? Or Stephen again? Suppose it's Sam?"

"Sure, any of that's possible. But what are you going to do? Give up? Leave town?"

Joe's face hardened. "You know me better than that."

"So what are you saying?"

"That I don't want you and my children in danger. Maybe you should stop working here."

"Look, Stephen will probably leave as soon as he gets well enough to go. I don't figure some city dude like him is going to hang around after getting shot at. But I'm not leaving. Sam can take care of himself, and so can I. You won't see the day when I start running scared. I'm staying right where I am."

Joe gave her a long, hard look, then grinned. "I reckon I knew that before we ever started talking."

"Then you might as well have saved your breath."

"Blast it, I want to know how a sweet woman like your mama ever managed to have a daughter as mule headed as you."

Jessie chuckled. "You don't know Ma very well if you think that. She may wear skirts and smile at you pretty, but underneath she's made of iron."

The older man's smile grew wider. "I reckon you're pretty right about that, too."

Stephen slept most of the day, and every time he awoke for a few minutes, there were Charles and Mrs. Randall, poking a few more spoonfuls of broth down him. He had no interest in eating, and his stomach remained unsteady all day. But Mrs. Randall wasn't about to let him get by without taking some nourishment. In the middle of the afternoon, the doctor came in, examined his wound and left him a bottle of laudanum for the pain. After Mrs. Randall gave him a spoonful of the liquid, the throbbing in his shoulder quieted down, and his sleep was easier and less troubled by the hot, fierce, senseless dreams he had experienced earlier.

When he awakened the next time, he could see by the darkened window that it was evening, and instead of Charles sitting in the chair beside his bed, it was Jessie Randall. He blinked, trying to clear his fuzzy mind. His shoulder was burning again. "Hello." He disliked how weak his voice sounded.

"Hi." Jessie rose from her chair and came over to the bed. She leaned down and placed her hand across his brow. Her skin was deliciously cool.

He liked the feel of her hand on his face. He wished she would leave it there. His eyes closed. Somehow he felt better with her there, silly as that seemed. Yet at the same time, it embarrassed him that she should see him so weak.

"You may have a bit of fever," Jessie said crisply. "I'll get you a cool rag."

She went to the washbowl and wet a rag, then wrung it out and placed it on his forehead. It was cool, but not nearly as pleasant as her touch.

"Are you feeling pain?" she asked. "Mama said you could take some more of the laudanum now, if you want."

"No. Maybe later." Actually, he would have taken the medicine gladly if it had been anyone else offering it. But knowing how poorly Jessie thought of him, he couldn't bring himself to admit to his pain. He could hold on for a while longer.

Jessie returned to the chair and sat, hands clasped together in her lap. She looked at Stephen. His eyes were closed again, and she wondered if he was sleeping. She wished that she had something to do with her hands, but she had never taken up any of the womanly skills of sewing or knitting or needlepoint, and she wasn't much for books, either. She was used to being up and doing things. The waiting was difficult. Sitting by a sickbed was something she wouldn't normally do, and she didn't know why she felt compelled to stay by Stephen's. She supposed it was because she had failed to protect him. She felt responsible for what had happened to him.

"Where's Charles?" Stephen asked, startling her.

"What? Oh. I said I'd spell him for a while. He's been looking after you all day long. I figured he needed a chance to rest and eat a little, maybe get outside for a walk."

"That was kind of you, to think of him."

Jessie shrugged. She wasn't about to tell him that she really hadn't considered Charles much when she had offered to relieve him of his patient-sitting duties for the evening.

To have something to do, she got up, rewet the rag on his forehead and laid it against his skin again. Stephen's cheeks were flushed, and there was a sparkle in his eyes. They were caused, no doubt, by the fever, but Jessie couldn't help but think how they intensified his handsomeness.

As she drew back, Stephen's hand came up and curled around her wrist, holding her there. Startled, Jessie went still, her heart speeding up strangely. His hand was warm around her wrist, and his grip was amazingly strong. With his hand wrapped around her arm like that, she felt, for a moment, strangely fragile.

"Jessie? Don't go just yet. I want to tell you something."

"I'm not going anywhere."

"Good." His fingers slipped from her arm almost reluctantly. "I want to thank you. For saving my life."

Jessie shook her head deprecatingly. "It wasn't anything."

A smile edged his lips. "It was to me. I'm rather fond of being alive."

"I didn't mean that. I just meant—I would have done it for—" She stopped abruptly, realizing how rude her response would sound.

"For anybody," he finished for her with a grimace. "I'm sure that's true. But you happened to do it for me, and I want to thank you. I'm indebted to you. You were quick and smart and courageous. I don't think most people would have thought or acted as fast as you did."

Jessie shrugged, embarrassed. "I had a good teacher: Sam Ferguson."

Stephen was aware of a twinge of irritation. Her hero worship of his brother was beginning to annoy him. He gave a short nod and turned his head from her.

Jessie started toward her chair, then stopped and turned to look at Stephen again. "I—I ought to tell you something, too."

Stephen glanced at her curiously.

"I—you hung in there, and you never even complained. You were a lot tougher than I thought."

Stephen's lips twitched. "I'll take that as a compliment."

Jessie's eyes narrowed with suspicion. Was he laughing at her? When she'd been trying to say something nice about him! "Take it however you want."

"No, wait. Don't get huffy. I appreciate what you said, I really do."

"Well, it doesn't matter. I wasn't looking for thanks or anything. I just wanted to let you know. You were brave."

He wondered if he had been as brave as Sam would have been, but he kept the barbed thought to himself as he watched Jessie return to her post in the chair. They stayed in their positions for a long time, not saying anything. The more time that passed, the worse his shoulder felt and the more he thought about it. The more he thought about the pain, the worse it grew. He felt hotter, too, all the time. But he wasn't about to admit either of those things to Jessie— particularly after her approval of his bravery, however grudging.

After a while, Amanda came in with one of her unending bowls of broth. She took one look at him and cast a stern gaze toward her daughter. "Jessamine Randall, what are you doing, just sitting there? Isn't it obvious that this man is in pain? Not to mention running a temperature? Did you give him any laudanum, like I told you?"

Jessie bristled. "He told me he didn't need it."

"Oh, pooh! Men!" Amanda made a gesture of dismissal. "Their pride hardly ever leaves any room for sense. Of course he'd deny needing it. It's up to you to see that he takes it anyway." She nodded toward the tall chest in the corner as she set down the tray. "Fetch me that packet of powder over there, Jess. The doctor left it for the fever. Then get the laudanum and give him a spoonful."

Stephen was glad for Amanda's intervention. He'd been gritting his teeth against the pain for too long. He had been on the verge of giving in and asking Jessie for a dose. Now he struggled awkwardly up onto one elbow to take the spoonful of liquid that she poured and held out to him.

While Amanda was dumping powder from the packet into a glass of water and mixing it, Jessie took hold of Stephen's good arm and tried to help him into a half-sitting position, plumping up the pillows and stuffing them behind him. He didn't get comfortable—he didn't think that was possible—but at least he would be able to drink the other medicine and the ever-present thin soup.

Amanda held the glass to his lips, and he drank, grimacing at the taste of the powder, much of it still gritty in his mouth. "Good Lord, Madam. Are you trying to kill me?" he asked testily when Amanda took the glass away to allow him to breathe.

"Quite the opposite," she responded calmly. "Now finish the rest."

"I'm not sure I can."

"Of course you can." Amanda smiled coaxingly. "Now, open your mouth."

Stephen released a heavy sigh and made himself drink the rest. He considered heaving up the contents for a moment, but closed his eyes and breathed shallowly until his stomach calmed down.

Amanda smiled. "There. You did just splendidly." She glanced at her daughter. "See? You have to lead them a little and force them a little. Men make the worst patients. Now, you do the same thing with this broth."

Jessie looked at her uneasily. "But, Ma . . . I thought you were going to do it."

"I haven't time. There are the supper dishes to clean. And Joe will be coming up soon. We want our patient looking as healthy as possible for Joe, don't we?"

"Well, sure." Jessie looked at Stephen, half-lying, half-sitting in his bed. The thought of sitting on his bed and feeding him made her uneasy. "But I've never done this. I don't know how."

"You'll get the hang of it quick enough. It isn't hard."

Jessie picked up the soup bowl and sat down gingerly on the bed. She dipped the spoon into the bowl and brought it up to Stephen's lips. It seemed as if half the broth dribbled down his chin and onto the bedclothes.

"Oh, dear." Jessie looked at the spots in dismay.

"Not such a full spoon," Stephen said quietly.

"What? Oh. I see." Jessie blushed a little. She hated to look incompetent in any matter. Why had she agreed to do this? Or, to be more honest, why had she volunteered to relieve Charles? She took a more modest spoonful.

"Your mother sets the bowl in her lap and holds the towel under my chin."

It worked far better that way, Jessie quickly discovered, and after that it wasn't so bad. It was almost—well, not fun, of course, but enjoyable in some way. She had never taken care of anyone before, and she was amazed to find that it could actually feel good to do so, not as if she was a drudge. She cupped her hand beneath his chin, holding the towel, and tipped the spoon up to his lips again and again, all the while looking into his face. There was nowhere else she could look. She'd never stared at a man's mouth before. Stephen's lips were firm, the lower one a trifle full. Now and then a drop of broth settled on his lower lip, and his tongue came out to sweep it up. Once or twice he smiled at her, and she saw the flash of white, even teeth. The longer she watched, the more tightly she clamped her own lips together.

Finally Stephen shook his head and refused to take another spoonful. Jessie set the bowl and towel on the tray, but she didn't yet rise from the bed. Stephen lay watching her. His eyes were foggy, and Jessie knew that the laudanum was taking effect. She reached out and laid her hand to his forehead, as she had earlier, to check his temperature.

"That feels good," Stephen murmured, then was amazed that he had said it to her. His tongue was thick, and he had the disconcerting feeling that he wasn't entirely in control of his brain. He hoped that Jessie would leave her hand where it was. His eyes went unconsciously to her throat, exposed by the open collar of her mannish shirt, and to the soft swell of her breasts beneath the flannel. "You have a gentle touch," he commented. "I'm surprised."

Jessie jerked her hand back. She felt very awkward suddenly. Stephen's voice had been low and faintly slurred, almost…caressing. Something quivered deep inside her. She glanced around, annoyed to feel a blush rising up her throat. "Well, I'm surprised, too," she replied, struggling for a light, flippant tone. "I'm more used to working than sitting in sickrooms."

Stephen looked at her. He felt too tired to do anything else, even to turn his head away. Besides, she was pleasant to look at. Not pretty in that cool, cameo way that Elizabeth was. But there was something intriguing in the big, frank blue eyes and the wide mouth, the triangular face, the spattering of golden freckles across her nose and cheeks. Her hair was the color of flame, and even though she wore it pulled back tightly into two pigtails, she could not completely restrain it; fine hairs around her face had pulled loose and curled around her features. Stephen suspected that when her hair lay loose across her shoulders, it was a glory to behold. He wondered if any man had ever seen it loose. If any man had ever turned her soft.

"Why do you try to hide what you are?" he asked softly, almost as if he were thinking aloud.

Jessie stiffened, and her eyes turned suspicious. "And what's that?"

"A woman." His brain was growing more and more numb, and he struggled to find the words to express what he meant. "You know, dressing like that. Acting tough."

"I *am* tough." Jessie crossed her arms over her chest and stared at him with blazing eyes. "I'm not trying to hide anything."

"But you're very pretty. You could look…enchanting."

*Enchanting!* The word stunned Jessie into silence. No man had ever even suggested such a thing. Finally she said, "You must be delirious. Your fever's worse than I thought." But her dry, cynical words came out a little breathlessly, and there was a funny, tight feeling in her chest.

Stephen smiled and shook his head. His eyelids drifted closed, and he pulled them open again. He wanted to say something else, to counter her self-deprecating words, but his mind had become too groggy. He wet his lips. "Jess…"

"Yes?" She leaned a little closer. His voice was slurred and almost too low to hear.

"What's your real name? Not Jess."

"Oh." Jessie grimaced. She had always disliked her full name. It was too prissy, too flowery. "Lots of folks call me Jessie."

"Not Jessie, is it?" His eyes were dark and velvety in the dim light of the kerosene lamp, the pupils huge. "Your real name?"

"No." She found she couldn't lie to a man who was lying there so weak. "No, it's not. It's Jessamine."

"Jessamine," he repeated, smiling. "Jessamine." Jessie squirmed under his repetition of her name. "Pretty. Pretty Jessamine."

He sank into sleep, a faint smile on his face.

Jessie sat through the evening, watching Stephen sleep. Normally she would have been bored silly, but tonight her brain was too active, returning again and again to what Stephen had said about her. "Enchanting." She wasn't used to men who used words like that. What had he meant by it, exactly?

It must have been the fever talking, she told herself. No one in his right mind would look at her in an old flannel shirt and denim pants and laced-up work boots almost to her knee and call her enchanting. Hell, she didn't even look like a woman, let alone a pretty one.

But, then, he hadn't said she *was* enchanting. He'd said she *could* be, if she tried. That meant if she'd wear skirts and arrange her hair up on her head and adopt a sweet, submissive face. Well, she wasn't about to do any of those things. Not for any man, and certainly not to impress one like Stephen Ferguson.

No doubt he liked women with lace frothing out of their cuffs and collar, and sweet little strings of pearls around their necks. He'd want the kind who flirted with him from behind their fans and who had all kinds of fancy, complicated rules for how people should behave, like those silly women in the books her mother liked to read. He'd thanked her for saving his life, but he still thought her unfeminine.

Jessie barely restrained a snort. She'd like to see how much good one of those frilly ladies would have done him last night on the trail when someone was shooting at them. Oh, no, he'd been glad enough then that she was tough and unwomanly and had gotten him out of there instead of falling into hysterics. But now, of course, he was rebuking her for her unfeminine dress and behavior. Well, let him. She shot a fulminating glance at Stephen's sleeping form. He was nothing to her. And what he'd said about her looks was nothing to her, either.

Still, a few minutes later, she couldn't stop herself from tiptoeing to the small mirror above the dresser. She turned her face from side to side, trying to see it from all angles in the poor light. *Enchanting.*

Jessie sighed. She couldn't see it. All she could see was carroty hair and thin red-brown brows and freckles splotched across her nose. Blue eyes were good; she'd always heard that men like blue eyes. But she didn't think that the direct, frank gaze in those blue eyes was what men wanted. No, it was vague, limpid blue orbs like Gertie Haskins down at the bakery had, the kind that glanced down modestly, then turned to gaze at a man with awe.

Jessie grimaced at her reflection. What in the world was she doing, mooning about in front of a mirror? She had far better things to do with her time than this. It didn't matter to her what Stephen Ferguson thought of her looks—or lack of them.

She returned to her chair and flopped down in it, stretching her legs out in front of her. She leaned her head back against the rocker and waited for Charles to relieve her. She didn't know what she was doing here, anyway.

## Chapter Seven

By morning Stephen's fever was better, and he continued to improve all day. Even the burning pain in his shoulder subsided somewhat. By the time Jessie came home the next evening, he was awake and alert, and he had several questions to ask her about what had happened to him.

"Looks like you must be feeling better," she said when she came in, nodding toward where he sat against the headboard, propped up by pillows.

"Yes. Charles helped me sit. It improved my mood considerably."

Charles, like the well-trained servant he was, glided noiselessly from the room upon Jessie's arrival, leaving the door open slightly for decorum's sake. Jessie watched him go, then turned, shaking her head.

"Doesn't he ever say anything?"

"What do you mean?"

"Hello, excuse me, so long. That sort of thing."

"Of course, if he's addressed."

"Huh? You mean, he doesn't say anything unless you say something first?"

"Yes."

"Why?"

Stephen looked puzzled. "He's supposed to be unobtrusive."

"What does that mean?" Jessie wondered if Stephen always talked like this, or if he did it just to make her feel ignorant.

"Not noticed. You know. As if he weren't there."

"Why?"

"Because he's a servant. He's—it was part of his training." Stephen gave up trying to explain it to her. Obviously she would never understand being a servant.

Jessie shrugged. She walked to the bed, holding out an envelope. "You got a telegram. Mama said she thought you were feeling well enough to read it. It came to the telegraph office in Missoula, and they brought it on the stage today. They delivered it to the mill because those are the only Fergusons they know."

"A telegram?" Stephen frowned, reaching for the envelope. He tore it open and read through the message quickly. "Damn!" He read it again. It didn't make any more sense the second time.

"What is it?"

"My fiancée. She wired to say she's taking the train from St. Louis to Missoula. She's leaving tomorrow."

"Fiancée!" Jessie's eyebrows flew up. He was engaged! She didn't know why it surprised her so much, but she felt as if she'd suddenly lost her breath. "You're engaged?"

"Yes. But I can't think why she'd take it into her head to come here. Elizabeth's usually a very levelheaded woman."

Yes, and no doubt she wore expensive, beautiful, very feminine dresses and smelled like lilacs or attar of roses or some such thing. "Doesn't she say?"

"No. Just that she has to come and to please meet her."

"Maybe she figures you're running out on her."

Stephen gave her a repressive look. "Elizabeth would never be that foolish. She's known me all my life."

"Maybe she can't wait to see you. Maybe she's ready to get married."

Stephen's lips quirked up at the thought of calm, proper Elizabeth rushing out to the wilds of the Montana Territory because she couldn't bear to be away from him. "It seems unlikely."

Jessie glanced at him oddly. He hardly sounded like a man who was about to see his fiancée again. She would have expected him to be excited and happy, not calm, almost amused. "I don't understand."

"You'd have to know Elizabeth. She's very much a lady, very correct and—even dignified."

Dignified? It seemed even more peculiar for a man to describe the young woman he loved as "dignified."

"She simply wouldn't do something as rash as this without an extremely good reason." His frown returned. It must have something to do with Elizabeth's stepmother. Netta must have done something so intolerable that Elizabeth could not bear to remain in the same house with her until Stephen returned to St. Louis. But why hadn't she gone to stay with his grandparents? And how could he possibly meet her train in Missoula? "I can't let her arrive with no one there to meet her."

Jessie shook her head. "You can't ride a horse in your condition. You haven't even gotten out of bed yet."

That was true enough. He would be lucky to get up and walk around the room tomorrow, let alone ride a horse for several days. "But what will I do about Elizabeth?"

"Couldn't she take the stage?"

"By herself?" His eyebrows shot up. "Oh, no, I don't think so. Besides, she will expect me to be there. After all, she sent me a telegram days ago. I'm sure she had no idea how long it would take to reach me. And certainly not that I would be injured and couldn't meet her!"

"You could send a message to her. I know! Sam is going to Missoula with Burley and Jim Two Horses to pick up the new saw blade. He came into town this afternoon, and he'll leave for Missoula bright and early tomorrow morning. He

could take a message to your fiancée. Better yet, he could
bring her back here.''

Stephen hesitated. It would be the next best thing to es-
corting her himself for Elizabeth to travel under his
brother's protection. "But would Sam be willing to? He—I
got the impression the other day that he wasn't happy to see
me. That he wished I'd never shown up. He might not want
the burden of looking after someone for me.''

"No. Sam's somebody you can always count on. He
wouldn't refuse to escort his brother's future wife, no matter—'' Jessie stopped, suddenly realizing how tactless her
words would sound.

"No matter how much he dislikes me,'' Stephen finished
for her. "Right?''

Jessie squirmed a little. "I didn't say that.''

"You didn't have to. It was obvious that Samuel's feelings toward me were, at best, ambivalent.'' Stephen's face
was cool and polite, a social mask he had learned to wear
long ago. "It's all right. It has, after all, been over twenty
years. One can hardly expect a brother's feelings not to
change. I was aware of that fact when I came here.''

He was a cool one about everybody, Jessie thought. His
fiancée. His brother. She wondered if he lacked feelings for
anyone but himself or if he was simply very good at hiding
what he felt. She was used to men who didn't talk much,
especially about painful things, but at least they usually
showed excitement and anger and happiness in their faces,
if not in their words. She was having a hard time, though,
guessing what Stephen Ferguson was feeling at the moment.

"Well,'' she said, "you might as well ask him. I don't
know how else you're going to get the lady here if she can't
ride the coach alone.''

Jessie was right. Much as he hated to ask Sam a favor,
given the way Sam had received him, it would be far worse
to leave Elizabeth stranded in a wild Western town.

"Yes, you're right. I'll have to ask him."

"Then I'll send him up when he comes to supper." Jessie backed toward the door. She wasn't sure what to do. When she had come up here, she had expected to sit with Stephen through the evening, as she had the night before. But he was so much better that it would be pointless for her to do so. It left her feeling awkward.

"Thank you." Stephen watched her make her way to the door. She looked almost as if she didn't want to leave, but he was sure that couldn't be true. It was simply that she was utterly lacking in social graces. He could imagine what Elizabeth's reaction to her would be. The thought was enough to make him smile.

Jessie left, and Stephen lay dozing, drifting in and out of sleep. Once, when he awoke, he remembered that in his astonishment and worry over Elizabeth's unexpected telegram, he had forgotten to ask Jessie about the circumstances of his shooting.

The next time he woke up it was because there was a knock at the door. He watched Charles go to the door and open it a fraction, blocking entry into the room. Stephen heard the murmur of low voices. "Who is it, Charles?"

His valet turned his head toward him. "He has not given his name, Master Stephen."

From outside the door he heard a rough, sarcastic voice say, "It's Master Samuel Ferguson of the Nora Springs Fergusons. Do I need an appointment to see my brother?"

Stephen smiled, and his chest felt suddenly lighter. Sam *had* come to see him. He had been afraid that he would not, despite what Jessie had told him. While Charles greeted Sam formally and ushered him into the room, Stephen pushed himself higher in the bed. He hated to look so weak before his brother.

Stephen dismissed his valet, and Charles exited the room quietly. Sam tossed his hat onto a chair near the door and came over to the bed. He stood, looking down at Stephen awkwardly. Stephen motioned toward the chair beside his bed. "Sit down, Sam."

Sam took a seat, clearing his throat. "Sorry about the ambush," he said finally. He sounded as if the words had been dragged out of him. "Somebody may have thought it was me riding with Jessie."

Stephen nodded. There was silence. "Does this sort of thing happen often out here?" He strove for a light tone, to break the ice.

"Not often, but occasionally." Sam looked at him. Suddenly a grin split his face. "Damn, but you sure had one hell of a welcome to the territory."

"I did at that," Stephen replied with a laugh, and they settled down to talk much more companionably.

By the time Sam left two hours later, they had learned a good deal about their separate pasts, though each carefully avoided any mention of their mother. Sam had also agreed to escort Elizabeth to Nora Springs, though Stephen had inadvertently upset Sam by offering to pay for the task. Sam was obviously very touchy. However, Stephen had smoothed it over with him, and they had parted on friendly terms.

Stephen smiled to himself. Sam wasn't an easy person to get to know, but they'd made a start. He was no longer the cold stranger he had been the other day at the lumber camp. It might take a while to reestablish their relationship completely, but at least now Stephen knew that he had his brother back again.

Stephen dreamed that night. He was in his home in St. Louis, but Jessie was there with him. They were in a dark hall. She was ahead of him, and he was hurrying to catch up with her. Suddenly, there was a man with her, struggling with her. She called Stephen's name, straining toward him, and he could see her pale, frightened face. He ran to help her, but for some reason he could not go forward. He ran desperately, reaching out for her, but she and her assailant remained in front of him. It was as if his feet were stuck in molasses, or as if the distance between them somehow grew. She screamed, and he called out her name, reaching, reaching...

The pain in Stephen's shoulder and side brought him to consciousness. He was struggling to sit up, reaching out one hand. His wound was on fire. He sucked in an agonized breath and flopped against the mattress.

*It was a dream. Nothing but a dream.* It had seemed so real and horrible. He closed his eyes. His heart was racing, and he was bathed in sweat.

The door opened, and a woman came in softly, hesitantly. She was carrying a glass kerosene lamp, and as she held it up to throw light over the room, he saw that the woman was Jessie. But this didn't look like the Jessie he knew. She was dressed in a long, heavy robe, belted at the waist, and when she moved across the floor, it separated in front to reveal flashes of pale nightgown beneath it. Her hair was loose, lying around her shoulders and spilling down over her back and breasts. Her tresses were a dark red in the dim light, flashing copper where they caught the light.

It was the first time Stephen had seen her dressed as a woman. And her hair—it was as glorious as he had suspected, a thick, rich fall that shone like satin. "Jessamine." Her name came out a whisper.

"Stephen?" She tiptoed closer. "Are you all right? I thought I heard you call out." She didn't add that it was her own name she had heard.

"Yes. I'm fine. I must have been dreaming."

Jessie nodded and set the lamp on the small table beside his bed. She reached across the bed and laid her hand on his forehead. It was damp with sweat, but not abnormally hot. She turned down the sheet to expose his shoulder and held the lamp closer to inspect his bandage. Jessie shook her head a little, tsking. "Looks like you tore open your wound a little.'' Her hair brushed against his arm and chest. It tickled his skin. It was as soft as the finest silk he'd ever touched.

She unwrapped the wound quickly, trying to keep her fingers light and steady, and pulled the bandage carefully away, grateful that it didn't stick. Then she folded up another bandage and placed it on him, winding a long strip of cotton around his chest to hold the pad in place.

Jessie felt uncomfortable, though she never would have admitted it. She was very aware of the fact that his torso was bare. She touched his skin time and again as she put the bandage in place. His flesh was smooth, and her fingers tingled strangely every time she brushed against it. She was also embarrassingly aware of her own attire. It wasn't proper for her to be here like this with a man, even if he was flat on his back with a gunshot wound. But that thought made her feel even more like a fool. Since when had Jessie Randall worried about whether what she was doing was proper?

''What did you dream?'' she asked, hoping that conversation would diminish the awkwardness.

''I don't remember.'' Stephen wasn't about to tell her that he'd been frantically trying to save her. The helplessness of the dream still tasted bitter in his mouth. Besides, Jessie would only laugh and remind him that she didn't need anybody to save her, that she could take care of herself.

No doubt she could. She'd not only taken care of herself when the shooting started the other day, she'd taken care of him, as well. The thought galled him.

''Well.'' Jessie tied the ends of the bandage and stepped back, picking up her lamp. The bandage was a trifle loose and far sloppier-looking than her mother's, but she thought that it would hold until her mother could put on a fresh one. ''That's done. I'll let you go back to sleep now.''

She turned to leave, but Stephen reached out a hand and grasped her robe. ''No, wait. Please.''

Jessie turned, her face questioning. "What's the matter?"

"Nothing. I wanted to ask you something. I forgot to earlier."

"All right." She waited a little uneasily.

"That shot. How'd it happen? Who did it?"

"I don't know." She shook her head. "The marshal's investigating it."

"But—was it deliberate? Does the marshal think it was on purpose or an accident?"

Jessie squirmed inside. How was she supposed to answer him? She didn't want to alarm or upset him, not in his condition, but she hated to lie. "He doesn't know yet," she equivocated finally.

Her silence had told Stephen what he wanted to know. "They meant to shoot me, didn't they?" His forehead creased in thought. "They shot at me more than once. Isn't that right? They kept on trying to kill me. It wasn't an accident."

Jessie hesitated, then nodded. "Yes. They kept on shooting. But we don't know who they were. Why would anybody in Nora Springs want to kill you?"

"I don't know. I don't know anyone here except my father and Sam."

"Well, it wasn't one of them." She shrugged, moving away. "We figure it might have been that they mistook you for Sam. You'd look enough alike from a distance."

"I know. Sam suggested that to me." He paused. "But does anybody hate Sam that much?"

"Somebody crazy. Anyway, we've been gossiping like crazy, Joe and Mama and me, getting the word out that you're not Sam. We figured then maybe he wouldn't try to shoot you if he saw you again."

"But what about Sam? He's still in danger."

"He'll be okay. There are two good men with him, and he's out of town. Joe and I figured he's about as safe as he can be."

"I see." Her words confirmed what he'd been thinking. Yet he sensed that she was still not telling him the truth, at least not all of it.

"Don't worry about it," Jessie assured him. "When the man who shot you learns who you really are, he won't try again."

"But what about Sam? What about when he gets back to town? The killer *will* go after him!"

Jessie nodded. "Maybe." She wasn't about to explain to him that she and Joe thought the attack was probably against the business rather than against Sam alone. Joe would have her head for worrying Stephen about such things when he was still so weak. He wouldn't like her telling Stephen as much as she had, but she didn't know what else to do, the way he kept asking her questions.

"Then something must be done. We have to find out who did it. What about the law? Is that marshal doing anything?"

"Sure. He's looking for the killer. He found where the man was hiding when he fired at you, and he followed the tracks for a ways, but he lost them."

"So he's learned nothing." Stephen frowned. "I don't like the sound of this. Perhaps I ought to send for a detective. We hired one in our business once, and he found the thievery we'd suspected right away. I could send a telegram to him."

"What good would he do out here?" Jessie asked scornfully. "A city man in the mountains?"

Stephen's lips twitched a little in irritation. It was obvious what she thought of the abilities of a man from the city. "Perhaps he couldn't track him through the wilderness, but I would think that finding motives and clues would be pretty much the same, whether one is located in St. Louis or Montana.''

"Well, Joe and Sam wouldn't stand for it."

Stephen thought about his brother's prickly pride when he'd offered him money to rent a conveyance for Elizabeth. He suspected that Jessie was right. Sam would be too proud to let him pay for a detective, and he would probably be embarrassed that people might think he couldn't handle the matter himself. Being completely self-sufficient seemed to be the thing the people out here prized most. "All right. I won't send for the detective—yet. But in the meantime, we can find out some things on our own."

"Things like what?"

"Like who would have a grudge against Sam? Who's he fired recently? Or refused to hire? That's a good place to start. You handle the money records for the lumber company. You ought to be able to determine that."

Jessie tried not to let her surprise show. She would never have guessed that Stephen Ferguson could come up with an idea that practical or sharp. Why, she hadn't even thought of it herself.

"Of course, it could be something personal." Stephen glanced at her uneasily. "Perhaps that's something you shouldn't delve into."

Jessie grinned. "Too nasty for my little ladylike eyes and ears?"

Stephen grimaced. "You, needless to say, don't think that's possible."

"I'll tell you what I think's possible. That my mother and your father will give me holy hell for talking to you about all this when you're supposed to be resting and mending. It's the middle of the night, you know."

"I know." His eyes flickered involuntarily to the neck of her bed robe, where the white of her nightgown showed above the collar.

One of Jessie's hands went to the top of her robe, clutching the two sides tightly together, and she colored a little. Her reaction surprised her, and she felt ridiculous for being embarrassed by nothing more than a man looking at her in her bed robe. Why, he hadn't even said anything suggestive. She made her hand relax and drop to her side, and forced her eyes to meet his coolly. "Good night."

"Good night." She started out the door. "Miss Randall!"

She paused and looked at him over her shoulder.

"Thank you for coming to see about me. You take good care of your patients."

His words warmed her inside, but Jessie just shrugged. She didn't know how to handle a compliment, especially from this man. "It wasn't anything. You go back to sleep now."

"I will. Good night."

She slipped out the door, and the room was plunged into darkness. Stephen lay looking out the window at the cold quarter moon. He wondered where Elizabeth was and why she was coming here. He wondered why someone had taken shots at him—or Sam. And he wondered what Jessie Randall looked like beneath that robe.

Stephen was a healthy young man, and he healed quickly. Soon he was getting out of bed with his valet's help and making his way slowly around the room. Every day he would sit up in a chair by the window, and with each day the time he spent there grew longer. But he still felt absurdly weak, and, to his impatient spirit, it was taking far too long to get well. His mind was fully alert and active despite his body's weakness, and he was bored.

Joe came by to see him every evening. They spent most of their time chatting about the sawmill and the lumber business. Stephen was curious about it, as he was eager to learn about most businesses, and Joe was more than happy to talk about it. Except for Sam, the lumber business had been Joe's life; he loved it with a feeling that ran far deeper than most men's attitudes toward their jobs. He was a part of it— the land, the trees, the vibrating hum of the mill. There was no job in the industry that he hadn't worked, no aspect of it he hadn't seen. And he loved every bit of it.

He told Stephen stories about the old days in the timber business, when the lumber camps had been smaller, primitive affairs, usually with only one building. He talked about the exhilaration and danger of driving the logs downriver, risking death with any slip of one's feet. He talked about starting the mill, and about the time it had caught on fire a few years ago, the sawdust sending it up in flames in an instant. It was one of the many hazards of the business, and he and Sam had simply started over. The more he talked, the more intrigued Stephen became. He chafed at his weakened state, feeling eager to get down to the mill again and take a tour with his father.

It was a wonderful thing to be with Joe, to be able to talk and joke with him. Stephen loved his grandfather, but Grandpapa was a distant, formal man, not given to affection or close companionship. Elizabeth's father had been the nearest thing he'd had to a father, and he had often gone to him for advice and sometimes even for comfort. But neither of them was the man Joseph Ferguson was; neither of them was the warm, laughing, rough yet tender father Stephen had known for the first five years of his life. They could not substitute for the man who had held Stephen on his lap and told him stories about daring, strong men and their impossible feats, who had whistled as he moved around the cabin, and who had been prone to burst into song on a long, cold winter's evening and grab his wife and whirl her around the room in a vigorous dance.

It was this man whom Stephen had never forgotten, whom he had held always in his heart, and it was like a miracle to be with him again. Sometimes Joe talked about his business or his love of the land; other times he recalled moments from Stephen's or Sam's childhood. He talked about his parents, long dead, and he talked about Eleanor as she had been when they fell in love. The more Stephen was with him, the more memories he dredged up from his youth, and with each new recollection, each remembered feeling and incident, he grew closer to his father.

Jessie visited Stephen, too, though not as often as Joe did. She rarely had much to say, just asked how he was doing and stood there awkwardly, until finally she left the room. Stephen felt like a fool at those times. Never before had he been so unable to carry on a conversation with a woman. He had been in hundreds of social situations, and he had always managed to keep the flow of talk going smoothly, no matter how tongue-tied or boring the other person might be. Every hostess in St. Louis considered him an asset. Yet here he was, unable to think of anything to say to a backwoods girl who dressed and acted like a man! It was absurd.

Stephen wanted to talk to her. Except for the visits from Joe, Stephen's days were deadly dull. Charles would have been shocked down to his toes had Stephen tried to chat with him, and Mrs. Randall was too busy to stay and talk. He quickly went through the single book he had brought to read, and he found that there were no books at all in Mrs. Randall's house except for a few old schoolbooks. When he was able, he went down to the garden to sit, but the late September weather was already too cold for him to remain outdoors comfortably, and he usually returned to the house quickly. He spent most of his time sleeping or staring aimlessly out the window.

He would have welcomed any diversion. But that wasn't the only reason he wanted to talk to Jessie. He was intrigued by her. She was such an odd creature, and, for reasons he didn't delve into, he wanted to understand her. But he could think of nothing to say that would interest her. He was sure she would react with scorn to any of the customary polite chatter he used with women. Nor did she seem to be curious about any of the places he had lived or the things he knew. In fact, he wasn't sure what she would like to talk about, but he was certain that it would be something he knew nothing about. Given the silence and uncomfortableness that usually lay between them, Stephen sometimes wondered why she came to see him at all.

He didn't know it, but Jessie frequently wondered the same thing. It was obvious that Stephen was healing; there was no need to check in on him every night. And the visits certainly weren't enjoyable. Yet somehow, she couldn't keep her steps from turning to his room every evening when she came home—anymore than she could stop thinking about what he had said that night when he'd been dosed up with laudanum. He had said she could be "enchanting."

It was an idea that scared Jessie, yet it drew her, too. Before this, she would have said that she was utterly unconcerned with her looks. If anything, she wanted to be plain; it drew a lot less talk and jests from the men. But ever since Stephen had spoken that night, she found herself glancing at her reflection whenever she passed a mirror. Sometimes in the evening, in the privacy of her bedroom, she would go to her mirror and stare into it, studying each feature carefully. Was there beauty lying dormant there? Could that face, that form, attract a man? A man like Sam Ferguson?

Jessie had never fooled herself. She had adored Sam for years, first with the love of a kid sister and then with more adult, confused feelings, but she had never expected Sam to feel anything for her. She was a tomboy, slender, not billowing like the floozie she'd caught sight of Sam walking with one time. She had a redhead's skin, marred with freckles across her nose and cheeks, and her hair was the color of carrots. She wasn't feminine the way a man wanted a woman to be. Hell, she didn't even know how to pretend to be feminine. And she didn't want to be, not really. Not if it meant simpering and giggling like Mr. Swenson's daughter, Olga. Or wearing constricting skirts and silly hats. And yet . . .

She would never forget the shock in Stephen Ferguson's eyes when he had realized that she was a woman, not a boy. That horror galled her, ate away at her inside in a way that the other men's jokes and insults never had. Clear as day, he'd hardly been able to believe that she was a woman. He had been disgusted; she remembered just as well the cutting remarks he had made about her lack of femininity. Of course, she didn't *care* what someone like Stephen Ferguson thought about her. Still, it hurt; she couldn't deny the little ache in her chest. And she couldn't help thinking what pleasant balm it would be to her soul to have Stephen look at her with admiration. Was it possible that she could get him to look at her that way?

She couldn't help wondering if maybe she had missed out on something other women, like her mother, knew. She couldn't help thinking about how she would look in a dress, with her hair piled up on her head. What would Sam think if he saw her that way? Might he stop thinking of her as just an amusing little sister? What would it be like to have men glance at her in an entirely new way? Would they smile and flirt with her—or would they guffaw at the sight of her all gussied up?

Such thoughts occupied her mind more and more as the days passed. Once she even sneaked into her mother's room and tried on one of her dresses. But she couldn't tell much about how she would look, since her mother was a larger, more buxom woman, and the dress hung loosely on her, about as attractive as a sack. Obviously it wasn't something she could go at halfway. And it took more than a dress and a new hairdo; she knew that. It would mean acting differently, talking differently. She wasn't willing to do all that, of course, just for this silly whim. And even if she was willing, she wouldn't know where to start, or how to tell if she was making progress or just making a fool of herself. She would need help, and there was no one in the whole town to help her.

Except Stephen Ferguson.

Jessie rejected the idea as soon as it popped into her head. That was crazy. There was no way she'd let that snobby man view her stumbling, bumbling efforts to be feminine and pretty. If anyone would laugh at her, he would. Why, he knew beautiful and sophisticated women, the kind of women who bought dresses that cost more than her whole salary, and who draped themselves with jewels. He was used to women who knew how to flirt and what to say to a man, who knew how to make a man come running with merely a quirk of one eyebrow. Women like his fiancée. He would think Jessie was ridiculous, and that her efforts to look pretty were pitiful. Stephen Ferguson was the last man to whom she'd expose such foolish, fragile seedlings of hope.

On the other hand, she didn't care what he thought, did she? He didn't matter to her. And he was the kind of man who would know what she should be like. If she asked someone like Sam, he'd probably just shrug and say a woman was "like...well, a woman. You know." No, she didn't know. But Stephen Ferguson did.

He would be willing to help her, too. He was grateful to her for saving his life. If she looked like a fool in front of him, it wouldn't really matter, because he'd be gone in a few weeks.

The idea began to take root in her mind and grow. Finally, one evening, as she lingered by Stephen's door, unable to find anything to say yet reluctant to leave, she drew a deep breath and said abruptly, "Stephen, do you reckon you could make me into a woman?"

# Chapter Eight

Stephen's jaw dropped. "Pardon?" She couldn't possibly have said what he thought she had.

"If I wanted to—*just if!*—I wanted to, you know, act like other women, could you teach me how? How to talk and act and everything?"

"Oh." For one flabbergasted moment, he had thought Jessie was asking him to take her to his bed. Of course she would never... and *he* would never...

"Well? Could you?" Jessie prodded, feeling more and more foolish for having asked. It had been a stupid idea. Stephen wouldn't do it. He couldn't; nobody could accomplish miracles. Besides, she didn't really want to change, anyhow.

"I—I don't know. You've deprived me of speech for the moment. I never dreamed..."

Jessie shrugged. "It's not important. You don't have to answer. I was just curious." She turned as though to leave the room.

"No! Wait. Don't go! It must have been important or you wouldn't have asked. I would think it took quite a bit of courage. Give me a minute to assimilate what you said. You want me to help in—in appearing more feminine?"

"I guess. I don't know. I just kept thinking about the things you said about me not being like a woman."

"I'm sorry. I shouldn't have said that. I was irritated with you, and I lashed out. You have a remarkable ability to irritate me." He smiled.

Jessie grinned back. "You're not the only one I have that ability with."

"I'm sure not." Stephen swung his legs off the bed and stood. He wore a dressing gown of heavy quilted satin over his bedclothes. He had another one, Jessie knew, of deep blue velvet, because she had seen him in it, too. Why would a man take two robes with him when he traveled? Jessie would have been surprised to learn that Sam had even one robe, let alone two. And certainly none like these! She had seen such rich fabrics only on the banker's wife, and then just on special occasions. The robe suited him, though; he looked more handsome than any man had a right to be, especially a few days past a gunshot wound.

Stephen walked over to her. "First of all, I'm not sure I can help you. I'm not privy to all the secrets and rules of ladylike behavior."

"But you know enough. You know that I'm not one. You must know how I should act."

"Perhaps some basics, but...are you sure you want to do this? Why, suddenly, do you want to act like a lady?"

Jessie's color rose. She wouldn't admit to him how intrigued she had been by his remark that she was enchanting. Nor was she willing to tell him that his insults about her lack of femininity had stung. And revealing the vague yearnings she had inside for a home, husband and family was out of the question. She shrugged and started to turn away. "If you won't do it, that's all right."

"Wait a minute." He reached out and grabbed her wrist, holding her still. "Are you always this difficult to talk to?"

She swung to face him, her chin up. "I reckon."

"Frankly, I don't see how I can help you if every time I say something or ask a question, you threaten to leave. I have to have your cooperation, you know."

Jessie looked at him suspiciously. "Does that mean you're going to do it?"

He sighed. "I'll do what I can. I'm not promising anything. I'm not a lady's maid or a deportment teacher. But I'll tell you everything I can think of. On one condition."

Her face closed up even tighter. "That's what I figured."

"And that is: you have to do what I tell you and not argue."

"Do what you tell me!" Her eyes opened wider. "What does that mean?"

"Nothing reprehensible, I assure you."

"Dang you, I can't understand half of what you say. What do you mean?"

"I mean, I have no intention of asking you to do anything wrong. But I refuse to put myself through the ordeal of arguing with you over every little thing I tell you to do. I've been around you enough to know that you will."

"I won't! Why would I ask you to teach me something and then not do it?"

"I don't know why, but I feel certain that you will. I'll tell you a lady does such and such, and you'll say, 'Why, tarnation, that's stupid!'" He mimicked her voice so effectively that Jessie had to giggle.

"So you're going to tell me to do a bunch of stupid things?"

"I imagine you'll think so."

Her expression wavered; then she set her jaw. "Well, I may not like it, and I may think it's stupid, but I won't argue."

"And you promise that you'll do it?"

"All right. I promise." Her mouth turned mulish. "But don't you go putting any jokes over on me, understand?"

"Jokes?"

"Yeah, like getting me to do ridiculous stuff, telling me it's what ladies do."

"Jessie! I wouldn't do that." He looked at her, puzzled. "Why would I want to make you look ridiculous?"

"I don't know. But men are always pulling that kind of thing."

"Well, I promise you that I won't. So, do we have an agreement?"

Jessie swallowed. She was scared of entering the unknown. Maybe she ought to forget the whole thing. But she couldn't. For whatever crazy reason, she knew she just had to do this. "All right." She wiped a nervous palm down her pants leg to remove the telltale dampness, then stuck out her hand. "It's a deal."

"It's a deal," he repeated and shook her hand. He'd never shaken a woman's hand before, only taken one to bow over it in greeting. Her hand felt odd, pressed palm to palm in his, so small and delicate, yet hardened with calluses and firm of grip, as well. He thought of how she had looked the other night when she had come into his room. He remembered the thick red hair hanging down around her shoulders like a silken cape. He had wanted to touch it. He still wanted to.

Stephen realized that he had held her hand longer than was customary, and he dropped it quickly. He backed up a step. It was crazy that he should feel even a twinge of desire for this girl. She wasn't at all feminine; she had none of the grace or culture Elizabeth had. They were as far apart as the poles. The only reason desire had rippled through him at the thought of touching her hair, he told himself, was that she was the only woman he'd been around for days, besides Mrs. Randall. It was only proximity and a lack of any other sort of female companionship.

He wondered what Jessie would do if he kissed her—or even ran a hand over her fiery hair. Probably send a right uppercut straight to his jaw. He smiled a little at the image.

"Well?" Jessie said brightly. "Where do we start?"

Stephen glanced at her. "You mean now? You want to begin right now?"

"Why not? No use wasting time. I mean, you'll only be laid up a few more days, and before long your fiancée will be here."

And Sam would be back. Stephen suspected that his brother was the man Jessie had decided to impress with her newly acquired femininity. He had seen the adoration in her eyes when she looked at Sam at the lumber camp. It made him feel a little strange to think that he was going to coach her so that she could pursue his brother. "All right," he replied, revealing none of his thoughts. "Where shall we start?"

"I don't know. That's why I asked you to teach me."

He crossed his arms and studied her. "Well, there are the obvious things. Your manner of dress, for instance. Ladies don't wear trousers."

"I don't have any dresses."

He blinked. "None?"

Jessie shook her head. "None that'll fit me. Last time I wore a dress was when I was fourteen years old."

"I see. Then, perhaps you could make one?"

He knew what her answer would be even before she began to shake her head. "Nope. I never learned."

"Well, it's hopeless if you aren't going to dress like a woman. We might as well save ourselves the trouble."

"I can wear some of Mama's clothes, I guess. And there's a woman in town who takes in sewing. I could pay her to fix up a dress for me."

"Good. That's a place to start. And you have to stop swearing. Ladies don't curse."

"I don't cuss all that much!" Jessie retorted indignantly.

"At all. Ladies don't curse at all. And your speech is—" he paused, groping for what he meant "—too rough. Too inelegant. You speak too bluntly and openly."

"I'm not sure I understand."

"We'll work on it. Also—and this is very, very impor- tant—ladies do not spit."

"Spit! I don't—" Jessie started to deny indignantly, then remembered her behavior when he'd met her. "Oh. Well, I don't do that normally. I just did it that day because you were so uppity."

"Uppity?"

"Yeah, you know—you acted like you were better than anybody else. And you looked so—so shiny and polished, like a doll in a store. It got the better of me."

"So you did it to shock me." Jessie nodded. "You did that, all right." He chuckled softly.

Jessie was surprised that he wasn't mad. Even as she was saying the words, she had been afraid he would explode. Instead, he had laughed. She found herself almost liking him.

"However." Stephen tried to pull his face back into stern lines. "Shocking people is not something ladies do, either."

"Sounds to me like ladies don't do anything."

"Of course they do things. They dance, sing, converse, laugh, have fun—but they do them in a softer, more gen- teel way. I think the difference is more one of attitude than conduct. I think you've tried very hard for years to make people believe that you aren't a woman. You've tried to think, talk and act like a man. Being a woman is natural to you, but you've done your best to hide it, even from your- self."

Jessie frowned. "I don't know what you're talking about."

"Take your name, for instance."

"What about my name?"

"Jessie. It sounds like a man's name. Sometimes it's even Jess. But, in fact, your real name is Jessamine. It's a lovely name, graceful and feminine. You've denied that name and substituted one that's masculine."

"The hell you say!"

"Jessie . . ." He looked pained. "I told you, ladies don't curse."

"Not even a 'hell' or a 'damn'?"

He shook his head.

"Not even sometimes?" Jessie frowned. "Well, he—I mean, what do they say when they get mad?"

He paused, nonplussed, trying to remember a time when he had heard his mother or Elizabeth angry. "I'm not sure. The normal things, I guess. But they don't scream or curse. Or threaten to punch someone in the nose."

Her eyes narrowed. "I never—at least, you never heard me say that."

"Maybe not, but I suspect you have. Hitting people is not particularly ladylike, either."

"I suppose shooting a gun isn't, either."

"Not that I've noticed," he agreed.

"Then how does a woman protect herself?"

"That's what men are for."

Jessie snorted. "Well, who else does a person need protection from, except men?"

"Not all men will protect a woman, of course. But a gentleman should protect a woman from danger and—and trouble, unpleasant things, the harsher aspects of life."

"I reckon I don't know many gentlemen, then. 'Sides, I'd rather depend on myself. It's safer. I'd think a man'd get tired, always running to some woman's rescue."

Amusement quirked one corner of his mouth. "Some women take less rescuing than others."

"Yeah, and some never get rescued at all."

"I'm sure you're right." He paused. "But I think we're getting a little far afield here. Aren't we supposed to be discussing how you should act?"

"Yeah." Jessie sighed. "I'm just not sure I'll like how I turn out."

"You can always change back, in that case. Look, if you don't want to go through with it, we don't have to."

"No." Jessie set her chin. "I made up my mind I was going to do it, and I will. Go ahead."

"All right. Jessamine."

Teaching Jessie how to be a lady was a slow and often frustrating task, but Stephen found that at least it kept him from being bored while he recovered. The next evening she appeared at his door after supper dressed in a calico dress that obviously belonged to her mother. It hung loosely on her shoulders, and the sash around her small waist made the material pucker and gather. It was not a pretty dress by any means, but it gave her a softer, more feminine look.

"Very nice," Stephen told her.

Jessie smiled a little at his words and entered the room. It occurred to Stephen that she was shy about being seen this way. She glanced into the hall and closed the door behind her, confirming his guess. "Do you really think so?"

"Yes. You already look more like a lady." But he couldn't help thinking of the way her denim trousers had outlined her legs and bottom. The dress hid everything except the daintiness of her waist.

"It's one of Mama's dresses." Jessie looked doubtfully at the garment, pulling out a piece of the loose bodice. "It's kind of big. I just took it out of her wardrobe and threw it on." She lifted the hem of her dress and petticoats to reveal her usual laced boots and, above them, the cuffs of her trousers.

Stephen pressed his lips together to hide his smile. "I'm afraid—" It was a struggle to keep the amusement out of his voice. "I'm afraid the shoes will have to go, too. It's hard to walk like a lady in work boots."

Jessie grimaced. "I figured that. But I didn't have anything else, and Mama's feet are smaller than mine. I guess tomorrow I could go buy some—some high button shoes."

Her cheeks were faintly flushed. "That embarrasses you, doesn't it?" Stephen asked in amusement.

Jessie shrugged and looked away. She didn't like to admit to weakness. "I guess."

"But why? You *are* a woman. Why would you be embarrassed to buy women's shoes?"

"I don't know. I guess I'm afraid they'll laugh."

"Believe me, no one who's trying to sell you a pair of shoes will laugh at you."

"Yeah. But they could tell other people. Somebody might see me doing it. And the men at the mill would snicker about it. 'Why, lookee there, ole Jessie's decided she wants to be a woman now!'" She mimicked a man's teasing voice. "'Reckon she's found herself a man?'"

"Oh, Jessie." Stephen impulsively took her hands. "What does it matter if a few buffoons laugh? All it proves is that they're ignorant, ill-mannered fools. How you look or what you do is none of their business. What *you* think is what counts. Besides, they'll get used to it in a few days."

Jessie looked at the floor. "I suppose."

"Come on." Stephen put a finger under her chin and tilted her face so she could look at him. "Since when is Jessie Randall scared of a few louts? I thought you believed in doing what you wanted and letting the devil take the hindmost?"

She smiled faintly. "Yeah. You're right." Her chin came out farther. "It's my business, not theirs. And if they want to make something of it, I'll pop 'em in the jaw."

"Oh, Jessie, no," he started, then saw the twinkle in her eyes and realized that she was joking. He chuckled, and Jessie joined him. He felt suddenly warm and close to her. He gave her hands a squeeze and let them slide from his fingers. His own hands felt strangely empty suddenly. "All right. Now you need to learn how to walk."

"How to walk! I already know how to walk."

"Not in a dress. You strode into the room like this." Stephen walked away with long, purposeful strides.

"Yeah, and these dang skirts and petticoats kept getting in the way."

"That's precisely my point. You don't walk like that in skirts. Your steps should be shorter, daintier, more—"

"Ladylike," Jessie finished for him in a singsong voice. She sighed. "All right. How's this?"

She came toward him slowly.

"Better. But you need to take short strides. You don't have to be so slow, just take shorter steps."

Jessie grimaced. "Sounds like more work to me." She tried a few mincing steps.

"Much better."

"I was joking."

"Well, it looked good."

Jessie rolled her eyes.

"Now, as you walk, you need to sway a little."

"Sway?" Jessie began to weave. "Are you crazy?"

"No, not like that. Like this." Stephen folded his hands demurely at his waist and began to walk, trying to gently swing his hips.

Jessie burst into laughter at his ludicrous portrayal.

Stephen turned and fixed her with a falsely stern gaze. "Please, I'm trying to be serious here." She responded with another hoot of laughter, and he grinned. "All right. All right. You know what I mean."

"Oh, sure," Jessie gasped. She managed to straighten up enough to walk across the room, swinging her slender hips exaggeratedly. Her skirts swished and curled around her legs. She paused, posing, one hip thrown out and her lips pursed in a mockery of seductiveness.

Stephen groaned. "No, no, no. I didn't say walk like a—a..."

"Slut?" Jessie suggested, ruining her pose by grinning. "Spoiled dove?"

Stephen shook his head. "You're hopeless."

"I think you're right." Jessie plopped down on the mattress in a very unladylike manner and hooked the heels of her boots on the side rail of the bed.

"No. I didn't mean that. You'll learn to do this—I intend to make sure of it. But you obviously aren't going to make my task any easier."

"Well, you started it."

"Started what?" Stephen asked with an air of accused innocence.

Jessie cast him a disgusted look and bounced to her feet. "Okay. Here we go." She began to walk carefully, taking short steps and making her hips sway back and forth. But she couldn't get the movement coordinated, and she stopped, crashing a heel onto the floor and growling, "Oooh! I can't do it!"

"Just keep on trying. Don't think about it too much, that makes you awkward." She began again. "Better. But you're still moving too much." Stephen came up behind her as she walked and put his hands on her hips to hold her down to exactly the right amount of sway.

Heat surged through Jessie; she was sure her face must be flaming. She couldn't think about anything but his fingers curled lightly across her hips, his palms flat against her. She lost her concentration and took a misstep, stumbling and almost falling. Stephen grabbed at her waist to keep her upright, his fingertips digging into her flesh. Jessie was aware of each separate finger; her skin was suddenly hot in each spot.

"Are you all right?"

Jessie nodded. But she wasn't, not at all. She had the strangest feelings running through her, all tingles and prickles and shivers, and she wasn't sure whether she wanted to giggle or run.

Stephen moved his hands down to her hips. "All right. Let's start again." His voice sounded deeper and huskier. Jessie wondered if he felt anything at having his hands so intimately on her body. She was amply protected, of course, by the padding of petticoats, skirt and trousers, but still, it wasn't the sort of place where people of limited acquaintance touched each other.

She began to walk, struggling to concentrate on her steps rather than on his hands. It wasn't easy. His fingers were long and slender, and there was a surprising firmness in his grip. Her flesh pushed against one or the other hand with every step.

"Good. Very good." His hands slid from her hips in a movement that was almost a caress. Jessie's heart jumped into a fast, irregular beat. Her skin burned where he had touched her. She kept her face turned away from him for fear that he would see in her expression how his touch had affected her.

"Now, when you are walking with a gentleman," Stephen said, coming around to stand beside her, "you put your hand on his arm, thus." He took her left hand in his and brought it up to rest on the inside of his arm, just above his elbow. He held his arm bent, his elbow jutting out from his body. Jessie curled her fingers around his arm. "That's right. Now, we will walk together."

They walked around the room. It took Jessie a few moments to get into the rhythm of walking with him. It was strange to be walking this close to a man, her hand on his arm. The fact that Stephen was wearing a dressing gown instead of street clothes made it even more peculiar. The satin was slick and cool beneath her skin; she had an urge to slide her hand up and down it, to sink her fingers into it. She had never felt anything this opulent. Her senses seemed more alive than usual, especially her sense of touch, and it took a great deal of restraint to keep her fingers from exploring the soft, alluring material.

Stephen looked at Jessie. She kept her eyes on her feet. "Look up, not down," he told her, reaching over to tilt her chin up.

She glanced at him. Her eyes were wide and luminous, the blue dark in the lamplight, and there was an open, soft quality to her face that Stephen had never seen there before. His breath stopped in his throat. She was lovely.

It was nothing to do with her dress or her newly acquired walk. It was an innate beauty that Jessie usually kept tamped down, under control. But something inside her was loosening, changing. For the moment her guard was down.

Or was it that his own guard was down? That he was seeing her for the first time without being deceived by her clothes and manner?

Stephen stopped abruptly, and Jessie followed suit, surprised. They gazed at each other for a moment that could have been one heartbeat long or a hundred. Stephen stared at her, seeing her soft, wide mouth and the glow of her skin, the curves and lines of her features.

Stephen broke the gaze first, turning his head away. Jessie came to with a start, for the first time realizing how close they had been standing and how long she had been looking into Stephen's face. She backed up quickly. He glanced at her and away, then cleared his throat.

"Uh, I, that's enough for tonight." Stephen felt suddenly, surprisingly weak, as he had when he was first recovering. "We'll try it again tomorrow."

"Of course." Jessie nodded. Stephen looked odd, as strange as she felt herself. "Are you all right?" She made a move toward him. "Is your wound hurting you?"

"No, I'm fine. Perhaps I overdid a little today. I feel suddenly tired."

"Shall I send for Charles?"

"No. I'll be all right. I'll simply rest for a minute." The last thing he wanted was to have his servant fussing over him.

"All right. Then I'll go. See you tomorrow night?"

He nodded, and she left the room. Stephen noticed that this time she swept right out into the hall without stopping first to see if anyone was there.

Stephen sank down into his chair with a sigh and closed his eyes. What a bizarre turn of events. He wanted Jessie. No, Jessamine. Surely that was who he desired, the woman hidden inside her. Not the prickly, pants-wearing, cussing tomboy Jessie. How could he desire a woman, a girl, really, who wore faded denim trousers and worn work boots? Who pulled her hair into tight braids like a schoolgirl? Who could handle a horse and a gun and account books with equal ease? She wasn't the sort of woman he was used to. She had no understanding of the world in which he lived. He felt sure she would have no interest in a good book or fine music. She had never attended a play or an opera; she hadn't danced at a ball. She didn't flirt; she didn't entice, even in subtle ways. No perfume drifted on the air around her to awaken his senses.

Then why had he felt that hot, bemused moment of desire? And, admit it, it hadn't been the first time; it hadn't come upon him without warning. There had been other flashes of passion. But why?

Stephen thought of the curve of her leg and derriere beneath her trousers. He thought of the way the denim pants cupped her body where her legs met, emphasizing the very threshold of her femininity. He squirmed in his seat. Damn! Just the thought of her was making him hot.

He remembered the intimacy of seeing her in her night robe, her hair down. Her hair had been a dark flame, thick and soft, and he had wanted to sink his hands into it. He had wanted to bury his face in it. He thought of her waist, cinched in by the sash of her mother's dress. Her breasts, with the soft flannel of her man's shirt pulled taut over them. The white column of her throat where she left the top button unfastened.

Jessie had hard edges, God knows. She was tough and smart, and she knew how to take care of herself. She was no fragile flower. Yet there was a sort of shining innocence about her. Wouldn't it be a sweeter victory to win her than an ordinary woman?

Stephen shook his head hard, as though clearing it of his thoughts. It was absurd to think this way. He might see something desirable in Jessie, but she wouldn't be interested in him. She didn't think of him as a man but as some sort of foreign dandy. She was in all likelihood in love with his brother. And even if those things weren't true, she simply was not the kind of woman for him. She would never fit into his world. Nor was she the kind of woman to whom a man could offer less than marriage. She might not personify his idea of a lady, but he knew that she was a woman of high morals. Most important of all, he was engaged to be married to another woman!

He thought of Elizabeth, whom he loved, whom he had asked to be his wife. She was the proper wife for him, the one who should be at his side throughout his life. He had loved her for years; they understood each other. Yet he couldn't deny that in all the years he had known Elizabeth, he had never felt that sudden, vibrant flash of desire that had ripped through him a moment ago when he looked at Jessie. He had to admit that while he loved Elizabeth, while he knew that they were suited to each other, he did not feel passion for her. But he knew many people who had not married for passion; among people such as himself and Elizabeth there were other considerations—matters of business and society and leading the right kind of life. There was the promise he had made to Elizabeth's father.

Stephen rose and went to his bed, unfastening his robe as he walked. He felt very weary. Perhaps it had been too tiring to teach Jessie; perhaps he should stop. Yet he knew he would not.

He got into bed and lay down. The wound in his shoulder itched beneath the bandage, and, tired as he was, he found it difficult to sleep. His mind kept going to Jessie. And to Elizabeth. He thought of his brother. Sam, he knew, wouldn't worry about the proper thing to do. If he didn't desire a woman, he wouldn't marry her. Nothing would stand in his way. Stephen wondered how it would feel to be like that, to operate on instincts, to always be the first man in a fight. And, for a moment, he wished he was his brother.

# Chapter Nine

Stephen awoke the next morning feeling restless. He dressed and went downstairs for his breakfast, as he had done for the past two days. Everyone was gone except Mrs. Randall, who was busy washing dishes in the kitchen. He ate in solitary silence, plagued by a nagging boredom. Perhaps he ought to try a longer walk today. He had taken to walking close to the house over the last few days, each day stretching the distance a little farther. Yesterday he had walked halfway to the mill. Maybe today he would go all the way there.

A smile touched Stephen's lips. He liked a challenge, and he was bored stiff with coddling himself. After all, the doctor had said that his shoulder was almost completely healed. It had been over a week since he'd been shot. He needed to release the energy that had been building up inside him.

His valet helped him into his coat. "Sir, are you certain you should venture out today? It seems rather cold for a man just out of his sickbed."

"Yes, I'm certain. Don't fuss, Charles." Stephen thought that it could be quite irritating having a servant help you to dress. It would be so much faster to throw on his coat himself rather than wait for Charles to bring it and hold it for him. He wanted to be gone.

"Yes, sir."

Stephen sighed. "I'm sorry, Charles. I'm irritable these days. I'm tired of being cooped up."

"Yes, sir, I know. And, of course, I wouldn't presume, except that the weather here is unseasonably cool."

"I know. I didn't realize it would be so much colder than at home. Silly. We are practically to Canada. I must buy a warmer coat, I suppose."

"Here?" Charles looked appalled. "Oh, Mr. Ferguson, I'm sure this town couldn't possibly have a garment of the style and quality to which you are accustomed."

Stephen grinned. "You're probably right. But right now I'm more interested in warmth than style and quality."

"But—will we be staying that long?"

Stephen's grin widened. "What's the matter, Charles? Are you finding the West not to your liking?"

"Well, frankly, sir, it is a bit primitive. That wasn't apparent in the stories I read. And in the books it seemed much more—exciting."

"You mean my getting shot wasn't exciting?"

"No, sir, that was quite enough excitement. But I found that it was more frightening than enjoyable. In the stories, it was, well, it sounded different. Better."

"I've never read any of your stories, I'm afraid. But, you know, I've found that I like it better than I had imagined I would."

"Sir! But you were shot!"

"I didn't like that, of course. But there's something about this country that's...intriguing."

"Indeed." Charles's tone indicated that he found that highly unlikely.

"Indeed." Stephen smiled again and started toward the front door.

"Sir? Shall I accompany you?"

"No. I think I'd like to be by myself today. No need for you to go out in the cold, too."

"Thank you, sir."

Stephen stepped outside and started toward the mill at a brisk pace. It was, in fact, colder than it had been the past few days, but he found the weather invigorating. He felt almost his old self again, healthy and strong, and there was a spring to his step. It made him happy to think of going to the mill. He looked forward to seeing his father and the surprise that would be on his face, to seeing the mill in operation after days of hearing his father talk about it. To seeing Jessie.

Not, of course, that that was why he was going.

Jessie found herself doodling on the paper before her and realized that she had been doing nothing for several minutes, just staring blindly at a letter and absentmindedly marking on it. She sighed in exasperation and seized an eraser to get rid of her drawing, an entwining of hearts, leaves and flowers. What a stupid thing to do!

She didn't know why she had been unable to keep her mind on business today. She had already made three mistakes in addition and had had to go over her figures countless times to find the errors. She had managed to waste so much time that she might as well not even have come to work. Thank goodness Joe had ridden up to the camp to check on it in Sam's absence and hadn't been here to see how poorly she had been working.

Jessie pushed back her chair and began to pace around the office. It was all that damned Stephen Ferguson's fault, she thought in irritation. No, she mentally corrected herself, that *darned* Stephen Ferguson's fault. Or maybe even *darned* was too harsh a word for a lady to use. What should one say?

Oh, hell, what did it matter, anyway? That was precisely the kind of thing that was getting her into trouble. All this worrying over what was proper and what wasn't and how she should act—all this *damned* lady-fying that Stephen Ferguson was putting her through.

Satisfaction poured through her at her mental use of one of the forbidden words, and Jessie smiled as though she had somehow outwitted her teacher. She conveniently ignored the fact that it was she who had asked Stephen to help her act like a lady. Instead, she recounted to herself the many sins that Stephen Ferguson had committed over the past few days, the humiliations and idiocies he had put her through. *"Do this. Don't do that."* Why, he had her so twisted around that she hardly knew whether she was coming or going!

She had stayed awake for hours last night, thinking about Stephen and his lessons, remembering his arm under her hand, his fingers digging into her hips as he showed her how to sway. Her nerves had been so jumpy and her stomach so churning that she hadn't been able to sleep. She felt strange around Stephen, confused and on edge. He was making her distracted and nervous, and if she had any sense she'd put a stop to all this "lady training" silliness right now!

The door to the office opened, breaking into her thoughts, and Jessie whirled around. Frank Grissom stood there. He grinned and leaned against the doorjamb, crossing his arms. "Why, Jessie, you jumped like a scared rabbit. What's the matter? Nerves jangling? I could help you relax."

Jessie grimaced. Grissom's leer raked her already irritated nerves. "There's not a thing on earth you could help me with!" she snapped and marched to her desk. "Now, what do you want?"

"Nothin' in particular. Just wanted to see you. Ain't seen you around much lately."

Jessie shrugged. "I've been busy."

"Yeah, I heard you been waitin' hand and foot on that sissy fella up at your ma's house, the one that got hisself shot. What happened? Did he shoot hisself in the foot tryin' to figure out which end of a gun was which?''

Jessie's mouth thinned, and she planted her hands on her hips pugnaciously. "No, we got ambushed, that's what happened to him, and you good and well know it. It's been all over town the whole week."

Grissom shrugged. "I don't much listen to gossip, least-ways not about him. You're what interests me, Jessie, not some city slicker that can't take care of himself in the woods."

"I'd like to know who could keep from getting ambushed?" Jessie retorted hotly. "I was with him, and *I* sure couldn't do anything about it."

"For God's sake." Grissom pushed himself away from the door frame and started across the room toward her. "Stop yammering about that fool. I didn't come here to argue about him."

"I know. You came here to see me. Well, you've seen me. Now you can leave."

"You know something? You're a hard woman." Grissom stopped on the other side of the desk. His eyes moved slowly down Jessie's body, bright with lust. "But you've got a fine shape on you. I reckon you know that, the way you prance around in them tight trousers." His gaze fastened greedily on the V where her legs met, and his hand cupped his own crotch. "I reckon you know what you do to a man, walkin' around like that."

Jessie's throat went dry. The look on the man's face sickened her. "Get out of here, Grissom. And in the future, keep your dirty talk to yourself. I don't want to hear it."

"Like hell." His tongue crept out to wet his lips, and his eyes stayed glued to her body. "Why else you wear them pants, showing your body to the world? You're just crying out for a man."

Jessie swallowed. Her face flamed with embarrassment and anger. She had never thought of her attire in that way.

It had seemed to her that dressing in a man's clothes was the opposite of being feminine, exactly the sort of thing that would *not* arouse lust in a man. "I've never cried out for anything, least of all you! Now get out."

"Uh-uh." He swung his big head slowly from side to side. "I ain't leaving. Not until we've got this thing settled. Joe ain't here to interrupt us, so you and I got plenty of time."

"Ha!" Jessie's lips twisted scornfully. "You and I have no time." In her anger she leaned forward, planting her hands flat on her desk. "I don't need Joe to protect me. I can do it myself!"

"Oh, yeah?" Frank smiled. "Good, then, let's go at it, just you and me."

Faster than she could move, Grissom grabbed her arms and jerked her forward over the desk. His mouth came down hard on hers, and his arms went around her in a grip so crushing Jessie could hardly breathe. She struggled impotently. His grasp held her arms tightly against her sides, so that she was unable to move them, and the way he had pulled her across the desk left her feet dangling off the floor, able to kick nothing except her own desk.

Even though it didn't help, Jessie kicked, flailing her feet against the hard wood, desperately seeking some purchase that would give her leverage against Grissom. He bent her backward, making it even more difficult for her to breathe and starting an agonizing pain in her spine. His tongue pushed into her mouth, thick and wet, and Jessie shuddered in horror. She thought she might be sick. She felt the rumble of his laugh at her helpless struggles. He kept her pinned with one arm, and his other hand shoved itself between her legs, rubbing harshly.

Her legs thrashed even more wildly at his obscene touch, and he pinched her inner thigh hard. It hurt, even through the protection of her trousers, and tears sprang into Jessie's eyes.

Grissom lifted his mouth, and Jessie gasped for air. "You want to play rough, huh? That's fine with me. You need somebody to take you down a peg. A man should have taken a hand to your backside a long time ago." His hand squeezed her bottom hard. "I reckon I'm the man to do it. By the time I'm through with you, girl, you'll be begging me for it."

Jessie sucked in another gulp of air and screamed.

Grissom chuckled. "Go ahead. Scream all you want. You think anybody can hear you over the sound of that blade?"

His hand slid up and around to her breast, and he pinched her nipple. Then he shoved his hand down the front of her shirt, popping off several buttons, and clutched her breast. "Mmm. You got more of a handful than I thought, girl." He chuckled again. "You and ole Frank are going to have a good time, a good, long time."

Jessie shrieked again and again, writhing desperately. Why had she been so foolishly sure of herself? If only she hadn't leaned forward! Why hadn't she reached into the drawer instead and brought out the pistol she kept there?

There was a roaring in Jessie's ears, and she knew she was close to passing out. She had wasted her breath in screaming.

Jessie didn't hear the sound of footsteps running in the hall, but she felt the impact when something smashed into Grissom from behind. Suddenly his grasp loosened, and Jessie jumped back from him, panting. It took a moment for her jumbled mind to make sense of the scene before her. It was Stephen! Stephen Ferguson had come flying into the room and hit Frank Grissom hard enough to knock the wind out of him.

"Stephen!" Tears filled her eyes, and Jessie had to clench her teeth to keep back the hysterical, joyous laughter rising in her throat. Stephen had saved her!

Stephen's eyes flickered from the man he had just hit to Jessie. He wasn't fool enough to let his gaze remain on her for longer than a second, but it was long enough to see the fear still in her face and the state of her shirt, hanging open halfway down the front, the cotton chemise beneath it ripped. He had heard her screams when he stepped inside the mill, and he had run to her, fear pounding through his veins so hard he had forgotten his weariness. When he burst into the room, he had acted on instinct, slamming his fist hard into Grissom's side almost before his mind registered what was going on.

But now, realizing what Grissom had been doing to Jessie, a cold, fierce anger flooded Stephen, and he turned to the man, his hands tightening into hard fists, his body automatically falling into the loose, prepared stance of a fighter. Forgotten were the bullets that had laid him low for a week, and the long, tiring walk to the mill. The only thing in his mind was the determination to make this man pay.

Grissom recovered his breath and whirled, growling low in his throat. He was a huge man, and few men ever crossed him. Those who had had soon been laid out with a blow from his hamlike hand. It was rare that anyone even got a punch in against him, so that he was furious not only at the interruption of his plans with Jessie, but also at the idea that anyone would dare oppose him. When he saw who it was, his grin broadened.

"Well, now, is it a man? No, I think it's too pretty for that. You fool with me, boy, and you won't be neither one much longer. Come on." He raised his hands in a mocking come-here gesture, wiggling his fingers.

Stephen hardly heard Grissom's words. His eyes were intent on judging the man. He was big, but heavy. Stephen suspected that he would deal crushing blows, but would also move clumsily. Stephen came in slowly, circling, testing Grissom, waiting for the right moment to dance in and land his first blow. He had no doubt that he could beat him. Whatever advantage Grissom had on him in size, Stephen knew he made up for it in skill and speed. He had learned the manly art of fisticuffs when he was in college at Princeton, and he had been acknowledged the champion of the school. He didn't even think about his recent illness or the resulting weakness; there was too much angry strength pouring through his veins now.

But Jessie thought of it. He had barely healed; he was too weak to fight anyone, let alone a monster like Frank Grissom. Even if he hadn't been laid up in bed for over a week with a gunshot wound, she knew that Stephen would be no match for Grissom. Stephen was shorter and a lot lighter, and he would know nothing about fighting. He was, after all, just a gentleman who had been brought up in the lap of luxury. Grissom would kill him! "Stephen! No!"

Jessie's shriek distracted Stephen for a vital instant. Involuntarily he glanced at her, and Grissom lunged forward, his huge fist connecting with the side of Stephen's face. Stephen stumbled backward under the force of the blow and crashed into the wall. He shook his head to clear it and started to rise as Grissom lumbered in to finish the job.

"Frank, no! Don't!" Jessie ran across the room and flung herself between them, spreading her arms out to the sides as though to protect Stephen. "Please, no. Think, Frank! He's Joe's son. Sam's brother. They'll kill you if you—"

"Damn it, Jessie, what the hell do you think you're doing?" Stephen staggered to his feet and reached out to push Jessie aside. She was trying to protect him! She thought he was such a weak, useless excuse for a man that he couldn't even hold his own in a fight! Fury surged through him.

Grissom grabbed Jessie's arm and tossed her aside. "Can't hide behind her, boy. She's too skinny."

Stephen's mouth tightened, and he almost rushed the other man in his anger, but he controlled himself. He could not let Grissom take charge of the fight. He moved in lightly, feinting, and landed a jab in the other man's stomach, then bounced out of reach. Grissom's eyes widened in surprise, but he was a tough man, and the blow didn't affect him much. Stephen hadn't expected it to. He was merely sounding Grissom out, testing his reflexes, his timing, his skill.

A thin smile touched Stephen's lips, chilling in its coldness. Grissom had confirmed his opinion of the man's fighting skills. Stephen moved in, ready to start the fight in earnest. Just as he did so, a loud boom reverberated through the room, and something thwacked into the ceiling above them. Both men froze. A gun had gone off.

"Hold it!" Jessie shouted, leveling her pistol at Frank Grissom. As soon as Frank had shoved her aside, she had again remembered the pistol she kept in her desk drawer, and she had run to it and whipped out the gun. She whirled and fired into the ceiling to get Frank's attention, and now she aimed the gun with calm purpose at his midsection. "You stay right where you are, Frank. I've got this gun trained on your stomach, and you know you're too wide a target for me to miss."

Frank raised his hands in a gesture of surrender. "Now, Jessie, don't get in an uproar."

Stephen went white with humiliation and rage. He began to curse, violently and at length, too consumed with outraged pride and fury to even make a coherent statement.

Jessie ignored him, keeping her gun fixed on the other man. "All right, Frank. You go back to work and cool down. Then you think on it. You just might realize that I saved your hide from Joe and Sam. You know what Sam said he'd do if you came around me again. Think how he'd feel if you beat his brother to a pulp."

"Jessamine Randall!" Stephen thundered. "That's enough! More than enough. Put that gun down this instant, and—"

"Oh, hush, Stephen." Jessie didn't even spare him a glance. "This is no time to get on your high horse."

Stephen's jaw dropped, and for an instant he was speechless. Frank shrugged and sidled toward the door. "Okay, Jessie, I hear you. I won't hurt Pretty Boy." He threw a contemptuous glance toward Stephen, then looked at Jessie and grinned slyly. "You and me—we still got something to settle. We'll have our time. You wait and see."

"It'll be a cold day in hell before you get near me again!"

Grissom grinned and backed out the door, letting it slam to behind him.

Stephen stalked toward Jessie, his feet thudding down in grim emphasis to his words. "Just what the hell did you think you were doing? How dare you interfere between me and that—that throwback to the Dark Ages!"

His nostrils were pinched, and deep brackets tightened around his mouth. His eyes glowed red.

Jessie looked at him and sighed exaggeratedly. "Well, if that isn't just like a man! Here I save your hide, and you're yelling at me!"

"Save my hide! You didn't save anything! I had everything under control. I was going to—" He made a noise of disgust and turned aside. "Oh, the devil with it. I can't expect a woman to understand the sport."

"The sport? Sport? Are you calling brawling all over the office a sport? Having your head bashed in? Breaking your nose and splitting your lip? Being beaten black and blue and having your wounds reopened? That's sport?"

"*I'm* not the one who would have had his head bashed in. You don't believe I can do a thing, do you? You think I'm nothing but a weakling, a poor clumsy soul who cannot ride or fight or shoot a gun or do any useful thing. Isn't that right? You have to protect me. You have to jump into the middle of a fight, guns blazing, so that some oaf won't beat me to a pulp! Well, thank you very much, Miss Jessamine Amazon Randall, but I have somehow managed to take care of myself for over twenty-seven years without your protection. Damn it, woman, I came in here to protect you. I was

in the process of teaching that scum a lesson for what he did
to you when you decided to take over—''

"I didn't ask for your protection!" Jessie retorted hotly,
stung by his words, doubly so because she knew, with
shame, that she *had* indeed needed help. "I can take care of
myself."

"Like you were doing when I came in? You screamed,
and I took that for a plea for help. Next time, believe me, I
won't bother!"

Jessamine's chin went up proudly. Stubbornly. "Please
don't." Her hands curled around the front of her shirt,
holding it together, but her expression was that of a queen
dismissing a forward servant.

Stephen grimaced. He slapped the dirt off his trousers and
started toward the door. The wound in his shoulder was beginning to throb. Damn, he'd probably reopened it. And,
now that he thought about it, his muscles were queerly
shaky all over.

Jessamine watched him until he was almost at the door.
"Will you—" she asked his back, and there was the slightest quaver to her voice "—that is, you won't tell anyone
about—about this, will you?"

He swung to face her, shocked. "No! How could you
think that I would?" He saw then that there was an odd
glitter in her eyes, almost like tears. A small bruise had already formed on her neck. And her hands on the shirt's
sides, holding it together, looked frail and pitiful. He swallowed, his anger seeping out of him. "I'm sorry. I lost my
head. I apologize. I shouldn't have yelled at you. You've
been through a horrible ordeal."

Jessie ducked her head, ashamed to let him see the tears
in her eyes. "I'm all right."

"What nonsense." But his voice was light and concerned, no longer angry. "Did he hurt you? I mean, did
he—''

Jessie shook her head quickly. "No! No! It was just that I was so stupid. I had a gun in the drawer, but I didn't pull it out when he came in. I never suspected that he would actually try anything like that!"

"Passion has been known to destroy a man's reason."

"But for me?" She tilted her eyes up at him comically. "Looking like this?" She swept her arms wide to indicate her faded, mannish trousers and too large shirt, the heavy work boots on her feet. But her gesture released the buttonless sides of her shirt, and it fell away, leaving her exposed to Stephen's gaze, with only the torn chemise for cover.

He could see the soft white top of her bosom, and where the tear in the chemise lay folded back, the full luscious curve of one breast was visible. Her nipples were darker shadows beneath the thin cloth. He gazed at her; he couldn't help it. His eyes seemed glued to the soft flesh. Her breasts were fuller than he had imagined; her large shirts had hidden them. And they were high and firm, the nipples large. He found himself wanting to slip his fingers beneath the torn edges of the cloth, to slide them down and around and cup the orb in his palm.

Jessie saw where his eyes had gone, and she blushed fiercely and snatched the edges of the shirt together. Stephen looked away, and a faint line of red stained his cheekbones.

"He tore the buttons," she explained, her voice abnormally small.

He felt like a lecherous cad, enjoying the view that another man's bestial lust had exposed. "Forgive me." He shrugged out of his jacket and lightly draped it around her shoulders, pulling it to in the front. "I should have thought. You need a wrap."

Jessie swallowed. His kindness almost undid her where anger and harsh words had not. "Thank you."

Nor had he thought when he'd begun to fight the man, Stephen reminded himself. Now he considered her reputation, which should have been uppermost in his mind. No woman of good name would want to have a common brawl explode in the room with her standing there, her blouse ripped open, obviously the object of attempted rape. A gentleman didn't protect a lady's honor by forcing the knowledge of her near-dishonor on the world. What if the men in the mill had heard the fight and come in?

The incident would have been all over the small town in hours, and Jessie would have had to face the shame of being whispered about, no matter how innocent she had been. Stephen might not know this part of the country, but he knew gossip, and it was the same the world over. *It was her own fault,* people would say, shaking their heads. *Sashaying around town in those pants and working alongside the men in a sawmill.* They would sagely admit that they'd been surprised it hadn't happened long ago, that Jessie had been asking for it.

No, the last thing Jessie needed was for him to beat up that great hulk, with her virtue as the obvious reason. She had been wise to end it, however hurtful to his pride that ending had been. Now that Stephen was thinking more clearly, he knew that he must not follow Frank out of the office and demand satisfaction. No, he would bide his time, wait for an opportunity to arise—some insult or argument that had nothing to do with Jessie—and then he would make the man pay. He would see to it that Frank didn't get away with it, but he would do it discreetly, as a gentleman should.

Right now the important thing was to take care of Jessie. She had been so capable and so aggravating, as usual, that he hadn't even thought about how shaken she must be. "Come. I'll take you home."

His arm slid around her shoulders. Jessie, who until now had ignored the turmoil of emotions within her, surprised herself by leaning gratefully into his supporting strength for a moment. She closed her eyes, breathing in the reassuring masculine odors of tobacco and shaving soap and sweat. She couldn't seem to control the trembling of her limbs.

"Poor Jessie. I'm sorry." His lips brushed her hair. She couldn't identify the touch and wondered what it was; it seemed to make her tremble even more, but somehow in a different way.

Jessie drew a ragged breath and pulled herself upright. It was stupid to fall apart over something like this. After all, Frank hadn't actually done anything to her except scare her. She wasn't physically hurt. She had been scared before and lived through it. She would live through this, too. And she certainly wouldn't let the world know she had been frightened. Nor would Grissom find out. There was no way she was giving that snake the satisfaction of being intimidated.

"I'm all right," she told Stephen stiffly and stepped out of the circle of his arm.

He let his arm drop to his side, suddenly feeling empty. Jessie faced him squarely, her eyes looking straight into his. "I have to ask you another favor."

"Of course. What?"

"When I said, don't tell anyone, I meant *anyone*."

He frowned. "Not even my father?"

Jessie nodded emphatically. "Especially not him."

"But he would want to know. He would never allow that man to work here if he knew what he'd done to you."

"Exactly."

"And you want Frank to continue working here?" Stephen's eyebrows vaulted up.

"Not because I like him," Jessie snapped. "I assure you. Nor because I welcomed his—his advances."

"That was obvious. Then why do you want him around where he could try again?"

"Joe needs him here, especially while Sam is away. Joe often has to be up at the camp, overseeing that operation, and he needs someone here who knows the business and has complete control of the workers. Frank Grissom does. If Joe knew what Frank tried to do, he'd throw him out immediately. Then he'd run himself into the ground trying to manage both operations.''

"Surely he could let one place or the other slide for a few days...."

Jessie shook her head firmly. "No. This is a very important time of the year. We have to get the trees in and sawed and shipped before we're shut down by the snows. Winter comes fast here. And when it comes, it's heavy. Joe can't afford to lose the time.''

Stephen frowned. He couldn't believe that it was so important to get out every last piece of lumber, even to the point of risking Jessie's safety. "Will you promise to stay away from the mill?''

"No!" Jessie looked horrified. "Joe needs *me* here, too. I couldn't desert him now.''

"It would hardly be deserting him." Stephen couldn't imagine why Jessie reacted so strongly to the thought of spending a few days away from the mill. "I don't understand.''

"Of course not!" Jessie responded crossly, irritated that Joe had made her swear not to tell Stephen about his financial troubles. Without knowing that, she supposed it did seem a little bizarre that it was so urgent to keep the mill running at top speed. "You never had to work for a living, did you? You don't know what it's like to have to make money to keep food on the table all winter and warm clothes on your back. But there are those of us who don't sit around surrounded by piles of money waiting to be counted.''

Stephen grimaced. It was the very devil to try to talk to this girl sometimes. She seemed to be prickly about anything and everything, and one never knew when she was going to attack with some barbed remark. "You haven't the faintest idea what I know," he responded, keeping his voice mild with some effort. After all, she had just had a bad time of it, and he must try to coddle her, however much she might shrug it off. "All right. If it matters that much to you, I promise that I shan't tell Father." He would just have to figure out a way to make sure she was protected from the ruffian at the mill without letting Joe know, but he wasn't about to tell her that. No doubt she would rise up in anger at the thought that she might need protection. "Now, will you allow me to take you home? You can take off at least a few hours from this job, I presume."

Jessie shot him a fulminating glance for his sarcasm and, in answer, marched across the room and out the door. Stephen sighed and followed her. He suspected that it was going to be no easy task to keep Miss Jessamine Randall under his watchful protection.

# Chapter Ten

Jessie slipped down the hallway to her small bedroom at the rear of the house, just beyond her mother's room. Fortunately, her mother was at work in the kitchen, and Jessie was able to make it to her room without Amanda knowing she was there. Jessie was grateful; her mother would have been full of questions as soon as she saw that Jessie was wearing Stephen's coat over her shirt. She was also glad that Stephen hadn't been full of questions and reproaches on the way home. She knew Sam would have chewed her out for getting caught alone with Grissom and then for not having the sense to pull her gun from the drawer before she faced him. But, except for his anger when she stopped the fight, Stephen had been only quiet and sympathetic.

It surprised her, now that she thought about it; she was actually glad that it had been Stephen and not Sam who had rescued her. Jessie slipped out of Stephen's coat and folded it carefully, then laid it across the foot rail of her bed. Her hand lingered on it for a moment. It was made of silk, soft and elegant. She had never owned anything made of a material that fine. She thought of Stephen and how he had looked in the suit jacket, the glossy brown color almost the same as his eyes.

She wondered if there had been many women back East who had their lures out for Stephen. There must have been, before he became engaged. No doubt he had been considered a fine catch—wealthy, impeccably dressed, handsome. Of course, such things didn't count with her, but they would be all that mattered to a city girl. A lady.

Jessie glanced at her gaping shirt, and her mouth tightened, thoughts of Stephen and the women in his life fleeing. Quickly she undid the last two remaining buttons and wadded the shirt up. She stuffed it in the rear of one of her drawers. Later she would pull it out and replace the buttons, but she couldn't bear to even touch it or see it now. It was too strong a reminder of Frank Grissom and what he had almost done to her. Hurriedly she unbuttoned the cotton chemise and shoved it into the drawer after the shirt. She would mend it, too, when she got around to fixing the shirt.

She poured water from the pitcher into the bowl and, taking up a cake of soap, lathered her hands, then scrubbed her chest and face, everywhere he had touched her. Damn that man! It made her skin crawl just remembering his hands on her flesh. She toweled herself dry, rubbing until her skin was red. Then she pulled another chemise and shirt out of her drawer and put them on. She sat on the bed. Now what was she going to do?

It was still an hour until supper, and she didn't want her mother to know that she was home. She couldn't go out and help Amanda in the kitchen, therefore. Nor did she feel like going into the sitting room, where the men gathered before supper. The last thing she wanted was to deal with their usual quips and teasing.

Jessie rose and walked to the window. How could she just sit in her room, twiddling her thumbs? She wanted to go somewhere, do something. She wanted not to have to think about Frank Grissom and his nasty, searching hands.

Her mind skittered away from that subject, and she thought of Stephen. She remembered the relief that had flooded her when he came in. Jessie grimaced. It wasn't any good to think about that, either. She shouldn't have been so

happy to have a man rescue her; she should have been able
to take care of herself. She felt ashamed that she hadn't. The
only thing that made it bearable was that Stephen had been
the one who found her. At least he hadn't thrown it up in her
face. Most of the men around Nora Springs would have
teased her unmercifully.

Then there was the heart-pounding fear she'd felt when
Frank had knocked Stephen down. She liked to think of *that*
even less than the other things. She had had a vision of
Grissom pounding Stephen's face to a bloody pulp, and it
had filled her with horror. She didn't want to remember it,
and she certainly didn't want to consider why it had scared
her so.

Jessie whirled away from the window. She didn't want to
be alone with her thoughts, yet she hated the idea of talking to anyone, pretending that she was fine when all the
while she was churning inside.

Stephen.

Stephen knew all about what had happened to her, and he
had already proved that he wouldn't question or scold her.
She wouldn't have to pretend for him; she wouldn't have to
lie. And she had a reason to go to his room. He was in-
structing her in the art of being a lady. She could run up the
stairs to his room and forget her problems by taking a lesson from him. She had found during the past few days that
Stephen Ferguson always managed to keep her mind fully
occupied.

Jessie plopped down on the bed and began to untie the
laces of her boots. Ten minutes later, she was tiptoing up the
back stairs to his room, dressed in another one of her
mother's gowns, with a pair of soft bedroom slippers on her
feet. She tapped softly on Stephen's door and heard his
voice bid her to come in.

Stephen turned toward the door, and his face went blank
with astonishment when Jessie came into the room. He
never would have dreamed that she would visit him for a

lesson in gentility tonight, after what she had gone through this afternoon. Yet surely that was why she was here, given the fact that she was wearing a dress. "Jessie? What are you—are you sure you want to do this tonight?"

"Of course." She carefully kept her face cool and unconcerned. She would never admit that she was still frightened and nervous and didn't want to be alone, that she wanted something to take her mind off the events of the afternoon. "I'm not going to hide in a closet just because of Frank Grissom." She made his name a sneer. "I'm not afraid of him."

"But shouldn't you rest, or—or something?"

She cast him a disparaging look. "I'm tough, Ferguson. Remember?"

"How could I forget?" he murmured. "All right, then. Let's begin." He moved away from the window, where he had been standing since he returned home, blankly staring out, thinking dark thoughts about the future of one Frank Grissom.

Jessie looked better in this dress, he noted. It fitted her, at least, even though the style was years out of date. And she had slippers instead of boots on her feet, even if they weren't exactly what a lady of fashion would wear. He made a mental note to find a seamstress tomorrow and have her a proper dress sewn up, one that was stylish and fitted and of a color and material suited to her looks and youth.

"You look very nice in that dress," he told her. "Now let me see you walk." She sauntered slowly across the room, her skirt swaying gently. "Much better. Much, much better." He didn't add that the soft motion of her hips beneath the skirt started a fire in his loins.

Jessie turned and cocked her head saucily. "I'm turning into a regular lady."

"A veritable belle. A debutante."

"A what?"

He shrugged. "It's not important. The next problem is your hair."

Jessie sighed. "I know. It's the same color as smushed carrots. But there's nothing I can do about that."

"No. No. I didn't mean the color. The color is beautiful. It's the color of fire." He came closer to her, and his voice softened. "Or a sunset." He stretched out a hand to graze her hair. "Any man would be—" He stopped, realizing that he was getting himself into treacherous waters. "That is, it wasn't the color of your hair to which I was referring. It's the style. Pigtails are for little girls in short skirts and pinafores. Women wear their hair up."

"But it's a bother to do that. And it's always falling down. Isn't it?"

"Not that I've noticed."

Jessie's voice dropped, and she looked away. "I don't know how to do it."

"What?"

She turned, gave him a flashing glance and raised her voice defiantly. "I said, I don't know how to put it up. Where does it go? How?"

He gazed at her, nonplussed. How could a woman live as many years as she had without acquiring the most basic womanly skills? "Heavens, I don't know. I've never done it." He thought of the thick golden hair of an actress who had once been his mistress and how he had often brushed it, loving the silken, sensual feel of it gliding through his hands. "That is, well . . ." Stephen broke off, appalled at what he had almost blurted out. It was so easy to forget what he was doing with Jessie and just say the first thing that came into his head. He cleared his throat. "First, you must take it out of the braids."

"Oh, all right." Jessie made a face and grabbed her left braid, beginning to untie the bow. "I'll do this one. You get the other."

Stephen's eyes widened. He'd never thought that he might have to touch her hair. It wasn't a wise idea. Just thinking about her hair lying loose around her shoulders started his blood humming. It would be foolish to take it down. Too tempting.

Yet he could not seem to stop his fingers from moving to her long, burnished braid. He lifted the thick rope of hair in his hand and untied the knot of the flannel strip Jessie used in place of a ribbon. The ends of her hair slipped apart some, but the plait remained mostly intact. He would have to separate the strands with his fingers. Stephen noticed that his fingers were trembling slightly as he reached out. He sank his fingers into her braid, wiggling the strands free. Her hair was cool and thick, soft to his touch. It slid around his fingers silkily, and his breath came faster in his throat.

Her hair was lovely. The color of burnished copper. "How can you even think of disparaging the color of your hair?" he murmured. "It's like liquid fire. A man dreams of warmth like this."

Jessie glanced up at him, startled. His eyes were dark and intense, alive with an inner heat. Her thoughts scattered like leaves on the wind. She could only look at him.

His fingers drifted through her hair, and she felt the gentle tug against her scalp. Her eyes dropped to his mouth. It was a wide, generous mouth, the lower lip sensually full. She thought of that mouth against hers, and she wondered how it would feel.

Jessie tore her gaze away and moved apart from him. The funny, sizzling feelings inside her body shocked and alarmed her. What was the matter with her? Why did this man have such a strange effect on her? "I—I need a brush."

She glanced blindly around the room.

"On the dresser."

Jessie hurried to the dresser. A silver-backed man's hair-brush and a silver comb lay beside a shaving mug and sil-ver-handled razor. Even the sight of such masculine toiletry articles shook her. She curved her hand around the brush. All she could think of was Stephen's hand on the same brush, lifting it to his own head. The silver was cool against her hot skin. She raised the brush with shaky fingers and pulled it through her hair. The curling, tangled strands were stubborn and caught on the bristles. In her haste, she jerked on the brush, bringing prickles of pain to her scalp.

She looked at herself in the mirror above the dresser. There must be something wrong with her, to even be thinking about a man's kiss after what had happened to her this afternoon. She looked at the bruise, already widening, on her neck. Her lips looked a little swollen, and there was a red, raw patch above her upper lip where Grissom's stubble had rubbed against the tender flesh. She thought of his wet, disgusting lips, of his tongue filling her mouth, and her stomach turned.

"Is it always like that?" she asked, her voice so low it was almost a whisper.

"What?" Stephen, watching her brush her hair, was brought out of his heated, sensual reverie with a start by the sight of her suddenly white face and wide, frightened eyes. He moved toward her instinctively. "Is what always like that?"

"When a man—when a man kisses you." She turned to face him. Her eyes were soft and vulnerable. "Is it like it was with Grissom?"

"Oh, Jessamine, no." His heart clenched inside his chest. She looked so achingly young and unsure. For all her air of unfeminine toughness, Jessie was really an innocent, naive girl. It was obvious that she knew nothing about the touch of a man. Desire coursed through him, and Stephen wondered how he could feel gently protective toward her and yet at the same time want to grind his body into hers and kiss her until her innocence fell away. "With a gentleman, a man who loves and respects you, it's entirely different."

"How?" She walked over to him and looked intently up into his eyes. "What's different?" Jessie could feel her heart hammering inside her, so loud she almost couldn't hear. She wanted to know about the other kind of kiss. She wanted to taste the kiss of a gentleman.

"Well, uh..." Stephen tore his eyes away from hers. It was almost too much for him to look into them, to see the questioning, the trace of anxiety left from Grissom's attack. "It's not rough. That is, well, perhaps sometimes it can be a little rough, but... but not in a hurtful way."

"What do you mean?" Jessie looked puzzled.

"Well, like—like when you love someone a lot and are very, very happy to see her, you hug her so hard that it hurts. But neither of you cares about the pain because it's so wonderful to hold her."

"I understand. So you can kiss hard, but it feels good?"

Stephen could feel the heat rising in his face, and he wasn't sure if it was from embarrassment or passion. "Yes. It's, well, it's an expression of love. Of desire. A man who loved you wouldn't want to hurt you or to gratify himself at your expense. He would want you to enjoy it, too. He would make sure you did."

"How would he do that?" Involuntarily, Jessie's eyes flickered to Stephen's mouth.

He found it difficult to breathe. "He would... be gentle. Slow. He would say sweet things to you. Tell you what you did to his heart and mind. Tell you how he could think of nothing but you."

"And then?"

"And then he would put his hands on your arms." His hands went to her arms and slid up them to her shoulders. "Gently, letting you know that if you didn't want him, you were free to pull away, to leave."

"And if you didn't?" Jessie breathed, staring raptly into his eyes.

"Then he would bend down, slowly." His actions followed his words. "And he would touch his lips to yours."

Stephen's mouth brushed against Jessie's as softly as the touch of butterfly wings, and she shivered all through in a delicious way. Stephen spoke, his breath fanning her lips. "Then he would kiss you again."

His lips closed the short distance between them, pressing into hers gently but insistently. It was nothing like Frank Grissom's kiss, she thought. Nothing. Then she was lost to all thought as his kiss deepened. She was aware of nothing but the scent and taste of him, the delightful fizz and sparkle that ran through her veins and along her nerves, the hot heaviness that mushroomed in her abdomen.

Stephen's mouth was searingly hot; his lips moved against hers, teasing them open. His tongue edged her lips and slipped inside her mouth. Instead of the disgust that had filled her at the touch of Grissom's tongue, Jessie felt only a delicious quiver of desire dart through her, and the heaviness in her abdomen leaped into flame. Her hands came up uncertainly and curled into the front of his shirt, innocently holding on to the joy that was sparking all through her.

Stephen's arms went around her, and he pressed her closer to him. Her arms went naturally around his neck. She could feel the hard warmth of his body all the way up and down hers, the strength of his thighs and the unyielding hardness of his chest. His arms were tight around her, but Jessie felt not even a flicker of fear. She liked the pressure of his arms around her body and the tightness with which he held her. Her body was like liquid, and she wasn't sure she could have remained standing without his support.

Stephen broke their kiss only to change the tilt of his head and kiss her again, his lips pressing harder against hers. His hands slid down her back, pressing her into him. The obviously inexperienced but hungry response of Jessie's kisses enflamed him. He was a man of the world, used to the skills and beauty of expensive prostitutes and sophisticated, restless socialites, but none of the women he had ever known excited him as this innocent, unfeminine girl did. He wanted her, here and now, with every fiber of his being.

"Ah, Jessamine," he sighed, his lips leaving hers and trailing down her throat, tasting its tender flesh. "Jessamine. Beautiful, beautiful Jessamine."

His mouth met the top of her bodice, which effectively stopped him. He felt like reaching up and tearing it apart so that his voracious mouth could reach her breasts. He wanted to pull her down on the floor and yank her clothes from her. He wanted to take her, to make her his. Just thinking about it made him tremble.

But he did none of the things he wanted to. Instead, his arms loosened around her. "Oh, God." He rested his cheek against her head and drew a long, steadying breath. "I'm sorry." He waited for his blood to cool enough that he was capable of pulling his arms away from her and stepping back. "I'm sorry," he repeated. "You . . . wanted reassurance, and instead I—I . . ."

"No! I wanted exactly that!" Jessie burst out, reaching out with one hand to take his. She squeezed his hand hard. "Don't apologize. Please, don't apologize." Her breath was unsteady, too, and she struggled to control it, to regain command of her mind and body. She wanted to tell him that she had been asking him to kiss her, to wipe away the memory of Frank Grissom, even though she hadn't been aware of it, but she couldn't get her tumultuous feelings shaped into thoughts and words. She felt as though she might fall into uncontrollable laughter or tears with equal ease.

Jessie raised a shaky hand to her face. Her cheek was as hot as fire. She swallowed, unable to think of anything to say. She could only stare at Stephen with wide eyes. In the space of a few minutes everything in her world had turned upside down—or perhaps she had just realized that it had been turning that way for the past couple of weeks. Ever since she had met Stephen Ferguson. "I don't know what's the matter with me."

Stephen shook his head. "It's my fault. I knew you were in a vulnerable state. It was the act of a blackguard to take advantage of that. I hope you will forgive me. In time."

He turned away. He thought that if he continued to look at her for another moment, his control would snap and he would pull her into his arms and not let her go until he had possessed her completely.

Jessie looked at his rigid back. Hurt sliced through her. He didn't want her; he had turned his back on her. She clenched her fingers in the folds of her skirts. At least that was something a dress was good for, giving one something to hold on to when one felt as if one might fall to pieces. She started to speak, but she couldn't, for there were tears swelling in her throat.

"Perhaps it would be a good idea if we discontinued our lessons," Stephen said stiffly, still turned away from her.

Jessie looked at him for a moment, then whirled and ran out the door.

Stephen heard her leave. His body went limp, as though all energy and life had drained out of him with her departure. He turned and looked into the empty hall. Slowly he walked to the door and closed it, then returned to his bed. He flopped down and lay back, crossing his hands under his head and staring at the ceiling. He was still on fire with longing; it would have taken almost nothing to have sent him running down the stairs after Jessie. God, he wanted her.

But he was engaged to Elizabeth! His duty, his love, his responsibility, were all to her. They must be. No matter how much desire he felt for Jessie, he could do nothing about it. Elizabeth was to be his wife; he was promised to her. He had given his word to her father, and Stephen never broke his word. He had betrayed both Elizabeth and Jessie by kissing Jessie; he had betrayed all three of them.

With a groan, he rolled off the bed and walked to the window. He was far too restless to lie still. He stared out sightlessly at the cold September evening. He wondered when Elizabeth would be here. He would marry her and leave as soon as Sam arrived with her. He'd tell Sam about Grissom's attack on Jessie and leave the girl in Sam's capable hands. He'd let Sam wreak revenge on Grissom. He could not stay to do it himself. He had to leave. He had to get as far away as he could—as soon as he could. Or he might just find himself forgetting all about honor and duty.

Their lessons in deportment might have to stop, but Stephen intended to start walking to and from work with her.

She came in to eat breakfast the next morning and saw him already sitting at the table, eating and talking with the other men and her mother. It surprised her. She had rarely known him to be up this early.

Jessie gave him a nod when he said hello, then slid into her seat. No doubt it was easy for him to talk to her as if nothing had happened, but she knew she wasn't sophisticated enough to behave that way. She had spent half the night tossing and turning and thinking about their kisses. She had been aghast that she had kissed Stephen Ferguson—and even more aghast that she had enjoyed it so thoroughly.

How could she feel attracted to a man like that? He was not a man she respected, not the kind of man she could possibly love. Not a man like Sam. She had always thought that a good woman was not supposed to feel desire for a man she didn't love. Well, if the truth was known, Jessie hadn't even known that such sizzling desire existed in a woman. Certainly she had never felt it before. She wondered if that meant she was a wanton. Would she feel the same about any man's kisses? Well, she hadn't felt that way about Frank Grissom's kisses, that was for sure. Maybe it was only with a man she liked.

But did she like Stephen Ferguson? She wouldn't have said so, but now that she thought about it, she had to admit that she did. Over the past few days, as he had helped her, they had drawn closer. She had realized that there was a kindness in him, a warmth, despite his rather formal manner. And one could get used to his politeness; it hardly made her feel strange anymore for him to jump to his feet whenever she entered the room or held her chair out for her to sit down at the table or stood aside to let her pass through a door first. He had a sense of humor, once she'd gotten to understand it, even though he often still said things she didn't understand. He had even shown some depth of character when he'd gotten shot. And, God knows, he was certainly pleasant to look at. She had gotten to where she sort of enjoyed being around him. Well, face it, she *did* enjoy being with him; she *did* like him.

But he wasn't the kind of man for this country. He wasn't tough enough, hard enough. He wouldn't know how to get by out here. He wouldn't stay for any length of time.

He was engaged to another woman.

It was that thought, which had kept coming back time and again through the night, that had made her cry, much to her chagrin. It had been wrong, very wrong, of him to kiss her when he was engaged to another woman. It showed a lack of morals, of honor, of respect for her. A good, solid man wouldn't kiss another woman if he was engaged, even if his fiancée wasn't around.

Of course, if that made him a scoundrel, what did it make her? Jessie didn't like to think about that. She had known that Stephen was engaged to that woman Sam was bringing home; Miss Elizabeth Hightone would be right here in town in another day or two. Why, she had been enjoying the kisses of an almost-married man! It was a horrifying realization that she hadn't even given that other woman a thought while he was kissing her. Hell's bells! She hadn't given anything a thought! She had acted like an empty-headed ninny. Jessie was ashamed of herself.

She was more ashamed because even though she was sitting several chairs away from Stephen, she felt not only the embarrassment she had expected, but also a new upsurge of those confused, exciting sensations she had known the night before. She blushed to her hairline and hoped no one was watching her. How could she, at this hour of the morning, right there at the breakfast table, be thinking about the way Stephen's arms had tightened around her, or the velvety pressure of his lips on hers? How could she actually feel the sudden tightening of her nerves all over and the heavy, heated yearning deep inside her? It didn't seem right.

She shoved her thoughts and feelings aside. The only thing to do was ignore them. She couldn't go around with this turmoil showing, especially not when Stephen was so cool and unconcerned, so natural-acting. It just went to prove that he must be a scoundrel inside, Jessie thought resentfully as she shoved a forkful of eggs into her mouth. A good man would be as embarrassed and awkward as she was.

It didn't take her long to eat. She had no appetite, and she was desperate to get away from the table, so as soon as she had made enough show of eating that her mother wouldn't start questioning her about it, she pushed her plate back and jumped up from the table.

"Are you off to the mill, Miss Randall?" Stephen said, rising from his place, too.

"Yes."

"Then I'll walk with you."

Jessie stared. "You're going to the mill?"

"Yes. I was going to talk to Joe."

"This early?"

Stephen shrugged. "It's as good a time as any."

Jessie frowned. What was this? Was he planning to try to sweet-talk her into something? But then, if he had evil designs on her, why had he stopped last night? She couldn't understand what kind of a game he was playing. Still, she was sure that he must have something up his sleeve.

"All right," she replied ungraciously. "I reckon you can come with me."

"Jessie!" Amanda reprimanded her, a shocked look on her face.

Jessie grimaced. Obviously Stephen had worked his spell on her mother. Jessie clumped out the door with Stephen behind her. When they got out of the house and were walking along the street toward the mill, she glanced at her companion. He was silent and appeared as cool and calm as ever, but she could see the tight lines around his mouth and eyes. He was feeling some strain in the situation, too. Then why had he forced himself into her company? It didn't make sense.

Stephen didn't talk to her much that day or the next, making only the few remarks necessary not to appear rude in front of other people. At the mill he spent most of his time in Joe's office, talking to him, or in exploring the sawmill with Joe, poking into all the different aspects of the operations. Jessie found his interest in the place distinctly annoying. Why should some rich Eastern dude find a poky little sawmill in Montana so absorbing?

However, it was even more annoying when he wasn't with Joe discussing the mill, for then he planted himself in the large outer office where Jessie worked and just sat there, saying almost nothing. Sometimes, when he sat like that, he watched her, and she found that the most unnerving thing of all. Finally, after five days of it, her nerves snapped, and she swung around to face him, snarling, "What in the blue blazes are you doing, sitting there? Why are you here all the time? Why don't you go home?"

Stephen's eyebrows rose lazily. "You don't like my company? I'm hurt."

Jessie grimaced. "You know good and well I don't like it, and you know why, too."

His face fell into a stiffly polite mask. "I assure you, you have nothing to worry about from me. I apologized to you for my behavior the other night. It was unforgivable. But I promise you it won't happen again. I'm not a Frank Grissom."

Jessie's eyes narrowed. "That's why you're here, isn't it? Because of Grissom! You think you're protecting me!"

"You have a strange way of putting it, but, yes, since you refuse to tell my father, I am obliged to watch out for you myself. I can hardly let you work here every day with that animal around, waiting for an opportunity to attack you again. I must afford you some protection. I can't always be sure that Father is in the office with you. He goes to the camp frequently."

"You can hardly let me work here?" Jessie repeated in a dangerous tone. "What makes you think you have any power to let or not let me do anything?"

"Of course, I have no rights over you, but I certainly have an obligation to see that you are not mistreated by Frank Grissom again."

"Why?" Jessie asked bluntly.

"Why? What do you mean, why? Because you are a lady, and I wouldn't be worth much as a man if I allowed a lady to be assaulted."

"I'm not a lady, and you know it. I wear pants, and I swear, as you yourself pointed out. But, more importantly, I can take care of myself. I don't need you to protect me." Her words mimicked his tone viciously.

"Mm. No more than you did the other day, no doubt. As I recall, you found my protection then not quite so contemptible."

Jessie ground her teeth. It was just like him to remind her of that. "I have a gun, and I will use it. I am on guard now."

"So am I."

Jessie felt like growling. "You are the most annoying, frustrating, bothersome man in the world! Why won't you leave me alone? I don't want you hanging around all the time!"

"It is not precisely enjoyable for me, either," Stephen threw back at her. "As for frustration and bother, you have no idea what that is until you've tried to deal with *you*! There is no woman in the world as irritating as you are. You're a wild, red-haired witch, and I wish to God I'd never met you!" Stephen's voice rose thunderously. Never before in his life had he yelled at a woman, but it seemed as if Jessie could bring him to that loss of control in the twinkling of an eye. His nerves were shredded because of her. He'd hardly slept at all the past couple of nights for thinking about her, wanting her and struggling to overcome that desire. Then, during the day, he'd felt honor bound to watch over her until Sam got back so that Grissom couldn't attack her again. It was torture to be in the same room with her the whole day. Yet, instead of appreciating what he was doing for her, Jessie sniped at him for it! The most infuriating thing of all, what he simply could not comprehend, was how he could desire a woman who was so thoroughly exasperating.

Tears sprang into Jessie's eyes at Stephen's words, but she blinked them away. Damn it! She was *not* hurt by his open dislike of her; she had heard worse things than that about herself from other men. She was just angry. He was unreasonable and stubborn.

Stephen thought he saw the glimmer of tears in her eyes, and his rage abruptly left him. Good Lord, had he made her cry? "I'm sorry." He wanted to go to her and take her hand, but he didn't dare. Touching Jessie was a dangerous thing to do. "You know, there's a simple way to get rid of me. Just tell Joe what happened."

"No! Absolutely not. He's worried enough as it is."

"Why?"

"Uh . . ." Jessie shifted. Now she'd done it. Joe would be hoppin' mad at her if she let Stephen know either of the reasons he was worried. "Well, he's anxious about the saw blade. He needs it."

"Jessie . . ." Stephen frowned. "Give me a little credit. I'm a businessman. I understand having to meet schedules. But I would never for a moment allow you to be in danger in order to do it. I can't believe my father would, either."

"He wouldn't. That's the point. He'd fire Grissom just when he needs him the most. But I don't want to be responsible for it."

"For what? Ferguson Mill's not sending out its last shipment of lumber for the year? It doesn't seem that important. And why has my father been so jumpy today? That frown hasn't left his face, and he must have been outside at least ten times." He stopped, realization dawning on him. He went cold inside. "It's something about Sam, isn't it? He thinks something's happened to Sam and Elizabeth."

"Now, wait, don't get in an uproar about it. It's bad enough to have Joe practically pacing the floor. They're just a little late, that's all. It's happened before. Normally Joe wouldn't even have worried about it. But he needs that blade so much. He knew Sam would do his best to get the blade here fast."

"How late are they?"

"Normally they would have gotten in yesterday. But Sam was going to push it and try to make it in the evening before."

"And they still aren't here. That makes them two days late."

"Men!" Jessie exclaimed disgustedly, shaking her head. "You're exaggerating, too. They're only one day late, really, and there are all kinds of reasons for that. Just having a lady with them probably slowed them down."

"Even though Sam was trying to hurry?" Stephen sensed the underlying anxiety in her voice, despite her optimistic words. "He doesn't strike me as someone who'd let much of anything slow him down."

"Sometimes you can't help it." Jessie's voice lacked conviction. She was beginning to be worried, too. When Sam hadn't shown up yesterday, she'd simply blamed it on Stephen's fancy fiancée. But she knew exactly how much Joe and Sam needed that blade here, and she was certain that Sam wouldn't let some lady's silly fears or complaints slow him down this much. "All kinds of things can happen."

"I'm sure that's exactly why my father is worried." Stephen was swept with guilt. What if something had happened to Elizabeth—while he had been here in Nora Springs lusting after another woman!

Jessie looked at him. Stephen was sick with worry; she could see it in his face. She'd known he would be, but she had hoped she wouldn't have to witness it. He was afraid for the woman Sam was bringing. The woman he loved. Her own heart twisted inside her. Yet, at the same time, she felt sorry for him. She wished she could give him some comfort, say something that would make him feel better. But she couldn't think of anything, and after a moment, she returned quietly to her work.

The rest of the day and night dragged by. Stephen was tortured by guilt and worry. He kept picturing the terrible things that could have happened to his brother and Elizabeth—and all the while he had been so wrapped up in himself and the disturbing longings he felt for Jessie that he hadn't even realized it was past time for Sam and Elizabeth to return to town. Mentally he berated himself for so forgetting himself and his duty. Elizabeth was his responsibility, yet he'd hardly spared a thought for her since Sam left to get her. In fact, if he was utterly honest with himself, he knew that he had been happy that Elizabeth was not here yet, for her arrival would mean an end to his time with Jessie. He hadn't wanted to think about why she wasn't here or what might have delayed her.

Even now, as he worried over Elizabeth, he couldn't keep the thought of Jessie out of his mind. All too often, he found that his mind drifted off, picturing Jessie, remembering the softness of her lips beneath his, the yielding eagerness of her body. He was, he thought, an utter scoundrel to desire her when the only thing that should be on his mind was his fiancée.

He ought to get a horse and ride along the road to Missoula until he found Sam's party. But if he did, he would be leaving Jessie unprotected at the mill. He simply could not do that. He reminded himself that he had no obligation to Jessamine Randall; all his duty was owed to Elizabeth. Elizabeth would bear his name; she had had his love for as long as he could remember. But Jessie—ah, Jessie. He thought of her hair, the color of fire and the texture of silk. She sparked a wildness, an eagerness in him that Elizabeth never had. He wanted her with a thick, hot yearning. He felt torn between them and wicked for feeling that way, when there was only one path that was right and honorable. He lay awake far into the night, and when he woke the next morning, he felt as guilty and indecisive as ever.

Stephen walked with Jessie to the mill, as he had the past few mornings, and sat down to wait again. He found it almost impossible. Neither Joe nor Jessie seemed to be able to settle down to their work.

In mid-morning, there was the sound of a shout, barely heard above the pounding and whine of the mill machinery. All three stiffened, suddenly alert. They waited, listening intently. The sound came closer. Then there were boots in the hall, and one of the men who worked in the lumberyard stuck his head inside the door. "The wagon's coming! They're back!"

Stephen jumped to his feet. Relief flooded him. Elizabeth was safe. He looked at Jessie. The relief was joined by reluctance and regret. He knew that when he went out the door to meet Elizabeth, he would have to leave Jessie be-

hind him forever. Suddenly he wished he could slip out the
back way.

But Joe was already hurrying through the door, his face
eager and happy. Jessie followed him. She turned and
looked at Stephen. "Come on. They're back."

She stood there in trousers and a shirt, her hair hanging
down her back in a thick, straight braid, and Stephen
thought he had never seen anyone more beautiful or desirable.

"Yes," he said. "I'm coming." He started forward on
feet that had turned to lead.

## Chapter Eleven

⁓⁓⁓⁓⁓

There was a large freight wagon in the lumberyard, and the mill workers were crowded around it. As Stephen came out, two men, one an Indian and the other the bearded older man named Burley Owens, were climbing down from the high wagon seat. They laughed and talked to the men, gesturing toward the huge crate in the back of the wagon. The Indian went around to the back and began to unfasten the ropes that held the crate in place, while Burley shook hands with Joe and began to talk.

Stephen glanced around. There was no sign of a buggy. He frowned. He wouldn't have thought a light buggy would be slower than the heavily laden wagon. He walked out of the yard into the street, shivering a little when the cold wind cut into him. He looked up and down the street. Where were Sam and Elizabeth?

He turned back to the yard, where the men were busy unharnessing the team of mules and unloading the heavy saw blade. Joe, directing the unloading, turned and saw Stephen. He left the men and came over to him, smiling broadly.

"I should have known Sam would come through. They just got slowed down a little. Seems the stage line has a rival that blew up a bridge or two along the way, so Burley

and Jim Two Horses had to come the long way around.
Nothing to worry about." He chuckled.

"But where are Sam and Elizabeth?"

"Don't worry. They'll be here in a few days. Seems your
fiancée got a little sick along the way, so Sam sent the wagon
on without them. They'll be following in their rig."

"Sick? What's the matter?"

"Don't get all het up about it. There's nothing to worry
about. Burley says your girl's fine, just a mite under the
weather. Seems she got a little boil or sore or something that
made it hard to sit in the buggy all day. She just needed a
few days to let it heal up, so she and Sam stopped at a
homesteader's cabin, and Sam sent the men ahead with the
blade. He knew how much we needed it."

"I see." The tension oozed out of Stephen, and he smiled.
There wasn't anything seriously wrong with Elizabeth. It
was probably just that the trip had been a little too rough for
her. But she was at someone's house, with the homesteader's wife to look after her while she got well, and with a little rest, she'd be fine. "Then there's no need to worry, is
there?"

"Nope. None at all. Sammy'll make sure she's well before they set out again." Joe smiled broadly. He glanced at
the wagon. "No, wait! Don't touch that blade!" He loped
to the wagon to supervise.

Stephen watched him go, aware of the new lightness in his
chest. The only problem was, he wasn't sure if his relief was
because he knew that Elizabeth was safe—or because it
would be a few more days before he had to face her.

It was music to Joe Ferguson's ears when the new, bigger
saw blade was attached and started up. Its shrill, mechanical whine shattered the quiet of the mill, and the men
cheered. Quickly the first log was guided toward it in the log
carriage, and the blade cut into the wood. Chips flew; saw-

dust filled the air. Joe turned to Jessie and Stephen, standing beside him, and grinned.

"We're in business again!" he shouted.

They had to guess at what he said. The noise was deafening. The thrum of the machinery vibrated through Stephen, and the excitement of the moment gripped him. He knew, at least in part, how his father felt. He'd had moments of triumph in his business, but this was somehow more exciting, more immediate.

They watched for a few minutes, then turned and walked toward the office. When they reached the door, Joe turned to Jessie and Stephen and said, "You two go on in. There's someone in town I need to see." The grin that had rarely left his face from the moment the saw blade arrived flashed again.

Stephen glanced at him, surprised. He would have thought Joe would want to sit down with them and babble out some of his excitement over the new blade. But Jessie wasn't surprised; she knew exactly where Joe planned to go. He wanted to tell Elias Moore in person that the blade had arrived and the mill's note would soon be paid.

Joe left the sawmill and walked down the street, whistling. He didn't notice that he'd forgotten his coat or that the chill north wind was slicing through him. He pulled his watch from his pocket and looked at it. It was late in the afternoon; the bank would be closed. Well, old man Moore would simply have to open up for him. This was one bit of news that couldn't wait. He suspected Elias Moore wouldn't resent making this exception; after all, he stood to gain a few thousand dollars. The old skinflint.

Joe wondered if he would finally manage to put a smile on Moore's sour countenance. Probably not. He didn't think the man knew how to smile.

It took a few minutes of tapping at the bank's locked and barred door before a clerk showed his face, and then a few more minutes of talking before Mr. Moore himself finally opened the door and let him inside.

"What is it, Ferguson, that couldn't be discussed during business hours?" Moore asked crossly as he led Joe across the bank lobby into his office. "We were about to leave."

"Well, it's still business hours most places," Joe retorted jovially. "The rest of the world works, you know, long after the bank closes its doors." He grinned. "I reckon that's 'cause we all have to sweat to make sure the bank gets our payments."

Mr. Moore frowned. He was a thin, spare man with a long, somber face. A large nose dominated his features, and atop it sat little spectacles. He had a habit of looking over the spectacles at someone until he began to shrivel and remember every sin he'd committed in his life. Mr. Moore tried the trick now with Joe Ferguson, but Joe grinned irrepressibly.

"I figured you'd want to hear my news. It might make your evening more pleasant."

"The only thing that would do that would be for you to pay off your note, which, as you well know, is already in arrears. If I don't receive your payment by the end of next month, I—"

Joe waved aside his words. "Hold your horses. No need to start threatening. You don't have to. You'll get your money. I came to tell you that we got the new saw blade today. It's in operation, and that means we'll get our shipment out in time."

Mr. Moore's mouth snapped shut. He blinked. "Well. I must admit you have surprised me." He smiled thinly. "Congratulations. Now both of us will profit." He rose and extended his hand to shake Joe's.

They continued to talk a few minutes about the new blade and Joe's estimation of how long it would take to finish their final shipment and receive payment. Then Moore escorted him to the front door. All the other employees had already gone, and the bank was empty.

The banker went outside with Joe and locked the door carefully behind him. Joe strode off toward the mill, and Moore began to walk in the other direction, toward his house. However, halfway there, he took a small detour down a side street. He took a piece of paper from inside his jacket and wrote a short note on it, then stuck it under the door of a small, shabby house.

That evening, after supper, when he was sitting in his study, there was a light tapping on the window. Moore arose and went immediately to the kitchen door to open it. A huge figure detached itself from the shadows and stepped inside.

"You wanted to see me?" Frank Grissom asked.

The banker glanced at him with cold eyes. "I can assure you that it was from necessity, not preference, that I sent for you."

"Huh?"

Mr. Moore grimaced. "Come with me. We can't talk here."

Grissom followed the thin man down the hall and into the study, his work boots clumping heavily against the hardwood floors. Inside the study, Moore locked the door and turned to his companion. "Well, you've certainly managed to make a mess of things."

Grissom shrugged. "I did what you told me. First I made sure the blade broke. Then you told me to take care of Sam, 'cause they couldn't meet the deadline without him. So when I saw Jessie ride out to the camp I reckoned Sam'd be coming back with her for the payroll. How was I supposed to know it was his brother? Nobody even knew there *was* another Ferguson kid."

Frank scowled. He wished he *had* killed the man, mistake or not. Then the weasel wouldn't have been around to interrupt him the other day with Jessie. Ever since then the dude had stuck to her like glue. Not, of course, that *that* would stop him from taking her if he wanted to. The city-bred Ferguson wasn't anywhere near his size, and it was obvious, looking at him in his fancy clothes, that he wouldn't last two minutes in a fight. Still, he was a bother. And what if he told Joe? Grissom sure didn't want to be kicked out while Elias Moore was willing to pay him for hurting the mill.

"I don't want any of your self-serving excuses." Elias's sharp voice intruded on Grissom's thoughts. "I want results! So far, you haven't shown me any. Sam went riding off to Missoula without a hitch, and now he's brought the blade back. Joe Ferguson was in the bank today, bragging to me about how he'd be able to pay off the note. Damn it, man, what do you think I'm paying you for? I want that sawmill shut down."

"I can't see why you'd want to keep somebody from paying you."

Moore's lip curled. "You wouldn't. Just trust me—that mill is worth far more to me than what I'll be receiving when Ferguson pays off the note. Now, I want business at that sawmill to cease immediately. Do you understand?"

Grissom shrugged. "Sure. But it's gonna seem awful suspicious, after them other things."

"Make it look like another accident. No one will be able to tell for certain. That's what you should have done with Sam. Look, I don't care how much people suspect. Just don't get caught, and no one will be able to prove anything."

That was easy enough for *him* to say, Grissom thought resentfully. Moore wasn't the one risking his neck betraying the Fergusons. But he kept his thoughts to himself. "What do you want me to do? Mess up the new blade?"

"No. Too obvious. Besides, there's no sense in ruining a new saw—it'll add to the place's value." He thought for a moment. "What powers the blades?"

"Huh?" Grissom stared at him blankly.

Moore sighed. He hated dealing with fools. "What makes them run?"

"Oh. Well, the engine. The steam engine."

"One central engine?"

"Yeah. It runs everything."

"Could you put it out of commission?"

The big man shrugged. "Sure, I reckon. It wouldn't be too hard. And nobody knows enough about it to fix it, except maybe Sam."

"I thought Sam was back."

"Nah. He won't be in for a while. He got stuck on the trail, something about his candy-ass brother's woman." He snorted. "I don't know what woman would have that one."

"All right." Moore ignored Grissom's extraneous comments. "That sounds good. Do something to the steam engine. Immediately."

"You're the boss."

Moore handed him a packet. "There's half the money, as usual. You'll get the rest when you've finished your job."

Grissom stuffed the envelope into a pocket of his jacket. He didn't like the way the banker paid, half and half. Last time the cheat had refused to give him the whole second half just because he'd shot Stephen instead of Sam. Hell, it was a mistake anybody could have made. Dealing with Moore was like handling a snake—a touchy one, at that. He'd be glad when he finished. He would have enough money then to get out of this town and start over someplace else. Considering the Fergusons, Grissom reckoned that'd be the safest thing to do.

Two nights later Stephen was awakened by the babble of excited male voices downstairs. He sat up, disoriented for a moment. It was pitch black, the middle of the night. He frowned and fumbled in the dark to light the oil lamp by his bed. By its dim light he picked up his watch from the table and opened it. It wasn't quite midnight. No wonder he felt so groggy. He'd been asleep hardly more than an hour.

Curious, he climbed out of bed and wrapped his heavy dressing gown around him, then went into the hall and down the stairs. In the back hall, he found a group of men clumped around one of the doors. Stephen had never been in this part of the house and wasn't sure what the room was. One of the men turned, saw him and stepped back.

"Oh! Mr. Ferguson. I'm sorry, sir. I didn't even think." Around him other men turned and drew back, opening a passage for Stephen into the room.

"What is it? What's the matter?" He walked past them into the room and came to a dead stop.

He was in a large bedroom, obviously a woman's room, but it was not a woman who lay on the bed. It was his father, stretched out on top of the covers, fully dressed, his eyes closed. "My God! What happened?"

Stephen covered the distance to the bed in two long strides. "Father? What's the matter with him? What happened to him?"

Blood clotted Joe's hair and oozed onto his forehead.

A woman reached out and gently took the lamp from Stephen's hand. He glanced at her and for the first time realized that Jessie was in the room.

"Jessie!" Instinctively his hand went out to her, and she clasped it tightly. "How—what?"

She shook her head. "I don't know. They just brought him in."

He noticed now that Amanda was there, too, on the other side of the bed. She was wringing out a cloth in a basin of water, and she leaned across the bed to dab at the bloody wound on Joe's head. Stephen saw tears in her eyes.

He drew a breath and turned to the men crowding into the room. Burley Owens stood at the foot of the bed, twisting his hat between his hands, his worried eyes on Joe's still figure. Stephen was glad to see him; from what little he had seen, Owens appeared to be a man of sense, however rough he might seem. "What happened?" he asked, directing the question toward Burley.

The man glanced at him; he looked every bit his age tonight—and more. "I don't know, rightly. I just found him like that. I went by late tonight, after the saloon closed to see Joe and maybe have a little celebration drink over the new blade. I went to his room at the mill, and he wasn't there, so I waited a while. Finally I got up, and for some reason I walked into the mill. Guess I wanted to see how the new blade looked. Anyway, that's where I found Joe. He was down by the engine, just layin' there. Like that. His head was bleedin', and I couldn't rouse him. Maybe the engine blew up on him or something, 'cause it was a mess, too. Or maybe he was trying' to fix it and—" He frowned and finished lamely, "I don't know."

At that moment the doctor elbowed his way into the room and hurried over to the bed. "Well, Amanda, looks like I might as well set up residence in your house, too, the way you keep giving me business."

He bent over the bed and probed gently at Joe's head wound. He opened one of Joe's eyelids. "Concussion. What hit him?"

"We don't rightly know," Burley replied. "Maybe it was a piece of metal from the engine."

"Well, it didn't crush the skull. We can be thankful for that. With luck he'll wind up with nothing more than a gigantic headache."

He dug in his bag for his supplies and began to clean the head wound. "There's nothing any of you can do for him here. Might as well get out and go back to bed. It may be quite a while before Joe wakes up. I won't really be able to tell anything about his condition until he does."

"He's right," Jessie said softly to Stephen. "The men needn't stay here."

Stephen understood what she didn't say, that all of them would be more of a hindrance than a help. "Yes." He turned around, naturally assuming command. "You men, go home and get some rest. Whenever we find out anything, we'll let you know."

Several of the men nodded, and they began to file out the door. Soon the room was almost empty. The doctor turned toward Stephen. "He was hit twice, whatever it was."

"What?"

"There's a large bump on the back of his head, as well as this one closer to the front. The front wound bled more, so we noticed it first, but I wouldn't be surprised if the rear one was the harder blow."

"It wasn't that the engine blew and he got hit by a flying piece of scrap, was it?" Stephen asked, watching the doctor's face intently.

Dr. Holzworth frowned. "Well, I don't know if I could say for sure, but I think it's unlikely. There's the position of the two wounds. How could the engine, flying apart, hit him both front and back?" He paused. "If I had to make a guess, I'd say somebody hit him hard with something big and blunt. It looks like a lot of wounds I've treated. Somebody picks up a bottle or a gun and whacks another man on the head with it. There are no other cuts or contusions, no sign of flying shrapnel. Besides, wasn't the engine cut off?"

"Yeah. It should have been." Stephen glanced at Jessie, then at Burley. They both nodded.

"I don't see any way," Burley said in a low voice, "'cept some son of a bitch attacked Joe."

The doctor shook his head. "I'd say someone's after you Fergusons." He narrowed his eyes. "You better watch your back, son."

Stephen looked again at Jessie. She avoided his gaze.

"I've done about all I can for the present," the doctor went on. "Or anyone else can, either. You might as well get some rest. Especially you, young man. As I remember, you're only a couple of weeks out of bed yourself. You need your sleep."

Stephen started to protest, but Amanda cut in smoothly. "I'll sit up with Joe tonight. Why don't you go to bed, Stephen? I'll wake you if anything happens."

"No, I couldn't let you. It's too hard for you, ma'am."

"Stephen..." Jessie tugged at his hand, pulling him toward the door. He glanced at their linked hands, surprised. He didn't remember taking Jessie's hand, let alone holding it for so long. But it felt so good and comforting in his that he didn't let it go. "Ma knows what she's doing better than you or me. She's the one to stay with him."

"Yes, but that's too great a burden for her," Stephen protested. Then he remembered the way Amanda had looked at his father as he lay motionless in the bed. She loved Joe; Stephen was sure of it. She would insist on taking care of him. "All right. But she must let me relieve her later."

"Of course," Jessie assured him as she led him from the room. She, too, knew how her mother felt about Joe. She'd known it for years. More than that, she knew that right now, more than anything else, Amanda needed to be alone with Joe, to be able to cry and fuss over him without anyone there to observe. As for Stephen, for all his calm, there was a pale tightness around his mouth and eyes that she didn't like. He'd had a terrible shock. He had probably never seen a man injured before. Besides, he was Joe's son, his flesh and blood, however newly discovered; it must cut him more deeply. In Jessie's opinion, he needed the Western cure-all: a good, stiff drink.

Stephen followed her out of the room and down the hall to the kitchen. "Here, sit down," Jessie ordered, pushing him toward one of the plain wooden chairs at the small kitchen table, then went to the cupboard for a bottle of Irish whiskey that her mother kept hidden for Joe's occasional visits.

"She loves him, doesn't she?" Stephen asked.

"What? Oh. You could see that?"

"Yes."

"Yeah." Jessie found the bottle and uncorked it, then poured him a healthy shot of whiskey in a water glass. After a second's thought, she took down another glass and poured herself a small shot, too. "Does it bother you?"

Stephen glanced up, surprised. "No. Why should it? My mother's dead, and she'd been gone many years before that. There's nothing wrong in him finding happiness and love somewhere else."

Jessie set the drinks on the table, looking away as she said, "But she's not—not quality, like your mother was. I reckoned you might not think she was good enough for your father."

"Jessie!" Stephen's hand lashed out and grabbed her around the wrist, pulling her around to face him. "Is that what you think of me? That I judge people by whether or not they're in the social register in St. Louis? Amanda Randall is quality. And I've known women of great prominence in social circles who were no better than the most common tramp."

Jessie's eyes flew up to his. It was on the tip of her tongue to ask tartly how he knew the state of those women's morals, but she clamped her lips over the imprudent words.

"Your mother is a lady. She's made of purest sterling. And so are you." Stephen's eyes bored into hers. "Don't ever think otherwise, Jessamine."

Jessie's knees trembled a little, as they always did when he said "Jessamine," and she sat abruptly to hide that fact. "I didn't know how you'd feel about it, especially if he'd—if they'd—"

"Slept together?"

Jessie nodded. "I don't know that they have. I just suspect. They're very circumspect. Joe would never do anything to damage Ma's reputation in town. But once I woke up in the middle of the night and heard his voice at Ma's door. They were saying goodbye." She glanced sideways at him, wondering what his reaction would be. She wasn't sure why she had told him; she had never revealed what she thought to anyone else, even Sam. But for some reason it was important to her to find out what Stephen thought.

"I'm happy for him, for both of them. Your mother is a generous and loving woman. And every inch a lady." Stephen reached out and took her hand, lacing his fingers through hers. He held on lightly, his thumb softly rubbing the back of her hand. "More to the point is how *you* feel about it. Whether you resent my father."

Jessie shrugged, surprised that he would even think of that side of the matter. She knew that it was always the woman who was considered immoral in such things, not the man. "Maybe a little, at first."

"I'm sure he meant no dishonor to her. He wasn't free to marry until Mother died."

She nodded. "Yes, but I didn't know that until you came into town. Mother certainly never talked to me about Joe or his marriage. And it was a forbidden subject with Sam. But I liked Joe, and I realized that he did his best to see that Ma was never hurt by it. He didn't treat her like a mistress. He made sure no one knew. He's a good man. And I was old enough, when I figured it out, to know how it is with a man."

Stephen grinned. "Oh? And how is it with a man?"

Jessie blushed and cast him a disgusted look. "You know what I mean." She jerked her hand away from his. The way he was caressing her made her feel strange inside, as if she wasn't quite in control of herself.

Stephen watched her, thinking how pretty she looked when she blushed. It made him want to lean over and kiss her pretty little upturned nose. And her forehead, her cheeks, her lips. Desire surged unexpectedly in him. He turned away and tossed down a slug of whiskey. What a time to be panting after a woman! His father was unconscious, possibly dying, in another room, and he was thinking about kissing Jessie!

He curled his fingers tightly around the glass, staring at its contents while inside the whiskey trailed fire down his throat and settled, flaming, in his stomach. "What if he dies, Jess? I've barely found him. What if he dies now?"

Jessie's heart went out to him. Stephen's usual polite social mask was gone, and there was stark pain on his face. She got out of her chair and went to him, bending to put her arm around his shoulders comfortingly. For a moment he was stiff beneath her arm. Then, with a hoarse noise, he turned to her, burying his face in her warmth and wrapping his arms tightly around her. He did not cry, but Jessie felt the shudders running through him as he fought to control his tears. Tears sprang into her own eyes, and she curled over him, laying her cheek against his head. His hair was soft beneath her skin.

"Don't worry," she whispered. "He won't die. Joe Ferguson is a tough ol' coot. It'd take more than somebody busting him in the head to make him give up the ghost. Once, when I was little, I saw a tree fall on him, and he got out with just a few scratches."

Stephen nuzzled into her, seeking the warmth and sweet, feminine comfort she offered. For a moment he let himself float in that state. God, she felt soft. She smelled good. What bliss it would be to stay like this, wrapped together with her, to soak up her strength and warmth.

But he knew it could not last. At any moment someone could walk into the kitchen and find them this way. It would not matter that she was only comforting him; merely the position would compromise her. And Stephen knew that before long it wouldn't be mere comfort, either. Not with her body so soft and warm in his arms, and her skin separated from his lips by only a nightgown and robe. Not with her breasts pressing into him. Already his blood was beginning to course more warmly in his veins.

He straightened and released her. Jessie turned away, moving jerkily, as if someone was pulling her on strings. With her back to him, she picked up her glass and downed the whiskey. Stephen watched her. He'd never seen a woman drink whiskey before. He expected at least a gasp at its fiery strength. But there was no sound from Jessie.

Stephen smiled a little. Why would he expect anything else? Even if Jessie had never drunk whiskey, she would never let on. His eyes trailed down her back and caressed the curve of her buttocks, barely hinted at under her belted robe. He cleared his throat and turned away. This would never do. Could he not even accept her kindness without turning it into desire? Being around Jessie seemed to bring out the lecher in him—even with his father in such a grave condition.

He sipped at the whiskey and tried to focus his mind. There were many things that needed thinking about, things that needed to be done. Perhaps if he concentrated on them, he could keep his mind off his father's health—and off Jessie.

She turned to look at him. He wasn't watching her. It must have been her imagination that she could feel his eyes on her. Imagination and her own wayward lust. She had gone to Stephen feeling only compassion and a need to help him, but when he had pressed his face into her, his arms holding her tightly, heat had sprung up all through her. Her skin had begun to tingle and her blood to race, and a hot, heavy knot had formed deep in her abdomen, aching and pulsing. She had wanted to turn Stephen's face up to hers and kiss him, kiss him deep and hard, as he had kissed her the other day. She had wanted to nip at his neck, to sink her fingers into his hair, to twist her body against him. How could she think of something like that at a time like this? Did she have the soul of a strumpet? Was this how her mother had felt about Joe all these years? Lord, if it was, she didn't know how Amanda had managed to keep from openly becoming his mistress.

The thought shocked her. Good Lord! Could she be thinking about becoming the mistress of this man? Throwing away her good name for the sake of a few days of passion with him? Why, only a couple of weeks ago she hadn't even liked him. She tried to summon up the way she had felt about him then, tried to recall that his elegant clothes and manner were sissified, that he wouldn't be worth a damn out here on his own, that he wasn't husky, hard, the way a real man was. He wasn't Sam, and Sam was her ideal.

No, he wasn't Sam. Jessie smiled a little. He wasn't like Sam at all. But she had never had feelings remotely like these for Sam. Right now, she had trouble remembering Sam's face. All she could see was Stephen.

"Well," she said, running her hands down the sides of her robe. Her palms were sweating. "I guess I'll go to bed. I'll trade watches with Mama after a while."

"Then call me to relieve you." He did not look at her, but kept staring into his glass as though it held the secrets of the world.

"I will." Jessie hesitated, then turned away and left the room.

Behind her, Stephen crossed his arms on the table and sank his head onto them with a sigh. *Ah, Jessie.* What was he going to do?

# Chapter Twelve

Stephen!" a voice hissed, and a hand shook his shoulder.

Stephen made a low noise in his sleep and flopped over onto his back. The persistent prodding at his shoulder continued, and finally his eyes opened a slit. Jessie was leaning over him. She was dressed in nightclothes, and her hair hung loose in vivid red waves. The ends brushed the covers over Stephen's chest.

Still foggy with sleep, not even thinking, he lifted his hand and wrapped it around several strands of her hair. Caressingly his hand slid down over the soft waves, letting them slip out of his palm. He didn't stop to wonder why Jessie was at his bed in nightclothes and with her hair invitingly unbound. He reacted instinctively. His hand went around her wrist and moved slowly up her arm. Jessie's eyes widened. She could have jerked back from his touch, but she did not. She stayed as motionless as a statue, barely breathing. His hand curled around her neck, then went up to curve over her cheek and jaw. He smoothed the hair from her face, and his hand remained there.

"Beautiful," he murmured, and his smile was slow and sensual.

A quiver ran through Jessie. All she could think about was lying down on the bed beside him. She wanted him to kiss her. She wanted to feel his hand on her skin. Suddenly her flesh was searing hot, as if a fire had exploded into life beneath her skin. Deep inside, a throbbing started, an aching emptiness that yearned to be filled.

Stephen's hand pulled her head down, and he rose up to meet her. For a moment, they were motionless, gazing deep into each other's eyes, their lips only a breath apart. It seemed like forever. The sound of her pulse roared in Jessie's ears as, gently, Stephen touched his mouth to hers. He kissed her, then kissed her again and again, pulling her onto the bed with him, until finally she was stretched out atop him, his tongue plundering her mouth. She dug her fingers into the covers, kissing him passionately.

All sleepiness burned away in the heat of his desire. Every inch of him was alive and alert now. But Stephen did not think of the miracle of Jessie's appearing in his bed; he did not consider the wisdom of what he did. He knew nothing but his need and her welcoming flesh.

He rolled over, pulling her beneath him. The bed covers lay between them, frustrating his desire to have her body directly against his, but he pressed into her, too eager and desperate to move away enough to pull off the covers. His pelvis ground suggestively into her, and even through the bedclothes, Jessie could feel the thick, hard length of his manhood. She whimpered and moved her legs restlessly, trying to get through the barriers that separated them. She twined her arms around his neck, clinging to him as they kissed endlessly, mindlessly.

With a growl, Stephen shoved the covers down to her waist, and his hand slid into her bed robe and cupped her breast. There was still the material of her gown between him and her skin, but it was thin, and through it he could clearly feel her heat and the hard tightness of her nipple. He caressed her breast, his breath ragged in his throat. He had to touch her, had to feel the satiny texture of her skin. With trembling haste his fingers unfastened the line of small pearl buttons down the front of her nightgown. He pushed the gown and robe off her shoulders and looked down at her.

Jessie's breasts rose up, full and firm, topped with the cherry points of her nipples. Her head was thrown back, her eyes closed, and her lips were slightly parted, moist and dark from his kisses. She was the picture of a woman lost in passion—erotic, seductive, compelling. Stephen caressed her breasts and cupped one in his palm. His fingers drifted teasingly over her nipple, and desire stabbed him, hot and intense, as the small bud hardened even more. He bent and kissed the supremely soft flesh. When his tongue came out to curl around the nipple, Jessie moaned aloud. The noise was a spur to his desire, and he pulled the nipple into his mouth.

Jessie arched her back, and her hands dug into Stephen's hair, clenching and unclenching with each new wave of desire that his mouth created in her. She writhed, lost to everything except the sensations shooting through her. She wanted to scream and cry. She wanted to feel him inside her. She wanted him to never stop touching and kissing her.

"Stephen. Stephen." Her breath was panting. Her hands slid down to his back and dug in.

Stephen groaned. His mouth widened, feasting on her breast.

There was the sound of a cough in the room next door, and Stephen stiffened. For the first time reason penetrated the haze of desire that surrounded him. He remembered where he was. He remembered that Jessie's body was not his to delight in and never would be.

He wanted to curse and rip the rest of the clothes from her; he wanted to make her his, so completely his that nothing could take her away from him. He wanted to damn the future and live only for this one moment.

War raged through him, reason and instinct struggling for control. As it always had with him, his mind finally won, and he rolled away from Jessie. He flung one arm across his eyes, blotting out everything, and a stream of vicious curses fell from his lips.

Jessie opened her eyes, dazed. She stared at him. A blush rose up her throat as she realized her nakedness. Hastily, ashamed, she yanked up her clothes and pulled them together across her chest. She scrambled out of bed, tears starting in her eyes. Once again she had forgotten everything under the force of passion. It had been Stephen who had had the strength and morals to stop—or perhaps it was only a lack of interest. That was an even more humiliating possibility.

"I came to wake you." Jessie spoke in a low, hurried voice. Tears clogged her throat. "You said you wanted to take over watching Joe. He's—I'm going to my room now."

She fled out the door and down the stairs.

"Jessie!" Stephen called after her, sitting up, but it was no good. She was already gone. He'd lost her. He'd given her up. He felt empty and aching inside. He wanted her so badly it was all he could do not to get up and run after her.

She must hate him. He'd handled things wretchedly. Never before in his life had he been so clumsy, so bestial, so lacking in smoothness and sophistication. It seemed insane that all his intelligence and skills should vanish when he was with the woman he desired more than he'd ever desired anyone. The woman he loved.

Stephen groaned and rolled over, burying his face in the pillow. Love. He couldn't be in love with her. It was too crazy, too horrible, too painful. He couldn't have her without marriage, because he loved her too much to disgrace her. Yet he could not marry her, because he was sworn and bound to marry another woman. And he could not bear not to have her.

No. It couldn't be love. It was just passion, if somewhat more extreme than what he usually felt. It could not be love. She was a strange, wild girl from the back of nowhere. She had no social graces to speak of and never worried about the correct thing to do. She had no use for fine clothes or food or art. She wore men's clothes and behaved in a completely unfeminine way. She never turned to him for help or gazed at him with soft, beguiling eyes. She was contrary, exasperating and stubborn.

She was also bewitching. Beautiful. Strong. Intelligent, impish and natural. She was warm and generous, kind. He could go on listing her attributes. It was easier to say what she was *not*, which was dull, boring and silly. Kissing her was like tasting the finest liquor—exciting, fiery, exquisite. No other woman had ever affected him so strongly, made him want her so much. But it wasn't only desire. It was far more than that.

Face it, he told himself. Admit it: you love her. He was in love with her in a way that wasn't even close to the lukewarm, fond emotion he had for Elizabeth. This love was intense and passionate, hot and unsettling.

It was also impossible.

He could not have her; he could not take their love to its final, right conclusion. He was engaged to Elizabeth, bound by his promise to her and his deathbed promise to her father. He had been reared in a society where honor and duty and doing what was right were the cornerstones of philosophy. A man did not run away from his responsibilities. The head ruled, not the heart. And wild, impulsive actions were avoided like the plague. Turbulent emotions were for common people, not people like the McClellans or the Caldwells. If one were unfortunate enough to feel such things, then one certainly did not act upon them. Emotions were never allowed to interfere with what had to be done.

He had to marry Elizabeth. To throw her over—especially now, when she had run away from St. Louis to marry him—would be the act of a scoundrel. Her reputation would be in shreds unless he married her; she would never be able to return to St. Louis. He would ruin her life if he refused to marry her. He could not do that to Elizabeth. His love for Jessie must be *his* burden, *his* pain, not Elizabeth's.

Stephen sighed and swung out of bed. He knew what he had to do, how he had to act. He had to avoid Jessie as much as possible, and when he was forced to be around her, he must not touch her; in fact, it would be best if he looked at her as little as possible. Stephen began to dress, sternly avoiding thinking about his decision. But inside his chest, his heart lay like lead.

It was broad daylight when Jessie awoke. The curtains across her windows were heavy, to help keep out the winter cold, but in spite of them the room was light. She jumped out of bed and ran to the window to shove aside the draperies. The pale winter sun was shining almost directly overhead. It must be close to noon! She couldn't remember when she had last overslept so badly.

She dressed hurriedly and ran downstairs, where she found the men already gathering for the noon meal. Good Lord, she'd missed a whole morning's work. She rushed into the kitchen and began filling her plate directly from the pots and pans before she remembered that there was no work this morning. The mill was shut down today, dead without the heartbeat of its huge engine. The engine was broken, and only Sam could fix it.

She ate some of her food, standing in the kitchen, then dumped the rest in the garbage pail. She no longer felt hungry.

Jessie went to her mother's room. The door was closed, and she eased it open and stuck her head inside. Joe was lying still on the bed, eyes closed, and her mother was sitting beside him, her hands busy with the sewing in her lap. Trust her mother to never be completely idle.

"How is he?" Jessie whispered.

Her mother turned and smiled. "Hello, dear," she answered in a normal tone. "No need to whisper. It would be far better if we *did* awaken him." She sighed. "He's no better, as far as I can tell. It's so awful. I can do nothing to help him!"

"I know, Ma." Jessie went over to her mother and patted her on the shoulder. "But he'll get better. Joe's tough."

"Of course. Of course. I'm being foolish."

Jessie stood for a moment, looking down at Joe. There was a battalion of questions inside her, all about confusing things like love and desire and the behavior of members of the upper crust. For once in her life, she had no idea what she should do or how she should act, and she needed her mother's knowledge and experience desperately. But she could not bring herself to ask Amanda such things now; they seemed so trivial compared to the life-and-death struggle going on in the bed before her. It would be cruel to burden her mother with questions at a time like this. She should be helping her, not adding to her problems.

So she said goodbye to her mother, pulled on her coat and, without really thinking about what she was doing, walked to the mill. As she moved down the hall toward the office, she heard a clanging sound in the huge room where the machinery lay silent. She stopped short. Someone was there. Why? Her heart began to pound. Could it be the person who had been causing all their problems?

Cautiously, Jessie crept through the double doors. The silence was eerie. There was another noise and a muffled curse. It came from the center of the room, where the steam engine was located. Jessie tiptoed closer.

In front of the engine was an oil lantern, burning brightly. A man sat beside it. He was dressed in rough clothes, and there were dirt and grease on his clothes, his hands and his face. Tools lay scattered around him. Jessie's jaw dropped.

"Stephen!"

The man glanced up. "Jessie! I didn't expect you to be in today." He rose smoothly from his cross-legged position on the floor.

"You scared me out of a year's growth! I heard a noise in here."

"Why did that scare you?" he asked.

Jessie hesitated. "Well, uh, because I thought it might be a stranger, and, uh . . ."

"Maybe you thought I was the person who did this." He gestured in the direction of the mighty engine.

"Did what?"

"Jessie . . . don't play games with me. There's no time for that. I'm not an idiot, though you seem to think I am. Apparently my father does, too. Why hasn't either one of you told me what's been going on?"

"I don't know what you're talking about."

"Will you please drop the act? When I arrived here, the saw blade had broken recently." Stephen began to tick off his points on his fingers. "A couple of days later you and I were ambushed, and I, who somewhat resemble my brother, was shot. Now, as soon as the new saw blade is brought in, the engine that powers the machinery is mysteriously disabled—and my father with it. It strains coincidence to the limit. Not only that, when I checked the engine, I found that it had obviously been tampered with. It didn't just happen to break. It had a lot of encouragement. My father must have heard the intruder and come to see what was happening, and the man hit him. Or perhaps he meant to put my father out of commission, too." Stephen paused. "Now . . . who is he?"

Jessie sighed and sat on the steps. "I don't know. I wish I did. Maybe I could have stopped it."

"How long have you known?"

"I suspected from the start, from the minute I saw that blade. The cut was too clean. It had been weakened deliberately. But Joe wouldn't tell either you or Sam. He didn't want you to worry, and besides, what could you have done?"

"Sam doesn't know about this, either? He thinks the blade was broken naturally?"

"I guess." Jessie shrugged. "But Sam's sharp. I imagine he'll put it together."

"Joe has no idea who's doing it?"

"Somebody with a grudge against him or Sam, I guess. But we can't figure out who would have that much bitterness toward either one of them."

"A grudge?" Stephen looked skeptical. "I don't think so. Maybe one incident. But three? It's hard to picture a mere grudge carrying a person to those lengths. My guess is there's another reason, and I suspect it has something to do with money. Things usually do. Who would profit by this mill being closed down?"

"That's just it!" Jessie raised her hands helplessly. "Nobody! In one way or another, most of the people in Nora Springs depend on the mill. They work here, or transport goods for us, or they sell things to the workers. The landowners sell us the trees, or lease us the timberland. Except for a couple of ranches in the valley, practically everything around here is connected to the sawmill. If it failed, the whole town would more or less die."

"What about a business rival?"

"What business rival? There isn't another sawmill for miles and miles. And there's plenty of business for more than one mill in this part of the country. The demand for lumber just gets bigger."

Stephen frowned. "It doesn't make sense."

"I know."

Jessie looked so woebegone that Stephen wanted to take her into his arms and comfort her. Sternly he rejected the impulse. He had made a decision to stick to business whenever he was around her. If he got personal, he would be on dangerous ground. As it was, just looking at her, he was having trouble keeping his mind on the problem before them.

"All right. Let's start at the most basic level and build up. What will happen now that the engine's broken?"

She gave him an odd look. "The mill can't run, obviously."

"Ever?"

"Not until Sam gets back. He's the only one who knows enough about the engine to even figure out what to do."

"So at least a few days."

"Yeah."

"And if it needed a certain part, it could be two weeks, or even more."

"Sure, if a part had to be shipped here."

"So what happens if the mill is closed down for a few days or a few weeks?"

Jessie looked uncomfortable. "We couldn't fill our orders. They'd have to buy from somewhere else, and we'd lose a lot of business."

"And what would the result of that be?"

Jessie squirmed. "Why do you have to know all this?"

"Because I am trying to ascertain a motive. There has to be one, or someone wouldn't have tried three times to stop the mill from operating."

"Joe'll kill me if he knows I told you."

"Told me what?"

"If we don't make the deadline on our orders, we're out of business."

"Completely?"

"Yes. Joe and Sam have a note at the bank. They got it to make improvements a few years ago, and then, when the blade broke, Joe added to the note, borrowing money to buy the new blade. Right now is when our cash is the lowest, right before we get paid."

"And the note's coming up soon, and Ferguson Mill won't have the money to pay it unless they fill their orders, right? Which they can't do if they're shut down."

Jessie nodded. "Yeah. The bank would get the sawmill."

"Then someone would profit, or rather, some*thing*—the bank."

"Not really. The bank would get the mill, but they'd have to run it, and the people at the bank don't know anything about that. I would think they'd rather just get the money paid back, don't you?"

"Usually. Besides, it seems very unlikely that the employees would care enough about the bank's profit to do something like this. It's hard to imagine this as the work of an institution. Maybe—maybe it's someone who thinks that if Joe is facing ruin, he would sell the mill to him at a good price. Or that the bank would sell it to him at a good price, that they'd discount it."

"Yeah, but nobody's tried to buy it. Wouldn't you think they'd at least make an offer before they set out to force him to sell?"

"Maybe. Maybe not. Well..." He shrugged as though dismissing the matter. "At least I can take care of one problem. I'll make the note payment for my father."

Jessie groaned. "He'll kill me. Joe doesn't want your money. He's afraid you'll think he was glad to see you just because he needed your money."

Stephen grimaced. "I wouldn't have thought that. Did he actually believe I'd rather see him fail than pay a debt for him?"

"He's a proud man. He wouldn't like taking charity."

"It's not charity. I'm his son. I'd give him whatever I had, and I think he'd do the same for me."

"He would."

"Then why should he object if I do it for him?"

"He's proud. Maybe it has something to do with your mama being rich, you know, and Joe taking her away from all that, then her going back to it."

"But she didn't leave because Joe didn't have enough money for her. She didn't care about the luxuries. I think she was just too gentle, too soft a woman to survive here." He sighed. "But I can understand how my father feels." He thought for a moment. "Surely we could work something out, a business deal so my father and Sam wouldn't have to feel it was charity. I could lend them the cash—or maybe I could buy a share in the business. It would be an investment for me."

Jessie brightened. "Hey! It might work. Joe might agree to that, as long as you were getting something in return."

"Good. How much is the payment?" Jessie told him, and he nodded. "That's fine. I have a letter of credit from my bank in St. Louis, and it will cover that." He paused, thinking. "But that may not stop the accidents from occurring. If it's a buyer who wants to force them to sell, he could continue to attack the business until Joe and Sam couldn't make a profit and would have to sell out."

Jessie nodded. "That's true."

"And something else—if I make the payment, and because of that there are no more accidents, we'll never find out who has been causing them. Not for sure, anyway."

"That's right. He would be able to get away with what he's done to Joe. And you."

"Right." A devilish light danced in Stephen's eyes. "What would you say about setting a trap for him?"

A wide grin split Jessie's face. "Sure! How?"

"Suppose I don't pay off the loan until the last minute and don't make it known that I intend to? Whoever is doing this will assume that the loan won't be paid unless the mill manages to meet their schedule. Then suppose that the mill goes back into operation quickly? He would have to strike again."

"And we'd catch him at it."

"Exactly."

"Let's do it!" Jessie crouched beside him on the floor. "We'll set up a secret watch, so he doesn't know we're here."

"We? No. Absolutely not. *You* are not going to be on the watch. I will do it—and perhaps another man or two. Who can we trust?"

"What do you mean, I can't?" Jessie exploded. "There's nobody here you can trust more than me, and that includes you! Just because Frank Grissom got the drop on me the other day, don't think I'm no good in a fight. He caught me off guard, that's all, and I'll be prepared for this one. I can shoot a pistol as good as anybody, and I can—"

"For heaven's sake, I'm not questioning your ability or your trustworthiness. You won't be there because you might get hurt!"

"So might you, or anybody else. As I remember, you didn't fare too well the other day when you took on Frank Grissom."

Stephen flushed. "I'm aware of your opinion of me, Miss Randall. I admit that the weakness from my injuries made me slow and careless, and Grissom did land a punch. However, I am quite recovered from my wounds now."

Now she'd injured his pride, Jessie knew. If she was her mother or one of those women Stephen had tried to teach her to be, she would try to placate him now. But, darn it, she didn't want to be cut out of his plan just because she was a woman! She wasn't about to sit meekly at home and hear about things secondhand. She crossed her hands over her chest and glared stubbornly at Stephen. "You can't keep me out. You have no right. I'm going to keep watch, too."

"You are not," Stephen ground out through clenched teeth.

"I am. You can't tell me what to do."

"Well, somebody certainly needs to."

"I'll come anyway, whether you say I can or not. You won't be able to keep me out without my creating such a huge fuss that the person who's doing this will guess something's up."

For a long moment they glared at each other mulishly. Then Stephen's lip began to twitch and, surprisingly, suddenly, he grinned. "Damn. I bet you would at that."

Jessie grinned back in a self-satisfied way. "You're right."

"You'll get yourself killed someday."

"Maybe so, but at least my life won't have been boring."

Stephen shook his head, half amused, half exasperated. "All right. You can watch with me. At least that way I can keep my eye on you and make sure you don't do anything too stupid."

Jessie chuckled. "And here I was going to say the same thing about you."

Her statement surprised a laugh out of him. "Oh, Jessie, what am I going to do with you?" He couldn't imagine having this sort of conversation with any other woman. She was so annoying. She was so lively and fun. Life with her would never be dull. What would it be like, he wondered, to wake up to Jessie each morning? To laugh and talk and fight with her? She made everyone else seem tame.

Sternly Stephen pulled his thoughts from the direction they were taking. He was not supposed to be thinking this way. He had promised himself last night that he would avoid Jessie. That was one reason he had come down to the mill this morning to look at the engine. Yet here he was, wanting to kiss the impish grin from her face and thinking about spending his life with her.

He turned away and jammed his hands in his pockets to keep them from reaching out for her. *Damn it! Keep your mind on the subject.* "What about the others?" he asked in a remote tone. "Who else can we trust?"

Jessie felt suddenly deflated. "Well, uh, Burley Owens, of course. He's been with Joe ever since the beginning. If we can't trust him, there's nobody we can trust. And Jim Two Horses. Sam likes him and trusts him."

"Okay. Good. We'll switch off with them, then."

"Wait a minute. Don't you think we're getting ahead of ourselves? I mean, what's the point of all this planning? The mill's crippled with the engine down. There's no way to get it operating again quickly."

"That's simple. Repair it."

"How? Sam's the only one who knows anything about the engine. I could probably repair half the machines in here myself, but not the steam engine."

"Ah, that's why you're lucky I happen to be here."

"*You* know how to fix a steam engine?" Jessie stared.

"Yes. Don't look so astonished. It's impolite."

"But you—you're so fancy!"

Stephen glanced at the rough garb he was wearing, now liberally smeared with dirt, oil and grease, then looked at her sneakingly. They both laughed.

"You know what I mean, though! You're rich. You don't work with steam engines."

"I do work, contrary to what you think. I've worked in my grandfather's business since I was fifteen. And before that I was always hanging around it. Do you know what my family's fortune is founded on?"

Jessie shook her head.

"Shipping. *Steam*ships."

"Oh." Her mouth opened, and hope rose in her eyes.

"That's right. Oh. I've been inside the engine rooms of more steamships than you can imagine. Large and small. When I was a boy, I was fascinated by the machinery of the ships far more than by their cargo or their profits. I spent a lot of time with the men who worked them, and I managed to learn a good bit. This engine is not precisely like the ones I am accustomed to, but it's close enough. I've found the problem, simply a damaged pipe or two. I think I can repair it easily enough. I may not be able to put it in perfect condition—we'll need to order a part to replace the damaged one. But I can put something together so that it will work until the new part gets here.''

''Oh, Stephen!'' Jessie wanted to throw her arms around him with joy and kiss him soundly. But she made herself stay where she was, letting her happiness show only in her blazing smile. ''That would be wonderful.'' She clasped her hands together tightly. ''Joe will be so happy.''

''How is he? Is he awake?''

She shook her head. ''No. He's the same. I'm sorry.''

Stephen returned to the engine and picked up a wrench. He squatted and began to work. Jessie stood for a moment, watching him. There was no reason for her to stay, but still she lingered, unwilling to leave him. She watched his hands as they worked. They were stained with dirt and oil, no longer carefully manicured. His fingers were long and slender, supple. They moved quickly, his touch delicate and deft. Jessie remembered the way they had felt on her skin, exploring her with the same gentleness and care.

Tendons moved and tightened in his hands and arms as he turned the wrench forcefully. There was strength in him. Jessie had felt the same strength in his arms last night as he had held her. When she had first met him, she had thought that Stephen was soft and weak, but she had been wrong; she knew that now. She had been fooled by his lean build and his manner, by his clothes and too-handsome face. She had been wrong, too, about his uselessness; he was not an idle, ignorant rich man. He had worked for a long time; he had experience and knowledge. He also had grit, determination and courage.

Nor was he the ice-cold man that his carefully controlled expression usually indicated. Jessie was positive of that, passion burned in him like a sawdust fire—fast, explosive, searing. She smiled, thinking about that passion. It had raged nearly out of control early this morning. But at the last minute he had been able to stop it.

She should be glad, of course. After all, he was an engaged man. He loved another woman, would marry another woman. There could be nothing more for them than a few nights' pleasure, so it was far better that they had stopped. Still, she couldn't help but feel a little piqued that Stephen had pulled away from her. She couldn't help but wonder why. Had it been out of love for his fiancée? She found that that idea caused a burning, itching sensation somewhere in the region of her heart. Or had it been because he would not dishonor her? That thought was much more attractive. Of course, there was still another possibility—that he simply didn't find her desirable enough. Jessie didn't like to think of that at all.

"Stephen? Why did you stop kissing me last night?" Jessie had always been a direct and honest person; she saw no sense in beating around the bush on any subject.

Stephen's wrench fell to the ground with a clatter. His head snapped around. "What? What the devil kind of a question is that?"

"I don't know." She shrugged. "A simple one?"

He made a noise of disbelief and bent to pick up the dropped tool. "Nothing is ever simple where you're concerned."

"Me? Are you joking? I think I must be painfully plain compared to the women you're used to. All those things they have to remember about walking and talking and everything, the hundreds of little tricks and deceits."

"I'm more accustomed to them. But you—well, usually I find myself lost." He went back to his work.

"Well?"

"Well what?"

"Aren't you going to answer my question?"

He sighed. "That's not the kind of question you ought to ask a man."

"Why not? It's what I want to know." Jessie leaned forward, staring at him. "Stephen Ferguson! Are you blushing?"

He shot her a scornful glance. "Of course not."

She chuckled. "Yes, you are! I thought you were supposed to be a man of the world."

"I'm not generally accustomed to being asked such questions. Hasn't anyone ever pointed out that you're too bold?"

"Mmm, lots of times. Now, quit trying to wriggle out of it and tell me why you stopped."

"All right." He set the wrench aside and turned to face her seriously. "You're a beautiful woman, Jessie, and I want you very much. But it would be wrong for me to take advantage of you. You're an innocent. If I seduced you, I would be a cad, a scoundrel. Surely you can see that."

"Because you love someone else."

He hesitated, then said carefully, "Because I am pledged to someone else. I gave her my promise, my word. I can't go back on that. I can't marry you. And a woman like you should settle for nothing less."

A bubble of emotion swelled in Jessie's chest. She wanted to cry, but she wasn't sure if it was out of sadness or pleasure. She ducked her head and blinked back the tears. "Thank you." She forced a smile. If she asked for the truth, it wasn't fair to start crying when she got it. "You're a good man, Stephen Ferguson."

"And you're a beautiful lady, Jessamine Randall." For a moment they gazed at each other. Finally Stephen pulled his eyes away and went back to his job.

Jessamine stood, dusting off the seat of her trousers. "When shall I tell the men to start work again? I imagine most of them will be dropping by today."

Stephen frowned at his work. "Tomorrow morning. I'll be finished tonight. And we'll have a guard to make sure nothing else happens."

"All right."

She walked out of the room and down the hall to the office. The quiet was eerie. She thought that if she was alone she might have been a little afraid, given the strange things that had been happening and the emptiness of the place, but it was comforting to know that Stephen was not far away. He would come running if she called.

Jessie shook her head. She must have lost her senses. Never before had she wanted a man's protection. And even if she was scared enough to want protection, she wouldn't have figured that Stephen Ferguson would be the man she'd pick to provide it.

Most of the workers dropped by throughout the afternoon, inquiring after Joe's health, and Jessie told them that they would be able to start the mill again the next day. Frank Grissom didn't drop by, and Jessie was glad. She didn't relish being alone with him, even if she did have her pistol close at hand.

But Grissom showed up the next morning, and the moment Jessie saw him, she knew that he brought trouble. She had awakened early and hurried to the mill, carrying a couple of cold biscuits in a napkin for her makeshift breakfast. She was nervous about running the mill without Joe, and she wanted to be there to meet the men as they came in the door, to reassure them that she was responsible and in charge. Another, unexamined reason for her early departure from the house was that she didn't want to have Stephen walk with her to the mill as he had done ever since Grissom's attack. She had thought about the matter long and hard the night before, and she had come to the conclusion that Stephen was right. There could be no possibility of a romance between them. Therefore, the best thing for her to do was to avoid being around him as much as possible.

Now she stood at the front door of the mill, greeting the workers as they walked up the stairs. The early morning air was chilly, even though she had on her heavy wool jacket and cap, and her breath crystallized in the air in front of her. In a few more weeks the snow would start falling, beginning the process that closed them in for the winter. The men seemed in good spirits, calling out greetings to her and each other, joking and laughing. She guessed that they must be grateful to be able to work; they must have feared, as she had, that the mill would be shut down for weeks. No one questioned her authority.

Until Grissom came up. She saw him approaching out of the corner of her eye, but she didn't turn to look at him. If she was lucky, she thought, she'd manage not to have to speak to him.

She wasn't lucky. Grissom walked straight to the bottom of the stairs and planted himself in front of her, his fists bunched on his hips pugnaciously. His eyes burned with resentment.

"What the hell do you think you're doing, anyway?" he roared. "Ordering my men back to work without a word to me!"

"I wasn't aware that you were in charge of whether or not the mill employees worked."

"I'm the foreman here, and with Joe down, I'm the one who'll be giving the orders. Not some split-tail in pants!"

"Is that right? Well, I never saw anything that put *you* in charge, either. I'm taking over until Joe is well enough to come down here himself, and I'm doing it because I'm his assistant. I know what Joe wants."

Grissom uttered a coarse curse. "You don't know nothin' missy, or you'd have talked to me before you went around telling all the men to come back to work. 'Cause I'm ordering 'em out of here!"

Jessie straightened, her eyes shooting sparks. "They aren't going. They're not your employees—they're Ferguson Mill employees. And why are you so all-fired eager to make these men lose another day's pay?"

"I'd rather see them lose a day's pay than an eye or a leg or maybe their life."

"What a ridic—"

"The hell it is," he charged on. "I heard that engine was stone dead. Who fixed it? I'll tell you who—that stranger! That fancy pants from back East. What does he know about a sawmill? There's no telling what he did to rig that engine back up to work. It'll probably explode any minute. I don't want my men working in a dangerous place."

More and more men had gathered around them, some stopping on their way into the mill and others coming out to find out what the ruckus was. Jessie could sense their growing restlessness, and she knew that the men were leaning toward Grissom's side. They didn't want to lose pay, but they distrusted the city slicker, and Grissom had gotten them thinking about the possible danger. Panic rose in Jessie. What could she say to make them stay?

"Mr. Ferguson may not know much about sawmills, but he knows steam engines. He fixed it, and it'll run as good as new."

"Well, I don't know, Jess," one of the men put in slowly, pausing to spit a stream of tobacco over the railing. "I ain't sure I want to risk my life on that young feller's say-so. I'm thinkin' we might orta wait till Sam comes back."

"That could take days!" Jessie protested. "Look, I'm telling you, it's safe now!"

"That's what *he* says."

"I don't know as how we can trust him."

"Maybe we better wait."

The statements came from all around her, and the men began to shift, moving away. Jessie dug her nails into her palms, watching helplessly. Damn that Frank Grissom! He would spoil everything with his hardheadedness.

"Wait!" The clear, confident male voice carried across the lumberyard. "I believe I'm the subject of this discussion. Perhaps you gentlemen should be talking to me, instead.''

Jessie swung around. Stephen stood at the entrance to the yard. He looked cool and calm, and his clothes were as neat and elegant as always. He looked like a gentleman of leisure out for a stroll. But his eyes were hard and cold as he stared across the yard at Grissom. ''Grissom, do you have some complaint? I realize that you would probably rather bully a young woman, but I suggest that you take any problems you have with this mill or that engine up with me. Am I making myself clear?''

''Yeah.'' Frank grinned ferally. His eyes were lit with an unholy light. ''I'd be real happy to take this up with you.'' He started across the yard toward Stephen, his fists doubling into knots.

# Chapter Thirteen

Stephen waited for Grissom calmly. Jessie's heart began to thunder in her chest. Grissom wanted to fight Stephen; she had seen the blood lust in his eyes when Stephen appeared. If he managed to goad Stephen into a fight, Frank wouldn't stop until he'd maimed or killed him. Grissom was the biggest, meanest man in the area, and no one would dare to make a move to stop him.

Grissom stopped directly in front of Stephen and stared into his face. It was an intimidation tactic he had used successfully in the past. Stephen, however, did not flinch or look away. He simply gazed back, and there was something in his face, a kind of smug superiority, that made Grissom's blood boil.

"The engine is in good working order. It's perfectly safe. I give you my word."

Pointedly Grissom turned aside and spat on the ground. "Your word?" He laughed. "Well, now, ain't that something? I always would trust the word of some fancy-pants stranger." His eyes narrowed, and his voice turned harsh. "Who the hell are you to be coming down here trying to fix things and handing out orders about when we'll work? Who are you to tell us that the engine's safe? What gives you the right to stick your nose into our business?"

"Our?" Stephen repeated, his tone faintly amused. "I wasn't aware until now that Joe Ferguson had taken you on as a partner." He dismissed Grissom with a glance and turned toward the other men, his gaze sweeping over them slowly, confidently. "My name is Ferguson, and that's what gives me the right to get Ferguson Sawmill running again. It is my father's business, no one else's. Ordinarily he would give the orders, and if he couldn't, then my brother, Sam, would. But Joe has been struck down by the vicious person who tried to ruin the steam engine. The person who is trying to stop Joe Ferguson's mill from running. If Sam was here, he wouldn't let that happen. But he's not here. So that leaves me. I'm Joe's son, and, just like Sam, I intend to make sure that whoever tried to kill my father and ruin his business won't succeed. That's what gives me the right. I don't think there's anyone here who has a better one."

His eyes settled on Grissom, cool and challenging. The men began to shift uncertainly and murmur among themselves. Jessie smiled. He had a beautiful way with words, that Stephen Ferguson. He'd obviously made the men start to rethink their decision to leave with Grissom.

"I realize that you men don't know me," Stephen went on after a moment. "But I am a Ferguson, and I think that name stands for something around here. I have done and will do nothing that will lessen that name. Now, if any of you are interested in putting in a day's work and getting paid for it, let's go inside."

Stephen started to move around Grissom toward the mill, but Grissom planted himself in front of him again, blocking his path. "Just hold on a damned minute! You can't go giving my men orders!"

"I will if they're working for me. That includes you, if you want to continue to work here."

"You can't fire me!"

"You want to stay and work? Fine. I'd like to see you do it. I was under the impression that you were refusing to work. That you were too scared to."

Jessie sucked in her breath. Now he'd put the fat in the fire. Grissom was already on the verge of exploding. Why was Stephen goading him? Didn't he realize what Grissom would do? He wouldn't stop just because Stephen was Joe's son, not if he was mad enough. He'd pound him into a pulp.

"What?" Grissom's voice was deadly. Stephen gazed at him, contempt tinging his face.

Despite what Jessie thought, Stephen knew exactly what he was doing. It was obvious that Grissom would use his influence with the men to keep them from obeying Stephen and Jessie. He could stop the mill more effectively than any tinkering with the engine had—unless Stephen cut his power out from under him. His power was his brute strength; let Stephen beat him in a fight, and the men would swing over to him, not Grissom. Stephen had seen as soon as Grissom arrived at the mill that this confrontation would have to end with one of them establishing superiority over the other. What was more, this was a perfect opportunity to give the boor the thrashing he deserved for his attack on Jessie without exposing Jessie's name to any scandal.

Stephen was ready for Grissom to swing at him. He wanted it.

"Are you calling me a coward?" Grissom went on.

Stephen shrugged, letting his body fall into a relaxed, even careless posture, while inside every sense was alert, every muscle and nerve ready and waiting. "You're the one who kept talking about how frightening it would be to work in the mill. I would say that speaks for itself."

Grissom's eyes flared red. "Nobody calls me a coward!" he roared. He swung his huge fist at Stephen.

Jessie's heart leaped into her throat. She wanted to cry out to Stephen to watch out, but she didn't dare distract him. She gripped the railing and leaned forward.

Grissom's fist would have knocked most men to the ground—if it had hit. But when it reached Stephen's face, Stephen was no longer there. He bobbed aside, and as he moved, he sent his fist into Grissom's belly with all his strength. Air whooshed out of Grissom, and he looked comically surprised.

Stephen stepped back and shrugged out of his coat and the suit jacket beneath it. A man in the crowd reached to take them from him. "There, that's more suitable attire for fisticuffs," Stephen said, raising his hands and taking a professional stance. "Well?"

Grissom recovered his breath. "Why, you little son of a—" He charged, lowering his head to butt his opponent, a tactic that usually resulted in at least a broken nose for the other fellow, but once again Stephen neatly sidestepped, and this time Grissom stumbled past him and fell to the ground.

He jumped up and whirled around immediately, rage pouring from him. Still cursing, he came at Stephen, punching.

"Stop!" Jessie screamed. She looked around frantically for help and caught sight of Burley and Jim entering the lumberyard. They stopped, interested, and began to watch the fight. Jessie wanted to scream at them for their stupidity. Why didn't they do something? Didn't they realize what was going to happen? Not even glancing toward the fight, she hurried down the stairs and pushed her way through the spectators to get to Owens. "Burley! Burley, please, you've got to stop it. He'll kill him!"

Burley shrugged. "That's no loss to the world. I never did like him anyway."

Jessie's mouth dropped open in horror. "No! You can't mean that. He's Joe's son! Sam's brother."

Burley gave her an odd look. "I didn't mean Ferguson. I was talkin' 'bout that bastard Grissom. Looks ta me like Ferguson's goin' ta clean his clock. Ain't that right, Jim?"

The Indian grunted his agreement, intent on the fight.

Still Jessie stared. "What? You mean Stephen's—" She whirled around. She couldn't see through the tightly packed crowd. She scrambled up onto the gate to see the fighters.

There was a livid red spot on Stephen's cheekbone that would soon turn into a bruise. But Frank Grissom's face was far worse—bruised and smeared with blood, one eye swelling badly. He was huffing like a locomotive, while Stephen was barely breathing hard. He danced in and out, dodging Grissom's heavy fists while he jabbed and punched. He was fast, and his fists hit hard. Grissom looked dazed, and he swung wildly, his blows rarely landing.

Burley was right. Stephen was winning the fight!

It was difficult to absorb that fact; it was so completely the opposite of what she had expected.

"Damn good fighter," Burley commented beside her. "I reckon he must have trained for it." He chuckled. "Well, that'll surprise ol' Sam, I guess."

No more than it surprised her, Jessie thought, numbly watching as Stephen hammered at Grissom. Burley was right. Stephen must have studied with a professional. She had seen men get into countless brawls over the years. Some were better than others, but she'd never seen a man, even Sam, who fought with Stephen's precision and speed.

Stephen landed a hard right to Grissom's jaw, and the other man staggered and fell heavily to the ground. He didn't get up. Silently, calmly, Stephen rolled down his sleeves and retrieved his coat and jacket from the man who had held him. All around him the ring of people stood, openmouthed, staring at the body of Frank Grissom stretched out on the ground. Stephen could barely restrain a chuckle at the looks of amazement on everyone's face. It was clear that no one had expected him even to put up a decent fight, let alone knock out the local bully.

He climbed the stairs to the mill entrance and looked back. "Now, I'm ready to work. Who else wants to earn an honest dollar?"

"I'm with you, Ferguson!" shouted a man in the crowd below. "Hell, anybody can see you're ol' Joe's son, through and through."

"Good. Then let's get to it." He turned and strode through the door, and the men pushed through behind him.


"Sit still!" Jessie snapped, dabbing at the scrape on Stephen's cheek. "I'm just putting some medicine on you, for Pete's sake. You'd think that after you'd whipped Frank Grissom into the ground, a little sting wouldn't bother you."

"Ow! Don't you think you're applying that a trifle roughly?"

"Don't be such a baby." Jessie gave his face a final dab and stepped back. "There."

"I'd rather face ten Frank Grissoms than one woman with a medicine bottle." Stephen grinned and slid off the desk.

Jessie grimaced and slammed the bottle down.

"You know, one might almost think that you were sorry I didn't lose that fight," he told her teasingly.

She shot him a flashing glance. "That's silly. Of course I didn't want you to lose."

"You don't act like someone who's happy."

"I'm happy. I'm very happy." She stalked to her desk, then whirled to face him. "Why didn't you tell me?"

"Tell you what?"

"That you could fight like that? Why, I'd almost think you earned your living doing it."

"Hardly. I doubt I could even stay in the ring with a professional pugilist. But I did study it when I was at Princeton." He struck a pose. "The noble art of self-defense. I had an excellent teacher. We used the Marquis of Queensbury rules, of course. But the tactics are the same, even when you're in a street fight."

"You knew you could whip Grissom."

He shrugged. "I guessed it. The brief sparring match we had in this office told me what kind of a fighter he was. He depends on his strength. He has no speed. He gets in close and batters his opponent. I knew that if I made him move, if I avoided his punches, I could get in enough blows of my own to eventually get the best of him. If nothing else, I'd tire him out."

"But you didn't bother to tell me! Why? Did you want me to worry? I guess you thought it was really funny when I pulled a gun to protect you from him."

"No. I didn't think it was funny. Jessie...what is it? Are you mad because I didn't tell you earlier?"

"Oh, no! Why should I be mad? Just because you didn't bother to inform me that you could defend yourself against that brute. Just because you let me worry and stew about how to make sure Grissom didn't jump you and beat you into a pulp. Just because—"

"All right, all right. I'm sorry. I didn't realize it would upset you so."

"Upset me! Damn it! I was scared today! I thought for sure that I was going to see you beaten to death right in front of my eyes. I could picture the blood all over you, and—" Her voice broke, and she turned away.

"Oh, Jessie..." Stephen came up behind her and put his hands on her arms. He leaned down to rest his cheek against her hair. "I never thought. It was stupid of me. I didn't realize you cared."

Her heart began to hammer in her chest. His breath ruffled her hair, and she felt it along every nerve ending in her body. "Not care!" she exclaimed, trying to keep her voice even. She *would not* let him affect her so. She had promised herself that she wouldn't get herself in this position again. She had been furious with him only moments before. How could she now feel as if her bones were melting and all she wanted was to turn in his arms and press her body against his? In the past few minutes she had flown from fear to anger and now to desire. It was all too fast for her. She felt breathless and shaken and vulnerable. It wasn't a way she was used to feeling.

"Stephen, please." She pulled away from him.

Stephen's arms fell away from her quickly. He had gone to her and held her so instinctively that he hadn't really realized what he was doing. He recalled his vow to stay away from her. How soon he had broken it! He was going to have to be much more disciplined from now on if he intended to keep his promise.

The problem was that she had felt so good in his arms. He had been flushed with victory, still pumped full of energy and excitement. He had wanted so much to share it with her, to make her smile and laugh and enjoy his winning as he did. It had seemed right to hold her, and for that moment everything had been perfect. But now his arms were achingly empty. The knowledge that he was doing the correct and honorable thing didn't begin to fill the void.

He turned away, shoving his hands into his pockets because it was difficult to keep them from reaching for Jessie. He cleared his throat. "I'm sorry. It won't happen again." For a moment there was silence.

Then Jessie said in a businesslike voice, "Well, we'd better decide what we're going to do now, since we no longer have a foreman. How will we keep the mill running?"

Stephen turned, relieved to have a topic to pursue. "I don't think we'll find that there's another man who can do the job equally well, so we'll simply have to make do without a foreman. We'll keep a close eye on the men ourselves. After all, these jobs are skilled. The men know what they're supposed to do. The foreman is there to make sure they work and to resolve whatever problems might arise. I think for a few days, until Father's better, you and I could do that. You know all the facets of the business, don't you?"

Jessie nodded. "Yes. I know how everything works and what everyone is supposed to do, though many of the jobs require such strength that I've never done them. I'd know if the workers were shirking or doing something wrong. But the problem is that they won't want to take orders from me."

"But they will from me. I've earned their respect in the quickest way possible—beaten the man they feared. So if you need to order someone to do something, I'll do it. We'll be a team, and together we ought to be able to fill one man's shoes, don't you think?"

Jessie thought of spending all her time with Stephen for the next few days, working closely with him. It was exciting and scary. She wasn't sure she could handle it. Yet she knew she wouldn't pass it up for anything in the world.

"All right," she replied, hoping that what she felt didn't show on her face. "Let's do it."

Jessie and Stephen spent most of the next two days together, until Joe finally regained consciousness. Unfortunately, he was unable to give them any information about the person who had attacked him. He had heard noises in the mill and gone to investigate, and someone had struck him down from behind with a heavy blow to his head. Joe remained weak, foggy and plagued with violent headaches for several more days and was unable to return to work, so Jessie and Stephen continued to carry on the business for him.

They walked through the mill several times each day, checking on the speed and quality of the work. To Jessie's surprise, the men worked as well as they had when Frank Grissom was overseeing them. If anything, they seemed to go a little faster. Perhaps they were doing it because they liked Joe and were aware of his financial problems. Or maybe it was more pleasant to work without Grissom's presence. But she also was sure that the men felt respect for and confidence in Stephen, despite the fact that all of them knew more about sawing lumber than he did. Jessie had thought that Stephen would be remote and dignified around the men, but she found that he had a friendly, easy manner, though he always retained a certain bearing that proclaimed him the man in charge.

Every moment that Jessie didn't have to spend working she spent trying to teach Stephen the business. She took him through the mill, explaining each process. Though Joe had taken him on a tour of the sawmill before, he hadn't shown him everything in such detail. She showed him the bookkeeping records, the payroll work and the correspondence that constituted most of her job. She explained who the mill's customers were and how much each usually bought, and she showed him the mill's bills for various expenses.

Fortunately, Stephen was sharp and caught on quickly. Also, he clearly had a base of business experience that enabled him to grasp "all those damned number things," as Joe called them. Stephen enjoyed learning the business. In fact, he soon had ideas for improving it buzzing around in his head.

For Stephen, perhaps the headiest, most wonderful sensation came from working so closely with Jessie. They worked together well, each one often seeming to sense what the other was thinking, and they spent endless hours discussing things. One of the things Stephen had always liked about Elizabeth was that she was a woman he could converse with intelligently, but even she had been bored by conversation about the steamship line. But Jessie was happy to talk about the mill—or dozens of other things that he had never dreamed of discussing with a lady, such as his interest in boxing, or mechanical things. She even asked him to draw a diagram and explain the workings of the mill's steam engine to her, and they were lost in the subject for one entire evening, oblivious to the fact that everyone else had left the mill long ago and that they were missing supper.

At night they often went back quietly to the mill to stand their watch for the culprit who had hurt Joe and tried to wreck his business. They had collected a group of four trusted men besides themselves and set up watch in three groups of two. Stephen and Jessie took the first shift each night, sitting silently in the darkened mill or talking in low whispers. Nothing untoward happened, but Stephen found that he enjoyed his time in the quiet dark with Jessie. It seemed almost as if they were the only people in the world; everyone and everything else were far away.

He couldn't deny that he was happy, though he felt guilty for feeling that way when Joe was ill and they were struggling to save his business—not to mention the fact that his brother and his own fiancée still had not arrived. Still, he awoke every day with a sense of excitement and eagerness. There were times when he daydreamed about remaining in Nora Springs. He imagined waking every morning to the fresh, pine-scented air and walking to work at the mill. He would buy into the business with Joe and Sam and spend the rest of his life here. He would marry Jessie and build a beautiful house for her. He would...

But it was only a dream. In reality it couldn't happen. Because in reality Elizabeth would be arriving any day now, and he would be marrying her, as he had promised. There would be no happy life with Jessie in Nora Springs or anywhere else.

That realization kept him in constant turmoil. He had never known before how important a woman could become to a man, how he would rack his brain for a witty remark just to see her smile, or how just the sight of her could raise his spirits. But that was how he felt about Jessie. He wanted to be with her all the time, and when he wasn't with her, he thought about her. He loved to watch her, to talk to her, to see her flash him a grin. He loved her thick red hair and her eyes as blue as the Montana skies. He loved, in short, everything about her. All the things he had once found irritating or even horrifying now struck him as endearing, intriguing, challenging.

So, loving her and placed by fate in direct contact with her daily, yet having to refrain from caressing her, kissing her or telling her of his feelings, was torture for Stephen. He found himself infected with a strange possessiveness; he wanted to snarl at any man who stood too close to Jessie or looked at her with too much interest. He couldn't stop himself from watching her as she worked. When she stood or walked, his eyes were drawn like magnets to her slender, shapely legs, perfectly delineated in the worn denim trousers, and his hands ached to reach out and slide over the pert curve of her derriere. Inevitably his thoughts became more and more lustful, until he was thinking of sliding his hand between her legs and up the smooth cloth all the way to the top, and then of unfastening the trousers and peeling them down, his fingers exploring her soft flesh. By that time, of course, he had become so heated that it took several minutes of concentrating on numbers before he could even decently leave the concealment of his desk.

Always, without ceasing, even when he wasn't clutched in the hot talons of desire, there was a low, constant thrumming in his blood, a banked fire ready to flame up at the slightest provocation. Stephen had never known such tormenting, insistent passion before, a lust strengthened and multiplied by the love he felt for Jessie. Before this, he would have scoffed at the idea of such desire. But now he knew exactly how real it was and how much he was at its mercy.

He would have been astounded to learn that Jessie was suffering much the same torture that he was. She had known that she desired Stephen, but she hadn't even guessed that she loved him until his fight with Grissom. Then, with fear and panic surging through her, blinding her to what was happening in the fight, she had realized that she had fallen in love with Stephen. It had been easier to deal with her desire.

How could she love a man who was so different from any she'd ever known, any she'd ever thought she could love? What about Sam? She had believed for years that she was in love with him. Had it not been true? Worst of all, how was she to control this alien, explosive feeling?

She spent time sifting through her emotions, trying to figure them out. When she was fourteen or so, she had developed a crush on Sam. The intense emotion had quickly worn itself out, but she had continued to love him. Jessie realized now that the love she had felt for Sam had not been romantic love, as she had thought. She had been naive and inexperienced. What she had felt for him didn't have the same spark, the same excitement and rushing joy, that blossomed inside her when she thought about Stephen. Perhaps she loved Sam more as a sister loved an older brother.

She looked at Stephen and remembered the man she had thought he was when she first met him. She had assumed he was idle, incompetent, weak and foppish. But he had shown her that he was tough and enduring. He had courage and determination. He was honorable; he was hardworking; he was inventive. The things she had held against him had been only appearances, not his inner spirit. She had simply been too prejudiced and set in her ways to see that. But now she knew that he was exactly the kind of man she could love.

All that was beside the point, of course. It didn't matter how much she loved him. The fact remained that he was engaged to another woman. No doubt he loved his Elizabeth; no doubt she was a beautiful, feminine creature who would not embarrass him in the elegant world in which he lived. Even if Elizabeth hadn't existed, Jessie knew that marrying Stephen was out of the question. He might desire her, but he would never accept anything less than a lady as his wife. And Jessie was not a lady, never would be. She couldn't live in the city, in his world. She couldn't wear skirts all the time and sit just so and keep her mouth shut about the things that were improper for a woman to have an opinion on—or even to know!

She had no chance of winning Stephen's love, or being his bride. And she had too much pride to settle for anything less! She would not allow herself to be his mistress, even if she did love him. She could not sleep with him. Therefore, she had to avoid getting into situations like the one the other night, when her passion had been so aroused that she hadn't even thought of stopping him. Unfortunately, she couldn't remove herself from temptation. What with working together and standing watch at the mill, they spent almost every waking minute of every day in each other's company. But Jessie was careful not to touch him, not to reach out and place her hand on his arm when she had something to show him, for example. She kept as much space as possible between them as they worked.

She had never dreamed it would be so difficult. There were times when Stephen would come and stand beside her, leaning over her, to see something she was working on. He would plant one of his hands flat on her desk and the other on the back of her chair, bending down so that his head was near hers. She could see the impossibly long curl of his eyelashes, the curve of his cheek, the faint shadow of his beard late in the afternoon, only inches away from her. She could smell the tang of his cologne and the subtler scent of his skin. She could feel his strength, his masculinity. And she longed to reach out and stroke her fingers down his face, to follow the curve of his eyebrows or the line of his mouth. She wanted to touch his thick hair, black as midnight. She wanted to stretch up the few inches it would take and press her lips against his.

She knew how his mouth would feel on hers, how warm and coaxing, how tender and passionate. She knew how his arms would tighten around her, pressing her into him, all the way up and down their bodies. He would pull her up out of her chair, his mouth digging into hers, and . . .

Then Jessie would shake herself out of her dream. She would tighten her fingers around her pencil and will her body to obey her head. After a moment Stephen would walk away, leaving her shaken to the core. She kept telling herself that with practice it would become easier. Instead, it seemed as if the opposite was true. With each passing day, she wanted him more.

The longer she was around Stephen, the more she talked and listened to him, the more she watched him, the more she fell in love with him. She saw him as he was: curt and harsh with a shirker, compassionate with an aging worker who could no longer keep up the pace of his job, smiling, swearing, frustrated, eager. And she loved him. At times he had an almost childish enthusiasm for learning this new business. At other times he exhibited a shrewdness that was deeper than that of most men twice his age. He was not a simple man; Jessie suspected that she could spend years with him and still discover new things about him. But she would never get that chance. Her time with Stephen was limited to mere days.

Her heart ached at the thought of letting him go, of watching him walk away with another woman. She wanted to reach out for him and pull him into her bed. She wanted to beg him to make love to her, to hold him and bind him to her in any way she could. Her attitude amazed her. Surely this was not really her, thinking of using her body, feminine trickery, *anything*, to keep a man with her. She wouldn't do it, of course. She couldn't live with herself if she did. She couldn't bear to face Stephen, knowing what an honorable man he was. But even the fact that she felt tempted was shocking to her. She would never have believed that she could feel such torment and longing for a man.

At night Jessie lay in her bed and thought about Stephen, dreamed of lying in his arms, and she smiled a little, secret smile. Then she would think of the long, lonely years stretching ahead of her, and she would turn her face into her pillow and weep.

# Chapter Fourteen

Jessie raised her head from the row of figures she was adding and stretched, rolling her head to ease the tension in her shoulders and neck. On the other side of the room Stephen chuckled. "Are the numbers beginning to cross your eyes?"

Jessie smiled. "No. Though they are getting blurry." She wasn't about to add that the long columns of figures in the ledger weren't the only things that had made her tense. She was all too aware of him sitting in the room; often this morning she had thought she felt his eyes on her, though she refused to look up. It was hard to keep her mind on her work when Stephen was around.

She made herself glance at him impersonally. It was harder to pull her eyes away. After a few days of working in the mill, Stephen had given up wearing his flawless suits, which were often covered with sawdust or spattered with dirt or grease by the end of the day. He had begun wearing the heavier, rougher clothes that most of the men wore. Today his legs were encased in denim, and he wore a flannel shirt with a heavy sweater over it. His hair was getting a trifle long and shaggy. He looked rougher, looser—happier.

That thought surprised her. She hadn't thought of Stephen as being unhappy when she first met him. But there was an elusive something in his face now—a sparkle in his eyes, a relaxation of his mouth, an expression of interest in his features—as if he enjoyed life. It had not been there before.

Realizing that she must have been staring, Jessie jerked her head away. She rose and walked to the window to cover her awkwardness. Suddenly she gasped. "Look!"

"What?" Stephen was by her side in an instant. "Why, it's snowing!"

Fat, puffy white flakes were floating down outside, most of them disappearing as they hit the ground.

"But it's too early." He turned his head toward Jessie. "Does it usually snow here this early?"

She shrugged. "Not usually, but sometimes there'll be a snow in late September or early October. I thought this morning that it looked like it might be snowing higher up in the mountains."

"I imagine it's beautiful here when it snows."

Jessie smiled. "Oh, yes. When the mountains are covered with white, and snow hangs on the pines and the firs, it's lovely—especially when it clears up, and the sky's blue, and the sun makes everything sparkle. Everything looks brand-new and clean then, even this dirty old mill." She turned impulsively and took his hand. "Come on."

"Where?"

"Outside." Jessie pulled him down the hall. By the time they reached the door, they were almost running, and they burst outside gasping and laughing as the frigid air hit them.

They hurried down the steps and into the yard, away from the protection of the building. Snowflakes splashed them, wet and cold. Jessie tilted her head back to let them catch her full in the face. Stephen watched her. Her cheeks were pink with the cold, her skin glowing. The snowflakes kissed her skin and clung to her eyelashes. She was beautiful, and he thought of kissing the snowflakes from her face. He could almost taste her warm skin and the icy contrast of the snow, feel the wetness on his tongue, melting. Desire stabbed through him, so fierce that he almost trembled from the force of it.

Jessie opened her mouth to catch a flake on her tongue, and Stephen shivered, though not from the cold. At the moment all he felt was the heat rushing through him. He thought of kissing Jessie, his tongue following the snowflake into her mouth. He thought of opening her shirt and seeing the snowflakes touch her breasts, her nipples hardening in the cold. He would take each snowflake from her skin with his mouth, coming at last to her nipple....

He swallowed and whirled away. Lord! In another moment he would embarrass them both by seizing her and kissing her right here in public, where anyone walking by or glancing out the window might see them. Her reputation would be in shreds. And he might very well be lost to all reason.

He cleared his throat. "It's cold out here."

Jessie turned to him, making a face. "Sissy! I always knew you fancy Eastern dudes couldn't take it."

Her face was laughing and warm, teasing. He ached to respond. He wanted to grab her, knowing that she would start to run and he would chase her. He could feel the excitement bubbling in him, the laughter that would tumble out as they ran like children playing tag. But they weren't children, and he knew what he would do, what he would not be able to keep himself from doing, when he caught her.

He shook his head slightly. "Let's go inside."

There was disappointment in Jessie's face, and something else, too—the knowledge of why Stephen had stopped her. "All right."

Jessie turned and walked into the building with Stephen following her. He hated himself for causing the laughter and light to die out of her face. For all that he loved her, he had brought her nothing but unhappiness.

They worked through the rest of the afternoon, hardly speaking or looking at each other. Stephen immersed himself in some of the files, Jessie in her ledgers. Neither of them paid any attention to the snow falling harder and harder outside. However, late in the afternoon, the sharp whining of the wind around the corner of the building at last penetrated Jessie's consciousness.

She looked up, frowning. "Did you hear that?"

"What?"

"The wind." She pushed her chair back and walked to the window. What she saw outside was a different world from what it had been a few hours earlier. The snowflakes were no longer drifting down. They were falling so fast they almost obliterated the leaden sky, and a wind blew in spurts, swirling them around. She frowned. "The wind's really kicked up."

Stephen joined her at the window. Just as he did so, the office door opened and Will Coggan stepped in. Will was the head sawyer, the most highly skilled worker in the mill, and he had more or less assumed the role of representing the workers since Frank Grissom's abrupt departure. He nodded toward Stephen and Jessie. "Mr. Ferguson. Jess. The weather's gettin' right bad out there. We're thinkin' it's nigh onto a blizzard. Maybe we oughtta shut down early and get on home whilst we kin still see."

"Is it that bad?" Stephen asked.

"Yes, sir, I'm afraid it is."

"Then close it down, of course. Let the men go home."

"Yes, sir. Thank you, Mr. Ferguson."

Coggan hurried out the door, and Stephen turned to Jessie. "Perhaps you should go, too."

"I'll wait for you. I know the way better."

Stephen stared. "Really, Jessie, I'm not a complete fool. I've walked the route a few times now."

"No, don't take it that way. I know you're anything but a fool." For a moment her eyes rested on his face in a soft, caressing way that made his heart speed up. "But you don't know how disorienting a blizzard can be. Things get confused with all that snow whipping around. It's easy to get lost, even right on the street."

Stephen still looked a little disbelieving, but he said only, "All right. We'll both go. Let me put up the files."

While Jessie closed her ledger books and straightened her desk, Stephen replaced a stack of files in the cabinet. He went to his desk to pick up the stack he had not yet read and glanced at the top file. Written in his father's large, scrawling handwriting were the words "Moore Note." Stephen's hand paused in the motion of picking up the stack of files. He frowned at the folder for a moment, then reached for the file and opened it.

"What did you say the banker's name was?"

"The president of the bank? Elias Moore. Why?"

"I'm not sure." Stephen flipped aside a page of numbers and began to read the legal-looking documents behind it. "There's something strange here."

"What?" Jessie walked over to him, intrigued. "Something about the loan?"

"Yeah. Didn't you say the loan was with the bank?"

Jessie nodded. "Sure. That's where Joe's always gotten money."

"Not this time."

"What? What are you talking about?"

"Look." He held out the file for her to read. "See this? It's a promissory note signed by Joseph Ferguson, but it's not made out to the bank. It's to Mr. Elias Moore personally. And see the deed of trust?" He flipped the note up to expose the security agreement. "This property is put up as security for that loan. To Elias Moore, not the bank."

"I don't understand."

"I'm not sure I do, either. Here, hold this." He shoved the file into her hands and strode over to the filing cabinet. He pawed in the drawer for a moment, then pulled out another brown folder. He opened it and quickly flipped through it's contents. "Here it is. The note to the bank was cancelled earlier this year. July 6."

"That's when he added to the loan. When the saw blade broke, and he had to borrow more money to replace it."

"Then he must have signed a new note to replace the old one." He turned the pages, his eyes scanning them quickly. "Yes! Here's a letter from Elias Moore explaining that the bank cannot add to the present loan, as the security is insufficient. But he knows Joe Ferguson and knows that he will repay the debt, so he offers to lend him the money *personally*."

Jessie snorted. "I'll bet it's at a higher rate of interest. That old goat never did anyone a favor."

"No. It's at the same rate." Stephen looked up at Jessie. "Moore isn't a friend of my father's?"

"No. I mean, they've done a lot of business over the years, but that's all. Joe doesn't especially like him. In fact, he usually calls him an old skinflint."

"I think we're onto something."

"What? I don't follow you. What difference does it make whether the bank or Mr. Moore gave Joe the loan?"

"It could mean a great deal of difference." Stephen took the file she held and put both folders on the desk. In his excitement, he took her hands in his. "Remember the other day when we were talking about who might want to ruin my father's business? You said that the bank would get it if they foreclosed because he couldn't repay the note. But it seemed too crazy, remember?"

"Of course. Why would anyone go to all that trouble and take all that risk just so a bank could get a piece of property? I mean, the whole bank couldn't be in on a conspiracy to ruin Joe."

"Right. Even if Elias Moore would profit from his business getting the property, it's still very indirect. But it's an entirely different thing if he has made the loan himself. *He* gets the mill if he forecloses, not the bank."

"Of course! That makes it much more likely! It gives Moore a better reason." Jessie's face lit up; then she frowned. "But Elias Moore? I can't see him creeping around in the dark dismantling steam engines or breaking saw blades—or hiding in the brush and ambushing us, either."

"It doesn't have to be him doing it. He's a wealthy man. He can hire someone."

"Who?"

"I don't know. Maybe someone with a grudge against your father. Or just someone without scruples."

"You think you know who, don't you?"

"I have no way of knowing, but I suspect someone, yes."

"Who?"

"The person who's been a troublemaker ever since I arrived here. A man who covets you and probably resented Joe and Sam for standing between him and what he wanted."

"Frank Grissom?"

He nodded.

"But why? If he stopped it, he wouldn't get paid—oh, of course. If Moore was paying him enough, he wouldn't care about his salary."

"And if anything happened to Joe or Sam, he'd have the added benefit of getting you."

Jessie snorted. "No man would do something like that to have me."

"No?" Stephen glanced at her, and suddenly the light in his brown eyes was hot. "I think there are any number of things a man would do in order to have you."

Jessie suddenly found it difficult to breathe. She swallowed and glanced around, trying to think of something to say. The room was silent around them; she could hear the blood thrumming in her ears. Then she realized how odd it was to hear the quiet in this room. "The machines are off. I forgot, everyone must be gone."

"Yes." Stephen dropped his eyes from her face. "I'm afraid I got so interested in the files I forgot what we were doing."

"We probably should leave now—the snow."

Stephen nodded and glanced at the large clock on the wall. "Of course. We've been here much longer than I thought." He set the files in one of the cabinets and locked the drawer.

They pulled on their coats and hats and left, carefully locking the office behind them. They walked to the front door, and Jessie reached out to push it open. It didn't budge. She turned the handle again and pushed harder. The door opened a few inches, then slammed shut again in her face.

"What the devil?" Stephen asked, coming up to help her.

"It's the wind. It's gotten worse. It must be blowing against the door."

Stephen put his hands on the door and pushed against it with her, and it began to open. Suddenly it snapped wide open, nearly breaking its hinges, and Stephen and Jessie tumbled into the snow. It was already thick on the ground and stairs, and it swirled around them blindingly.

Stephen bit back an oath. "I can hardly see a thing."

"I know." Jessie had to cup her hands around her mouth to make her voice carry to him in the wind. She groped forward to the railing and began to carefully feel her way down the stairs. Behind her Stephen struggled to close the door. When he turned, Jessie was nowhere in sight.

"Jessie? Jessie, where are you?"

"Right here!" she called from the stairs. "I'm three steps down."

"I can't even see you!"

"Feel your way down with your feet and hold tight to the railing."

"That's fine here, but what about when we reach the yard?"

"Maybe it'll be a little clearer down there."

Stephen doubted that, but he shrugged and followed Jessie down the steps. When at last he reached the ground, he was able to see Jessie who was standing just in front of him, her hand around the bottom post of the rail. She looked at him, and he could see the doubt in her eyes.

"It's bad!" she shouted through cupped hands.

The icy wind cut through Stephen's coat and the sweater beneath. He already felt chilled to the bone. He wondered if he'd be able to reach Mrs. Randall's house before he froze. "Can you find your way?" he yelled.

"I'm not sure." Jessie edged away from the stairs. The swirling, stinging whiteness swallowed her up.

Icy, unreasoning fear clenched around Stephen's heart when she disappeared. "Jessie!"

"Here!" Stephen couldn't tell how far away she was. In another moment she appeared in front of him. "It's no use! Go back!" She motioned up the stairs.

"What? But—" Stephen realized the futility of discussing their situation out here in the cold and wind, and he closed his mouth and turned to climb the stairs.

It was as slow going up as it had been going down, and it seemed to take even longer to pry the front door open wide enough for them to squeeze through. Inside, they stamped their feet and brushed at their clothes to get rid of the snow, shivering in delayed reaction to the cold.

"We can't make it," Jessie said, her teeth chattering slightly.

"But we have to."

"I can't see a blessed thing. Even knowing the way home as well as I do, I'm not sure I can keep on track. We could walk a few steps off course and get so muddled we would wind up freezing to death right on the street. Believe me. It would be like asking to get killed to try to walk home in this. We'll have to wait until it stops, or at least slows down."

Stephen thought of spending hours alone with Jessie; he couldn't stand the temptation. He started to protest that they could make it, but then he remembered the fear that had seized him when she had disappeared in front of him in the snow. She could get killed trying to get through the blizzard. It was insane to risk that. He nodded. "Of course."

They went to the office, and Jessie lit the lamps. Stephen stoked up the fire in the cast-iron stove and added more wood to it. "Well, at least we have plenty of wood for the fire," he joked lightly, sweeping his hand toward the lumberyard outside. "We won't have to freeze."

Jessie smiled slightly. "That's true. But I'm afraid it doesn't help my stomach." She patted her middle. "I'm already hungry." She, too, was very aware of the fact that they were the only two people in the place and that it could be hours, perhaps the whole night, before the snow and wind died down enough for them to make another attempt to leave. She wanted to keep the light, inconsequential chatter going.

"I am, too, but I imagine we won't be here long enough to starve."

"No." She glanced around. "I suppose, since we're stuck here, we could get back to work."

"Yes. You're right. I'd like to look over those notes again more carefully."

The two of them settled down to work. Jessie found it difficult to concentrate on her figures, however. The room was unnaturally quiet. She was used to the pounding of the machines and the steam engine, and the high-pitched whine of the huge buzz saw. The complete silence made her even more acutely aware of Stephen's presence. She could hear his every movement—each stirring in his chair, each rustle of a page turned, each sigh from his lips.

"How're you doing?" she asked, turning to look at him, unable to sit still any longer and pretend to be adding up numbers. She had to talk to him; anything was better than this nerve-racking waiting.

Stephen shrugged. "There's really nothing here that we didn't see before."

"There's still something I don't understand. Why would he want the mill? How would he profit? Mr. Moore doesn't know anything about lumber or running a mill. He doesn't know the men. Why wouldn't it be a better deal for him to collect the interest?"

"You're right. It'd make more sense if there was someone who wanted to buy it at a high price." Stephen sighed and pinched the bridge of his nose. "I'm through reading, anyway. The lamps don't provide enough light."

He was right. The light from the windows was growing even dimmer as evening approached, and their two lamps made only small glowing circles in the huge darkness of the room. The office simply wasn't equipped for the nighttime work.

Jessie closed her ledger book. For a moment they looked at each other. She was afraid that he might hear the terrible pounding of her heart from where he sat. Why did being alone with him have to have such an effect on her?

Suddenly she brightened. "I just thought of something! I'm so stupid. Why didn't I think of it earlier?"

"What?"

"Joe has a room downstairs. You know, he's been staying here the last few weeks. He brought in a stove and some furniture. I'd lay you odds he also has some food stashed there."

"You think so?" Stephen stood. "Let's check. At least it'll give us something to do."

After extinguishing one of the oil lamps, Stephen picked up the other one to light their way, and they ventured into the darkening hallway. At the end of the hall there was a small staircase down to the floor below. There, walled off from the machinery at the other end of the building, was a small hall with a few doors opening off it. One of them proved to be a supply room, and another was a small closet containing brooms, mops and cleaning materials. The third door led into a small room where someone had obviously been living, at least part of the time.

There was a round table with a single chair against one wall, and directly across from it was a set of shelves containing a few books and several jars and cans. In the center of the room stood a small Franklin stove, with wood piled beside it. There was also, across the back wall of the room, a narrow iron bed topped with blankets. Stephen's eyes went immediately to the bed, and he glanced away again just as quickly. Seeing the bed had brought flashes of thoroughly indecent pictures, all involving himself and Jessie, to his mind. He hoped the thoughts didn't show on his face.

Since he avoided looking at her, he didn't see that Jessie's reaction was much the same as his. A flush climbed in her cheeks, and she looked away from the bed, glancing at everything in the room except it.

Jessie went to the stove and began to build a fire. Stephen walked to the shelves, hoping to put the bed out of his mind, as well as the insidious, insistent thought that he and Jessie were alone in the building. "You're right. He does have some food. There's even a plate and some utensils. Let's see." He bent and began to pick up the jars and cans, examining them. "Beans. Pickled beets. Something I can't identify—and don't care to. Chokecherry juice. That doesn't sound too promising, does it?"

"Oh, no, chokecherries make good juice. Syrup and jelly, too. That looks like some of Ma's. That's wonderful—we need something to drink."

"I suppose." He gave the jar another doubtful look and set it down. "This appears to be preserves of some sort." He picked up a squat jar and read the label. "Barb. jelly?"

"Creeping barberry. That's Ma's, too. It makes delicious jelly. We can put it on these crackers. Look, a bowl of hard candies.'' She smiled. ''Joe obviously didn't want to pass the long nights without something to nibble on.''

''Doesn't make for a square meal, exactly, but at least we won't go hungry.''

They opened the jars and cans and put them on the table, then sat down to their odd repast. There was only one of everything, so they shared the plate, and Jessie took the spoon, Stephen the fork. Half the time they used their fingers. There was only one battered tin cup, which Jessie filled with chokecherry juice. She drank from it first and held it out to him, smiling, the juice slightly staining her lips. Stephen took the cup and drank from it, very aware of the fact that her lips had just touched it. He knew he should drink from the opposite side, but he couldn't bring himself to. He wanted even this hint of her taste.

It was an intimate meal. They couldn't rid their minds of the fact that the narrow bed was the major furnishing in the room. With only one chair, which Stephen politely gave to Jessie, he had nowhere else to sit except on the edge of the bed. At first he stood, but that was awkward, and besides, he would have to sit on the bed sometime. He couldn't spend the whole evening standing up or sitting on the cold, unwashed floor.

He watched Jessie eat, watched her lips part and her white teeth bite into a piece of what looked like crisp, uncooked okra. He could almost taste her mouth, almost feel it. It was all he could do to stop from running his tongue across his lips. He thought of her earlier this afternoon, catching a snowflake on her tongue, and of how he had wanted to kiss her, to feel the tantalizing combination of the warmth of her mouth mingling with the icy snow.

Jessie glanced at him. ''What?'' she asked doubtfully.

Stephen shook himself from his reverie. ''Pardon?''

''Why were you staring at me?''

''I was, uh, wondering what that was you were eating.''

''Oh. Pickled okra. Want one?''

He cocked an eyebrow. "I don't think so."

"Come on, try it." She smiled and held out the remainder of the okra to him.

His heart slammed in his chest. The thought of her feeding him was something he couldn't resist. "All right."

He opened his mouth, and she slipped the crisp morsel onto his tongue. Her fingers brushed his mouth, and he wanted to close his lips over her fingertips, to take them into his mouth, too, and slowly, gently...

Stephen turned his head away. He had to stop thinking like this. He would never last the evening if he continued to conjure up erotic images of Jessie. On the other hand, he couldn't imagine being this close to her for hours without conjuring up erotic images.

He chewed the tart, crunchy vegetable and swallowed. "Thanks. I think I'll stick to what I have on my plate."

"Coward." She held up a small, reddish-purple beet. "Sure you wouldn't like to try one of these?"

"It's pickled, too? No, thank you."

Jessie giggled. Beet juice was beginning to drip down her finger, and she scooped it up with her tongue. Desire sizzled through Stephen. All he could think of was that pointed pink tongue snaking across his skin.

Jessie bit into the beet, and the purplish juice stayed on her lips for a moment. Stephen clenched his hands on the bed beneath him to keep from leaning across and licking the drop from her lips. He could feel his mouth loosening, his blood pumping thick and hot through him, his manhood pulsing—the signals of his desire, the warning that it would soon carry him away if he wasn't careful.

"Come on." Jessie held out the beet again, almost to his lips. There was something a little hot and reckless in her eyes, too. She touched the food to his lips, moving it a little.

Stephen opened his mouth and seized the beet, and as he did, his tongue ran across her fingertips. Jessie's eyes widened a little. They continued to stare into each other's eyes, their breathing turning rapid and uneven. Then, silently, Jessie extended her fingers toward his mouth, bending them a little as if showing them to him. Traces of the purplish liquid still clung to the tips of one finger and her thumb.

Neither of them spoke, but their eyes burned into each other's. Still without a word, Stephen opened his mouth and closed his lips around her finger, sucking the drop of juice from it. His tongue circled her finger greedily, tasting the tartness and the salt and the unique taste of her. He turned to her thumb and did the same.

His heart was slamming wildly in his chest. He wanted to grab Jessie and pull her across his lap. He wanted to hold her and kiss her until she was limp and moaning in his arms. He wanted to roll onto the bed with her and make love to her so thoroughly that neither of them would ever forget it.

Jessie gazed into his eyes, unable to look away, her lips parting slightly. She wanted him to kiss her. She wanted to feel his hands on her body. She wanted—oh, a hundred things so wild and wanton she hardly knew what they were. But she knew how much her whole body hungered for them.

Stephen's eyes went to her lips. It was impossible to look at that soft, sensuous mouth and not want to kiss it. He wanted her so much that he felt as if he might explode. It was hard to breathe. Hard to think. "Ah...I...maybe we should check outside. See if the snow's died down."

Jessie nodded slowly. "Yes."

Neither of them made a move to leave.

Stephen stretched out his hand and laid his fingertips lightly on her jaw, and Jessie's eyes fluttered closed at the gentle, intensely sensual touch. His fingers drifted down her neck, and her skin flamed to life. He touched the hollow of her throat, where her flannel shirt met her skin, and paused for a moment; then his fingers moved lower, onto the shirt, down to the swell of her breast. Caressingly, his hand rounded her breast. Jessie moaned low in her throat.

"Jessamine." Her name sounded like poetry when he said it. "You are so damnably beautiful. A man could consign his soul to hell for you."

"I . . . wouldn't . . . ask that of you." Her breathing was labored and uneven.

"You don't have to ask." His hand tightened slightly, and his thumb rubbed across the center of her breast. His eyes glazed with desire. God, he had to touch her, had to taste her. Had to see her.

He reached out for her and pulled her into his lap. "Please stop me, Jessie. Stop me," he mumbled as he buried his face in her neck.

"I don't want to," she whispered, moving her head so that more of her neck was exposed to his predatory mouth.

It was an invitation he hadn't the willpower to resist. With a groan, Stephen began to kiss the soft flesh of her throat, arching her back over his arm. His free hand came up to cup her other breast, kneading and stroking until her nipple was a hard button pressing through the cloth of her shirt. Jessie whimpered and squirmed on his lap. Passion burst white-hot in him, and suddenly he was past all hope of stopping.

He murmured her name over and over as his hand gripped the back of her neck and turned her lips to his. He kissed her fiercely, deeply, his tongue laying bold claim to her mouth.

Jessie quivered, and her hands curled into his shirtfront, holding on. They kissed again and again, their mouths clinging hungrily, tongues twining in a dance of love. Stephen pulled back, sucking air into his lungs, and for a moment he just looked at her, drinking in the sight of her face, warm and relaxed with love, her eyes glowing up at him. There was love in her face, and beauty, everything a man could ever hope for in a woman.

His fingers went to the long braid that hung down her back and tugged loose the tie that held it. He sank his hand into her hair, separating the thick strands until her hair tumbled down in waves, filling his hand and spilling over it like molten fire. It was almost surprising that her tresses felt cool against his flesh, not hot. He clenched his fist, crushing the soft hair between his fingers.

"I love your hair." He brought his hand to his lips and gently kissed her hair. "I love it down. It's like fire. Like satin."

He combed his fingers through it. It fell past her waist, long and thick. He nuzzled into the hair at her neck, burying himself in its scent and texture. Passion pounded through him, heavy and hard. He knew in the back of his mind that the next morning he would regret what he was doing. But he also knew, with an instinctive, unthinking certainty, that right now there was no chance that he would turn away and not make love to her. In this moment she was his, and he was hers, in the most primitive and basic way. There was no room in him right now for refinement or courtesy or codes of ethics; there was only a driving need to love her that pushed everything else aside.

Stephen kissed Jessie's hair, her neck, her ear. His breath, hot against her skin, sent shivers running through her. Tentatively, her hands slid up his chest and onto his neck, gliding up the column of his throat to where his hair brushed her fingertips. She wasn't sure what to do; she felt clumsy and inexperienced. But she knew she had to touch him, had to feel his skin beneath her hands.

Stephen drew in his breath sharply at her touch, and Jessie froze. "No," he murmured hoarsely. "No, don't stop. Please."

"I wasn't sure. I wanted to—touch you."

"I want you to." His reply was shaky. "It's just—" He drew another breath. "It feels so good. Ah, Jessie..." He moved his head against her hand, seeking her caress.

Jessie moved her hands into his hair. It was thick, and softer than she had thought it would be. She combed her fingers through it, letting the strands slide across her skin, delighting in the sensations that ran through her.

Stephen nuzzled her neck, and his lips slipped downward to the hollow of her throat. His tongue rimmed the indentation and dipped into it. But when his mouth moved lower, he was stopped by her shirt. His hand went to the top button, pausing to curve over her breast on the way. He glanced up at her face, and there was a question in his eyes.

"Love me," Jessie whispered, answering his unspoken question, assuring him that she wanted him to take away her maidenhood. She raised her lips to his, murmuring again, "Please love me."

He kissed her long and deeply. His fingers shook a little on her buttons as he unfastened them. Jessie dug her fingers into his hair, passion surging through her, and she kissed him hungrily. His mouth dug into hers as if he would consume her. Jessie began to tremble, and she clung to him, awash in a sea of emotions and sensations that were entirely new to her.

Stephen parted her shirt and pushed it back on her shoulders, then raised his head and looked down at her. Beneath the shirt Jessie wore a plain white cotton chemise with only a single narrow strip of lace across the top. He had seen sheerer undergarments than this, and ones far frothier with lace or fashioned of the finest silk. But none had ever stirred him as this simple shift did. The cotton drifted across her breasts, exposing the soft, tremulous tops, and beneath the material the darker circles of her nipples showed, the tight little buds pressing up against the cloth.

He drew a calming breath, forcing himself to go slowly. He bent forward and drew a circle around her nipple with his tongue. Jessie stiffened, arching up a little. His tongue continued to play with the fleshy button through the cloth, teasing it into greater hardness. Softly he blew upon the wet fabric, and again Jessie tightened all over, a tiny moan escaping her lips. He went to the other nipple to work the same magic on it. Jessie stirred restlessly, moving her legs. He slid his hand down her stomach and between her thighs.

She made a sound of surprise low in her throat, but her legs closed around him, squeezing.

He lifted his head to look at her. Her eyes were closed, and her head lolled back. He moved his hand rhythmically between her legs, and her hips rolled with him. Where the chemise was wet over her nipples, it was almost transparent, and he could see the buds clearly. They rose up, taut and eager, hard with the desire he had aroused in her.

His own desire swelled in him. He was hard and ready. He wanted to thrust into her immediately and ride out his passion. But he knew he must go slowly, for Jessie's sake. Sternly tamping down his desire, he slipped her shirt the rest of the way off her body. He pulled down the straps of her chemise, uncovering her breasts completely. For a moment he simply looked at her, drinking in the sight of the lush, rounded globes that he had been thinking about, dreaming about, for weeks. Then he bent and pressed his mouth against the soft, quivering flesh. He trailed kisses over the curve of her breast, moving ever closer to her nipple, until at last his lips closed around the throbbing, puckered flesh.

He pulled the bud into his mouth, sucking and stroking with his tongue, teasing until Jessie was writhing beneath him, her breath coming in ragged spurts. His hand went to the buttons of her trousers and unfastened them, then slipped into the hot, damp center of her femininity. Gently his fingers explored the slick folds of flesh and slipped inside her.

Stephen groaned. He was on fire, and it was the most exquisite torture to hold back. Jessie moved her hands restlessly over him, digging into his arms, his back, his hair. She lifted her hips and moved against his hand, seeking a deeper fulfillment. Stephen wasn't sure he could wait any longer. He had to be inside her, had to know her completely.

Abruptly he stood, setting her on her feet on the floor, and Jessie blinked at him. Her eyes were dark and dazed with passion, and she looked the very picture of a woman lost in the throes of desire. The image sent a shudder of longing through him, and he had to reach out and cup her breasts in his hands once more and caress the jewel-like tips. He bent and kissed each nipple lightly, then pulled away from her.

"Stephen? What—'' Jessie felt bereft and lost. Surely he could not mean to stop! He could not leave her like this, poised on the edge of—well, she wasn't sure what, but she knew it was something grand, something magnificent, something she wanted more than she'd ever wanted anything in her life. She was aching and empty inside.

Stephen yanked his sweater over his head and began to unbutton his shirt, his fingers fumbling in their haste. A smile spread across Jessie's face. He was stopping to undress. She watched him as he took off his shirt and dropped it on the floor. His chest was leanly muscled and covered with a sprinkling of curling black hair. She wondered what it would feel like to touch it. She thought of running her hands across his chest, of circling those small, flat, masculine nipples. Would they tighten and ache as hers did when he touched them?

He struggled to pull off his boots, still standing up, then shucked off the rest of his clothes. He stood before her completely naked. Jessie looked, her heart skittering around in her chest like a wild thing. He looked primitive and powerful, no gentleman now, but a man intent on claiming his woman. And Jessie felt in her a breathless eagerness to be that woman, to receive him and pleasure him and make him forever hers.

She held out her arms to him, and Stephen crossed the space between them in a single stride. He swooped her up in his arms and kissed her, a dizzying, eternal kiss. She clung to him as to an anchor in a spinning world.

He lowered her onto the bed and undressed her, his hands lingering over the soft, white flesh he revealed. His hunger was so great that he wanted to tear the garments from her, but her body was so beautiful that he could only move gently over it, pausing again and again to caress her.

At last she was naked, and he shifted on top of her. Jessie drew in her breath at the feel of his hard, masculine body stretched out full length against hers. He was all bone and muscle, so different from her, so excitingly different. She twined her arms around him, seeking to pull him even more tightly against her. She wanted more, wanted all of him.

Stephen entered her slowly and gently, restraining himself with great effort so that there would be little hurt to her. Jessie moaned, arching her neck. There was some pain, but far greater than that was the intense pleasure, the satisfaction of feeling him inside her. He filled the center of her ache and her emptiness, stretching her unaccustomed flesh. She dug her fingers into his bare back, breathing his name as she thrust her hips up, opening herself more fully to him.

He shuddered at her welcoming passion and had to pause for a moment to regain his shattered control. Then he began to move slowly, thrusting with long, unhurried strokes, building their passion ever higher. Instinctively Jessie moved with him, with a combination of innocence and passion that vaulted Stephen past all reason and control into a realm of white-hot, shattering sensation. He thrust into her wildly. Pleasure exploded deep in Jessie's abdomen and swept outward, undulating through her. Stephen cried out, shuddering, as he poured his seed into her. They clung to each other, lost together in a swirling, mindless ecstasy.

"Jessie," he murmured. "My love, my love."

## Chapter Fifteen

A shaft of light from the small window above the bed fell onto Stephen's face, and his eyelids fluttered open. He lay for a moment in groggy contentment. He was squeezed against the wall, a warm body snuggled against his. Red hair tumbled over the pillow beside him, and a few stray strands had drifted across his cheek. Jessamine.

He closed his eyes, luxuriating in the smell and feel of her, in the delicious, satisfied languor that permeated his body. They had awakened twice during the night, each time making love again. It was impossible to awake with his hand curved around Jessie's breast and not want to make love to her again. In fact, he wanted to right now.

But it was morning and light, and somehow it was no longer possible to hide from the truth. He must not make love to her. He had been the lowest form of scum to do it last night. He was engaged to Elizabeth, bound to her. He could not marry Jessie; he could only dishonor her.

And he had done that.

Stephen sighed and sat up, running his hands through his hair. What was he going to do? He could not refuse to marry Elizabeth. He had a duty to her.

He looked at Jessie, still asleep, red hair spilling over her naked white skin. He drew his hand along the curve of her spine and hip. How soft her skin was. How vulnerable she looked.

She belonged to him. She was his. He had taken her body, her innocence. He had a duty to her, too. But there was more than that. For a few moments, the two of them had been joined in a way he'd never known with any other woman, no matter how desirable or skillful she had been. In one shattering instant, he had really possessed her. And she had possessed him. It had been as if they were a single body, an entwined heart and soul. How could he possibly give that up and settle for a lifetime of something less?

He groaned, digging his fingers into his scalp. Damn it! Why had he done it? Why had he given in? He wasn't usually that weak.

But then, he had never before been tempted by Jessie. He had never been tested by love. He continued to look at her, and a small smile touched his lips. He couldn't regret what had happened between them. It had been the most beautiful night of his life, the most thrilling and satisfying. He wondered how he could live without ever experiencing it again.

On the other hand, how could he marry Jessie? Even if he were to ignore the deathbed promise he had made to Elizabeth's father, if he were to abandon her and his honor for the sake of love, he could not marry Jessie. They would never suit. They were too different. Why, hardly a day passed that they didn't have an argument about something. Jessie didn't even know how to have a genteel argument. She didn't freeze up or talk in a furious, low tone, as most of the women he knew did. She expressed herself loudly and often wound up yelling or pounding something or even, on occasion, picking up an object and throwing it on the floor—or at him. Her eyes flashed, and her cheeks turned red, and her fiery hair seemed to crackle. She didn't stop to consider propriety or the presence of anyone else within earshot.

Of course, there was also the fun of talking to her, of watching those fine eyes light up with excitement or anger, of listening to her clever ideas or the funny things she said. She was so easy to talk to, so easy to be with; there was no constraint or awkwardness with her. There were even times when he found that he enjoyed their fights.

But that wasn't enough. Love wasn't enough. He had to think of how Jessie would feel. He couldn't marry her and take her home. She would never fit into his world; she wouldn't want to. She would be miserable in St. Louis or New York, as miserable as his mother had been here.

Careful not to awaken Jessie, he slipped out of bed and dressed. It was terribly cold in the room, and he went to the small metal stove and stirred up the coals inside. They sparked and glowed red hot, and he stuffed in a few sticks of kindling, then set some larger logs on top of them. Holding his hands out to the fire, he waited for it to warm him. And he thought.

With each passing moment, his guilt weighed more heavily upon him. His actions had been unpardonable. Lust, even love, was no excuse for the wrong he had done to both women. The two women in the world whom he loved. He had been foolhardy, selfish, unthinking.

By the time Jessie awoke, he had worked up an enormous case of self-hatred. He dreaded having to face her. In the sanity of daylight she was bound to regret what she had done. She was certain to despise him. Stephen didn't think he could bear to see her look at him with contempt.

When he heard her stirring, he was tempted to hurry out of the room. But he forced himself to stay. He deserved whatever she chose to do or say. After his base actions, the least he could do was let her vent her wrath on him. He made himself turn toward the bed.

Jessie's eyes were open, and she was watching him. Stephen thought he'd never seen anyone look as desirable as she did that morning. Her tresses were tumbled over the pillow and sheets, vivid against the blank white, and her eyes were big and luminous, the color of a spring sky. Her bare shoulders were visible, soft and curving, hinting at the naked body below. Even as contrite as he felt at the moment, Stephen couldn't suppress a sharp twinge of longing.

"Good morning," Jessie said softly. She felt shy and uncertain. It was strange to awaken naked in a room with a man. It was also exciting. Her body still ached a little in unaccustomed ways from what they had done last night. This man, in some ways still almost a stranger, knew her in a way that no one else in her life ever had. Ever would, for that matter, for Jessie was certain that she could never feel this way about any other man. Last night had been glorious and wild. Still, when she thought about what she had done, she couldn't help but blush. What did he think of her now? Had she been too bold, too brazen? Or had she been too inexperienced and clumsy? Last night he had seemed as enthralled, as dazzled, as passionate as she had been. This morning she wasn't so sure. She wanted reassurance.

"Good morning." Stephen's voice was low and rough, his words clipped. He sounded...almost angry. Jessie tightened up inside, bracing herself. "Jessamine, I—Lord, I'm sorry. I'm so sorry."

"Sorry?" Jessie sat up, which made her feel less vulnerable. She clutched the covers to her chest, covering her nakedness.

"Yes." Stephen looked away, unable to meet her eyes. "You must hate me."

"Hate you?" she repeated. She sounded like an idiot, she thought. A parrot!

"Yes. I quite understand if you cannot find it in your heart to forgive me."

"Forgive you for what?" Her voice sounded leaden.

"For—for what I did. For taking you. Despoiling you."

"Is that what happened?" She fought to keep the tears back. Was that how he viewed what had happened between them? Just lust and dishonor? To her it had been beautiful, thrilling; their lovemaking had seemed to touch her very soul. Yet Stephen apparently found it contemptible. "You were a blackguard out to steal my virginity from me?"

"Jessamine!" Her bluntness still had the power to startle him. "Of course not. I—" He stopped himself. This was no time for a declaration of love. That, too, would be the act of a scoundrel, to say he loved her when he could offer her nothing. It would only be self-serving; it wouldn't help her. "I'm sorry. What I meant was that to do what I did when I am affianced to another..."

Jessie's chin went a little higher. Her eyes were clear and dry, and her voice trembled only slightly as she said, "You are going to marry someone else. I knew that. I went into it with my eyes open. I wasn't exactly the victim of your wiles."

"You were an innocent. I was responsible. I knew. What I did was wrong. To place you in this kind of position, knowing that I could not do the honorable thing—it was despicable."

"The honorable thing!" Jessie flared. "Damn your eyes! I'm no obligation, no duty for you to perform so that you can still lay claim to the title of gentleman. Perhaps I was innocent physically. But I knew what I was doing. I was fully aware of the fact that you would not marry me. You love—Elizabeth." It was difficult for her to choke out the words. She had to pause a moment to take a deep breath. "I did not believe that being in your bed meant being your wife. You didn't deceive or seduce me. I wanted to. There's no need for you to do the honorable thing. I don't want you to. The fact is, I wouldn't be your wife if you had a gun to my head!"

Anger surged through Stephen, burning away his guilt and self-recrimination. "Is that right? You slept with me, yet you wouldn't marry me! What do you think that makes you?"

"A free woman!"

"Free! Alone is more like it."

"Maybe that's the only way a woman can be free."

Stephen was filled with a rage so intense, so fierce that he almost shook beneath its force. He wanted to roar, to grab Jessie and shake her until she admitted that she loved him, to force her to agree to be his wife. It was all he could do to keep himself from crossing the room and hauling her out of the bed. Instead, he swung around and slammed his fist against the wall. He stood for a moment, his back to her, battling his anger. The violence, the sheer magnitude of his feelings shocked him.

Finally, when he was sure he had himself under control again, he pushed himself away from the wall. Without turning to look at Jessie, he said in a flat tone, "I'll leave so you can dress. Then we'd better return to the house."

"Of course."

The evenness of her voice caused another small geyser of anger inside him, and he strode from the room, slamming the door behind him.

Jessie stared after him, filled with righteous indignation. Here she was absolving him from all obligation—how dare he think of her as a duty!—and all he did was get furious at her! It was enormously unfair. He acted as if she didn't care, as if *she* had hurt *him*. Yet *he* was the one who hadn't said a word about the beauty of what they had done, instead just talking about honor and obligation and how sorry he was. With a muffled, frustrated shriek, Jessie grabbed the closest thing to her, a book, and hurled it across the room. There was nothing else to throw, so she gripped the iron bedstead and shook it with all her might. Then she burst into tears and sagged against the headboard, weeping her heart out.

When Jessie joined Stephen in the office sometime later, she was white and silent. Neither of them said a word about what had happened last night or this morning; both were churning with new and volatile emotions, too confused to be able to speak coherently. They trudged home through the snow in a vast, uncomfortable silence, not even noticing the serene white beauty of the snow-covered town around them.

When they got back, Stephen was surprised to find that Amanda had little interest in their halting explanation of why they had been gone all night. "I figured that was what happened. I kept telling Joe you'd stay at the mill instead of trying to make it home through the blizzard. Come on up and see him. He's been worrying like a hen with one chick."

Joe was pacing the floor in the rear sitting room, and when Stephen and Jessie came in, he grinned widely and walked over to hug them both. Stephen tightened his arms around his father. He found himself wanting to pour out his troubles to Joe, but he reminded himself quickly that Joe was the last person he could tell about Jessie and what had happened. She was like a daughter to him.

Stephen stepped back. "How are you feeling?"

"Better. A lot better. Damn headaches have finally stopped. I'll be coming back to work now." He smiled and glanced toward Jessie's mother. "You haven't told them yet?"

Amanda blushed and shook her head. She crossed the room and slipped her hand into Joe's. "No. I'll let you."

Joe raised her hand to his mouth and kissed it. He looked at Stephen. "Amanda and me are gettin' hitched."

"Married!"

"Oh, Mama, that's wonderful!"

Jessie flew across the room and hugged her mother. Stephen looked surprised, then smiled and reached out to take Amanda's hand and bow over it in a courtly manner.

"I can't think of a more lovely addition to the Ferguson family," he told her. "I can only wonder why it took my father so long to ask you."

"I've been thinking about it ever since you came to town and told me about your ma." Joe shrugged. "I guess when I came to the other day, I realized how crazy I was to be shilly-shallying around about it."

"Congratulations." Stephen shook his father's hand. "I'm very happy for you."

Joe winked and squeezed his hand. "Thanks, son. Now, as soon as that rapscallion brother of yours gets back, we can have us a wedding."

"You can have a double wedding," Jessie suggested brightly, but there was a brittleness underlying her tone that caused her mother to glance at her sharply. "After all, when Sam gets back, he'll have Stephen's fiancée with him."

"Why, that's right." Joe was looking at his future wife and therefore didn't see the frozen expression on Stephen's face. "What do you say, Amanda? Shall we horn in on the young folks' hooplah? It'd be a bang-up celebration."

Amanda glanced at Stephen. "That's not really for us to say, is it, dear? Perhaps Stephen's fiancée wouldn't want to share such a precious moment."

"I'm sure it will be fine with Elizabeth," Stephen said tightly. "She's a very amenable woman." He couldn't keep from shooting Jessie a sideways glance. She was watching him, her mouth tight and her face as pale as a marble statue. She set her jaw even tighter at his words, and her eyes flashed. She whirled away.

"Well, I reckon I better find something suitably grand to wear for such an occasion," she commented and strode out of the room.

Amanda excused herself and slipped out after her daughter. Stephen let out a sigh and sat on the bed beside Joe.

"Anything wrong, boy?"

Stephen shook his head. "Of course not. I'm glad for you and Mrs. Randall." He paused. "Have you remembered anything about the man who attacked you?"

Joe shook his head disgustedly. "Nope. I wish I could. If I ever get my hands on that son of a bitch—"

"Why didn't you tell me?" Stephen asked quietly.

Joe sighed. "It wasn't anything against you. I just didn't want to worry you."

"You mean you were too proud to let me know you were having a problem."

Joe scowled. "I don't want any of your money, if that's what you're thinking of doing."

"Jessie told me you'd balk."

"What's the matter with that girl, anyway? She was acting awful peculiar a while ago, not like herself at all."

"Don't try to change the subject. I know you don't want any favors from a stranger. But it hurts that you consider me a stranger."

"It ain't that! And don't you go trying to manipulate me, neither. I'm not taking your money."

"Not even as a loan? I'll make the same arrangement you did with Moore—you can even put the mill up as security. Or I could buy into the company. There's nothing wrong with a third Ferguson having a share in Ferguson Mill, is there?"

Joe considered it. "Well, no, I reckon not. That is, not if Sam is agreeable to it. But what would you want with part of a mill so far away from where you live?"

"I've become rather interested in the business, actually. I wouldn't mind li—" He paused and seemed to mentally pull himself back. What was he thinking of? He couldn't live here. There was Elizabeth. There was his business. There was his obligation to his grandfather. "You're right. I would be far away from it. However, I think I could trust you and Sam to manage my share for me."

"Of course you could."

"Then it's settled." Quickly Stephen explained his plan to conceal his intentions of paying off the note in the hopes that they could catch the man who had engineered the mill's "accidents."

With the matter settled, he started to leave the room, but Joe stretched out a hand to him. "No. Don't go yet. There's something troubling you, isn't there? Why don't you tell me about it? Maybe I can help."

Stephen shook his head. "No. It's nothing."

"Is it the young lady you're worrying about? Your fiancée? Are you afraid she might be trapped out in this snow?"

"No." Stephen's eyes widened. "Good God, no! I hadn't even thought about it!" He was flooded with guilt. He hadn't even thought once about Elizabeth being caught in the blizzard. "If they were caught outdoors, they could have frozen by now. I must go look for them." He started toward the door, then stopped. "No. I haven't the slightest idea where to look. A search party, then. We should send out a search party."

"Now, now, I didn't mean to get you all het up. Just calm down. What I was trying to say was that you didn't need to worry. Sam's no fool. He knows this country. He'd have seen the blizzard coming. He wouldn't have missed the signs, and he'd take shelter. A cabin, a cave . . . if nothing else, he'd build a lean-to. She'll be all right."

"Are you sure?"

"Positive. Think I'd be so calm about my son lying out in the snow somewhere frozen? They're all right. The storm will just delay them for a while. But you'll see—give 'em a few days, and they'll come ridin' in, big as you please. No need to send out anybody to look for them. Nobody knows these mountains as well as Sam. Besides, we don't know where in tarnation they are. Burley said they had to stay off the road 'cause of the bridges.''

"Good. Thank heaven."

Joe studied his son shrewdly for a moment. "Well, if that wasn't it, what was making you frown so? Something's gotten under your skin like a burr."

Stephen shook his head. "It's nothing I can talk about."

"It's Jessie, isn't it?"

Stephen's head shot up. "How did you know?"

"Lucky guess. But it looks like I was right. What is it, boy? Did something happen between you two last night?"

Stephen cast him an agonized glance. "Yes. You'll hate me—and with good reason. I took advantage of the situation last night. Of Jessie."

Joe stared. "You aren't meaning to tell me that you forced her!"

"Good God, no! What do you think I am!"

"Then what happened? She was willing?"

"Yes." Stephen's voice was so low that Joe had to strain to hear it.

"It doesn't sound like it's all your fault. Sounds like Jessie had something to do with it, too."

"That's what she said." Stephen sounded exasperated. "But, damn it, I should have been more responsible. I should have kept the situation under control."

Joe smiled slightly. "I'd like to see anybody try to control Jessie. You know, son, I think you'll find women out here are a mite more independent than what you're used to. Especially Jessie. She's used to making her own decisions."

Stephen stared. "But don't you care? Aren't you angry with me? What I did was dishonorable."

"Of course I care. I'm fond of Jessie. But I know she does what she wants. And I know that when a man's in love, he doesn't always think straight." He paused, and his face became uncertain. "You do love her, don't you?"

"Of course I love her! How could I not love her? She's beautiful and generous and unaffected. She's strong, smart, funny. I want her so much I can hardly think straight when I'm around her. But what can I do about it? I'm engaged to another woman. Elizabeth and I grew up together. She trusts me, depends on me. Her father was—well, I was very close to him, and when he died, I promised him that I would marry Elizabeth. How can I break that promise? How can I fail Elizabeth? What kind of man am I if I turn my back on a woman who's given up everything and come halfway across the country on my word that I'll marry her?"

His father nodded. "I see your problem. Now, I don't hold much account with deathbed promises. They always seemed like threats to me. But you've made a commitment to that woman, and you owe her something. Only, tell me this, do you owe her the rest of your life? Is it going to make her happy for you to be miserable? A marriage without love is a sad way to live."

"But you and my mother loved each other, and look what happened."

Joe sighed. "Yes. Maybe it doesn't always work out. But I don't see how in the hell it's got a chance if you don't even have love. I've been fortunate enough to be loved by two wonderful women in my lifetime. Sometimes it was enough to break my heart. But I wouldn't have traded it for a loveless, bloodless marriage. Think about it, son. Duty is a fine thing, and so is honor. But they'll never keep you warm at night, and they'll never make a December day seem like April. Only love can do that."

Jessie and Stephen did their best to pretend that nothing had happened between them. Jessie was cool to him, but polite, and Stephen was the soul of courtesy toward her. But neither of them could look at the other without thinking of the night they had spent together and the soul-shattering passion they had shared. They could not speak without feeling the familiar upswelling of love inside them.

They were wise enough to keep their distance. Stephen moved into Joe's room at the mill, so he wouldn't have to sleep only a flight of stairs away from Jessie, and she no longer kept watch with him at night. But she often awoke, sweating and aching, from erotic dreams of Stephen's love-making. And during the day she found herself staring at him as he worked, remembering the smooth play of his muscles beneath his skin or the heat of his mouth on hers.

She wanted him. She loved him. There was no denying either fact, much as she might want to. But it was just as undeniable that he was bound to another woman. He might desire her, but his love was given elsewhere.

One afternoon, two days after their night at the mill, Jessie left work early, unable to remain in the same room with Stephen for another minute, and tromped home through the snow. Inside the parlor, she found Harmonia Taylor, the widow who earned her living as a seamstress in town, sitting waiting for her, a large box on her lap.

Jessie stared at Miss Taylor in surprise as the woman bounced up and shoved the box into her hands. "Oh, Miss Randall, I'm so sorry," the woman twittered, her girlish voice at odds with her hefty frame. "I had this finished three days ago, but I couldn't get over here earlier because of the snow."

"Of course. That's perfectly all right. But what is this? I didn't—"

The other woman smiled archly, managing to look both ingratiating and annoying in the peculiar way she had. "Of course not. It's a surprise. A gift for you."

"A gift?"

"Yes. There's a note inside. He left it for you."

"He?" Jessie was still puzzled.

"Yes." Harmonia smiled again and almost giggled. "That fine gentleman."

Jessie's eyes widened. "Mr. Ferguson?"

"Yes. Mr. Ferguson. Mr. Stephen Ferguson."

Jessie took the box upstairs, hardly waiting long enough to bid Mrs. Taylor a polite farewell. She laid the box on her bed and pulled off the lid. She drew in a sharp breath. Inside lay a dress of ice-blue velvet. With trembling fingers, she reached in and drew out the garment. She held it up in front of her and looked into the mirror.

It was beautiful. She had never owned anything of such richness and elegance. Champagne-colored lace frothed at the cuffs and accented the neck. The skirt was pulled back into a saucy bustle in the rear, and there, too, row upon row of lace tumbled down, just as it did below the draped velvet skirts in the front. Mrs. Taylor must have used up every scrap of lace in Swenson's store on this dress! And the velvet! It was so soft and rich, and it was the exact color of her eyes. Had Stephen realized that? Had he planned it?

She looked at her face in the mirror. Her eyes were huge, her mouth soft. She smoothed the dress against her body, her hand running lightly over her breast and stomach onto her abdomen.

Jessie froze. What was she doing?

She tossed the dress onto the bed. This was the kind of gift a man gave to a woman he knew intimately, to a wife...or a mistress. Stephen was trying to appease his guilt, she thought, to make up for taking her virginity when he could not marry her. Or perhaps it was a payment for her services.

She picked up the lovely dress and crumpled it into a ball, then heaved it across the room. Bitterly she cursed Stephen. Then she cursed herself for being the fool that she was. Finally, she plopped down in the chair beside the window and sat for a long time, staring out. She thought about Stephen and the night they had shared together. She thought about the beautiful dress lying in a mess on the floor. She thought about her mother and the years she had spent loving Joe Ferguson, as faithful and loving as a wife, with never a public claim on him. Had her mother's heart ached as hers did now? Had she cried into her pillow at night and awakened feeling empty and lonely? She wondered if her mother had thought it was worth it. She must have, even before he asked her to marry him. Jessie had never heard Amanda speak a word against Joe or show in any way that she resented her position.

The day darkened before Jessie's eyes as she sat there thinking. She heard the sounds of voices and cutlery in the dining room and knew that supper had been served, but she didn't move. She wasn't interested in food. She just sat, staring blindly.

It was a flicker of movement outside on the lawn that finally caught her attention, a furtive gliding that was different from the normal passage of people along the street. She straightened and leaned forward a little, wondering exactly what it was she had seen.

For a moment she could discern nothing but shadows; then one of the shadows dislodged itself from a tree, and she realized that it was a person. A man, lurking beneath the tree. She peered out, squinting her eyes, glad she had not bothered to light the kerosene lamp in her room as the day had dimmed. There was something so secretive about the man's stance that it sent a frisson of alarm up her spine. He was standing looking at the second story of the house, still and waiting.

The front door opened and closed, and Jessie heard the sound of steps going down from the porch. The shadow melted under the tree. She saw a figure leave the front yard and turn up the street. It was Stephen. No doubt he was going to sleep in Joe's room at the office again. A moment later, the shadowy man slipped out of the yard after him. For an instant the shadow's face was clear in the moonlight.

It was Frank Grissom.

Jessie stiffened, her breath hissing in. Frank Grissom was following Stephen, and she couldn't think of a single good reason in the world for him to do that. Fear stabbed through her. Frank hated Stephen; Stephen had bested him before everyone, had humiliated him. Stephen had fired him. And if Frank was, as Stephen thought, the one who was responsible for the mishaps at the mill . . .

Jessie jumped out of her chair and hurried to pull on her boots and coat. Stephen might be able to beat Grissom in a fair fight, but, knowing Frank, Stephen wouldn't have a chance this time. There wouldn't be anything fair about it. She ran down the stairs and pulled her mother from her dishes to whisper where she was going and why. Then she hurried into the snow and down the street toward the mill.

The mill yard was dark and silent when Jessie walked up. She moved across it quickly, her eyes alert for any sign of Frank Grissom. Her feet were silent on the stairs, and she opened the mill door and closed it behind her just as quietly. She paused for a moment, listening. She heard nothing.

She tiptoed down the hall to the office, unlocked the door and went inside. Aided by dim moonlight coming through the window, she made her way across the room to her desk and opened the top right-hand drawer. The revolver was there. She checked to make sure it was loaded, then tiptoed out of the office and down the stairs to the bottom floor.

If Frank Grissom had not followed Stephen, she was going to feel very foolish, she thought. Her heart was pounding like a hammer in her chest, and she felt slightly sick with tension and fear. Sliding along the wall, she made her way toward the light that spilled out of the open doorway of Joe's room. Still there was no sound.

Jessie stopped at the doorway and cautiously peered around the frame into the room. An oil lamp burned on the small table. The room was empty.

Suddenly, with a roar, the steam engine sprang to life somewhere behind her. Jessie jumped at the abrupt violation of the silence. She slumped against the doorway, her heart slamming inside her chest. Thank heavens, it was just the machines. The noise had nearly scared her to death.

But what were the machines doing running at this hour of the night? An even greater fear clutched at her stomach, and she ran down the hall to the mill. She jerked open the door, and as she did, she glanced at the floor. On the floor, liberally streaked with sawdust as it always was, was a cleared path. Something had been dragged along this way.

Stephen!

She burst through the door, heedless of any noise she made. The din inside the mill was too great for anything she did to be heard. There was a light inside, and she ran toward it. The high—pitched whine of the huge buzz saw filled the air.

Jessie saw a man's shape outlined against the glow of a lantern. He bent and hoisted the limp form of another man onto his shoulder and lumbered across the floor toward the log carriage. For a moment Jessie was struck numb with terror. Grissom was carrying Stephen, who could only be either unconscious or dead.

Grissom turned slightly, shifting his load, and the lantern light flickered across Stephen's head. His hair was wet and matted, and scarlet blood stained his face. With a grunt Grissom threw Stephen's body onto the log carriage. Then he turned to the lever and shoved it away from him. The log carriage began to rumble forward toward the buzz saw.

The sight freed Jessie from her momentary paralysis, and she screamed, "Stop! Grissom! Stop it!"

Grissom whirled and saw her. His jaw dropped; then he grinned. "Come to see your lover sliced up?" he shouted across the noise.

Jessie leveled her gun at him. "Stop it. Now! Or you're a dead man."

Grissom began to laugh. "Or you're goin' ta shoot me? Go ahead! A woman ain't got the nerve."

The carriage moved inexorably onward, carrying Stephen. Jessie knew she had to stop it. She drew in a breath, sighted and squeezed the trigger.

The crack of the pistol shot barely rose above the thunderous noise of the carriage and saw. The bullet hit Grissom in the chest, knocking him backward. Red spread across his shirt, and he stumbled and fell. Jessie didn't pause to watch. As soon as she fired, she started running forward. She reached the saw mechanism and threw the lever to stop it. But that wasn't enough, she knew; Stephen would still be carried right into the saw's deadly sharp teeth, even if they weren't whirling. She ran on, not sparing a glance for Grissom, who was scrabbling around on the floor, trying to rise.

She passed the moving carriage and ran alongside the track to the lever that would stop it. She grabbed the handle and pushed. It didn't budge. Frantically she pushed again. Finally, lowering her head, she planted her feet, wrapped her hands around the handle and threw her entire weight against the lever. It snapped forward, and the carriage shuddered to a halt.

Jessie leaned against the long handle, her knees suddenly weak. She turned, trembling, and looked back. The carriage—and Stephen's head—lay less than a foot from the sharp points of the saw. She wiped the sweat from her forehead. The muscles in her legs felt like rubber. She glanced at Grissom. He had given up his attempts to get up and had flopped onto his back. Blood soaked his shirtfront.

"Damn!" he whispered. "I never thought you'd do it."

Jessie wet her dry lips. It took all the strength she had to keep her voice even. "You're just lucky the light's bad in here. I was aiming for your head."

She turned and climbed onto the carriage. She would have to pull herself together enough to tie Grissom up and go for the marshal and the doctor. But first she had to see Stephen.

She bent over him and picked up his hand, pressing her fingers against his wrist. His pulse was uneven, but it was there. Thank God. He was alive!

# Chapter Sixteen

Stephen came to groggily. The room was dim around him, the only light coming from a kerosene lamp on the table, its wick turned low. A groan escaped him. His head was splitting.

His father was immediately beside his bed, grinning at him. "Stephen! You're awake. Well, it's a good thing you've got a harder head than I do. You've only been out a couple of hours."

"My head feels as if there are a hundred little men inside with hammers."

"That's to be expected. Frank Grissom can really crack a head open." He rubbed his own head ruefully. "I ought to know."

"Frank Grissom? He hit me? What happened?"

"You up to hearing the story?"

Stephen nodded, then immediately regretted the move. "Yes," he whispered. "Tell me."

"Well, you were at the mill last night, sitting at the table working on some accounts."

"Yes, I remember that."

"You had your back to the door." Joe clicked his tongue against his teeth in reproval. "That's something a man's got to learn out here: never sit with your back to a door, especially when you've acquired an enemy like Frank Grissom."

"He hit me over the head?"

Joe nodded. "Yep. Then he dragged you down the hall into the mill."

"Why?"

"Seems he wanted to get rid of you. It would have shut the place down, too, but I reckon he'd gone past carin' about that. Main thing he wanted was to get shed of you."

"What happened?"

Joe related the story of how Jessie had seen Grissom and followed him to the mill, then saved Stephen's life. "Burley and Jim arrived not long after that, and they hauled Grissom over to the doc's."

"He's still alive?"

"Yeah. Reckon he'll stay that way, too. Jessie says she's been kicking herself 'cause her aim was off. But it's better this way. When Grissom got to the doctor's he confessed everything. Said he'd arranged all the accidents at the mill, and your shooting. And he laid it all at Elias Moore's doorstep. So the marshal hustled over to ol' Elias's house. It seems that there's going to be a railroad spur coming up here from Missoula, so one of the big lumber outfits got interested in acquiring timber around here, and the person they checked with was the local banker. Our Mr. Moore. He didn't waste any time telling them that he would soon foreclose on a mill, and would they be interested in buying it? Seems they were. So Moore got busy setting me up." Joe chuckled. "Only he's the one that got caught. The marshal's still up there talking to him. I reckon he's thinking ol' Elias might have been involved in some other havey-cavey dealings along the way."

"A railroad. Of course. I should have realized. I was just thinking the other day about what we could do if we put in a railway line." He rubbed his hand across his forehead, frowning. "Where's Jessie?"

"Don't fret about her. She wanted to stay with you, but the marshal insisted on her coming down and telling her story. I tell you, that was one wrought-up young lady."

Stephen's eyes drifted closed. "I'd like to thank her." His voice began to slur.

"Sure. In the morning. Right now you go back to sleep."

He took a second look at his son. Stephen had already followed his advice.

When Stephen awakened the next time, his head felt much better. There was no one else in the room, and he cautiously slipped out of bed. His head spun for a moment, and his stomach rolled, but then everything settled into place. He went to the curtain and drew it back. It was obviously morning. He dressed, moving with great care so as not to disturb his head, and went downstairs. There he found only Amanda and her maid, bustling around in the kitchen, cleaning the breakfast dishes.

"Why, there are are! I was just going to come up and see about you." Amanda directed him to a chair at the kitchen table. "Sit down. Feel like breakfast?"

"Maybe. A light one." He glanced around. "Where's Jessie?"

Amanda shook her head. "That girl. I finally made her go to bed. I told her you weren't bad enough off for her to be sitting up watching you. She lay down around dawn. If I know her, it shouldn't be too long before she's up again and coming in to see you."

Stephen was disappointed. He wanted to see Jessie and talk to her, and every moment's delay seemed a huge waste of time. "Oh."

The biscuits and bacon Amanda set down in front of him helped calm his queasy stomach, and the headache powder she gave him did wonders, as well. By the time Stephen left the kitchen, he was feeling almost normal.

He climbed the stairs to his room and found his valet inside, fussing over one of his suits. Charles cast a look of disdain at the plain denim trousers, boots and shirt Stephen had put on.

"Is that what you're planning to wear today, sir?" he asked in a dreadfully polite voice.

"Yes, I rather think so."

"Very good, sir." Charles turned away and hung the suit in the wardrobe.

"I've found that sturdier clothes fare better here."

"Of course, sir."

"Charles . . . am I safe in assuming that the West has lost its appeal for you?"

Charles turned. "I have found it to be—rather different from what I expected, yes."

"Then you would be happy about going back to New York?"

The valet's somber face lit up. "Indeed, sir, I would consider it a privilege to leave this place."

"Good. I thought so. Well, you'll be getting your wish any day now, as soon as Miss Elizabeth arrives."

Charles couldn't suppress a smile. "Very good, sir. I will be happy to accompany you and Mrs. Ferguson to the—"

"Oh, not me. Or, at least, I hope I won't have to escort Elizabeth all the way to New York. That's one reason I want you to accompany her, to make sure she has a safe and pleasant journey."

"I beg your pardon, sir?"

"I won't be marrying Miss Elizabeth, Charles."

"You mean you won't be marrying her now? Here?"

"Now, here and forever, anywhere."

Charles stared, bug-eyed. "Sir!"

"I've had a change of heart, Charles—and mind, and most everything else, as well."

Charles pulled himself in order. "Yes, sir. Very good, sir." He bowed and left the room.

Stephen removed his boots and flopped on the bed, linking his hands behind his head. He winced a little at the soreness, but then he forgot it. He lay gazing at the ceiling, making plans and smiling.

It was some time later that there was a small, tentative knock at his door, and Jessie slipped inside, closing the door after her. She stood for a moment, looking at him. He stared back.

She was wearing the pale blue dress he had hired the local seamstress to sew for her. He had almost forgotten about it in the hectic events of the last few days. She looked even more beautiful than he had envisioned.

It fit her as her mother's dresses had not. The waist nipped in snugly, and the cloth outlined the generous curves of her breasts rather than hiding them. The velvet and lace added softening touches to her beauty, as did the way she wore her hair, piled loosely on the crown of her head, with curling wisps drifting down beside her face. She looked feminine and lovely, and her face glowed.

"Hello, Stephen." Her voice sounded oddly small and shy.

"Jessamine." He stood, pulled to his feet by the force of her beauty. "You are . . . beautiful," he said simply.

She smiled, dimpling, and color washed her cheeks. "Thank you. I'm so happy to see you up and looking so . . . so well."

"Thanks to you. You saved my life. Again. And don't say it was nothing. It was quite something to me."

"It was quite something to me, too." Jessie's voice was soft and slightly shaky as she continued. "I love you, Stephen. I came here to ask you to make love to me."

Desire clenched in his gut. "Jessie..."

Jessie wet her lips. Her hands were ice cold, and she couldn't recall ever feeling quite this scared. "I know you swore not to, that you were sorry about last time. But this time, you don't have to feel guilty for seducing me. I'm no longer inexperienced. And you aren't leading me astray. I want to."

She reached up and pulled the pins from her hair. It cascaded in rich red waves upon her shoulders. She smiled at him, and it was the knowing, beckoning smile of a seductress. Stephen could not speak, could only stand and watch her, his pulse throbbing, as she wove her spell of enchantment around him.

Her fingers went to the small pearl buttons that ran down the length of her dress, and she began to unbutton them, revealing first her throat, then the soft, tremulous tops of her breasts, and finally the white lacy camisole beneath. Stephen's eyes followed the path of her fingers, dwelling on the satiny skin and the clinging, revealing garment covering it. The cloth moved with every breath she took, tightening and loosening over her full breasts. Her aureoles were wine-dark circles beneath the sheer white, and the nipples hardened, pushing against it.

When her dress was unfastened, she shrugged out of it and let it fall to the floor. Then she unfastened the ties of her petticoats, and they crumpled to the floor atop the dress. She stood before him clad only in her underthings and stockings. Keeping her eyes on his face, she reached up and untied one of the pink bows that held her camisole together. Her fingers slid lower, and Stephen's eyes followed as she undid the next small satin ribbon. The garment gaped wider with every breath she drew, so that the beauty of her breasts was revealed little by little, shadowed and mysterious.

Desire sizzled through Stephen, enflaming every nerve, heating every vein. "You don't know what you're doing."

"Oh, yes, I do." Jessie's voice was low and breathy, arousing him even more. She strolled across the room to him, stopping only inches away. "When I saw you last night I didn't know whether you were alive. I've never been so scared."

She began to unbutton his shirt, her fingers slow and caressing. "I knew then that I loved you more than anything on earth. I can't live without you."

Jessie slipped her hands into his shirt and opened it, baring his chest. Stephen sucked in his breath. She looked at him. His eyes were glittering, his face flushed with desire. She knew that if she moved her hands down, she could touch the sure proof of his desire for her. He wanted her; that was all she needed to know.

She stepped closer and pressed her lips against one of his nipples, nestled in the hair of his chest. Stephen jerked and groaned. "Jessie..." Her name was half laugh, half moan.

Her tongue flicked out and circled the small bud. She could feel the heat flooding his body. "I wanted to do this the other night, but I wasn't sure if you would like it."

"If I would like it! You're going to make me explode."

"Good." Jessie smiled and began to nibble at his skin. "That's what I want to do. I don't want you to think about anything but me. I don't care about my name or my reputation. I know I cannot be your wife. But I can't leave you. I can't live without knowing your lovemaking again. Make love to me, Stephen." She lifted her clear eyes and gazed deeply into his. "Let me be your mistress. I'll follow you back East. I'll live wherever, however you want me to. Just love me, and let me love you."

Her eyes were luminous, her face glowing with love and desire. Her lips were moist and very kissable. Stephen was shaken to the core with lust and love. He bent and kissed

er, his hands clutching her hair. His lips dug into hers; his
ongue possessed her.

He kissed her again and again, murmuring her name and
oft words of love and passion. They pulled off their clothes
nd joined together stormily in his bed, wild with a hunger
estrained so fiercely for days. They rolled and tumbled,
kissing greedily, their hands exploring, stroking, gripping.
Finally he moved between her legs, opening her to his lov-
ng invasion, and plunged deep within her. Jessie gave a soft
ry and wrapped her legs around him, moving with him,
until at last their passion exploded, hurtling them into the
momentary oblivion of satisfaction.

Later, damp with sweat and shaken by the depths of their
ovemaking, Stephen lay curled up with her, cradling her in
his arms. Jessie nestled against him, utterly at peace.

"I love you," Stephen whispered.

She smiled faintly and kissed his chest. "I love you, too."

"But I have to turn down your offer."

Jessie stiffened, and her eyes flew open. "What?"

"I don't want you to be my mistress."

Hurt flooded her face, and she turned away, scrambling
o leave his bed. Stephen's hand lashed out and fastened
around her arm.

"No! Wait! I said that clumsily."

Jessie shot him a flashing glance. "How could you say it
smoothly?"

"No. I didn't mean that I don't want you. I do. I want
you and love you with every fiber of my being."

She paused, bewildered. "Then what—"

"I love you too much to make you my mistress. I would
never dishonor you that way."

"Honor be damned!"

His mouth quirked into a smile. "Would you please let
me finish what I'm trying to say? I love you. I don't want to

spend my life sneaking out to see you, hiding you away from the world. I want to spend every moment with you. I want everyone to know that I love you. I want you to be my wife."

Jessie's jaw dropped. "What?"

"I want to marry you. Will you marry me?"

For a moment she couldn't speak, could only gape at him, astonished. "But—but—what about Elizabeth? What about your promise?"

"I've been thinking a lot over the past few days. Last night, almost dying—well, it crystallized my thinking. It made me realize what an idiot I was. I don't love Elizabeth. I can't marry her, no matter what promise I made her father. I can't condemn myself to a lifetime of boredom and misery because it's the 'proper' thing to do. I won't let you go, and I certainly wouldn't ask you to bear the shame of being my mistress. Elizabeth is a good woman, and she doesn't love me any more than I love her. She will understand; she's been my friend for years."

Jessie looked doubtful. "I don't think I'd understand your choosing another woman. I think I'd slug her."

Stephen chuckled. "You probably would. But not Elizabeth. She doesn't want me. All she wants is to be able to live free of her stepmother. I do have a responsibility to her, but I realized this morning what I can do. I will explain it all to her, and I'll send her to New York. Charles is eager to leave here, and he can escort her. In New York, she can live with Isabelle Clampton. I don't know why I didn't think of it before. Isabelle is a distant cousin of Elizabeth's father and is living now as a companion to her sister. She hates her position, but though she is quite genteel, she has only a small portion from her father's will. She will be a perfectly acceptable chaperone for Elizabeth, and they will get along well. They're both educated and intelligent.

"Elizabeth has an income from the trust her father left her, and, as I am one of the trustees, I can easily increase the amount so that she and Isabelle can live comfortably. No one in New York will know that she ran away from her home in St. Louis in order to marry me. Her reputation will be secure. Perhaps Elizabeth will even find a man there whom she can love as she doesn't love me."

Jessie gazed at him for a long moment. "You're serious, aren't you?"

"Yes! Of course I am!" He kissed her hard. "Well? Will you marry me?"

Jessie began to laugh. She threw her arms around his neck and covered his face with kisses. "Yes. Yes, I'll marry you, you crazy man! And you'll see—I won't embarrass you when we go to St. Louis. I'll learn all about being a lady. You can teach me. I promise I won't cuss or throw things or shoot a gun."

"Whoa. Wait. Hold it." Stephen set her away from him, gripping her by the shoulders and gazing intently into her eyes. "We're not going to St. Louis."

"What?"

"You heard me. I'm not taking you to live in the city. Do you think I'd pull up a beautiful wild rose by its roots and stick it in a glass vase, just to watch it die? I'd never do that to you. We'll get married and live right here. I like Montana. I like the business. I don't have to go back to St. Louis. Joe will let me buy into the mill, I think. And if he and Sam don't want that, well, I'll find something else I can do. It's a brand new land. I can do anything I want to."

"But—but won't you miss it? Won't you be sorry?"

He shook his head. "No. I'd like to get to know my brother and father again. I'd like to help build something. There's nothing for me back home, except a stale life that someone else created for me. My grandfather will manage without me. He can find someone else to run the company.

Maybe he'll sell it. I don't know. But I do know I can't live for him. Here, with you, is where I've really lived. And I guarantee you, I won't miss anything or anybody as long as I have you."

Tears brimmed in Jessamine's eyes. "You are the best and kindest of men. And I love you to distraction. I love you."

She threw her arms around him and kissed him again, and for the next few minutes, both of them were pleasantly lost.

It was some long time later that they finally rose and pulled their clothes back on, talking and laughing softly. They had trouble keeping their hands off each other, and Stephen pulled Jessie back time after time to kiss her. When they were finally dressed, they strolled downstairs, hand in hand. Amanda, seeing their linked hands, raised her eyebrows but said nothing. They wandered into the parlor and sat down. They talked together quietly, making plans for their future, studying their linked hands with all the intensity that only new lovers have.

It was late in the afternoon, and Stephen and Jessie were still lost in each other's eyes, when there was the sound of feet pounding up the front steps and Burley Owens burst into the house. "Miz Randall! Where's Stephen?"

"In here, Burley."

Burley stuck his head into the parlor. "Say, you're lookin' mighty good for a man what almost got sawed up into two-by-fours last night."

"Why, thank you, Burley...I think. What's your news?"

"I was down at the mill. Guess who just rode into town? That ringtail rascal Sam Ferguson, that's who," he continued, answering his own question. "And he's got your fi—" He glanced at Stephen's and Jessie's linked hands, and his voice faltered. "That is, well, Miss Elizabeth's with him."

Stephen and Jessie looked at each other. Jessie's stomach tightened in fear, and suddenly she was afraid that this afternoon had been only a dream, that Stephen would stand up and walk out of her life.

But he smiled and squeezed her hand. "Come on. We'd better go face the music. Don't worry. She'll be fine."

He stood, pulling Jessie with him. "I'm glad they've finally arrived. All safe, I take it?"

Burley nodded, seemingly unable to speak.

Jessie hung back. "Stephen . . . are you sure?"

He turned, smiling slowly, and his eyes held a hot promise. "Yes. I'm sure. I love you, and I want to marry you. Damn the consequences." He leaned down and kissed her thoroughly. "Now, shall we go?"

Jessie's grin was dazzling. "Anywhere."

She tucked her hand in his arm, and they walked out the door together.

\* \* \* \* \*

*What becomes of Stephen Ferguson's roughneck brother Sam?*
*And what of Stephen's delicate, city-bred fiancée?*

*Coming next month, from* Harlequin Historicals, watch for Sam's exciting, action-packed story in THE HELL RAISER (#45), *from the pen of critically acclaimed historical novelist* Dorothy Glenn.

THE GENTLEMAN *and* THE HELL RAISER. *Each volume stands alone—together they're a dashing duet.*

Kristin James *and* Dorothy Glenn. *Two great authors— one unique publishing venture. Only in* Harlequin Historicals.

# COMING NEXT MONTH

### #45 THE HELL RAISER—Dorothy Glenn

Sam Ferguson scorned the fripperies and falseness of
Eastern society folk. But he'd given his word he'd escort
his city-bred brother's fiancée across the Montana
wilderness. So when Elizabeth Caldwell turned out to be as
tough—and true—as Sam, all hell broke loose!

### #46 TERMS OF SURRENDER—Mollie Ashton

Unhappy Julie Farroux had paid her price for escaping the
Reign of Terror's guillotine: a loveless union with a
scheming, greedy old man. Handsome Englishman
Sebastian Ramlin recoiled from the Devil's bargain Julie's
husband offered him. Yet when he looked into her eyes,
Sebastian knew he could never turn away.

---

**AVAILABLE NOW:**

#43 THE GENTLEMAN
Kristin James

#44 SUMMER'S PROMISE
Lucy Elliot

## Have You Been Introduced To
## THE GENTLEMAN
## Yet?

If you enjoyed Dorothy Glenn's THE HELL RAISER (HH #45), you won't want to miss its companion book, THE GENTLEMAN, by Kristin James.

As a boy, Stephen Ferguson was taken away from his brother and his western home, then raised with all the comforts that money and city society could provide. As a man, he longed to be reunited with the family he'd nearly forgotten. In THE GENTLEMAN (HH #43) Stephen finds not only his father and brother but something even more precious—the love of a woman who is every inch his opposite—and absolutely his perfect match!

---

If you missed THE GENTLEMAN (HH #43), and would like to order it, send your name, zip or postal code along with a check or money order for $3.25 plus 75¢ postage and handling ($1.00 in Canada), payable to Harlequin Reader Service, to:

**In the U.S.**
Harlequin Reader Service
901 Fuhrmann Blvd.
Box 1325
Buffalo, NY 14269-1325

**In Canada**
Harlequin Reader Service
P.O. Box 609
Fort Erie, Ontario
L2A 5X3

Please mention book title with your order.

HH45-1

# Have You Ever Wondered If You Could Write A Harlequin Novel?

Here's great news—Harlequin is offering a series of cassette tapes to help you do just that. Written by Harlequin editors, these tapes give practical advice on how to make your characters—and your story—come alive. There's a tape for each contemporary romance series Harlequin publishes.

**Mail order only**

**All sales final**

---

TO: ***Harlequin Reader Service***
**Audiocassette Tape Offer**
**P.O. Box 1396**
**Buffalo, NY 14269-1396**

I enclose a check/money order payable to HARLEQUIN READER SERVICE® for $9.70 ($8.95 plus 75¢ postage and handling) for EACH tape ordered for the total sum of $_____*
Please send:

☐ Romance and Presents     ☐ Intrigue
☐ American Romance          ☐ Temptation
☐ Superromance              ☐ All five tapes ($38.80 total)

Signature_____

Name:_____ (please print clearly)

Address:_____

State:_____ Zip:_____

* Iowa and New York residents add appropriate sales tax.

AUDIO-H

# Indulge a Little
# Give a Lot

---

## A LITTLE SELF-INDULGENCE CAN DO A WORLD OF GOOD!

Last fall readers indulged themselves with fine romance and free gifts during the Harlequin®/ Silhouette® "Indulge A Little—Give A Lot" promotion. For every specially marked book purchased, 5¢ was donated by Harlequin/ Silhouette to Big Brothers/Big Sisters Programs and Services in the United States and Canada. We are pleased to announce that your participation in this unique promotion resulted in a total contribution of $100,000.

*

*Watch for details on Harlequin® and Silhouette®'s next exciting promotion in September.*